PROTECTION

ALSO BY JACK KELLY

Apalachin

PROTECTION

JACK KELLY

E. P. DUTTON NEW YORK

PUBLISHER'S NOTE: This novel is a work of fiction.
Names, characters, places, and incidents either are the product
of the author's imagination or are used fictitiously,
and any resemblance to actual persons, living or dead,
events, or locales is entirely coincidental.

Published in the United States by E. P. Dutton,
a division of Penguin Books USA Inc.,
2 Park Avenue, New York, N.Y. 10016.

Published simultaneously in Canada by
Fitzhenry and Whiteside, Limited, Toronto.

Library of Congress Cataloging-in-Publication Data
Kelly, Jack, 1949–
Protection / Jack Kelly. — 1st ed.
p. cm.
ISBN 0-525-24778-5
I. Title.
PS3561.E394P7   1989
813'.54—dc19   89-1046
                                    CIP

BOMC offers recordings and compact discs, cassettes
and records. For information and catalog write to
BOMR, Camp Hill, PA 17012.

PROTECTION

1

"Forget about it, Lew, the son of a bitch is a sweetheart," the fat man said. "Sal Veronica is a fucking sweetheart."

"I heard—"

"You heard, you heard. The man is wide open. He's a human being. Huh? How many of those you meet nowdays? Fucking homo sapiens. Lots of guys, Lew, would be all gooseflesh, be sitting here waiting to talk to Sal Veronica. Understand me?"

"I am all gooseflesh, Vipe. Believe me I am."

"That's good. So don't start on me with you heard."

"What can I do?" Lew pleaded. "People talk, they talk. A guy was telling me about a guy. Something with Carolina cigarettes and an ice pick."

"Hey, don't start. I'm doing you a fucking favor here." Vipe waved to the waitress. Anemic amber bulbs illuminated the Sheepshead Bay bar. Buffalo nickels and Kennedy half-dollars were frozen in the urethaned tops of the knotty-pine tables. The olive shag carpet on the ceiling gave the place a hushed atmosphere. An orchestral arrangement of "Never on Sunday" was seeping from hidden speakers. The Rams were picking apart the Chargers' secondary on "Monday Night Football" over the bar.

"It's just," Lew said, "this guy got a chance to meet your man, too. And, your man's such a sweetheart and all, so he says put your hand out."

The waitress stood by their table. The set of her hips made her body smile. "Gents?"

"Another Pernod," Lew said.

"Mine's a White Label, Capri." Vipe turned back to his companion but kept his eyes on the waitress as she walked away.

Lew said, "Put your hand out, right? So the guy does and Veronica rams an ice pick through it, pins it right to the table, absolutely no reason. And he won't let him take it out. He has to sit there, look at it. I'm supposed to handle that, somebody does something like that? I couldn't handle it."

"Absolutely no reason? Come on, Lew."

"Because of these cigarettes, cigarette machines, all this, I don't know."

"That's theatrics, to make a point. Sal's into theatrics. Christ, ninety percent of what people do, what do they do it for? Effect. Theatrics."

"Me, I can't even afford to take my wife to a Broadway show anymore, the prices they're getting. But what I'm talking about, I'd go to pieces. My nerves are shot to hell to begin with. My business—"

Vipe closed his eyes and slowly shook his head. He'd been middle-aged since adolescence. A slender pencil mustache drooped down the sides of his mouth, four chins supported his lower lip.

"Boy, I don't get you," he said. "I arrange—and believe me it wasn't easy, Sal is busy—I arrange for you to sit down with him and talk, man to man. I save your goddamn life here, and you're going on about some rumor you heard, some jerk got his hand pricked."

"What save my life?" Lew said.

"Save your life, cover your ass—it's a way of talking is all."

"What do you mean, save my life? I want to know."

"Relax. You never heard of a figure of speech?"

"So help me, I'm going to make it all good."

"Sure you are."

"But I hear these things, I wonder. I hear something, the U.S. attorney, a dope rap. I have a respectable business, my clients, I have a reputation. Something like this comes out, indictments, whatever, it's no good."

"Hold it there, friend. Indictments? I can see your brain work, Lew. You've got a glass head. You think you're going to be saved by the bell here? You think something's coming down, you'll just stall it out? Because these things are par for the course, they don't mean shit. He's got lawyers take care of all that. That's just politics. Thanks, babe." The waitress arranged the new drinks in front of them. "How do you drink that licorice shit?" Vipe asked Lew.

"This woman I knew, we used to drink it together. She had eyes like—"

"Give me a break. What I'm saying is, you came to us. You wanted major capital. Remember? You were going to set up those fronts and move truckloads of shit off the books and all. You were all mouth back then, Lew." Vipe held up his index finger as if showing it off to the smaller man.

"It's cash flow," Lew said. "I mean, it's practically making me come down with a mental illness here, is what it's doing. I got crucified on earth tones. That's what I want to explain to him. My shop is profitable, I brought my D and Bs to prove it. But I took a bath on earth tones. I was so sure in my gut your sepias, your khakis, your russets were going to be the rage. I plunged. Isn't that what they say? Go for it? I went for it. What happens? They hit me in the face with primaries. Everywhere you look it's egg yolk, it's flame, it's cobalt. I've got bolts upon bolts of cinnamon corduroy—I can't stand to look at the stuff. But it's all cash flow. You walk up the Mount of Olives, take the kind of drubbing I did, it's gotta put a crimp in your cash flow."

"Sure."

"He'll understand."

"Sure he will."

"Won't he? I mean, there's no point in him—it's not in his interest. I want to pay, I can pay, I will pay. Vipe, I'm going to pay everything. Those deals I thought, they never came through. But I can pay it out of the shop, soon as we're back to the positive cash flow. I know what we agreed, but I didn't think you'd all of a sudden be calling me on it. God, it's hot in here."

"I ain't hot. Listen, there's something else we gotta talk about. Nuevo Zip."

"Nuevo Zip?"

"Nuevo Zip. Miss Unnameable? Big Coda?"

"What?"

"DeFacto Romance, off at seven to five? Nuevo Zip, a bay colt that paid five forty in a six-board claimer at Aqueduct? I'm talking about your action, sport."

"So? So, my action. I don't get it."

"You play with Stein. Who do you think Stein answers to? Huh? Forget about it. This is grave, Lew. I can't go to Sal, do the fifth act from the *Barber of Seville* on behalf of a poor schmo got ground up by his own cash flow—he's going to say to me, Nuevo Zip. Huh? Miss Unnameable. What about Miss Unnameable? How do I answer about a guy who plays heavy with Stein, can't keep up with the vig when you extend him capital—capital, Lew—to keep him out of chapter seven? Tell me. Tell me what I say when he asks, did you really recommend we back this asshole? This"—he shifted in his chair and farted—"this is grave."

"I had a bad week."

"You drop eleven hundred on the ponies with what you owe, I'll say you had a bad week."

"Ask Maury—week before I won six in one day." The memory flitted across Lew's mouth.

"You're playing with Sal's money, is what I'm saying. How the hell you think that looks?"

4

"Vipe, it's a tradition in the trade. You're dealing with buyers and cutters and factors all day, you're trekking the showrooms, you're up and down dingy offices and factories, in and out of sweatshops—you want to dream horseflesh. Your mind needs that. You go down Seventh Avenue—see if you can find one person there doesn't get down on the races."

"I hope you can convince him of that, Lew, I really do."

"Lookit, you don't think he'd really— 'Cause I want to pay. You know me, you know I'm a guy pays what he owes. Spring line, I've got some knit bottoms that are going to floor the specialty chains."

"Sal Veronica, I don't think, is all that interested in spring lines. I just gotta impress on you that what we're talking here is serious. He don't want to look at no D and fucking Bs. He wants cash. Now."

Lew gritted his teeth and scratched at the back of his hand.

"I need time."

Vipe shook his head. "Forget about it."

Lew's eyes were turning to raw egg white. He sipped his Pernod too fast. He choked briefly. He rubbed his mouth with a shaking hand.

Vipe said, "Here he is."

Lew stood and tried to smile at the man approaching them.

2

His fucking D and Bs he wanted to show you," Vipe was saying. He was relieved. The rag-trade guy had coughed up and it was okay. Four of them sat in the booth. Joey Skull was counting the money. Primo was periodically craning his neck to catch the score of the game. Over near the door, the kid, Sal's driver, leaned against the wall with his arms crossed.

"What'd you tell him, we were Merrill Lynch, Vipe?" Joey Skull asked.

Vipe grinned. "I knew he had it. The guy's a chalk eater from the word go. He'll take a chance, jerk you around, as long as he knows he's got the kicker. There you are." He pointed at the stack of bills.

"How's it look?" Sal asked Joey Skull.

Joey kept licking his thumb as he counted the money. He laid down the last bill. "Six big ones on the nose."

"And Thursday he'll have another six, maybe more," Vipe said. "Now he's thinking right, we won't have any

6

more trouble with him. Guys like Lew, they should be on the stage. Sitting there with six bills practically ripping a hole in his pocket and he's going on about how he can't come up with it and his cash flow and his boners in the trade, the earth tones and all. I mean real tears. Him getting down with Stein, that was how I turned his head around. If you're so flat, how come you're playing heavy with Stein? I asked him. Think Sal don't know about that?"

"I almost felt sorry for the guy," Sal said.

"Sal, forget about it. He heard I was bringing him to see you, that started him thinking straight. You handled him just right."

"Forget his D and Bs," Primo said, his voice sandpaper. "We oughta'a checked his BVDs, color of them. Heh."

They all laughed.

Vipe reported on the other Seventh Avenue dings he'd been after. This one, they padlocked his warehouse yesterday. Vipe didn't know why, there was nothing in it, the guy's fucking factored till Christmas of 'ninety-nine. This other one, he's got an insurance deal going, a step van full of chinchillas, he'll have the vig and half by Thursday. And so-and-so paid up, so-and-so took a powder, so-and-so, his wife's brother's going to kick in.

Sal listened, nodded his approval, raised an eyebrow, frowned. Vipe and Joey watched his features, searching for signs. Sal's face, when he looked at you, always seemed a few inches too close, even if he was across the room. It was a handsome face, handsome in a way that women called rugged, men coarse. A fifth-grade brawl over a penny-pitching contest had at forty left him a nose with a hint of a question mark. Except when he was very pleased, he smiled with only half his face. His umber eyes could not be called cold, but they had a directness that made him a difficult man to lie to.

Joey Skull said he was still trying to collect on that kilo of blow they fronted to the man on 145th Street. Vipe claimed the guy was a crackhead, everybody knew he'd gone to the moon, they never should have dealt with him. Joey said he'd get the money if he had to bust every head

7

in Harlem. They talked about the cowboys up there now, the automatic weapons, a guy who'd carved his initials into the back of some dude he killed over a burn—his goddamn initials.

Sal said he could see there were guys out there playing the waiting game. Vipe and Joey shifted in their chairs. No, Vipe said, nobody had mentioned the case. His man Lew never mentioned any indictment, not a word. They're waiting, Sal said, hoping the D.A. will cancel their debts for them.

They talked about Sal's case, what his chances were. Vipe said with Baylor Sal couldn't possibly be facing time. Baylor knew all the strings. Baylor could get anybody off of anything.

Yeah? Sal said. What about Abbie Shots? He thought they couldn't put him inside. But they told the jury that when he nodded to a guy in a restaurant it meant that he was giving the approval to move a dozen kilos of Palermo powder. And the jury bought it and Abbie Shots was in Atlanta waiting for the earth to circle the sun eight or nine more times.

"It's all politics," Sal went on. "Every election year, the politicians go into heat over drugs. Rest of the time, they're happy making money off it."

Anything but a coke rap, he said, and he'd have a chance. Sure, Baylor could talk about entrapment this, grounds for the warrant that, motions coming out his ass, the thousand ways he can fade the bet. But the case was shaping up as a game of hardball and nobody could say which way it was going to go.

Liquidity, that was what he needed. Call in as much money from the street as they could, get a war chest ready. This case was going to cost and nobody knew where it would end.

"Here's Bobby Eggs," Joey said.

People came and went for an hour. They would talk to the kid at the door when they came in. He'd make a sign to Joey Skull. When Sal was ready for them, Joey'd bring them over to the secluded booth, into the light of Primo's stare.

They went into Manhattan then for another round of meetings at a rug joint near the Midtown Tunnel.

It was nearly two in the morning when they finished their business. Sal said he was supposed to meet the trim an hour ago, they were going to Chinatown. He asked Joey if he wanted to come.

"I can't eat that stuff now—my ulcer," Joey Skull said.

"You'll check with the Jap about that kid who's giving Bobby a hard time in the market."

"I'm seeing him in the morning. No problem."

"Take it easy, Skull. Ready for some chow mein, Primo?"

Gripping her auburn hair, Vanessa leaned over. Her face rose up to meet her in the glass, the eyes set wide, the lips an eager red. Through a silver straw she inhaled a stripe of white sting. She raised her head, bit off a sneeze. She lowered it again to vacuum the other powdery line.

Her eyes watered. She licked her finger and wiped it over the mirror and numbed her gums with it. She gave herself a million-dollar smile, a professional smile.

She reached and pulled open the closet door so that its full-length mirror came parallel to the one on her vanity. A cascade of Vanessas swept into view. She smiled. Vanessas bared their teeth into the dim distance. She waved. A fan of arms mimicked her.

One of those images was her, she thought. But it was the one way down the line, obscured by all the others. She'd seen too many pictures of herself still to think of that face as her.

You could never see your own face, she thought. You were the only person in the world who would never see how you actually looked, only reflections. This fact thrilled her with its profundity.

He'd be here any minute. Soon, too soon.

Too bad she had to spoil her appetite. She loved

9

Chinese. She and Sal both did, it was something they had in common. And Sal always took her to the best places in Chinatown, where you could get the razor clams and the aromatic five-flavor duck. But she had to ruin her appetite with the coke because she needed to be up because this was going to be an acting job and she had to have her head in shape for it. This was going to be her greatest role.

Act? She could act. Redi-Wax proved that.

Redi-Wax! she hummed to herself. Twice the shine in half the time—looking fine with Redi-Wax! Redi-Wax!

That was acting, the little dance she did. She was still pulling residuals on that one.

They just wanted your cute navel. That's what Sal told her. Your sweet, sweet midriff. So what? Acting was something you did with your entire being, midriff and all. Another truth. She was sharp as a tack tonight.

No, she thought, admiring her left leg as she pulled the stocking over it. No, it wasn't all that inspirational stuff. Acting was nothing more than contacts, who you knew. That was how people made it in the business—contacts. And she was going to have all the contacts she needed after this, because Mickey knew Goldman. Mickey promised he'd introduce her to Goldman as his special friend if she did this for him, and Goldman pretty much pulled the strings at four different soap operas.

And it wasn't like she was committing a crime. It wasn't that serious, Mickey assured her. Because they just wanted to talk to Sal. You know, just talk kinda thing. And anyway, he doesn't love you.

Nobody was lucky or unlucky, you made your luck or you didn't. All those kids who flocked to New York to work as actors and pounded from one audition to another, hardly ever getting a callback, they thought it was luck, they were waiting for their lucky breaks. Ha.

She slipped her dress on, a sleeveless number that shimmered with blue sequins.

Little-girl shivers rushed up from her toes. The cocaine was filling her with electric helium. She skipped into the kitchen to wet her cottony mouth with Perrier.

Oh, where was he? Christ. She clasped her shoulders and hugged herself. They just wanted to talk to him, that was all. That was *all*.

She thought of when her career would be over. She'd marry, have a mess of kids, and drive a station wagon to the A&P. Her husband could introduce her as a former actress. She'd only tell her best friend.

She saw herself already. They'd be sitting over coffee, her and her girlfriend. And Vanessa would say, I had an affair with this guy Sal Veronica, a real gangster.

And the friend would say, no, Vanessa, really? My God, what was it like?

I can't describe it. I was so young then, a silly girl. You know how when you're young. But of course we came from two different worlds.

Talking about him in the past tense gave their affair an epic quality.

She went into the bedroom and slid more gloss onto her lips. She thought of laying out another line of coke. No. The tightrope was already so taut it trembled.

But he was cruel, too.

No man ever hit me before. You couldn't reason with him. He had this animal thing, this brutal brute force. And he made fun of my acting.

She was speaking to her future best friend in the mirror.

They just wanted to talk to him. He owed them money, probably. Gambling debts kinda thing. That was all. And Mickey would put her in with Goldman and finally she'd have the contacts she needed.

Where was he? When was he coming? Sal.

Her doorbell sounded its low pong.

Vanessa bit her knuckles. She took a deep breath, tugged down her neckline, sniffed twice, and stepped to the door. This was going to be a performance.

"A little leg, a little leg, he's going. And I told him, I said, what the hell is this, a skin flick? I thought I'm supposed to be a housewife, suburban kinda thing. You think they wear garters all day? Wear garters to the laundromat? But he says this is supposed to be the fifties. Before panty hose, remember? Remember? How could I remember? I said. I wasn't born until 'sixty-five.'"

Sitting beside Sal in the backseat of the Mercedes, Vanessa recrossed her legs. Coked up, Sal thought, as usual. And yapping as usual. But those legs.

Or maybe she's picking up on your nerves.

Christ, he liked looking at her. He loved to watch her lips, the way when she said some word they formed a little smile, as if her mouth were smiling at him on its own, anticipating. He loved the structure of her face, her elegant floating hands, the little-girl frown that never left a line on her brow. She was his principal distraction. She had a flair for the dramatic. For the melodramatic, really. It made her a clown on stage, but a powerhouse in bed.

She was the reason he'd taken the fall. Because Primo always warned him, never handle junk, never touch it yourself. But he'd dropped a half-ounce in his pocket as a surprise, one of the surprises she loved. And fate pointed its finger, and he took the fall.

Okay, so no blame. No regrets. Never any regrets.

Sal turned away, looked out the smoked windows for a sign. Of what? What was bothering him? The lights whipped by as they cruised down Second. The movie marquees danced yellow. At the entrance to the Queensboro, traffic slowed them.

The kid was a good driver, Sal thought. Kept it rolling at a light. Didn't let anybody pull up alongside. Slipped through obstacles instead of crowding these jerks and giving them the horn. Smooth with the car. Sal appreciated it.

Was it the rap? Baylor talked optimistic, but he was preparing the ground, dropping hints about ways they could play it, keep the sentence down. The federals were in it this time and they were turning the screws.

Shit, you're with Paulie Amato, this shouldn't be happening. Like a son, the old man told you once. Go anywhere in this country, anywhere, just say you're with Paulie from New York, people will crank their eyes down.

But this strike force pins you with the half-ounce and you're staring at ten years' flat time.

So what is it—fear?

He caught a glimpse of the United Nations a block away on First, glowing.

Call it fear. Call it something. You waded through it to make it to where you are today. Hustled your hustles. Put up with Paulie's bull for the last how many years? Kicked ass when you had to. Did your work. You're ready to start collecting on it all. And now you're facing the can.

Sal had to recognize his feelings in the way things looked, his reactions, his moods. He would read his moods like oracles. The nights he couldn't bear to have any lights on or any clothes touching him, he'd stand naked and stare out the window listening to Miles. That mood usually meant somebody was going to have to get clipped.

Ten years would do it for Gina. She might come to see him at first. Then she'd stop coming. Then he'd hear from her lawyer. Then she'd take Mario. Sal wouldn't be able to do anything about that. Mario would be eighteen when Sal got out. His little boy would be shaving, balling, drinking.

He should be spending more time with Mario now. His own son, and he might be on the verge of dropping ten years. But Sal just didn't get home that much and the kid was always off somewhere, school or camp or playing.

Paulie gave Mario a thousand every birthday. Why couldn't he put in the fix on this? Goddamn cops. Goddamn frame-up.

Hell, what can you do? You take your body shots, keep your eyes open. Isn't that what Primo said? If you close your eyes when the guy pounds your belly, the next one lands on your head, my friend.

Primo sat in the front seat studiously ignoring what the girl was saying, missing nothing. El Moledor, they called him, the Grinder. Light-heavy champ of Puerto Rico a lot of years ago. Contender, they said, but he copped a manslaughter rap over a bar brawl before he got a crack at Dick Tiger. Did time in Attica during the rebellion.

So you do your time. You do it standing on your head, it's over, you get out, you go on. Nothing to fear there. If Gina couldn't hack it, that's the way it would be.

So why did the world have this funny complexion?

"Aw, lookit the poor little fishies," Vanessa said.

Too many carp crowded the tank. The fish were breathless, swarming around the stream of bubbles, elbowing each other for a taste of oxygen. They writhed at the surface, their slick black backs forming a mass of darkness. Their tails lashed petulantly. Their unblinking eyes looked out at diners.

The three of them sat at a table in the corner opposite the tank. The boy waited in the car. Even at this hour the restaurant was filled with a buzzing clientele. Several groups of Chinese businessmen in identical blue suits were chanting to each other over tables crowded with dishes and platters. Some Oriental youths were smoking cigarettes and drinking cans of Budweiser as they nibbled peppers and snails. A black man in Eldorado duds was entertaining his slick lady.

"Amaretto?" their waiter repeated through clenched teeth.

"It's a lick-*cure*," Vanessa explained. "Amaretto."

"Sure, amaretto. You want on rocks?"

"No, I want it in a glass, like it comes in, with a stem."

"Sure, in a glass."

Sal answered the waiter's stare. "Cutty and water. Primo?"

Primo ordered a glass of vermouth.

Vanessa was laughing as she stood up. "Oh boy, I almost cracked up when he said that. I was going to say, on locks? No, I don't want it on my locks. I don't want you to pour it on my head. See? You want on the locks? he said. My God.

"Sal, I've gotta call my service, I just remembered. I

should have before I left, but I'm expecting this producer to phone from the Coast. I know what you're going to say, but I've told you and told you about the competition for these spots—a few minutes, a few seconds, can make or break your career right there. You have to keep on top of it. Okay? And then I'm going to the ladies', I hope to God it's cleaner than they usually are in these places. I mean, I know it's going to be a filthy hole, but when nature calls she doesn't take any prisoners. So order me something, I'm hungry as a palomino, but not the super-hot stuff this time, okay? Okay?"

Examining the menu, Sal nodded without looking at her. As she crossed the room, he checked the other eyes following her. Several men glanced from her sparkling hips to Sal, then quickly looked away.

"This one fight, I don't think I ever tell you," Primo was saying. "Was in Cuba, just before the revolution. I seen the boy fight before, a black boy with long arms. He seem, during the instruction, like he's sleeping. Bell rings, I see how slow he is, flat foot."

Sal was always impressed how Primo could relive fights he'd had thirty years earlier, and they were so fresh you could almost smell the rosin and sweat. He lit a cigar and tasted the scotch the waiter put in front of him.

Primo described the scene, the smoky arena full of pimps and panama hats.

"I'm just going to play with him, move move move. When I want to, stop and punish his body. First time I try it, he splits my cheek with his elbow. I complain, ref see nothing. Is hard to hit this boy, his arms always in the way."

Their waiter came back with a chrome pot of tea, a bowl of chow mein noodles, saucers of duck sauce and mustard.

"But this boy just warming up. Next round he stand on my foot and work a lace in my left eye. Ref wag his finger. Then the boy start pound my cup. Everything south of the border. I work in close, he jam his chin down on my shoulder."

Primo paused, wincing as if he could feel the sharp chin of the long-armed Cuban still.

"Fifth round, my eye all closed. Cut on my cheek bleeding bad. Arms ache from pounding. Bottom falling out down here. So I wake up. Primo, I say, ref mean nothing in this fight. This a real fight. This a fight like death. I feel is like a vision, like I see something. I see, I see— how you say?"

Sal smiled across at the older man. I don't know how you say, he was going to tell him. It was something you couldn't find a word for, something you had to get punched in the nuts a few times before you could learn, maybe.

Primo glanced quickly at his watch. The gesture touched off a nerve in Sal's brain.

The thought that came to Sal was a tantalizing one, because he understood, in the instant it entered his head, that it came too late. It happens. Things click into place at the exact moment when it no longer matters: the girl had been gone too long.

His eyes rose to see the two men halfway across the room. They were ignoring the waiter who was trying to point them to a table. Oblivious, they were bumping people.

Sal hadn't quite finished pouring tea into the small stoneware cup. His hand jerked on its own, practically before the idea of Vanessa's prolonged absence registered.

The teapot sailed through the air. A transparent sheet of hot liquid spread toward the closer of the two men.

Primo, his reflexes still hair-trigger, was already turning.

Next came the suspension. No sound, the teapot, the tea frozen. Colors soaring to a terrible brilliance. At the table beside them was a woman whose face Sal had noticed earlier. She had high cheekbones, cocky eyes, and a fine frame of straight blond hair. He'd traded looks with her twice since he sat down. Her features were now twisted with alarm.

During this brief suspension, the first man, the one in

16

the Mets cap, fired his pistol. As the bullet slapped the side of his chest, Sal cursed Vanessa. Condemned her utterly.

Then the rush. The explosion of the shots engulfed the restaurant. Tables went over. Glass broke. Some people dove to the floor. Others leapt to see what was going on. Screams erupted.

The tea caught the gunman square in the face. His second shot smashed the jaw of the blonde at the next table. His third shattered a fluorescent tube in the ceiling.

The other intruder, dressed in denim jacket and ski cap, had already shot Primo twice as the fighter spun. Primo managed to extract his gun. He sent off two shots. One punched into the chest of the man in the baseball cap. A mirror broke on the opposite wall, sending the image of the room flying to pieces.

Sal had to lean over to grip the off-duty pistol he kept in an ankle holster. He heard two more shots.

Primo was standing the way an old man stands. The gunman slammed one more slug into Primo's body. He tried for a head shot and missed. Primo fired twice wildly. He slumped over a table covered with steaming platters of food. He slid to the floor, pulling dishes of pork and chicken and clotted rice on top of him.

His left side on fire, Sal stood up. He held his pistol in both hands and squeezed off round after round. The man in the ski cap was firing back at him.

Sal's shots were more accurate. The man stumbled backward. His head split the fish tank. He slumped. The water gushed, diluting his blood. Four good-sized carp flopped frantically on the floor beside his body.

Sal's breath was wet. He leaned briefly over Primo, noting the boxer's eyes. They still stared relentlessly, now sightless. Sal stumbled on, through a door.

It was the wrong door. The kitchen. An overwhelming aroma of hot oil and boiling rice, fumes of garlic and ginger and sizzling meat threatened to suffocate him. Spectral Chinamen stared and blanched and ducked. The bare bulbs were emitting blackness. On a calendar beside the choking sign, a pink-nippled Chinese girl in cowboy hat and chaps was spinning a six-shooter.

Sal weaved. For a moment he couldn't find the door through which he'd just entered. Whispering in Chinese, amplified a thousand times, swelled his head.

Back out in the restaurant, patrons were rushing for the door. A scream, high and thin and icy, hung in the air.

Beside the kitchen an arrow and a silhouette of a man in a top hat and a woman in a party dress pointed to the rest rooms in the basement. Descending the stairs, Sal thought he was climbing them.

He reached the bottom. He kicked at the door of the ladies', missed, broke a toe. He threw his shoulder at it. He spun through, sliding onto his hip on the tile floor. The room smelled of chemical flowers. It was empty.

He pulled himself up by the sink. A madman's face peeked over the bottom of the mirror. The hand print Sal left on the porcelain was bloody.

Still using the sink for a support, he bent down. He looked under the doors of the stalls at no feet.

A rush brought him to the exit. He hesitated. With the precision of a drunk toeing the line for a traffic cop, he stepped to the farthest cubicle. He nudged the door. It swung easily. Inside, Vanessa was squatting on top of the toilet.

"I heard a noise," she said.

Sal spit blood. He grabbed her hair, her luscious, deep-mahogany hair. He wrapped it tightly around his hand.

She slipped. One foot splashed into the bowl.

He twisted her head. He pressed the hot barrel of the gun to the center of her frown. Pressed and pulled the trigger.

The gun clicked. He pressed harder and pulled again. Click. Again.

Her whimpering became darkness. He collapsed to the floor.

Later, a plastic surgeon would charge Vanessa $2,800 to remove the little *o* from her forehead.

At least this time it wasn't a woman, Gina thought as she steered her Marquis up the ramp of the Verrazano Narrows Bridge. The gray in the east was turning to an orange haze, promising a hot and dirty day. Gulls swooped above the cables and veered down across the harbor.

At least. At least the waiting was over. It seemed as if she'd been waiting for years.

That was the worst, the waiting. She remembered the first time, soon after they were married, when Sal didn't come home all night. Didn't come home, didn't call, nothing. No idea where he was. And brother she'd waited. She'd called her mother, her sister, her friends. Waited some more. Began to hope that something *had* happened to him. Hoped that he wasn't *doing* this to her, what no human being would do to their worst enemy. Wasn't putting her through this hell just out of carelessness. Wasn't with some woman, some whore.

All night she'd waited, while the phone swelled and swelled with the urge to ring and didn't ring. Waited, ruined her nails, smoked so many cigarettes her heart was doing somersaults in her chest. And still he didn't come home.

She wound down now off the bridge onto the Belt Parkway. At least at this hour the traffic was light.

Waited until he walked in at noon the next day as if nothing had happened, fed her the sly smile, the wink that he used to disarm her. She let him have it, all right. Broke things. Gina loved to break things. Smashed almost half the English bone china, the wedding present from Uncle Phil. Broke one window, a mirror, cups, glasses. The same as he was smashing their marriage, she broke things.

And he just told her she was full of it and walked. Didn't come back for another two days. But he called. At least he called. Told her she was a crazy wop, he was scared of her. That was a good one. Ho ho.

God damn it, the worry he'd caused her. Eight years of it. Nine years it'd be in October. She'd never gotten used to it. She'd always known—she'd *told* him over and over and over it would come to this. Rushing to a hospital at dawn, imagining the worst.

Last night was like the others. As always, she'd spent most of the evening on the phone talking to her girlfriends. They knew the kind of man Sal was, most of their men were the same, they weren't regular. No regular job, no regular hours, no regular habits. Restless, haphazard men—not workaday men.

"Gina Fratelli, what in the name of the Virgin are you doing marrying this man?" her mother had asked her. "You're twenty-four years old, you're a beautiful girl, you're smart, you could've gone to college, and he's a hoodlum, he'll never be nothing, a street bum, people know him in this neighborhood, he's no good, he comes from low people, he'll treat you low."

"Mama, he's the most beautiful guy I ever went out with, he's strong, he's gentle, he knows things, Mama, he's got this fire in him, he makes me feel like I never knew I could feel, he knows a lot of people, everybody, he treats me I can't tell you how good, Mama . . . Mama, I'm pregnant."

So now Mario was eight, eight already. Sal never did any of the things a father was supposed to, didn't have time.

Didn't have time for her, either, usually. She'd become accustomed to a kind of loneliness that she'd never known until she married.

The night before she'd put their son to bed. She watched TV and paced and smoked. She drank a black russian and dozed and watched more TV, waiting. Finally, she lay down in bed. Slept, but didn't sleep. Waited even in her sleep.

Yellow flashers blinked dumbly to mark a construction site. A hazy sun was just starting to slice through the gaps in the apartment houses along the parkway.

Okay, the life wasn't all bad. And Sal could still be the man she'd flipped over. Could still make her go molten with a word, a look. Could surprise her with his gentleness, the tender things he said.

But they had only emptiness before them. Sal had to build the bridge that was their future. And sooner or later he wouldn't be able to build it fast enough, and they'd go over.

As she approached the Battery Tunnel she had to fight a feeling she knew was wrong. But she couldn't stamp out the glow of satisfaction that at last this time the worst *had* happened, he *was* hurt. At least she hadn't spent the night agonizing over him while he frolicked with some slut in town, God damn him. She knew it was wrong to think such thoughts when he could be dying— Oh, Sal! At least she'd know where he was now for a while. As she'd known the time he'd had to go to prison for fourteen months. Now she could care for him, love him, without any of the bad thoughts.

If he lived. Oh, God! Oh, sweet God, please! The detective sergeant had told her only that Sal'd been hurt, shot, it was serious, he was in St. Vincent's.

She had been awake when the phone rang. Awake and petrified. *Before* the phone rang.

Right away she telephoned Denise to take care of Mario. Denise understood. She came right over and told Gina not to worry about a thing. Be brave, she said.

The noise roused Mario. She had to tell him.

"Daddy got hurt a little bit and I've got to go see him. You be a good boy. Denise will get your breakfast and you can stay home from school today and play. Won't that be fun?"

"What happened to him?"

"He got hurt, but he's going to be okay. The doctors are just making him all better."

"Did somebody beat him up?"

"No, they—it might have been an accident."

" 'Cause nobody can beat up Daddy. Can they?"

"No, dear."

She parked the car near the hospital and hurried across Seventh Avenue. The sun caught her as she passed a store window. She checked her reflection, stopped to put on lipstick.

She was an attractive woman. She knew it. She spent a lot of time on her looks, a lot of care. Why did he have to have others? Forget about that now. No, really. Didn't she please him? What was he looking for in them that he couldn't find in her?

Sal was in a private room on the eighth floor. A burly man in a gray suit sat outside the door reading a tabloid, sipping from a Styrofoam coffee cup. He stopped her. She told him she was Mrs. Veronica.

"See some I.D., please?"

"That's my husband in there. He's badly hurt."

"Driver's license, something."

She swore as she fumbled through her purse. He glanced at her license, pushed the door open for her, stepped inside behind her, and waited.

Sal was lying partially propped up in bed. His chest was wrapped. An I.V. tube was taped to his left arm. He looked pale, the shadow of his beard beginning to stand out, his lips slack, his hair matted.

She took his hand. She wanted to say his name, but the word caught in her throat.

His lids rose. He seemed to swim back into his eyes. He forced a half-smile.

"Close one," he said.

Gina couldn't hold her tears back any longer.

Sal waved at her and looked away. She pressed her hands to her mouth, held her breath, sniffed back her emotion.

He talked slowly. They'd given him a sedative. But the dullness, the thick speech made his anger even more frightening, more menacing.

He wouldn't go into the details of the shooting. That was history.

Primo was dead, he told her. It shocked her. Primo was one of the few real gentlemen among Sal's cronies. She remembered how Sal had always praised Primo to Mario. Look at the eyes, he'd say. A fighter's eyes never look away.

What he had to deal with now was Paulie. Paulie had

betrayed him. Paulie had set him up. Paulie was responsible for this. Paulie would pay. He spit out the name as if it tasted of bile.

Gina couldn't believe it. Why? Why would anyone? But especially Paulie. Mario's Uncle Paulie? That mild, gray-haired man?

Paulie thought Sal was a snitch. Paulie thought he would maybe run his mouth to avoid a sentence. The one-eyed son of a bitch didn't trust him. All he'd done for Paulie. All the grief. All the work.

Okay. Paulie was covering his own ass. Okay. So be it. Except—one little problem. Sal wasn't dead. Sal the Veil would ride again. And this time, no bullshit loyalty, no code, no silence, no honor.

He would talk. He would hand over all he knew on Paulie. He knew plenty. He could put Paulie away for ten thousand years on half of what he knew.

Paulie would learn. Shoot him down like a dog? Paulie would see. Paulie would pay.

"And then what, Sal?" she asked. "What about us? You and me and Mario? What are we going to do? We still have to live. You know what I mean? What's going to happen to us?"

"They have this program," Sal said.

3

The tadpole of Ted Reed's consciousness, lost in the great swamp of sleep, sprouted legs and began to crawl onto the dry land of a suburban Saturday morning. He found his bearings on this secure bank and shook off the clinging remnants of three A.M. doubts, the innuendo of dreams just beyond the veil of memory.

Lying in bed, he wiped grit from his eyes and thought about the couple he had to meet that morning. He would sell them. He would sell them today. He would, by sheer desire, by absolute mental dynamics, by the force of pure will transformed into irresistible salesmanship, force them to sign a binder on one of the Cedargrove properties. He would. No question. Done deal.

He actually smiled, calculating his commission on the transaction. This would be the beginning of a streak that would be talked about for years to come at Winner Realty.

He'd be the Winner Winner every month from now

till Christmas. He'd lead the board for so long they'd think he *owned* the board. Christ, he knew how to sell. Sell? He could sell refrigerators to Eskimos. Forget it, he could sell a teeter-totter to a hermit.

Yep, you had to go out there imbued with the kind of confidence that reached to the soles of your feet, that put a special spring in your step. You had to..

He swung his legs over the edge of the bed and walked stiffly to the bathroom. He was a tall man with a stoop. In school they'd called him Condor.

Not that he didn't have his little worries, his real worries. Once he was up he could catalog them. He no longer had to be afraid of confusing them with the primal terrors that stalked his nights.

Laura, his wife, that was one. Habit had taken over—as it did, he hastened to add, with all married couples sooner or later. Habit had worn the excitement off their lives. They'd become familiar strangers to each other. It frightened him, the distance between them. And it was his fault—no, nobody's fault. He knew it was something they should talk about, but they never talked about things like that.

And Jenny. Life was getting serious for his little girl. Things happened to other people's kids and things could happen to your kid. It was a prickly world out there: drugs, boys, the stuff at school, all the snares the world laid for the incautious fifteen-year-old.

Ted spit blood. Great. Every morning now he spit blood. He could already hear the dark-eyed hygienist with her "You haven't been flossing, Ted. Have you?" He'd have to confess. Maynard would start pressing him to have his gums flapped and the plaque scraped.

He couldn't bear the thought of it. Didn't he have enough problems? A salesman's lot was so goddamn precarious, did he also have to have bad teeth? He sucked a mouthful of Lavoris.

He arranged his hair. Shampoo, comb it right, nobody'd call him bald. Thinning, sure. But not bald. No way.

25

He was forty-three, after all. And baldness was a sign of virility.

He showered and shaved. Brushed with the electric toothbrush.

He tested his patented, cocked-eyebrow trust-me-with-your-life deal-closing hex smile. It fit his face like a glove. Better. Ted, you're a selling machine. They'll be dropping like flies, my boy, like flies.

Laura was still in bed when he came out. She was breathing deeply. She slept naked, a sheet draped over her. Ted's eyes studied her contours.

He sighed. He had responsibilities. No way he could afford to crawl back into bed. He had to land this couple—he'd already invested so much time in them, worked them for so long on the ten-pound test line, he couldn't let them slip off the hook when they were just coming in range of the net. He had to close them. Hell, he had to close something, just to keep up his confidence.

He thought with longing back to the time when he couldn't have stopped himself from crawling back into bed. Even now he still felt like a schoolboy sometimes when he looked at his wife. Still felt that lump of longing and fear, of confused arousal, of painful tenderness.

"Daddy, will you make Jenny get *out* of there? She's been *in* there for *hours*." Robbie was mashing grapes by the bathroom door.

"Jennifer, hurry please. Your brother wants to brush his teeth."

"I don't want to brush my teeth, Dad," Robbie pleaded. "I've gotta go. Bad."

"Hear me, Jenny?"

The girl's voice came through the door. "I'll be out when I'm done. Leave me alone."

"I can't wait, Dad."

"She'll be finished in a minute."

"I'm going to kill you, Jenny!" Robbie yelled through the door. "I'm going to napalm you, you gook!"

"Robbie, just keep cool, will you."

"Da-ad."

26

"Hurry up, Jen."

Down in the kitchen Ted ate his bran flakes and looked over the real estate ads while he waited for the coffee maker. Radford had a half-page spread with photographs. Tasteful, but drab. Winner's full page really caught your eye. He looked for his listings. "Aah-eee-aah" was the lead highlighted at the top. Beautiful. "Aah-eee-aah! Tarzan swing from trees around this five-bedroom colonial while Jane soak in modern spa. Boy (and Girl) romp on eight acres, gorgeously landscaped. Priced to sell at $356,000."

It was exactly the type of ad that would appeal to that market, those jokers with some coin to throw around, the new-money market, just learning how to spend it. Ted hoped to God he could move the place fast.

He skimmed the rest of the paper, picking out a couple of human-interest pieces as conversation starters. It was important to keep up a smooth flow of talk while he drove clients around to view properties. The guy was a sports fan, he knew, so he checked batting stats for both leagues. Christ, he imagined himself saying, did you see how many ribbies that Davis has got already?

"Jennifer," he said to his daughter as she wandered into the kitchen, "I want you to stay here today and help your mother. She has a lot to do around the house and in the garden and she has to get ready for the barbecue tonight."

"Dad—"

When Jenny was born, Ted wanted to name her Hermione, after a great-aunt of his who read Dante and had always been generous with the hard candies. Laura pointed out that she'd have trouble with kids making fun of her later, so they settled on Jennifer. Hard to believe their baby was fifteen already. Sixteen in December, she always pointed out. That was still six months away, but she was already studying for her learner's permit and referring to the family car as "wheels."

Fifteen. She had her mother's auburn hair and cheekbones. She was quickly developing a shape. She was going to be a very pretty girl.

Mixed blessing, Ted thought. She already attracted boys like flies. During the spring she'd been suspended from school for a day. The charge was improper behavior—"Doing nothing," was how she'd described it—with a boy in a deserted home-ec room. Laura had found cigarettes in her purse. Jenny insisted on listening to music by these groups that Ted suspected were satanic. Her friends, forget it. And she'd become just impossible around the house.

She'd discovered all of a sudden that she knew all there was to know. It was painful to see the wonder go out of her, replaced by the blasé certainty that, Ted supposed, was a requisite umbrella against the storm of adolescence.

Laura's approach to the matter made him uneasy. She felt they couldn't stop Jenny from having sex, so be open about it and make sure she uses birth control. But with all the nut cases running around, the diseases you could catch now, Ted worried about the risks.

"I don't want to hear about it, Jenny."

"I'm not staying home, Daddy dear." She bared her braces in an unctuous smile. "Michelle and I are going to the mall. We're meeting some kids there. I already told her."

"I'm telling *you.* You're going to stay here and help your mother."

She crossed her arms, a sign, Ted recognized, that meant she was digging in. She stood there with her girl's knees showing through precisely lacerated jeans. Her T-shirt, tied in a knot above her narrow waist, advertised a concert perpetrated by some bizarre musical group. From her checkerboard-painted toenails to her multiple earrings, her whole being blared teenage arrogance. She was drinking a Diet Pepsi for breakfast.

"Her mother's taking us," she said. "It's all arranged. I am not going to stay home and grub in the dirt. Do you hear me?"

"Look, it's a beautiful day out. You want to go and hang around inside? Just to go shopping? You should be out, get some color."

"Dad, sun causes skin cancer. It's going to get hot and I want to be in air conditioning."

"Gardening is a very healthy activity."

"What's she want to raise a lot of tomatoes for anyway? Why can't we just buy vegetables like normal people? Are we that poor, we can't afford a few measly tomatoes? It's stupid."

"It's because of the pesticides, Jenny," Laura said, entering. She was barefoot in shorts.

Ted looked at his wife's legs.

"There's nothing like the taste of a homegrown tomato," he said.

"And weed killers," Laura went on. "Commercial tomatoes are the worst for contamination. We raise ours organically."

"The ones you buy don't have any taste," Ted said.

"Who cares?" Jenny protested. "Who cares about a goddamn tomato? There's children starving in Africa. What about them? You people are dead in your minds."

Ted looked at Laura and raised his eyebrows.

"I hate tomatoes," Robbie said, pouring himself a bowl of Fruit Loops.

The discussion continued through breakfast. Jenny *did* have to have a new swimsuit. They *were* predicting a hot day. Laura played the good cop and they decided she could go to the mall if she'd help out with the celery and carrot sticks and dip for the barbecue when she returned.

Ted thought of bringing up the fact that she'd broken her curfew again last night, stayed out with that little bastard Hollis boy. But she'd only been a half-hour late. Anyway, he had to leave for work. He put it on the long list of subjects he was accumulating for that father-daughter talk he planned to have with her. Soon. Someday very soon.

Ted was finishing his second cup when Josh came in and said, "They're here."

No one ever guessed that Josh and Robbie were twins. When they'd lined up for dibs on the birth canal, Laura felt Robbie kicking poor Josh in the head. Ever since, Robbie had been bigger and brasher.

29

"Who's here?" Ted asked.

"Have they got any kids?" Jenny asked.

"Next door. Yeah, a boy."

"How old?"

"My age. About."

"That's all? Great. Another brat in the neighborhood. Maybe at least I can baby-sit for them."

"I'm going to do some recon," Robbie said.

"I think I'll go have a look." Jenny followed him out.

"Boy, it's going to be good to have somebody new in there," Ted said.

"I'm glad they have kids," Laura said.

"Anybody's got to be better than the Bennetts."

The Bennetts, an older couple who drove a Cadillac and kept two colicky poodles, had moved out three months ago. The feud between them and the Reeds had never quite reached epic proportions. But it had had a Hatfield-McCoy endlessness as an exchange over blowing trash followed one about baseballs in flower beds. The smoke from burning leaves was forever drifting in the wrong direction. Somebody's leach line was being fouled by somebody's tree roots. Children's yelling was repeatedly measured against dogs' sanitary habits.

Ted looked across at Josh, who was fingering the Matchbox Porsche that was like a security blanket to him. Josh was the quiet one, the one Ted hoped wouldn't turn out gay. He sometimes wondered how he'd handle it if it did happen.

"They are white, aren't they, Josh?"

"Ted, Jesus," Laura said.

"I'm just joking, for Christ's sake. You know I'm joking, don't you, Josh?"

Josh nodded. "He's got a girl's name."

"Who?"

"Their boy."

"You met him already?"

"Yeah. He doesn't know where he's from. He's got a girl's name and he doesn't know where he's from."

"What's his name? Sue? Boy named Sue?"

"No. Mary-O."

"That's not—that's an Italian name. Mario Lanza. What do you mean, he doesn't know where he's from?"

"I asked him, where you from? He said he forgot, he'd tell me later. Then he said his father could beat you up. His father could beat anybody up, he said. I said no he couldn't. I said you look stronger when you have your shirt off. He said his father was stronger, a lot stronger. He could mash you to a pulp, he said. He could kill you."

"Well, thank God you're not my manager, so we won't have to climb in the ring to settle the matter. It's good you'll have another kid in the neighborhood to play with, isn't it?"

"I want you to be nice to that little boy, Josh," Laura said. "He doesn't know anybody here, and you can help him adjust. It's very stressful to have to move."

"I know, Mom."

"Listen, Josh," Ted said, slipping on his sport coat and checking the contents of his briefcase. "They're having a meeting Monday night for all the kids who might be interested in going out for Pop Warner. Robbie's going. I thought maybe you'd—it might give you something to do during the summer."

"I don't want to play football, Dad."

"Robbie said the kids want you to play."

"So they can massacre me."

"I just thought, you know, get out there with the boys."

Josh ran his little car up and down the table. "I don't wanna, Dad."

"Okay, nobody's forcing you."

Jennifer returned to the kitchen.

"He's cute," she announced.

"Their boy?" Ted said.

"Christ, Dad, I don't mean their *boy*. He's another little brat, just what we don't need. I mean him, the guy. He looks like a movie star or something. Really."

"Wow, a movie star!" Ted mocked, stooping to give Laura the ritual kiss before heading out.

"I think we should invite them over for the barbecue," Laura said. "It would be a nice gesture."

"Tonight? No, they'll be all in from moving."

"So, it'll be easier than cooking or going out to eat. They can meet Maynard and Felice and that other couple. If they're too tired, they don't have to stay."

"Yes, Dad, I think you should invite them," Jennifer said. "They look very very interesting. They're probably more sophisticated than we are, but one has to expect that, doesn't one?"

"Yeah, Dad," Robbie said. "We want to get to go in their pool."

The Bennetts' inviting, unused pool had long been an object of envy for the Reed household.

"Oh, for the love of—"

"I'll ask them," Laura said, "if you don't want to."

"No, I'll talk to him. I'll mention the barbecue, see what he says. What's their name, does anyone know?"

The guy was standing on the front lawn directing the movers and giving instructions to a man on a ladder by the garage when Ted went over. Medium build, a little short. His dark hair recently barbered, his broad shoulders giving onto muscular arms. Ted, whose business depended on sizing people up by their appearance, noticed the tattoo, the gold chain showing in the neck of the Lacoste shirt, the cigar.

Stockbroker? he thought. One of these commodity dealers? Doing okay at it, whatever it was. Doing very well. Slick, even a little oily. Not a wise-ass, he hoped.

The man looked at Ted intently, shifting his weight, watching. No smile. Ted couldn't read his expression behind the dark glasses. The neat mustache and Kirk Douglas chin probably explained why Jenny thought he had star potential.

"Peace, friend," Ted said, raising his hand in an Indian salute.

A cold smile. They exchanged greetings, shook hands. The man's name was Sal Vincent. They'd moved out here

32

from Rochester. No, New York, not Minnesota. Yeah, you never knew how much junk you had until you moved, too true.

"You looked for a minute there like you thought I was from the IRS," Ted said.

"Not at all, babe. You aren't government, I can see that."

"Putting up some new lights?"

"For security."

"Yeah," Ted said. "I noticed a guy out here this week doing a major alarm job. We're a pretty low-crime community here."

"Good."

"Course, it doesn't hurt to be careful. Don't worry, the guy didn't blab. I just happen to know the kind of work he does, being in the business."

"What business is that?"

"Real estate. Fact, I almost sold this place. I was handling it on the multiple listing. I had a guy very interested, but he really rubbed me the wrong way. He was a computer engineer. Let me tell you, this guy knew it all."

"An asshole."

"Precisely. See, he didn't want to know about the heating system, he already knew everything there was to know about heating systems. He says, how's the crime around here? I say, beautiful. No crime. I'm going to check with the cops, he says. I say, I've got a wife, three kids, I live next door—think I'd live in a neighborhood wasn't safe?"

Ted had a sense that he was talking too much, but something about this guy made him uneasy, made him want to talk.

"But see, the point is, I could have sold this guy—a know-it-all's an easy sale. You just agree with him. Especially this place, this landscaping. But I don't want to sell him *this* house. I don't want to have to deal with the guy, have him next door. I've been through that—the Bennetts."

"Yeah, the ones we bought from."

"Right. Older couple. He was—I think he was one of

33

these Nazi war criminals escaped over here. He used to scream at the kids. They had a Frisbee sailed over the hedge there. He wouldn't give it back. I went over. He said it nearly hit him on the head. A piece of goddamn plastic. I got pissed—I have something of a temper—and told him maybe I'd knock his dentures out. He went and called the cops. When the prowl car arrived the deputies had quite a laugh."

"Sounds like a nice guy."

"We were thrilled when they decided to pack it in and move to Sarasota. But this computer engineer, I could tell he was another Bennett. I can usually tell with a person pretty quick. My business it pays."

"So what did you do?"

"Oh, I told him, I said, yeah, now that you mention it, there's some low-income housing going in up the road. That iced him. His wife's jabbing him to lock the car door as they're leaving."

"So you blew your commission."

"What's money?"

"I like that," Sal said. "What the hell's money? It's what you got between your legs that's important."

"Sure. What line of work are you in?"

"I'm retired, sort of. I've been doing some consulting. I'm looking around for the right setup at the moment. I used to work for Uncle Sam myself. In the service."

"I was in the Peace Corps, years ago," Ted said.

"Yeah, I kind of worked in army intelligence."

"You were—what do they call it?—a spook? Spy, sort of?"

"Sort of. I did some fieldwork. Mostly pretty mundane, pushing papers. Not an awful lot I can go into."

"I get you. Hush-hush."

They talked about the house, the neighborhood, the weather. Ted could see the guy had been around. Bright. A little mysterious. Nobody's fool. And something else. Something about him that made you want very much to have him like you.

Ted found himself mentioning his hopes for Golden

Age Estates. Strange, he usually made a point of never talking about something like that until it was a done deal. But he explained it to this stranger, told of his dream of a new kind of housing for older citizens. Not a nursing home. Not just condos. A real community. The potential, he said, was absolutely tremendous. Just look at the demographics.

"It would mean heading out on my own," he said, "starting my own development firm. But something like this could serve as the foundation of a whole real estate operation—I almost said empire. That's how I think of it. Think big, that's my motto. I'm a natural optimist."

"It pays to think big," Sal said, smiling.

Was the man making fun of him? Ted wondered.

"Of course," Ted continued, "there's always a lot of risk in these things, you have to hit it just right. But I have a friend who has a few extra bucks. He's promised to help bankroll the proposition with some seed money if I ever decide to take the plunge. Of course, with my responsibilities, family and all, I have to weigh it pretty carefully."

Talking too much, Ted told himself again. He extended the invitation to the barbecue that night. Very informal, he said, just two other couples stopping by. Grill some chicken, hoist a few.

Sal removed his sunglasses. He stared at Ted for a long time without speaking.

"Very informal," Ted repeated.

"Okay," Sal said.

"Great." Ted went off feeling relieved, as if he'd passed a kind of test.

4

"I am really going to do something with this house," Gina said. "It'll be a gem, something you can be proud of."

Their last place was a modest attached brick home in New Dorp, on Staten Island. Sal had never paid much attention to where he lived. Gina liked it there because her sister lived three blocks away and she had plenty of friends in the neighborhood. This, she felt, was her first "real" house.

"The big window in front there is no good," Sal commented.

"I'm going to make it into an honest-to-goodness home. It's so bright."

"But at night, I mean. Too exposed."

"You know what I'm going to make it? A palace. And you'll be the king."

"King?"

"Sal, please? Please. This has been hard for me, too. Just please go along with it, okay? Please try."

"I'm trying."

"I know you are. Here, I want you to see this." She led him through the bedroom. "Mario came in here looking around and he said, how come you've got two toilets? Did you know this was here? That's great. So French. Huh?"

"Yeah, very groovy, sure."

"Sal, can't you relax? You're making me nervous. We're here. It's over, all the bullshit. This is a new life for us. I mean that. I feel like a bride or something. You know?"

She flowed onto the oversized bed and propped a hand under her neck.

"I don't feel like no bride," Sal said. "I can tell you that. I feel like I'm in never-never land here. You know, where nobody grows up? Where Captain Hook's a storybook pirate? Where you can fly if you believe hard enough? This isn't my world. This isn't real. What am I going to do, one minute to the next? How am I going to act? Where am I going to get my kicks?"

"Oh, right, I forgot. Your kicks. Sal's gotta have his kicks. That's what's important. Stop the world, time for Sal to get his kicks."

"Don't—"

"You are one hundred percent responsible for us being here. You'd like some kicks? I—maybe I'd like to see my mother once in a while, or Lucy, or Denise. And I never will again. Ever! And *I* didn't do anything wrong!"

"Okay."

"I'm no criminal! Mario's no criminal! Your son, remember? What about him?"

"You're right."

"Sal, let's make it a chance. Let's really start something new. Look, see how my butterflies look in this corner? I'm going to have room to show off all my things."

Gina collected porcelain butterflies, porcelain horses, porcelain fairy-tale figures. She delighted in their delicacy.

37

"Just to be finally settled someplace permanent," she said. "All the moving around, living in motels, it was getting to me. To Mario, too. That was no good for him. And having those damn marshals around all the time. He picks up on things like that. I don't like the ideas he comes out with sometimes."

"He's a kid."

"You don't know him, Sal. Mario's not a baby anymore. Remember how you used to dote on him? But then you kind of lost interest."

"I didn't have time."

"You had time to hang out with Joey and Primo and them."

"That was business."

"You had time. For your women you had time."

"We going to run around that track again?"

"Hey—magic slate. Huh? You know Mario's magic slate, you pull up the cellophane and all the writing disappears? That's what I want, Sal. New. All new. New life, new house, new city, new us. We can find something together."

"Find? What are we going to find? We're nowhere. We're exactly, precisely in the middle of nowhere."

"Remember the good times we had? We can—don't you see this is a chance to wipe out all the hurt and all the betrayal and everything? Find ourselves, the way we were."

"The way we weren't."

Gina rubbed her mouth.

"You said once that no other woman could," she said.

"Could what?"

"Could . . . I don't know. You said, no other woman, Gina—I remember you saying it. The way you used to look at me."

"Hey, you were always it for me, baby. You were the ultimate."

"Yeah, were. When you'd take the time. Nine years, how many times have we had really to ourselves?"

"Course, we always had the kid around."

"Mario his name is. But you know how I used to talk

about a desert island, just us, where we could spend time and nobody to bother us and no worries? This is it. I'm not going to go on about the women."

"Oh, for Christ—"

"I said, I'm not bringing them up. I just want you to accept that we're out here together. You and me, Sal. This is our chance. Can't you let yourself see it as a chance?"

"For somebody else it's a chance. Not for me. Only way I can get in on it—stop being myself. That's the price of admission. You can have this life and still be Gina Veronica, only now it's Vincent. Different name, that's all. You'll gossip with the girls. You'll go shopping, beauty parlor, the mall. It's you, the old you in a new setting."

"Do you really think—?"

"I can't do that. I have to pretend all the time. Or I'm screwed. I have to live in a world that before I've just seen through glass. I have to accommodate people I always thought were jellyfish, nobodies, dings. Whole world full of them. Like the guy next door. He's a ding. Got his little family, his little job, his little dreams. He's a ding. He says, we'd like you to come over for a barbecue tonight. A fucking barbecue."

"Really, Sal? That's fantastic. We can meet the neighbors. Mario will have kids to play with—they have kids, right? I thought it might be hard to get to know people."

"You don't get it—he's inviting Sal Vincent. Sal Vincent's going, I'm not. I have to put myself away and be this other guy I don't even know. Fucking Clark Kent. And not just tonight—always, from now on."

"Wait—faster than a speeding bullet, wasn't it? More powerful than a locomotive?"

Sal laughed. He stretched on the bed beside her.

Gina said, "You're wrong, you know. It's not easy for me either. My friends, my family? You don't replace people with a bunch of new faces. Lucy and Denise? Patsy? Aunt Alice? I'm never going to see them again."

"Aw."

"Just have some consideration."

"I'll give you some consideration."

"Sal." She pushed his hand away.

"What?"

"Mario. The door isn't closed."

"You said I was the king, babe."

"Sa-al. Jesus."

Ted met his clients at the office. They were an eager young couple, the wife showing a volleyball belly under her blue summer dress. That meant they'd just have time to close, put giraffe wallpaper in the nursery, and make their first mortgage payment before the blessed event.

They were an easy sale, but Ted hadn't been able to sell them. He was taking them out to see their fourth executive ranch today. The developer had left some of the trees, so it wouldn't have that naked feel. A nice development, each house styled differently—not like the old suburban ticky-tack. You had a few Dutch colonials, some Tudor, a couple of saltbox replicas. But they were all new, all in a comfortably expensive range. There'd be plenty of kids. Perfect for a young married couple with dough.

They climbed into his car—the wife in front, the solicitous husband droning about Lamaze classes from the back.

The key to landing these people, he knew, was "value." He had to push value for all it was worth. They were value freaks. Yes, a home was more than an investment. Everybody knew that. You lived in it. It was a special place for you. But it *was* an investment, the most important one you'd make in your life. So value meant not just getting a good house at a good price, in a good neighborhood, with a good prospect for healthy appreciation over the near and long term. It also meant you had to love the place. Then it was a good investment and a good home, too. Then you were getting value.

They were clever buyers. They knew how to *avoid* buying. None of the houses he'd shown them had the right "feel." That's what they told him. This place didn't speak to her. That place struck him as impersonal. This other place, no charm. No realtor could argue with a buyer's feelings.

"I think you're going to find that there's something special about this place," he said, in his best soft-sell voice, as they drove out toward the development. "The location is what I like about it. And you know what you said about location, Roy."

"Location, location, location," Roy said. "That's the real estate game in a nutshell." He reverted immediately to his obstetrical monologue.

Location, you half-assed overachiever, Ted thought. How come lately he had to struggle with his resentment of the young and affluent types who were his best customers? Why should he care? They weren't taking any money out of his pocket. Just the opposite. They were the catch of the day.

But God, he got so tired of dealing with these people. Biggest investment of your life? A measly hundred and fifty thousand for a tract house in a hayfield? Didn't matter, the world has to stop for them to make up their minds.

Small time. Why was he stuck in the small time, when he could be casually pushing buttons that would set in motion developments valued in the tens of millions? Why should he still be worrying about paying his bills, about Jenny's orthodontist tab hanging over him? Why did he have to feel queasy at the articles he read that projected the cost of the twins' college at over eighty thousand dollars?

Ted didn't mind working. He liked to work. But this job was using only half his ability. He had to move on, but how could he get around the risk?

These people didn't realize. If he went cold, he had nothing to fall back on. Young people today, they're calculating pension benefits and dental plans before they're out of high school. They grab an MBA and start at forty grand a year. They have no idea what it is to go out and *earn*.

". . . says the schools out here are not the best," the woman said. "This was where they picked up those kids for drugs."

What? What the hell was she saying? You don't listen, you can't steer them around the snags. She's worried about drugs in a high school her kid won't be entering until sometime in the next goddamn century? And they'll probably send it to private school anyway, give the little bastard all the advantages. He had real worries of his own, God damn it.

Okay, Ted, hold on. You're slipping here. Get back in the groove. Empathize. Dream their dreams. Bare your choppers, boy.

He'd approached real estate with an initial enthusiasm. Opportunity? The way developers were submerging the city in malls and sprawl, it was wide open. He'd had his ups and downs, but lately he'd been on a plateau. He felt stale. He had to wind himself up just to keep even.

And you were always fighting competition. He was a pro, but these goddamn amateurs were constantly clawing at his commissions. Was there a retired bus driver in the county who was not out pushing real estate part time? Was there a bored housewife anywhere who had not answered the clarion call of some Century 21 franchise?

He could hardly believe he'd already put twelve years of his life into this racket. To be on his own, that was the real ticket. What the hell was he doing, Evelyn Winner ordering him around, doling out her puny bonuses to him?

The Golden Age idea could establish him on his own. It would be a real accomplishment, not some gross development, some overblown supermarket. Landscaped, dignified, affordable. He could point to it and tell his boys, your old man is responsible for that. Conceived it. Built it. Those old folks can thank me for the facilities, the whirlpool baths and the shuffleboard, for the community they've found in their twilight years, the dignity. That's the beauty of it. Not the money—okay, the money's nice—but the satisfaction of knowing that you've helped somebody else, made the lives of these others more dignified.

And that would be the keystone of his—empire.

Christ, he could do it, too. He could be the boss, be

somebody. It might blossom into a nationwide chain. But the risk, the damn risk.

He turned down Pineview Drive toward the house he intended to show the expectant couple. He'd forgotten to go around the other way, where you had to drive up the rise. That gave a better curb impression. Oh, well.

"This is it, Roy, Linda. When the grass comes in there, you'll have a beautiful lawn for the little one. The drainage here is terrific. That's important. And those sycamores will sprout up so fast, you'll have shade before you know it."

Linda had a toothache in her face that told Ted the sale was already as good as lost. Roy, an accountant for one of the big pharmaceutical concerns that the city had attracted with overly generous tax rebates, picked up a chunk of soil and looked at it with the eye of a dust-bowl farmer. They all went inside. Ted did a little dreaming for them, but they never looked in the closets.

"When they don't open the closets," Duncan Winner always said, "you can kiss your sale good-bye."

Ted had started with Winner five years before Winner died. Back in those days he'd been the firm's top producer. The prospect of a partnership had become a certainty in his eyes. But then the old man choked on a piece of sirloin gristle and had a coronary and his daughter Evelyn took over.

Evelyn was born-again. She'd found Jesus, now she found real estate. She was good. She had a kind of sincere, bubbling zeal that invariably infected her clients. The company grew. Now Ted was only one of a dozen agents.

Ted was waiting for Roy to finish inspecting the basement—Roy loved basements. He ran out of things to say to Linda. He couldn't remember the human-interest stories he'd read at breakfast.

He began to think about his new neighbor. What was it about the guy? Something deep. Most people were so shallow. Army intelligence. Must have seen a lot. Must know things. Yeah, he'd be an interesting guy to get friendly with. A natural.

43

Ted was glad he'd invited them over tonight. Sal was the kind of guy you could show off to your friends. A character. Somebody who'd done something in the world. Yeah, a genuine character.

"So you can see what I mean," he told them. "This is a very attractive property. Good value."

"Oh, I don't know," Linda said. "It's just—it doesn't . . ."

"I'd hate to see you lose this one," Ted said.

"But I think the layout—" Roy said.

"You're going to get a lot of light in these windows."

"If it was in a different school district," Linda said.

"Of course. I can really empathize with those types of concerns."

"It's a nice house," Roy said.

"It's lovely, but—"

"I think I'm getting a better sense of what you're after," Ted said. "Okay. There's one more place I want you to see. I think you'll be pleasantly surprised by this one. It just came on the hot sheet yesterday, and I'm sure, at what they're asking, it's not going to last. Yes, I think you'll be very surprised at the value of this one."

Robbie and Josh were crouching in the maze of shrubs that separated their yard from the one next door.

"Enemy at three o'clock," Robbie whispered. "We'll attack him on his right flank. First I want to soften him up with some artillery fire."

"That's Mario."

"Quiet! You'll give away our position."

"Hey, Mario!"

Josh rose and crossed to the open lawn. Robbie followed reluctantly.

It was a new feeling for them to be able to wander freely in the intricately landscaped yard next door. They had infiltrated the property repeatedly in the past, but always risking the awesome retribution of Old Man Bennett.

"What are you doing?" Josh asked.

"Nothing," Mario said shyly.

44

"Standing on your head and spitting mothballs?" Robbie asked.

"I'm not standing on my head."

"Don't you know where you are, soldier?"

"Where?"

"He doesn't know. Ha ha."

"I'm from Rochester. That's where I lived before. We moved a lot."

"I don't care where you're from, mister. I want you to know one thing. You're in the Nam now. You're in country. This is the death zone. So you'd better wise up or ship out."

"Says who?"

"This is my brother, Robbie," Josh said. "He's a nut case."

"That's right, I'm a nut case. I've got the thousand-yard stare because I've seen combat. I've seen things that would turn you to stone."

"Like what?" Mario asked.

"Lots of things. Guys blasted so bad their flesh is like pieces of bubble gum. You've heard of hell, haven't you? This is it. War is hell, and I love it."

"I saw a guy," Mario said, "and he got hit over the head by a bottle and he was all bloody."

"You did not. Where did you see that? Rochester?"

"No."

"Where? Liar. How do we know you're not a spy for the gooks?"

"He isn't a spy," Josh said.

"How do you know?"

"I saw him earlier. You want to see our tree house, Mario? We've got some magazines, pictures of women with no clothes on."

"Sure."

"Wait a minute," Robbie said. "That material is classified. For our eyes only. Anyway, he can't go up to the fort without basic training. Give me ten, mister."

"Ten what?"

"We've got cigarettes up there, too," Josh said.

"Push-ups, stupid," Robbie ordered.

"No," Mario said.

"You can't."

"Could if I wanted to."

"Bullshit. You're a liar and a yimp. A yimp is a wimp."

"I've got something you don't have."

"What?"

"Wait, I'll show you. They're in the house."

Mario ran toward the back door.

"You want to go swimming in their pool, you'd better be friendly with him," Josh said.

"Soon as he learns who his commanding officer is, he'll be okay."

Robbie tried unsuccessfully to do a handstand on the grass. Mario was back in a minute.

"Firecrackers!" Josh said.

"It's not a firecracker," Mario said. "It's an M-80. They'll blow a mailbox to pieces. They're so loud you can't stand it. I've got lots."

"Look, Robbie!"

"Big deal." Robbie eyed the little red bomb with envy.

"Can I come up and look at the pictures?" Mario asked.

"Do you swear to tell the whole truth and defend the rootin-tootin so help you God?" Robbie said.

"Yeah, I guess."

"Okay. Company, ho!"

5

"Sal, who are you?"

Wait a minute, Sal thought, I know this guy. The man had a bartender's face and cop's eyes. Unfashionably long sideburns ran down his fleshy cheeks. A dustbroom mustache hung over his upper lip.

"Who am I? I'm Joe Cool, man. I'm the Hunchback of Notre Dame. I'm the Man Who Broke the Bank at Monte Carlo. Who the hell you think I am?"

"No, really."

"I'm Sal Vincent."

"Yeah?"

"I'm a consultant. I been in the service. Army intelligence. I can't talk about it. Sorry, can't talk about it, babe. I'm sort of retired now. I'm looking around, something with high pay, easy work."

"You're kind of young to be retired, aren't you?"

Yes, he definitely knew this guy from somewhere before.

"Well, you burn out on that shit, the stress. I'm looking for something soft, something where I can be my own boss. I've had a lot of experience running things, but it's all, you know, covert."

"You're from Buffalo, aren't you?"

They were sitting across from each other in a small windowless room that contained a filing cabinet, a safe, and a gun-metal desk. The ceiling was acoustical tile, the lights buzzing fluorescent.

"Rochester," Sal said, snapping his fingers and pointing at the man.

"They show you where you lived there?"

"They showed me. I was out east of the city, place called Irondesquat."

"Irondequoit."

"Irondequoit. Conmar Drive. Nice development, good for the kid. We had a house there, three-bedroom job with a playroom and a deck."

"Sure you did."

The man's name was Fred Schimanski. Sal recognized his probation-officer mentality. These guys like to play tough. They talk the lingo. They think that because they're in contact with street people they know the streets. They're just like a lot of wine buyers he'd dealt with in the city. And nobody ever set them straight because why would you? They liked to pretend. Plus, they pulled all the strings. Better to humor them.

They liked a little show. They liked to see you dance, strut your stuff. If you were too reserved, they got the idea you had something to hide. They were guys who liked a situation, a role already prepared for them. The deck was stacked, but you still had to play out the hand.

Like the first one. After they got you on the rap for punching out the guy who owned the Buick. Underlined everything he said. Well, *Sal.* How's it *going?* Are we keeping out of the *shit?* Or are we being a little *prick?*

You were on the streets back then. You envied the kids with the sharp talk. The kids on the inside. You wanted to be in with them, with the smart guys. In the swing. In the know.

"You'll be receiving your stipend for a while longer," Schimanski was saying, sorting through papers in the file on his desk. "But I want you to start thinking about a job now. You ever work before?"

"I been working my ass off since I was fourteen. My old man was no Rockefeller. I worked."

"Pay taxes, I mean. Have you ever filed an income tax return?"

"No."

"You do know that things like income tax, FICA, state tax, all that comes off the top."

"I heard. It's a disgrace the way they run this country, the jack-offs they have on the payroll."

"Referring to anyone in particular?"

"Hey, don't get so sensitive, babe. I know you agree with me."

Schimanski smiled a humorless smile.

You knew who was in. They had the green. They had the bouffant babes and drove this year's car. At eleven o'clock in the morning you'd see them hanging out on the stoops at the Pacifico Club. Combing their hair and whistling their silent whistles. And your old man gone to hell to work at six thirty.

Precision. You learn it early. Big-muscled brutes swinging wild in a brawl. A tap that cracks a man's nose takes the fight out of him. A hammer right on top of the kidney, it slows them down.

Be precise. Be patient.

"I want to talk to you about attitude. See, we get these guys in the program, they often have bad work habits. They like the good life, but come Monday morning, they don't show up at the shop. The boss tells them to do something, they go, fuck you, Charlie. They think they know too much. You can't talk to them. Some guy opens his mouth, they punch his face in. They want something, they go out and steal it. None of that is allowed."

49

"What do you think I am, an animal?"

"I think you're dead, Sal. You don't know it yet, but Sal Veronica—remember him, you used to be so close?—he's dead. You're going to have a little grief over it, but you bury him and go on, you'll be all right. You try to keep him alive, you're going to develop a bad attitude."

Sal folded his arms and licked his lips. Let the guy mouth off about attitude. What the hell. Dead? He wasn't dead. Survival was his specialty. That's why he'd testified. This guy didn't know what he was talking about, dead.

Yeah, that's who he was like, like the first one. You can see the ding still, the fat ding probation officer. Sweaty fat ding trying to tell you what's what, the blood pressure in his face. You've got a *choice* to make here, Sal.

". . . been flying high. I have it all right here. But now it's time to come down to earth. Now you're going to have to deal with real life for a change."

"Real life?" Sal said. "Listen, baby, you want to have a relationship, don't start on real life with me. Okay? I've been there. I've been down in that pit—know that pit everybody's afraid of falling into? I've been down right to the bottom of it. I been where there ain't no more bullshit, no more pretending, no more illusions. I know what's in here." He tapped himself on the chest.

Your first score, the flowers. Hot-wire a van and you're flying across the bridge with a load of mums and dahlias. The smell of them. Up to East Harlem and unload them to the spics. Rositas, señora. You and Bobby Nap. Giving a dozen long-stems to a shy Spanish girl, her wisp of a mustache, her eyes. You ride home in a cab. First time you felt your pockets bulge with cash. A roll. A wad. All those flowers. The smell of them.

"Let me tell you something," he went on. "I've seen life stripped raw. So don't start snowing me with real life. Most people have no idea what real life is about. They're afraid of the dark. Know what I mean, the dark? And being afraid of the dark's only the first thing you gotta get over before you can get a taste of real life."

Or that other score, early on, and they ask you into

the storefront that night. Old guys playing checkers in the front. TV going. "Bonanza." Still remember "Bonanza" drifting through the curtain. They set it up for you to get laid. You popped a doctor's car and the trunk was full of sample cases. You grabbed a shitload of Tuinal, Demerol, blue morphine, and this is your reward. Redhead with lots of padding. Up on the pool table. Under the light. Everybody watching. Cheering. You'll show her. All the jokes. "Bonanza" in the next room. Summer night long ago. And she shows you. Even there. Everybody watching. She takes you. She takes you around the world and back again.

"You know," Schimanski said, as if Sal hadn't spoken, "it's a funny thing about recidivism. Your recidivism rate, especially for career criminals, it's horrendous, it's hopeless. Prison's a crime college, you know that. Guy's dumb enough to end up in the can once, he's going to end up there again and again and again. But in this program, Witness Security, which is ninety-seven percent wise guys, almost all of them hard-core repeat offenders, our recidivism is only about thirteen percent. We're the real solution to the crime problem, and the cost, compared to prison, is nothing. Some say it's because we give you people a chance to start over, to have a new life, to escape evil influences. I say it's because you're scared shitless. You screw up, you commit any serious crime whatever, you're out, you're on your own, no more protection."

"I've been on my own before."

"Yeah? Hear about your pal Joey Skull? Huh? Joseph Pitaro? No, you didn't hear, how could you? One of the best boys on your crew, wasn't he? Loyal. Hear what happened? It happened the day the jury came in on Paul Amato. They found Joey Skull up in the Catskills. He didn't have any hands. No feet. His nose was sliced off, his ears, everything. His tool. Joey was aerodynamic. So I understand, you've been to hell and back. You've seen reality stripped. You've killed people and you think you know life inside out. Joey Skull probably knew something about life, too. But he was on his own and look what happened. I'd suggest you think a long time before you decide you want to risk being on your own again, Sal. Don't be part of that thirteen percent."

Sal stared across the desk. He took hold of the sharp pain in his chest and ground it out as if it had been a cigarette. Sal wasn't the sentimental type. And he didn't need to sit in a cubicle and get a hard-on over somebody else's life.

"You were born in upstate New York, weren't you, Mr. Vincent?"

"Yeah. Little town. We went through there with the other guy."

"Deputy Kreiger?"

"He showed me the place on the way out here. Little wide spot in the road. Walworth."

"You're not likely to run into anybody from Walworth around here—or anywhere else. Another nice thing, Walworth High School burned down in 1976 and they merged with another district. All the student records were destroyed. Did you go to college?"

"You tell me."

"I mean really. I assume you didn't. Sal Vincent got a degree in English from St. Joseph Carpenter College in Utica. English is good. It dolls up your résumé, but it doesn't mean you have to know anything. Anybody asks, tell them you wrote your senior paper on 'The Wasteland.' "

"T. S. Eliot. Think I'm ignorant?"

"T. S. Eliot, huh?" Schimanski chuckled over some private joke.

He passed Sal some papers—his honorable discharge from the U.S. Army, his reserve credentials. "We've decided to give you the Distinguished Service Cross, for some of the undercover work you did with army intelligence. Here. Congratulations."

"My mother should be alive to see this."

Mario's school records, Schimanski said, had been shifted to a private school in a Rochester suburb. He passed Sal the boy's baptismal certificate from St. Ambrose parish in Irondequoit.

"You guys have connections, I can see that."

"This is your bank reference. That'll make it easier to open an account here. We're not allowed to set up any credit background. You'll have to start from scratch."

"What about a birth certificate?"

"You won't need it. You've got your driver's license. Only reason you might want a birth certificate is for a passport, and the U.S. Attorney doesn't want you to have a passport."

"Why not? Say I want to take my family to Europe?"

"Why? Because some people might have funds stashed in banks in Switzerland or in the Caymans, or some other convenient location. That money might well be the proceeds of criminal activity. And, all appearances to the contrary, we're doing our damnedest to uphold the principle that crime does not pay. I know you used your shy money to buy your house. Okay. But that's as far as it goes."

He told Sal that any mail would be forwarded to him from a drop box. After he read it he should destroy the envelope and anything that had his old identity printed on it. And destroy meant burn, not throw in the garbage.

He said they had a list of employers who were willing to cooperate with the Marshal's Service, to employ program participants. Applicants had to be qualified, of course, but the firms wouldn't insist on extensive background checks.

"I'm not sure what I want to do yet," Sal said. "I'd like something where I work with the public. I think I'd be good at that."

"Work with the public?"

Sal didn't pick up on Schimanski's wry smile. "That's right. Maybe real estate. I used to manage a few buildings Paulie owned in East Harlem. Pretty easy money."

"Maybe that wouldn't be a bad idea. Now, what else? If you have any old pictures around the house, get rid of them. Anything that connects you with your past."

"They already told me that."

"Here's a phone number I want you to memorize. It's a panic number. Any time, day or night, you come to the

53

conclusion your cover is blown, call. We'll establish an immediate security ring and go from there. If you're smart you won't ever need to use it."

Sal looked at the number on the piece of paper, handed it back to him. "I've got it."

"Your fingerprints will remain in FBI central records, but they'll be flagged. Any requests will be referred to us first. But we won't hesitate to provide information on your background if there's a criminal matter at stake. Don't get to thinking you're invisible. Guys used to do that in this program. They'd run up a load of debt or pull some kind of scam and then come crying about they'd been found out, they needed a new identity. We don't go for that anymore."

Sal stared at him.

"We do know there's a price on your head," Schimanski said. "An open contract."

"How much?"

"Enough. And one last thing. We protect you as long as you stay out of the danger areas. So far, we have a perfect record in this program. Nobody's been clipped who hasn't gone asking for it."

"I'm not asking. And I'm not planning any sightseeing trips to New York."

"It's not just New York. It's anywhere you might run into former associates. You used to do business for Amato in Las Vegas, we know that. Stay away from there. You took your vacations in Lauderdale. Don't go near south Florida. Whatever. If you know guys in Chicago, keep away from Chicago. Those are the danger areas for you."

"I'm not afraid."

"What I'm saying, you'd better be afraid."

"Let me explain something to you," Sal said, pointing his finger. "I'm no coward. I could face down Paul Amato and any ten guys whatever day of the week you name. I didn't squeal because I wanted to. He bought it. He lost his head. He was the one who was dumb. So he ends up in Atlanta and I'm cruising."

"Just remember, if you start to get restless, this is the

last stop. You dive back into the life, boy, it's a long swim to China."

"I'm doing this for my kid, for Gina and the kid. Except for them, I wouldn't be running and I wouldn't be hiding."

Schimanski rested both hands on his desk and leaned forward. For a minute, he and Sal locked eyes. Then the marshal said, "I'll tell you something. The danger areas aren't just out there. There in here, too." He tapped his temple. "Maybe it's a broad you can't get shut of. Maybe you've got a taste for dope. Maybe it's something even finer than that. A guy will get this feeling that he left something behind. What was it? He can't say. Where did he leave it? He's not sure, but it's somewhere in some danger area. See, it's himself he's missing. So he goes back looking for it. And he gets fucked."

6

The suburb where Ted lived was one of the older ones surrounding the city. The trees had reached middle age, some of them elbowing the houses they'd been planted to shade. Through their leaves was drifting the sweet smoke of briquettes, of fat sizzling on coals, of secret barbecue sauces, of charred steaks and succulent chickens and blistered hot dogs. Ice was clinking in glasses. The sun was blessing the scene with its red stamp of approval.

"Old old friend of mine," Ted was saying. "Maynard Barker. I've known Maynard since, hell, second grade I guess. This is our new neighbor, Sal Vincent. Moved into Bennett's place just today."

"Sal. Pleasure. Some new blood around here, that's great. We need it, right Teddy? That Bennett, he was a fun guy at a funeral."

They shook hands.

Ted said to Sal, "Maynard, of course, we always used

to kid him—Maynard G. Krebs. You know, the beatnik? Maynard G., on television?"

"Work! Work!" Maynard shrugged violently. His slightly protruding eyes and wiry blond hair made the gesture comical.

Ted answered Sal's blank stare. "You know. Maynard G. Krebs, on the Dobie Gillis show. Remember? With the little goatee."

"I guess I missed it."

"Well, we used to get on Maynard about it. And he could do that character so well. He's kind of a natural mimic."

"I'm not going to play the sap for you," Maynard said with a Bogart snarl. He jabbed a finger in Sal's face. "When a man's partner is killed, he's supposed to do something about it. It doesn't matter what you thought of him. He was your partner and you're supposed to do something about it. See, kid?"

Sal smiled. Ted smiled.

Maynard turned the talk to baseball. He referred to the glory days, the days of Musial and Ernie Banks. Sal told of having dinner once with Reggie Jackson when the slugger was with the Yanks.

"I told Reggie," he said, "I said, keep your weight back on your left foot more, you'll add twenty points to your average and hit for power, too. Of course he didn't want to hear that from me, but it was true. Next thing, he gets in that series, pops all those home runs."

"Actually had dinner with him?" Maynard said. "I'm impressed. Of course, Jackson was overrated. He had some good years with Oakland, but you look at his strikeout ratio."

"Overrated?" Sal said. "The guy's Hall of Fame."

"There's plenty of guys, should be in the Hall, aren't."

"The man struck out because he swung the goddamn bat," Sal insisted. "He was up there to hit the ball, that's the key thing."

"I always liked Pete Rose when he was playing," Ted said. "I mean, he really played. Baseball needs that. Remember the streak he had going, consecutive-game streak?"

"Charlie Hustle," Sal said.

"I bet you had dinner with him, too," Maynard said, snapping his fingers and grinning.

Sal didn't grin.

"Now, listen," Ted said.

"No, I never did," Sal answered.

"Well, I'll tell you," Maynard said, slipping back into his Bogart snarl. "I'm going to send you over. You'll get out in twenty years. I'll wait for you. If they hang you I'll always remember you."

Sal didn't respond. The three men stood in silence for a moment, each holding a glass of scotch. A bug zapper let out a delighted crackle each time a mosquito left the world. Its light seemed to concentrate the fading blue of the twilight sky.

Ted broke the awkwardness. "Maynard's a dentist. Painless, absolutely painless."

"Yeah, it don't hurt me a bit," Maynard said, finishing the stock gag.

"He was in the army, too," Ted pointed out. "Sal has a background in army intelligence."

"What was your unit?" Maynard asked Sal.

"Like he said, intelligence, I can't—"

"Made you sign the—yeah, I know. I signed it, too, but I've got nothing to leak. Used to sit over in Augsburg and listen to Morse code on the graveyard shift. Drove me bananas, but it was better than the alternative, am I right? You have buddies in Nam?"

"Yeah, sure."

"Oh, we had some of these gung-ho boys in basic, actually wanted to go over," Maynard said. "Fools."

"Why fools?" Sal said. "They put it on the line. They got killed, so what? We're all headed down the same road."

"That war was immoral, that's the point," Maynard said. "I'm not saying that in World War Two—"

"War is war," Sal insisted.

"Don't let him kid you about not knowing any secrets,"

58

Ted said to Sal, forcing a laugh. "Maynard knows the biggest secret of all. Tell him, Maynard. Come on."

"I shouldn't, but a bunch of us, we had some equipment over there in Germany, voice analyzers. And we put the original 'Louie Louie' through it. Remember, the Kingsmen?"

"He's one of the few people on earth who knows all the words to that song." Ted laughed.

"My face turned white," Maynard said. He did his imitation of a man whose face was turning white. "You know, like when the pope opened the secret the Virgin Mary told the kids at Fátima or Lourdes or wherever and he read it and his face turned white? It's quite a responsibility, knowing what I know."

"The man knows his trivia inside out, believe me," Ted said.

"Yeah?"

"What it is, I keep up on trends," Maynard said. "I'm into the sixties. I'm predicting the sixties are going to come back with a vengeance."

Ted asked Sal if there was anything at all he could tell them about his cloak-and-dagger experiences. Sal downplayed the danger he'd faced but let drop some of the locales that he'd seen during his service—Afghanistan, Cambodia. Ted said that was very impressive.

Robbie approached his father to ask if they could sleep out tonight. Ted told him maybe tomorrow.

"Afghanistan?" Maynard was saying. "Where were you in Afghanistan? I followed that conflict a little because I was struck by the parallels to Nam. I guess a lot of people were."

Sal insisted that he was trying to put it all behind him.

"Were you in Nam, Mr. Vincent?" Robbie asked.

"No, I wasn't, not in Vietnam itself."

"We play Nam a lot. That's my favorite. I want to be a Green Beret. Is that what you were?"

"No."

"What were you?"

"Robbie, come on now."

59

"Were you a spy, like?"

"That's enough, Robbie," his father said.

"I'll tell you sometime," Sal said.

"Neat."

"Don't encourage him," Ted said as Robbie ran off.

Gina and Maynard's wife Felice were helping Laura with the salads and silverware. Josh had taken Mario off to show him a garter snake in a shoe box.

They were waiting for the fourth couple. He was a real estate agent who worked with Ted.

"Don's—how shall I put it?—youthful," Ted explained. "Not that he's all that young, but he's one of these guys who never grows up. They razz him at work because he has this baby face. The New Guy—they've always called him that even though he's been with us over a year. You can't take him seriously. They invited us to their house, so . . ."

"You're a one-man welcome wagon here, Ted," Sal said.

"Well, with them, it's an obligation. You and Gina, we're glad you could come. Privileged. Kids love having another playmate, too."

He excused himself to go start the fire. Maynard and Sal both walked over to the picnic table, where the women were laying out food. Felice was talking about some people she knew who'd been married, divorced, remarried, and now it looked like they were headed for another divorce. Come on, she said.

She was a luxurious, chestnut-haired woman in her late twenties. Her summer dress kept busy covering her healthy physique. She had trouble with her spike heels sinking into the sod.

He'd always thought of Maynard as a confirmed bachelor, Ted had told Sal. But last year his friend had fallen overboard for this girl, sixteen years younger than he was, a real knockout. He'd replaced the crown on her right incisor and it was good-night-Irene at first sight. She was a minor local celebrity, did the weather on television.

"She's supposed to be a meteorologist," Ted explained to his new neighbor, "but when I asked her, she said she really didn't know that much about meteors. However, channel eight's got the highest ratings in the city for its news and she's two of the reasons why."

Sal watched her suck the filling from a deviled egg, retaining the flaccid cup of white in her fingers. Her lips pulsing, she saw him looking. She varied the voltage in her eyes, licked her lips, looked away.

Don, the New Guy, arrived with his wife Vera. He made a habit of thrusting his immature face at everyone he spoke to. She seemed always to be searching unsuccessfully for something to say and worrying about what time it was.

Ted handed around more drinks. Darkness settled in. The New Guy voiced his opinions with a zeal that was wearing. When someone disagreed with him, he reversed his position without slacking his enthusiasm.

When the meal was finally ready, Ted apologized for having let Laura talk him into chicken when they should by all rights be eating steaks, but he guessed there was something to this cholesterol business. Vera mentioned that Don's father had passed away from a massive coronary only last year. It really made you think, she said.

The kids were allowed to take their food up into a tree house that Ted had built for the twins. The grownups sat on the patio. Everyone complimented Ted on his Polynesian chicken.

After dinner Ted proposed a series of toasts. He flattered Sal and Gina mercilessly.

Don started a discussion of the tickle reflex. He'd heard it had something to do with sexual response. He and Ted maneuvered Felice, cruising on piña coladas, into volunteering to be the subject of a serious scientific experiment. They started with a feather applied to her toes and worked up to the intimacies of her armpits, by which time Felice was in hysterics.

"Hey, enough already," Maynard complained. "I mean it."

61

The general laughter ground itself out as Felice rear-ranged her neckline.

More drinks. Felice corralled Sal. All evening she'd been shooting him deep, meaningless messages with her eyes. She had to tell him, she said, about this book she'd been reading. It had to do with past-life regression.

As they talked she kept making a gesture, an idle caress down her neck and into the hollow above her collarbone. The movement reminded him of Vanessa. This girl, with her maraschino lips and loud figure, was an imperfect imitation of Vanessa. She had the same slender fingers, the same quick pointed tongue, the same airy self-confidence. Sal couldn't keep his mind from straying.

Was that just last fall when Primo was talking about some fight he'd had, some Cuban before Castro?

Vanessa. The girl wanted to be an actress. I'll coach you, babe, he'd told her. He used to have her read him the sports columns from the paper in that sexy voice she had. It would blow his mind. Sexy she could do, okay. But it was all she could do. You make tragedy sexy, it's just funny. She could run the gamut of emotions from A to B. Bedroom voice and that was it, though it was all she needed as far as Sal was concerned.

She certainly played some Oscar-winning roles for him. He remembered the way she used to dress up—cowgirl, depraved cheerleader, geisha, Cleopatra. Got hold of the costumes and really became the role. And drew him in. Made him forget who he was for a time.

Miss her? He hated her. First he took the fall bringing her her nose candy. Okay, that wasn't her fault, but still. Then she fingered him for Paulie. What the hell had they offered her to get her to do that? What difference did it make? His own fault for going apeshit over a broad. Wave a mink in front of her, or an ounce of blow, she'd finger her own father. Then after he passed out she just walked, apparently. Left him bleeding to death on the floor of the ladies' toilet.

Christ, he hated her. Hated her more than he hated Paulie, even. Paulie played the hand he was dealt. He didn't get to be a boss by being sentimental, by taking chances on people. Somebody was a threat, you got rid of him. Turned out he wasn't really a threat? Too bad, he was history. And Paulie was still around.

Paulie made the decision. And if that bullet had come from a slightly different angle, nobody would say the decision was a mistake. And Paulie would not be enjoying an extended vacation at government expense.

It was probably even a little hard for Paulie, Sal had to imagine, calling for the hit. Sal was one of his top earners. They'd been friends, honest friends, for years. Paulie had a brain. He wasn't some bonehead. He had feelings. He'd had Sal and Gina over for Christmas dinner three years running. He doted on Mario like a grandfather. He and Sal enjoyed good times together, did things that brought men close. It must have been hard for Paulie to decide Sal had to die. But not that hard.

Sal had enjoyed seeing Paulie squirm at the trial. Enjoyed knowing that Paulie had to face the fact that not only was he getting shafted by somebody in a perfect position to drive home the shaft, but that he had only himself to blame. He couldn't point the finger at Sal, though he did for show. He couldn't accuse Sal of going bad—that was the only opening he'd left for his lieutenant. Sal was dead on the streets, even more dead if he ever went to prison.

Sal was no rat. Sal did the right thing. He was stand-up, God damn it. Stand-up. Honor. Right guy. But how far did that go? How far did friendship go? How far did this "thing of ours" go?

Paulie had taught him something: it went just as far as your own life and no farther. He could remember the guys at the club laughing over some jerk who'd joined the army, some sucker. Go out and get your ass killed for nothing? It didn't make sense.

The same thing was true across the board. You do the right thing, up to a point. You're stand-up, but only so far. When your life is on the line, you cover your ass and the hell with everybody else. That was Paulie's message. Sal appreciated it. He'd almost learned it too late.

Talk? No problem. He sat on that stand and said the words that would send Paulie away, and enjoyed it. All he had to do was think about Primo. Those eyes. The man's face had always been a disaster, but the eyes were so full of keenness, of life. To snuff them out—that was what Paulie had done.

The hell with Paulie, with all his "like a son" baloney, all the kissing, the papal audiences. Sal liked to remember him whispering frantically to his lawyer while Sal wove the noose around his neck.

And, Mr. Veronica, when you say that the defendant ordered you, quote, to find Mr. DeGarmo, unquote, what exactly did that mean to you?

Find him, get rid of him.

To kill him? To find him meant—you took it to mean that Mr. Amato was ordering you to kill Mr. DeGarmo?

Sure.

And did you?

I did. The guy was always hanging out in a steam room. I went there and put two bullets in his head.

Put two bullets in his head. But that didn't say anything about it. You couldn't express it, walking up to a dangerous man in a crowded room and killing him flat out and then walking away. That's not the truth of it. Nobody could understand the truth of that one.

The funny thing was, the more he told, the harder it was for him to believe the stories himself. He knew what he was saying had happened. But his own words seemed to cast it into the realm of the absurd, to turn it into a fantasy. And the fantasies had been flitting around, worrying him lately in a way they never had before.

It had gone on and on. Paulie, the others. The juries and the legal wrangling, the testimony, the arguments, the motions. Finally the verdict. Guilty. Guilty.

At first he'd enjoyed being the star of the show. It was pleasant being the center of a storm, all these guys facing the can and you've cut your deal. He enjoyed the headlines, Sal the Veil, the prosecution's pet viper. Center of attention.

64

But after a while the strain had taken its toll. Always being hustled in and out of court in a bulletproof vest. The convoys. The marshals rousing them at two A.M. to change motels. Always waiting for some sniper with a scope on some rooftop to blast a hole in his skull.

Gradually the fear had taken over. All of them—Gina and Mario, too. The hiding, the long hours of boredom as they waited for Sal to testify.

Then it was over. And they picked a city for the climate. And the marshals took them from La Guardia to O'Hare, then switched them to another plane and on to here.

He hadn't thought much about Vanessa the whole time, about her games. But this broad reminded him of her. And he found that hating Vanessa didn't dampen her allure. If anything, he wanted her more now than ever before.

Felice moved her hand lower. Sal's eyes followed.

"What about your wife?" she was saying.

"My wife?"

"While you were with this Arab woman who was linked to the terrorists? Wasn't your wife worried sick? Or was it something you didn't talk to her about?"

What had he been saying? He'd been rambling about his exploits in the spy game. He found it foolishly easy to talk about this imaginary life, much easier than it would have been to discuss his real past.

"That's it, I kept her pretty much in the dark," he said. "These things—when you're in deep cover, you can do things and not be involved. You go through all the motions, but you don't feel it."

"It's like you're watching someone else live your life," she offered. "You're removed from it."

"That's right."

"Still, it makes me worried for you, just to hear you describe it. Those people could have killed you. It makes my heart go thump." She illustrated her palpitations with her hand.

Sal was still half absorbed in memories. The girl was

hanging on his arm, shining her melodramatic eyes toward his face.

"It was nothing, really."

"I know the feeling implicitly," she said. "Sometimes when I'm on camera talking about the latest cold front that's approaching, or the dew point or something, I go completely outside my own body. It's like I'm somewhere else, watching myself and saying, who is this person?"

"You're on television?"

"I told you, channel eight. You should tune me in. Not tonight, it's my night off."

"I will."

"I'll tell you something else," she said, pulling him closer. "I've lived before. In Atlantis."

"Atlanta?"

"Atlan-*tis*. Plus I was a knight in the crusades. And in one life I was the wife of a Druid. It's absolutely fascinating when you get into it."

"I'll bet. At least, all these other lives, you were white."

Felice started to chuckle, stopped abruptly.

"Having fun?" Gina said, approaching them from behind.

"Gina, your husband is a really remarkable man. They should do a piece on him in *People* magazine. I've never met anyone who'd actually . . . you know."

"Yes, I know. Sal, I think Mario's tired. We should really go, dear."

"Go ahead."

"Mario!" Turning back to Sal, "Together."

"I'll come over when I'm ready."

"Really, lover. Mario, we've got to go. You're tired."

"I'm not, Mom. We're playing Capture the Flag. Can't we stay? I'm not tired at all. Dad? This is the most fun I've had in my life."

"You go home with your mother, Mario," Sal said.

"I guess we can stay if you want to stay," Gina said. "We'll all stay until you're ready, Sal. Until you're finished."

Mario ran off. Felice excused herself and went to refill her glass.

"Don't do it, Gina," Sal told Gina in a low voice.

"I am doing it, my dear. And this is only the beginning. I told you, I'm not going to endure this stuff now. You screwed my life up, Mario's life. Okay. So we're starting over. But it's not going to be like before. You're not going to humiliate me. I can dial a phone, buddy."

"What's that supposed to mean?"

"It means I can give you up if I feel like it. Just like that."

"Go do it, if you're going to talk about it."

"You throw it in my face with a little cheap piece of fluff like that and I will. Believe it."

"You're tired, Gina."

"Tired? You're goddamn right I'm tired."

"Excuse me." Ted was grinning at them. "I want you to meet my daughter. My daughter who thinks she can stay out to any hour, to any and all hours, and to every hour."

"Dad."

"With everybody and anybody and whoever she damn well pleases."

"Dad, do you have to?"

"But who we love anyhoo."

Jenny rolled her eyes and told them she was very happy to meet them and would they please excuse her father, who'd obviously had a wee too much to drink. She was not a child and did not need to be treated like one.

Sal said he could see she wasn't.

This remark elicited a grin that tensed her entire neck. She said she hoped they would enjoy the locale but that she was afraid they might find it a little boring, as Paris it was not, not by a long shot. She wanted them to know that she was available to baby-sit whenever they needed her, all they had to do was to call.

Ted took Gina off to mix her another drink.

Jenny, left alone with Sal, played nervously with her

hair for a second, then backed away with an embarrassed giggle and ran to the house.

Sal sank down on the chaise longue. He would have gone home to bed except that Gina had made an issue of it. He watched Felice talking with Maynard and Vera, her body swaying in a kind of slow hula. Gina's scolding had pricked his interest.

"Let the word go forth from this time and place," Maynard was proclaiming, "that the torch has passed to a new generation of Americans, born in this century, tempered by war, disciplined by a hard and bitter peace—"

"Maynard has four highballs and he becomes JFK," Laura said. She sat on a lawn chair beside Sal. "He can go on like that for hours."

"Let every nation know, whether it wishes us well or ill, that we shall pay any price, bear any burden—"

"Does he think that's funny?" Sal said.

"What do you mean? Sure, I guess so."

"That's disrespectful. Kennedy was a man. Know what I mean? You don't mock him. He said things that were true. You don't spit on that."

"I never really thought about it before," Laura said.

"Some people think you can laugh at anything. Kennedy was a man, I tell you. Have a little respect."

"I guess I kind of agree with you."

"You know what happens to people who scoff, people who have no respect?"

"What?"

"They end up getting hurt. Or they should."

She looked at him. He smiled. She gave an uncertain chuckle.

"You're different," Laura said.

"Sure I am."

"No, you really are. You're a breed apart. I noticed that about you right away. You're a very complex person."

"There you're wrong. I'm really very simple."

She smiled. "Ted likes you. He's a good judge of people."

"That's—yeah, he seems like a—"

68

"I sometimes wonder if there are any coincidences. Ted's at a point in his life, a kind of crossroads. He started out to be a teacher. I often wish he'd kept at it, but financially he felt—and his destiny carried him on. He's had trouble finding himself."

"Well, I guess we all—you know."

"Mm-hmm. He really is a nice guy."

"You're kind of a nice guy yourself," he said.

Her eyes, for the first time, dropped away from his.

To break the tension he asked her if there were any good jazz clubs in town. One place, she said, brought in some decent acts, name acts. She and Ted had been planning to go there for months. Did he like jazz? Of course, he must. Her favorites were Sarah Vaughan and George Shearing.

Miles Davis was his man. He began to tell her about a time he was in New York on business and he ran into Miles in a bar. The man's eyes, he was saying, like a fighter's eyes.

Approaching them, Ted clapped his hands and rubbed them together. "Sal, my friend, your glass is empty. We don't allow that around here. That's a no-no."

Sal said he'd have to be heading home soon. With the move and all, they were pretty beat.

"Oh, *capisce*. Isn't that what you wops say?"

"Ted," Laura said.

Sal smiled. *"Capisce, amico mio."*

"Jesus, Laura, Sal knows I'm joking. Oh, that look. She thinks I'm overimbibing," he explained to Sal. "Don't worry, hon, I'm not drinking at all between drinks." Ted's smile was slightly too broad for his face. "But seriously, Sal, are you having a good time? I want you to have a good time."

"Good time."

"Good. Maynard's good people, Maynard and Felice. And what about this little package here? Huh? Talk about good people." He draped his arm over Laura's shoulder.

"You're a lucky man."

"Damn right I am. We're all, all lucky men. So let's drink to Caesar, not bury him."

Laura said it was high time the boys were in bed. She went off to fetch them.

"I've been thinking about what you said," Sal said. "About the old-age home and all, the commercial real estate. I'm looking to get set up in something myself. I'm thinking maybe it might suit me. I have to be my own boss. I've had some experience arranging deals. I managed a couple of multi-unit buildings at one time. I think real estate might be exactly the thing I'm looking for. Fast start and who knows where we might end up?"

"Hey, now you're cooking with grease."

"Maybe we should think about getting something going, if you're serious."

"Oh, I'm serious," Ted declared. "Seriouser than serious. This, I've thought about it for years."

"Good. I'll think about it, you think about it. Maybe we'll decide to give it a shot."

"Hey. Yeah, well, I don't know, I—"

"If the idea has as much potential as you say, it'd be a shame to let it go by the boards."

"Of course. Opportunity knocks, then the long silence."

"You said you had a backer."

"Maynard. You know how dentists are always looking for someplace to park their cash? He's ready and willing to back me, assuming the deal makes sense."

"Sounds ideal for everybody. That's a start, and we could look around for some investors. Must be lots of them in this city."

"Yeah. Of course there are. I mean, there's going to be risk, but still." Ted's face took on a grave look. "I've thought about this in a sort of blue-sky way for so long, it's hard for me to conceive of it in real terms. But, Jesus, you know, it really gets me considering. The demographics, you should look at the long-term demographics."

"I can see you've got a head for the business. I'm no real estate maven, of course, but I've done my share of hustling. I'm thinking, with your brains and my balls, we might make quite a splash in this burg."

"My brains and your—Christ, you've got me thinking here."

"Let me know."

"Hey, I will, buddy. I'll let you know for sure."

7

For years Duncan Winner had operated his real estate business out of his home. Now Winner Realty occupied the entire rambling Victorian house. The agents used the kitchen as a lounge.

Ted was preparing a cup of coffee.

Elliott Fishman, who'd been with the firm nearly as long as Ted, was giving the New Guy some sales advice.

"You grab them by the lapel, see? Not hard, but with a little tug so they know you mean business. You talk right in their face, close, so they feel uncomfortable, so they smell the garlic under the Tic Tac. You say to them, Bud, you don't know it, but I'm in the syndicate, the mob. I'm one of these wise guys you hear about."

"Wise guy." The New Guy chuckled. "But I'm not Italian."

"That don't matter. They let anybody into the mafia these days. I'm a wise guy, you tell them. And look, you're going to buy this here property and that's all there is to it.

You don't, I'm going to get a guy to come over to your house and break boat your legs. Like that, 'boat.'"

"And what if he still says no?"

"He still says no, you say, hey, so it's not exactly what you're looking for. I've got this other one. It just came on the hot sheet."

"You can't actually break their legs?"

"No, the board, they're touchy about something like that. Point I'm making, kid, soft sell's overdone."

"But I thought in real estate—"

"Real estate, anything. I hear all this, subtle, soft—it's just, a lot of times, you haven't got the balls to close. Guys don't want to close. I see it. Shit, they've got the customer, he wants to sign the contract, and they can't find a pen. They're all go-home-and-think-it-over happy. Listen to me, sales begins when the customer says no."

"But, a home," Don said. "People don't like it if they feel you pushing, is what I learned."

"No way. Forget about think it over. Close the sucker, any way you can. It's the same with anything. Don't say, a home, I have to be subtle, I can't close the jerk. Point I'm making—fear. You do whatever you can to put some fear in your people. It's the great motivator, fear. Fear and greed. Am I right, Ted? Fear and greed, right?"

In fact, Fishman's sales technique was the syrupiest of anybody's in the office. He wore green pants and a yellow knit tie. He had bad breath and he chain-smoked low-tar menthol cigarettes. He referred to everyone's children as "bambinos."

"And envy," Ted said. He liked Elliott, they shared memories.

"And envy, I forgot about that one. That's the voice of experience talking there. Hey, Mr. Experience, you get any activity on that Ferndale property yet?"

"By the tracks?"

"My Ferndale listing, that Tudor cottage. You said you had a serious prospect for that one."

"I showed it. People see those tracks, they don't like it."

"Hey, it's psychological, all the stuff about the other side of the tracks. Tell them it's this side they're going to be on. This side of the tracks."

"These people had a kid."

"There's a goddamn fence. Their bambino's not going to get run over by a freight train. Use some psychology, will you?"

Ted said, "Elliott, it isn't psychology. They don't want a goddamn train running eighty feet from their bedroom window. Bring me a deaf, dumb, and blind buyer and I'll use psychology on him."

The New Guy interrupted to say he had an appointment, he had to get going.

Fishman drained coffee from the urn into a paper cup and stirred in creamer. He made a face as he sipped. Winner agents prided themselves on having the worst coffee in the business.

"That guy," Fishman said, referring to Don. "You hear? He unloaded four of those new colonials out in Thornwood. Four of them in one week. What goddamn luck."

He lowered his voice. "Say, Ted, I wanted to talk to you on the Q.T. for a minute. I looked at a place yesterday, it's an old farmhouse. It's got some minuses but it's just the kind of place these young two-income types are looking for to fix up. Guy only wants a hundred thousand out of it. It's got six acres, the land itself is worth seventy. It's going to sell like *that* if only I can get some good leads, the right leads."

"Ask Evelyn. I can't—"

"No, no. You know how Evelyn is. I thought maybe you could talk to her for me. Just a few of the right leads and I'll have a binder on the place, I swear, inside a week."

"I'm not going to talk to Evelyn for you, Elliott."

"I need that commission. It's only a hundred thousand, but Jesus, I remember when you closed a hundred-thousand-dollar deal, you were riding high. I need it, Ted."

Ted gave in. He agreed to talk to Evelyn. He knew that Evelyn, at her core a completely unsentimental busi-

74

nesswoman, would refuse. And he knew, too, that he'd probably end up giving Elliott a few of his own leads.

Ted could empathize with Fishman. That was the problem. You're going nowhere fast and every little commission makes a difference. You get caught in the nickel-and-dime rut and you can't get out. You spend your life drinking bad coffee and waiting for things to happen.

But, no. That wasn't his fate. He wasn't an Elliott Fishman. He wasn't nickel-and-dime. Not inside. Inside he was a mover and a shaker. All he had to do was dare. All he needed was the balls to take a risk.

It was going to happen. Yes, it was. He was going to make it happen. Oblivious of Fishman's curious glance, Ted grinned to himself as a flush of excitement gripped him.

"He's God, Debi," Jenny said into the phone. "I mean, I'm telling you, he's absolutely, totally—he's God. I'm not kidding. You should see him. No, I mean, you shouldn't see him. Debi, you wouldn't be able to control yourself. I know you. You'd melt."

Saving money religiously from her babysitting, she'd had her own phone line put in when she was thirteen.

"No, he's not. He must have married very young or something. He's not old at all. Not like my father. He's very athletic. He put in a punching bag. I'm not kidding. I've seen him, punching and punching. He gets all glisteny, you know, from the sweat. It drives me insane. Really.

"And he's so nice. He always says my name. You know, not just hi there but hello, Jenny. And I say hello, Sal. Because they told me to call them Sal and Gina. Hello, Sal—I love it. And he says nice to see you, Jenny, and I think he means nice to *see* me, that he likes to see me, likes to look at me. I feel naked when I'm with him.

"Yes, alone. Lots. I'm going to tell you. It was a few days ago. I had on my bikini. The yellow one. And I saw him in their yard. He was lying on a chaise. And there's a place you can get through the bushes. So I just went. Shaking, that's how. And he's lying there, he doesn't hear

75

me coming. He has a hat over his face. I didn't know if he was asleep or what. I stood there, I was going to run back. But I said, Jenny, don't be chicken. Debi would. Well, you would. So I coughed like. Then, I was so brave, I touched him.

"No, on the shoulder, stupid. Oh my God, did he jump. He must be very nervous or something. He grabbed me, grabbed my arm. He was going to hit me. I could see he was ready to hit me. God, was I surprised.

"Well, he said he was sorry. He said I'd startled him, but he knew I didn't mean it. He was very very sorry and he hoped he hadn't hurt me. I said not at all. I should have—right, I should have said, yes, you hurt me, hurt me again, torture me, you brute. What? Yeah, ravish my flesh, you uncouth animal. But I don't know why he's so touchy.

"What? I shouldn't tell you, Debi. No, really, it might make you drop the phone. Well, it was one of those tight bathing suits that are like briefs. Huh? Not quite, but almost that tight.

"Oh, I said I had my junior lifesaving and if they wanted I could watch their little boy in the pool sometimes so they wouldn't have to. I wouldn't charge them because, I said, they were so nice to me when I baby-sat for him. The kid? He's a little brat about the same age as the twins. Actually, he's not so bad.

"No, they're very nice. They're adults, like. My parents are more like grown-up kids compared to them.

"So anyway, I said to him, I said I liked to get out in the sun to get a tan and I could sit around by their pool as easy as I could in our yard if they didn't have time to watch their boy and he wanted to go swimming and what did he think, was I getting a good tan? He said a beautiful tan. I said how about my legs? He said they looked nice and dark.

"Then, I was rubbing my arm a little and he said, was I sure I was okay. I said fine, only my arm, here, was a little, tiny sore. And he touched it. I mean, he's so gentle it's unbelievable. I could hardly breathe. I wanted to say it hurts here, too. And here and here and here. Everywhere.

"So we're standing like that and his wife comes out, Gina. She smiles, but I see that little bit of ice in her eyes. No, really. I'm taller than she is. And she had on Bermuda shorts and a blouse that didn't go with it—it looked terrible. And here I am, just my bikini, with her husband caressing my arm.

"Yeah, but let me tell you then. She says, we're having drinks, would I like a Coke or something. I said I'll have whatever you're having. She says do my parents let me drink alcohol? I said sure. Well, they do. And she doesn't want to, but Sal looks at me, right in the eye, and says, let her have one, a light one. So she gets another glass and they're having gin and tonic. I had some and smiled and said this is so nice on a hot day. No, I hate tonic, but I had to pretend. There we are, it was just like we were the two women in his life. And she's old. She's almost as old as Mom is. She has those wrinkles by her mouth, where it looks like she's disgusted with everything.

"Oh, Debi, I just dream and dream about it.

"Mark? I guess we are. He thinks we are. But he's such a boy. Really. I told him, I love you dearly but I don't have any control over the chemistry. How can you control the chemistry?

"I'm through with boys, Deb. This is a new phase in my life. I go next door and they treat me like an adult and we have gin and tonic and nobody's crude and it's—it's civilized. I'm too mature for those kids. Well, I am.

"Sure. He's married. Plus, you know, he's friends with my father. But these things are bigger than that, Deb, much bigger.

"So, did you get those shoes you were looking at?"

"You can rinse now," the hygienist told Ted.

Ted rinsed.

"I'm afraid you have some severe pocketing in your gums, especially around your lower molars," she told him.

"Has Dr. Barker explained to you how the bone that holds your dentition can become eroded?"

"Repeatedly, yes. I know I should be having something done about it."

"Teddy, how's it going?" Maynard said, entering and washing his hands. He and the brown-eyed woman exchanged a few cryptic words about Ted's teeth. She pointed out something on his X rays. Maynard thanked her and told her she could take off, this was his last appointment.

"Remember to floss, Mr. Reed," she said as she left.

"Oh, I will," Ted promised. To Maynard he said, "She's a pretty girl."

"Three kids," Maynard commented, continuing to study the X rays.

"You're kidding."

"We're getting on, Teddy. Judy Desmond, remember, from high school? Remember? She had hair down to here? Two grandchildren. Two."

"Christ, Judy Desmond, I remember her."

"I'll bet. I'm not going to give you the lecture again about periodontal disease, how many teeth are lost every year, all that. I just think you shouldn't let it go much longer."

"I won't, I'm not."

"Good. Let's go talk."

They went to a bar that had very healthy spider plants in the windows. Maynard ordered a martini, Ted beer.

As he unfolded the details of the plan, Ted felt himself growing tense, almost ecstatic.

"Just look at the demographics, Maynard. Look at the demographics. The over-sixty-five population has doubled since 1960. They're going to be the biggest and the richest age group within ten years. And you market this as a community. See? Not a nursing home. I've gone over this a million times on paper. You know that. How we talked about it, blue sky. But I mean it for real now. I think it can work. I can see it, like a vision, just as clear as I can see that waitress with the ponytail. In my imagination it's a done deal."

78

"Ted, you're preaching to the converted here. I've always said you should go out on your own. Haven't I? But is this the right way, the right time?"

"I'm ready, I really feel I'm ready now. Of course timing is the key. Haven't I always said, it isn't location, location, location in real estate. It's timing, timing, timing. Location, you can put it in black-and-white, anybody can. You can measure traffic patterns, comparable values, all that. But timing you need a feel for. And I have that feel, Maynard."

"I know that."

"These past few days, as I've thought about it seriously, it's become clearer and clearer to me. Pull it off and it will be a complete gold mine."

"The idea, I'm not saying it doesn't have a lot of potential. I like the idea, I've always liked it."

"You just have to market it right. A community. Not a nursing home where you go to die, a community where you go to live. I just wish there'd been someplace like this when my dad—you know what he went through, the joint we ended up putting him into."

"It's not the idea that gives me pause, Teddy. It's the circumstances."

"What circumstances? There's not going to be a better time. Interest rates are coming down. Everything points to it."

"I don't mean interest rates. I mean this guy."

"Sal? What?"

"Who is he? Can you trust him? I pick up some funny vibes around him, Teddy. Something, I don't know how to describe it."

"Okay, you don't know him that well."

"You do?"

"I've been talking to him. He's— Maynard, he's very very impressive. I've known a lot of people in my career, a lot of hustlers, a lot of bullslingers, a lot of phonies. This man has a kind of dynamism, a—I'd even call it charisma."

"Charisma? Like Kennedy, charisma?"

"I mean it."

79

"I don't know. To me, there's something odd about him. What is he, a soldier of fortune? It's too vague. I don't know why, exactly, but he just strikes me wrong. Something about him doesn't ring true."

Ted pushed out his lips and shook his head. "I can't agree. The man has opened my eyes. I mean, I'm going nowhere fast where I am, Maynard. I have to make a move."

"You're earning a living."

"Call it living? No, really. Talking to Sal has made me understand the concept of risk. You have to *take* the risk. The opportunity without risk, that's the one to be wary of. Risk is the sea. You want to sail to the new world? You have to launch out. Worry about what's going to happen, you never leave home. Sure there's going to be rough waters. Thing is to launch out and then deal with the storms as they come up."

"Very poetic," Maynard said. "But you're cutting out of one of the top firms in the city to try and make it on spit-and-a-shoeshine with a guy you met—what, a couple of weeks ago?"

"Stop worrying about Sal. This isn't about him. It's about me. I should have quit Winner years ago. Know why I didn't? Simple. I didn't have the balls. I wasn't willing to take the risk."

"Risk means you can fall on your face."

"Exactly. Maynard, I'm forty-three years old and I've done nothing in my life. I've accomplished nothing. You drift along, someday you wake up and it's over. I dread that. You know how time flies by. Tomorrow I'm fifty. If I don't do it today, it's too late."

"I always said I'd back you, Teddy. And I will. I just think you should maybe look a little more closely at who this guy is."

"Well, he has a résumé and references and all. And with my experience, I can sense a ringer. Sal's no ringer, I guarantee it."

"If you say so, Teddy. You know I'm with you a thousand percent."

They ordered another round of drinks. Ted went over the financial details, how he intended the business to be set up. Maynard proposed a toast to the new venture.

"Best of luck, good buddy."

"Not luck, my friend. Balls. Balls and brains. That's what it takes, believe me. It sounds simple, but it's true.

8

Oh, Sal's a real Don Juan, I can tell you," Gina was saying. "If it's female, he's interested."

"It doesn't, uh, bother you?" Laura asked.

"You get used to these things. At first it seems like the end of the world, you know. But after a while you don't take it so personal. It's almost like a compliment. Ready for another drink?"

They were sitting on the Vincents' flagstone patio. Laura had brought the boys over to swim. Josh was in the house with Mario. Robbie was having a cannonball contest with himself in the pool.

"No, no thanks."

"See, my theory was always—two things." Gina drained her glass. "First, who are these women he goes for?"

"Who are they?"

"Airheads, most of them. Dead from the neck up.

'Cause all he's interested in is the neck down. At least that's a consolation. Pieces of fluff. They don't *mean* anything to him, is what I'm saying. They're lightweights, they're not a threat, really."

"You certainly have a levelheaded approach to it. Ted—I don't know what I'd do if I found out."

"Come on, we're adults." Gina wasn't sure why she was taking this attitude. Maybe she was laying the groundwork for the time when Sal would start cheating. Maybe she was acting blasé in order to put on a front for the judging suburban eyes. Or to form a callus on her heart to insulate her from the pain she knew was coming.

Laura was the easiest to talk to. The others she'd met, she was afraid of them. Afraid they were waiting to make fun of her, whispering among themselves. Whispering, perhaps, about the dark, dangerous secret that Gina felt more and more desperate to conceal.

"The second thing," Gina said, lighting a cigarette, "is how are they harming me? One thing I have to hand to Sal, for all his faults he's a dynamo between the sheets. Absolutely. There's no stopping him. He's a legend in his own time."

Laura's mouth held its uncommitted smile.

"So it's not like I'm losing in the deal," Gina went on. "When it comes right down to it, the man is an animal. He's a machine. Know what I mean?"

"Well . . . ," Laura said with a shrug.

You had to be careful, Gina thought. Sal wasn't careful enough. You had to make a certain impression on these people. Even Laura. You couldn't let them start rummaging around in your secrets.

"Did I ever tell you about my sister's wedding?" Gina asked.

She hadn't told anyone. The story had just occurred to her in the past few days. Gina had felt embarrassed and uneasy to be in a situation where she had no family. It seemed to her not only odd but somehow disreputable. She could say they were all back east, but then why did they never come visit? She needed a better story.

83

She related the event to Laura in detail, the wedding, the great great guy her sister had married, their proud father, the elaborate reception that had been planned, how Gina had had to take Mario home because he was sick, the fire. Sal always told her to keep it simple, but she went on to relate the whole story of the imaginary tragedy that had taken the lives of all her immediate family, right down to finding the charred bridal bouquet.

Laura was appropriately shocked and sympathetic. The wound had healed, Gina insisted, but the emptiness, that would always be there.

"The world is such a dangerous place, Laura. I worry all the time, especially about Mario. I practically can't let him out of my sight."

"I think those concerns," Laura said, "every mother has them. You have to let go. And you have to realize that worrying itself does no good."

"When it's come to raising Mario, I've always had the burden entirely on my shoulders. Something as simple as having him baptized. What's the point, we don't go to church, Sal says. Well, just in case, I told him. First, it's a tradition. Second, the family, my family anyway. And third, what if there *is* original sin like they say? You want your son to rot in limbo? Do you? While you—at least you have a chance because your folks had you baptized."

"Ritual is good, it's important."

"Of course. But Sal hates priests. I guess one of them tried to goose him or something when he was little."

Laura shook her head.

"Course, I had the nuns," Gina added. "I suffered. I was somewhat of a hell raiser at that age. God, all the ups and downs of my life, Laura, I wish I could tell you."

"I guess we've all had them."

"Isn't that the truth? But Sal, he doesn't grasp what it means to have a kid. To him it's only a Christmas present here, a birthday party there, what school to put him in. I tell him, Sal, this person you're ignoring, he's your son. He lives here. All day every day. Sal doesn't pay any attention. Of course, he's busy, but—"

"They're always busy. Ted, same thing. He does try to be with the boys, but work comes first."

"Exactly. The bums. Get you another? Come on."

"Okay, very light."

Gina fixed two more gin and tonics.

"Yeah, the worries I've had," she said, sitting back down. "It's made me old before my time."

"Do you have that feeling?" Laura said. "Does time seem to be speeding up for you?"

"Speeding up? Jeez, I don't know."

"It's not getting older that bothers me. You expect that. It's the acceleration. I could handle aging gracefully. But for it to come at you faster and faster—it's scary. For me."

"You're crazy, how old are you?"

"Nearly forty."

"You don't look it at all."

"Thanks."

"No, really. Hell, I'm thirty-two. Never thought I'd see the day."

"I think for a woman—"

"Oh, definitely."

"I start thinking, I'm already older than my parents were when I remember them, when I was little. I used to always say, how old you'd think you were if you didn't know how old you were—that's what's important. And I'd say, I'd think I was nineteen. But Jenny's sixteen, practically, and it makes me realize I'm no teenager."

"You look like you're in great shape," Gina said.

"I do my aerobics. But, it's not that, not the gray hairs I'm finding, it's a feeling. I wish—"

"Mom, watch!" Robbie called. "*Big Bertha!* Bombs over Tokyo!" He flung himself from the diving board, his knees in his arms, and landed on his back.

"I have to tell you, Gina," Laura said, "I'm very very pleased that you and Sal have moved into our lives. I think you're both very fine people."

"You'll make me blush here."

"Seriously, I can't get over the change in Ted these

85

past couple of months. Getting involved in this business has been almost a dream come true for him. I can't remember when he was so happy."

"I know Sal's good at business."

"Ted says Sal's so persuasive. He just makes people do what he wants."

"You can't say no to him. It's been good for Sal, too, having a regular job, regular hours."

"It's one of those lucky twists of fate, I guess. One of those—"

Gina wasn't listening.

"Where's Mario?" she said, rising quickly to her feet.

" 'She was wet with her flaming, throbbing desire,' " Josh read. " 'His tongue inch-wormed its way up her silken thigh. Her love juices were the sweetest nec—' "

"What?" Mario asked.

"Nec-tar, sweetest nec-tar. You know what nec-tar is, don't you?"

"Sure. Don't you?"

"Of course."

"What?"

"I don't know."

"Me either."

Josh giggled. "Let's see. 'You are driving me insane, she moaned. I am on fire. Give it to me. I cannot wait.' "

"She's in a hurry, she has to catch a bus."

"Here it is. 'He eased his swollen member into her steaming love nest. Fireworks went off in her darkness. Slowly he drove his throbbing tool deep into her pulsating hunger.' "

"That's his weeny, his prick," Mario said.

"I know. Jesus. Isn't this great?"

"You didn't know about this before?"

"Sure, I knew," Josh said. "I mean, I don't know what nec-tar is, but I know you have to take off their clothes and—and kiss their boobies."

"Kiss their boobies and slam your flaming rod in until they say yes yes yes."

86

"Robbie drew a girl with no clothes on his arm once with a pen."

"Your mother see it?"

"Uh-huh. She says we shouldn't think it's dirty. She says the human body is natural. So Robbie says, how come we wear clothes all the time, then? And— Wait, I hear him coming."

Josh's brother waddled into Mario's room. He wore his frogman flippers. He was still dripping.

"Ten-shun!" he said. "At ease. What are you guys doing?"

"We're waiting for you," Josh said, "to show off your throbbing tool that you like to thrust into the wet nec-tar of Lori Bellingham."

"Get out of here, you queerzo. I can't stand her. What are you guys doing in here, anyway? Your mother's looking for you, Vincent. And we're supposed to be engaged in amphibious maneuvers."

"Mario has this really fantastic magazine. But you can't see it because you'll turn to stone."

"I'll never turn to stone. You can show me anything, a man eating a toad or anything, and it won't make me turn to stone. I've seen it all. Where did you get the con-traband, Vincent?"

"The what?"

"That kind of stuff's off-limits. Bad for morale. You get more interested in girls with their shirts off than in the orders of your commanding officer, such as to report for amphibious operations at oh two hundred hours."

"Mario says his father's got a gun," Josh said. "A pistol."

"That is a lie," Robbie said. "Let's see it."

"It's locked up," Mario explained. "But he's got one. A real one."

"Because he was in the army," Robbie said. "What is it? A .45 Colt? That's probably what it is."

"I don't know. He wears it sometimes. He has a holster on his ankle."

"You liar."

"He does. Because nobody in the world can beat him up."

"Can you get it? You have to get it so we'll know it's real, otherwise you're a goddamn liar and you have to do a million push-ups."

"I don't think I can, my dad would kill me."

"You're scared, that's why. If you can get it and it's real and it works and we can shoot it, you'll be promoted to major and get the Congressional Medal of Honor, maybe."

"Maybe I can."

"Hey, Robbie," Josh said. "Stop dripping your sweet nec-tar all over the floor."

Mario laughed.

Robbie said, "I'm going to kill you, you smerk."

9

Ted pinched his forehead and reached again for the computer software manual. He couldn't get this estimate spreadsheet to work right. The screen stared at him like a grinning puppy eager for its master's approval of the mess it had left on the living room carpet.

Ted had converted his den into an office. They'd originally talked about setting up the business in Sal's house, since he had more room. But Sal made the excuse that for some reason Gina was "paranoid" about having any clients coming in. They'd arranged for an answering service. Several clients from Winner had followed Ted. He'd rounded up a few small apartment buildings for Reed-Vincent to manage. Sal was taking courses to get his real estate license and canvassing for more management accounts.

Ted was spending most of his time getting the Golden Age project going. With Maynard's seed money they'd been able to obtain a number of bank loans. They were talking with additional private investors about backing. They'd taken an option on the land. The architects were finishing the preliminary sketches of the development. Now Ted was trying to work through a morass of permits and estimates, tax forms, zoning regulations, deed registers, and other deadening details that he had to pull together in order to work up a coherent plan for investors.

Once the Golden Age project was rolling, he would feel more secure. That would be their base, their cash cow. It would establish their credibility. He was already a little disturbed at some of the cost estimates, additional expenses that would raise the price of the units. But, Sal said, plunging ahead was everything. Yeah, that was the key. You had to stamp out all doubts.

He was surprised at his mixed emotions over leaving Winner. For years he'd griped about what a flake Evelyn was, her administrative clumsiness. Partly it was a matter of the security he was relinquishing, the enormous responsibility he was taking on his shoulders. It scared and invigorated him. He found himself getting up earlier, applying himself with greater concentration, and working later.

Sal was a phenomenon. He'd already closed one property at almost $400,000, though Ted had warned him that the real estate board wouldn't like it if they found out he wasn't licensed. Sal laughed it off, Ted handled the paperwork, and the business pocketed its first sizable commission.

When he wasn't selling, Sal was making contacts. He seemed to be everywhere at once, from a downtown racquetball club to a blue-collar lounge on the East Side. There he'd gotten talking to a rich Pole whose wife had inherited a run-down Victorian house on the edge of one of the suburbs. Sal had convinced the man to convert the building to apartments and let Reed-Vincent manage them. He even talked the owner into giving him the prime contracting role, drawing an uncannily accurate estimate out of the air and concluding the whole deal with a handshake over beer and pickled eggs.

Ted had imagined that Evelyn, a fiercely competitive

woman, would resent his departure. Instead of turning bitter, she personally arranged his farewell party.

Evelyn offered him an effusive testimonial. She went into his entire history with the company, how beloved he'd been by her father, what a fine man and upstanding citizen, and a lot more. Ted was embarrassed. She begged Jesus to help Ted and Sal in their new venture. Ted had always been a Winner Winner, she declared and, once a Winner Winner, could never be a loser. She ended with her trademark, a short sermon equating real estate and the Kingdom of Heaven.

She insisted that Ted give a farewell talk. He said that a journey of a thousand miles started with a single step and with the aid of their friends and colleagues he hoped they'd make it a thousand miles and anyway this was a good start. He introduced Sal. He said that Laura, his lovely wife, always insisted that nothing in life is a coincidence and he guessed that was true. The new firm, Reed-Vincent Properties, was meant to be. He was thrilled to have an opportunity to hook up at just the right time with such a compatible and dynamic partner.

Elliott Fishman had a few words to say about what a great guy Ted was and how they'd all miss him. He seemed genuinely moved. He said they'd chipped in and gotten him an appropriate gift. Ted opened the box and took out an Indian war bonnet. Him no longer brave now, him chief, Elliott said. Ted put on the headdress and gave a feeble whoop. Then Evelyn presented him with the "real" gift, a brushed-pigskin briefcase. Ted felt his eyes getting hot.

Ted knew this was a watershed in his life. As Sal said, you had to take your life in hand. Ted now saw he'd always been a drifter, letting circumstances carry him. At last he was paddling his canoe into the main channel. He was going to buck the white water and forge his own destiny. If he succeeded— No, no if. He had no choice. When you throw yourself into something like this fully, you make it, the gods see that you make it.

Ted was impressed, almost intimidated by how quickly

Sal picked up the nuances of the business. It was less a question of guiding him than of restraining him.

Sal wrung the banker's hand. They crinkled their eyes at each other. Sal had stopped in to drop off some additional financials the bank wanted. The loan committee, the banker was sure, would be very favorably impressed by the projections for Reed-Vincent Properties. Sal said they'd have to get together sometime, have a drink. The banker said he'd enjoy that.

Sal smiled to himself on the way out. He was actually getting to like this stuff.

Ted had asked him to stop and check a building they'd just landed a management contract on, look around the place, size up the situation.

He had to ask directions, but he finally found the building, a weathered three-story brick apartment complex. On the way in he passed a bulky young man in a cutoff sweatshirt and gold chains. He felt the man's eyes follow him through the door. In the foyer Sal found the name of the janitor, a Mr. Ramos. He pushed a button beside the name.

A voice answered. Sal identified himself. The door buzzed open.

Ramos's apartment was in the rear. Lounging against the staircase was another man, this one in mirrored sunglasses, his hands jammed into the pockets of his jacket.

Sal walked past him. He introduced himself to the wiry man who was waiting for him.

"The owner wasn't happy with the last managing agent he had," he explained. "Apparently there were some complaints. If there's anything we can do to fix things up, that's what Reed-Vincent's here for."

"Yes, okay."

"What's the matter?"

"Nothing." The man was still holding the door open.

"Why are you looking down there? Something about the squirt by the stairs?"

"Everything is fine."

"Something going down right now?" He was watching the man's eyes.

"Come inside, please."

They stepped into the man's apartment, which smelled heavily of bacon.

"People in this building are afraid," Ramos said. "There is a man in 2C, Davey Hicks, he deals drugs—crack, heroin. People are afraid. He works for Lard Lujak."

"So we throw him out."

"*You* throw him out."

"I will."

"Don't be crazy. You hear what I said? Lard Lujak. That name don't mean nothing to you?"

"I'm new around here. But I know one thing—these jerks are scum. Selling shit to kids? Fuck it. Two C?"

"No, mister, wait."

"This guy is causing a lot of the problems in this building, am I right? So, he has to go."

"No, no, no. It is not so easy."

"Anything's easy. You just put your mind to it."

"You're crazy. These people have weapons."

"I'm just doing my job, amigo."

Whistling, Sal left the apartment and walked toward the front of the building. He stopped and turned.

"Hicks upstairs?"

The man leaning against the staircase stood upright. He swallowed and said, "Beat it, he's busy."

"Let's go up and talk to him anyway, whataya say?"

The man smoothed the hair around his ear. When he went to put his hand back into his pocket, Sal grasped his wrist and twisted the arm into a hammerlock. In the same motion he thrust his own hand into the pocket. He tore the fabric extracting a stainless automatic pistol. He dug the barrel of the pistol into the flesh under the man's jaw.

"Change your mind?"

The man made a dry gargle in his throat.

Sal marched the man up the flight of stairs. He placed

him in front of the peephole in the door marked 2C and stood out of the way. He knocked. With two hands he aimed the gun at the man's head.

The man answered the muffled inquiry. "It's Mitch."

"I told you—"

Sal was inside the apartment, pushing Mitch in front of him, but pointing the gun now at the small man who'd answered.

This man had a snakelike appearance, short hair combed to a point over his forehead, small eyes, a reptilian upper lip that hung over the lower.

"Oh, shit."

"Don't try it!" Sal yelled at another man, who was beginning to lean over beside a desk in the corner. "Tell them to keep cool, Davey," he said to the small man, "or you're dead meat."

"What is this?"

"I'm the new managing agent for the building here, Davey. I'm going to be making a few changes. Some of them concern you."

"What are you, serious? Managing agent?"

"Change number one, we're not going to have any more monkeys hanging around the lobby with iron bulging their pockets."

"Hey, man, listen."

"Change number two, I guess the folks here just don't seem to want you for a neighbor no more. You're going to have to move along."

"Please put the gun down. It could go off, somebody could get hurt."

"Somebody? You say somebody, but it seems to be pointed right at your gut, Davey."

"Okay," he said. "I see your point. You're the managing agent. You want a little rent increase. I think we can arrange that."

He stepped over to the desk. He indicated a briefcase on top of it. Sal nodded. Hicks lifted the lid. Inside were neatly wrapped piles of bills. He lifted out one, two. He thought for a minute, smiled, added a third.

He offered the money to Sal. Sal shook his head. "Put it back."

"Maybe you like pussy, man?" said the other, a tall man with a large Adam's apple. "We can get you girls, young ones, all you want."

"I thought you looked like a pimp. Now, listen to me, I'm going to give you shitheads a chance to pack up what you can carry. It looks like you're just using the place to deal out of anyway. Then you're going to walk. You won't ever want to come around this building again. If you ever do come around, very bad things will happen to you. I guarantee it."

"I have a lease on this place," Hicks insisted.

A look of great surprise came over Sal's features. He glanced across the room at the tall man. At the same instant he pulled the trigger of the gun. The bullet sliced past Hicks and tore a hole in the couch. The blast left their ears ringing.

"Your lease is terminated, asshole," Sal said.

Hicks let out a breath very slowly.

"Okay," he said, "you hold the high hand today. I wouldn't want, however, to be in your shoes when certain people—"

"Lard Lujak, for example?" Sal asked.

"When certain people find out about this little escapade. You may discover—"

"Not that," Sal said, indicating the briefcase. "You're leaving that. You can have the suitcase your pal's been trying to nudge behind the drapes with his foot since I walked in. I never touch that shit."

The tall man picked up the suitcase. Hicks collected some papers from the drawers of the desk. They hurried out.

Sal dropped the gun into the briefcase and snapped it shut. He felt a delicious rush of adrenaline, a humming down his nerves that he hadn't experienced in months. On his way out he stopped at the door of the janitor's apartment and told him to change the locks on 2C.

Sal checked his watch as he got back into his car. He

95

had to step on it. Today was the day he planned to spring the big surprise on Ted.

Ted was still struggling to adjust the spreadsheet parameters when Sal arrived.

"Where have you been?" Ted snapped. "That guy you were supposed to show the storefront to, the guy with the laundry, he called and I had to take him myself. I was supposed to meet Anderson at two thirty. I had to put him off. That doesn't look good."

"Hey, slow down. Easy, boy."

"Well? I'm working my ass off here and you're—"

"I've been busy, too. Real busy. Took care of some junkies over in the Magin Street place. Had drinks with Deep Pockets at the club earlier. He's not ready to throw in with Golden Age just yet, but I'm working him closer. He's one of these guys likes to see momentum before he jumps on. Plus, I've been putting together a little surprise."

"What surprise?"

Sal insisted that Ted drop what he was doing and take a drive downtown. Ted reluctantly agreed.

In the business district the sun was raging over the decline of summer.

A surprise, Sal thought as they drove. Like that guy you set up, Baldy McComb. Told him he was going to get a surprise. Drove him across the Brooklyn Bridge and out to the Lizard Lounge, him thinking you were finally going to pay him for the load of clock radios and electronic shit he'd jacked. But Paulie had found out Baldy was talking to the man. They got him on an assault-with-deadly rap. He never called Baylor, but he was on the street next day. He told everybody the guy had dropped charges, but Paulie got from a clerk in the D.A.'s office that Baldy was saving his ass from a fifteen-to-life, trading a few names, just a few. Because if he wasn't, why didn't he call Baylor?

And you jollying him along. Big surprise, Baldy. Did he really not know? Or did he not want to know? Nobody wants to know once it's inevitable. They want to keep hoping.

Hand over his shoulder, coming out of the light into

the dark lounge. Surprise. Spinning him around. They've got the rope ready, the slipknot. And you and Billy on one side, Ack-ack on the other, pulling for all you're worth. Ack-ack laughing, the way Baldy's eyes popped. Laughing and yanking so hard. The rope dug in. Somebody yelled stop. Stop, his head'll come off.

And the smell of him. They cleaned up with bleach, but you could still smell it the next day.

"This is that White and Stanton project that just opened," Ted said. They'd parked in front of a glass needle of an office building. "Did you catch how much they spent on it?"

"It's a class joint," Sal said. There were still signs of the recently completed construction, burlap on the trees, workmen polishing some brass trim. "Check this lobby— or, wait, they call it an atrium. The waterfall, the trees. Class, am I right?"

"It's a showplace, no doubt about it."

As they took the elevator to the eighteenth floor, Sal refused to divulge who they would be meeting. It had to be a surprise. They turned the corner in the corridor and proceeded down to a pair of thick glass doors. A workman was kneeling in front of them, painting with black enamel.

"What the hell is this?" Ted said, frowning at the bold letters that spelled out "Reed-Vincent Properties." Grasping the significance, he was immediately torn in two.

You're letting things get out of control here, he admonished himself. This is serious.

At the same time, his heart was swelling. He'd never seen his name on a door, only on the two-inch plaque on his desk at Winner.

"It's class, babe. All the way."

"What? We have to talk about this. You rented this place?"

"Come on." Sal led him inside. The beige carpeting was practically alive. "What happened, I got to talking to this guy in a bar over in the Sheraton. He's a consultant. He's been doing good, but now the guy he worked with decides to take a job with their biggest client. He loses a partner and half his business like that. Turns out they'd just signed a ten-year lease on this suite. Prestige address. Decorated and ready to go. He wants out, he can't afford it."

"And we can?"

"Let me finish. I told him I had a client, I'm in real estate, I had a client who I was sure I could get to take the place off his hands, nominal sum. Of course, my man would want to put in his own fixtures, so he couldn't give credit for the paint job, the furnishings. We struck a deal right there. The place is perfect, we get it all fixed up for nothing, and he's paying us to assume the lease. How can you beat that?"

The suite held the clean smell of new paint.

"I think we should have discussed this."

"It was one of those things. You jump on them or they're gone. You and I talked, remember? We said class all the way. And we definitely need a place downtown."

"I'm referring to overhead. We're not bringing in enough to cover a place like this. Nowhere near enough."

"We will be. This layout will generate bucks, it'll pay for itself ten times over. Anyway, when Golden Age Estates comes through, we're going to be in the chips. We might as well get ready. Oh."

"Hi." The woman was almost as tall as Ted. She emerged from a short corridor on the left and stepped behind the oval reception desk. She had a wide jaw and global eyes. Her bangs and long wrists suggested a model. Flowers and spice filled the air. "Welcome to Reed-Vincent," she said.

"This is Reed," Sal explained. "Ted, Margot."

Ted forgot himself for a minute. He closed his eyes, grinned, ran a hand down his face, and shook his head.

"Are you all right, Ted?" Margot cooed.

Ted nodded, chuckling in his throat.

"I have the coffee machine set up, if you'd like some."

"No, thanks. I'm delighted to meet you, Margot. Sal?"

"Let me show you your office," Sal said.

The phone purred. Margot shook her long red hair

away from her ear and answered with a musical "Reed-Vincent Properties, good afternoon."

"What do we do, play football in here in our spare time?" Ted said, surveying the enormous corner office with its chocolate-and-tan color scheme.

"The beauty of this setup, they planned it for the two of them, these consultants, so the offices are essentially identical. Go ahead, try out the chair. That's real leather."

Reluctantly, Ted settled into the throne behind the broad modern desk. He glanced at the view.

"Look," he said, "I hate to be a party pooper, but I'm afraid you've gone way overboard here. I know we talked. I know we had big plans—someday. But you have to work up to it. The Golden Age project isn't a certainty. We're over our heads on that as it is. To take on this kind of expense, bleed our cash, it doesn't make any rational business sense."

"Sure it does," Sal countered. "Business is hype, man. You know that, but you don't know you know it. Look at your old place, Winner. They're nickel-and-diming it out of offices that say Winner's a loser. They get by, but they're always left out of the big deals. You jump in, babe. People with the bucks, they want to be sure they're dealing with a class outfit. It's a façade? What isn't? Anybody can rent a slick suite like this? Sure, but they don't dare. Who gets the business? We do. Why? They can see we're a class operation. It's all a head game."

"It's all a money game, is what it is. No money to pay the bills, no classy façade, no business."

"So we get more financing. I'm talking to people right now to come in as backers. You play with a minor-league mentality, you spend your whole career in Class A."

"And what about Miss High Heel Sneakers out there?"

"Part of the flash, babe. She's trained as a systems analyst and she's done some modeling. But because of our great profit-sharing plan, she's using her many talents here."

"What profits?"

"At least you didn't ask what talents. I mentioned to

her, you know, in vague terms about her getting a little of the equity. It'll motivate her."

"I'd be afraid of motivating her too much."

"I hear you, married man. She's a battleship, isn't she? People walk in—picture it, Ted—they come through the atrium down there, the waterfall and that, up the elevator, the hushed hallway, the big glass doors. They're impressed, okay? But those are just the body blows to soften them up. They walk in, they're face-to-face with this neon broad and suddenly they're in church. By the time they get to your very formidable office, they're down on their knees, hands folded, begging for a deal."

"Well, it's an interesting scenario, but I don't know—"

"Don't think I'm doing this for a goof. I'm looking at the business end first and foremost. Everything for the business. Return on investment, as you put it. Margot will return in spades, believe it. And the funny thing is, I really hired her for her brains."

"I can see that."

"I really did."

Ted puffed his cheeks and let out a sigh. "Okay. For now, okay, if we're committed. But if we don't boost our revenues quickly, if God forbid something happens to the Golden Age deal, we're going to have to retrench and fast. Understand? And in the future, I wish you'd clear these commitments with me before you plunge."

"I wanted to surprise you."

"I'm surprised."

Sal winked. "Class, baby, class."

Ted shrugged with his palms up. Sal left him alone. As soon as the door closed, Ted leaned back, crossed his arms, and put his feet up on the glossy desk. He couldn't keep himself from grinning.

After trying unsuccessfully to figure how to work the intercom, he went out and told Margot that he'd have some coffee after all.

10

Ted laid his bag on the edge of the trap and drew out his wedge. The sand, wet with dew, squeaked under his spikes. His ball nested in a little crater where it had landed.

He planted his feet and hefted the club over the ball, careful not to touch the sand. He swung. The sand gripped the chrome wedge. The white sphere skipped, nudged the edge of the bunker, rolled back down the slope.

Ted said, shit. He stepped over to the new lie. This time he buried the club closer to the ball. His Titleist 4 popped high, plunked cleanly onto the green, and dribbled to within five feet of the pin.

"Shot," Maynard said.

Ted dragged the sand rake over the depressions and footsteps.

"Can't take much sand when it's damp."

Maynard was already on the green. He putted, came close, tapped in for his par. Ted's shot skirted the rim, pranced a foot past. Ted said, shit, again. Maynard told him it was a gimme and replaced the pin.

"Can you believe this is the first time I've been on the course since I left Winner?" Ted said. He'd managed to fit an early morning game into his schedule. "I may have been small-time there, but I got in plenty of golf."

"Now you're chained to your office."

"And loving it. I don't have to tell you, being your own boss is the only way to go."

"I'm glad it's working out."

Maynard drove. Ted clocked his drive up the middle, but it hooked as it died and bounded toward the left rough.

Maynard was silent as they walked down the grassy slope. They split apart to their balls. Maynard hit a four-iron short of the green. Ted's took a lucky bounce over a creek and rolled to within good chipping distance.

"Listen, let me ask you something," Maynard said as he joined Ted on the fairway. "This will sound kind of funny, but we're—we've known each other a long time."

"Talk to me, Maynard G. You know you can."

"Felice is a fantastic girl. That's—I mean, no question about it."

"You'll get no argument there. Your waiting paid off. All the guys envy the hell out of you."

"Who?"

"Everybody. Like you won the lottery."

Ted's third shot caught the apron.

"Don't get me wrong," Maynard said. "She is a phenom. In bed? Couldn't be better. She's taught *me* a few tricks, if you can believe that one. But, I have to wonder. She's young. When we were dating, it was one thing. But when you have to relate on a day-to-day basis . . ."

"She loves you, that's what matters."

Maynard knocked his ball onto the far edge of the split-level green.

"She's a very friendly girl, Ted. She's vivacious. She's talkative. I see her talking to some guy, I start to wonder. I can't help myself."

"That all? You've got nothing to worry about, a stud

like you. What, you find briefs in your drawer, thirty-fours, you take a thirty-eight?"

"No, I'm serious. She knows so many people, has all these friends from before we met. Then, she does the eleven o'clock news, she's out every night, it's midnight, a lot of times it's two, three. She says they had a meeting or she went for drinks with people from the station. I have to be up early, I have appointments at eight. There's just too much opportunity there."

"You know we've been around this buoy before," Ted said. "When you were serious about that girl Fran, same thing. You fall, you get possessive. You get possessive, you get jealous. You get jealous, you start thinking. You imagine. You see signs. You convince yourself. You go apeshit. Tell me I'm wrong."

Maynard stepped across the glistening green and hunched over his ball. He stroked it. It almost ran out of gas before it reached the downhill slope. Then it rushed down and rolled straight into the hole.

Ted let out a congratulatory whoop. He three-putted.

"I know what you're saying, Teddy," Maynard said as they walked. "But I've caught her a few times. Nothing serious, but she's either disappearing with some guy at a party or she's wearing some kind of a getup you'd see a whore in."

"I can't believe you. She's a pretty lady. Why shouldn't she show it?"

"She's married."

"Everybody's got a fault—we wouldn't be human if we didn't," Ted said. "Some guys have the booze yen. Others, they gamble away the grocery money. You, it's the green-eyed monster. You have to stand up, say, my name is Maynard and I'm a jealous son of a bitch. You have to face it that it's inside you."

"Okay, maybe I've cried wolf before. But the whole point of that story, when the wolf did come, nobody believed the boy. But the wolf was there. The wolf was real that time."

"Leave it alone."

"I see things, very subtle things. Like, she's almost too careful to let me know where she's going to be all the time. But then I call up where she's supposed to be and she isn't there. But she always has an excuse."

"I think maybe you should go see a counselor. This is obviously something—"

"A counselor is fine, great—if she's not fooling around. But what if she is? Then, we go to a counselor, I pour my heart out, and she's laughing her ass off, doing it with somebody behind my back. I have a different idea."

Ted drove his ball from the tee. He shaded his eyes, looking into the low morning sun. Maynard sliced sharply toward the rough.

"What's your idea?" Ted asked.

"I was talking to a friend of mine—do you know Chuck? Anyway, he got a divorce last year. His lawyer told him to hire this detective. No, wait, I'm serious. He suspected the wife, who was suing him, was actually two-timing. So he got a complete report of her movements—guy conducted surveillance periodically over months. He walked into court with dates, times, photographs."

"Is this you? Is this Maynard Barker saying this?"

"I know it sounds weird, but it makes a lot of sense. Either way it makes sense. He comes back with a report that Felice is as pure as the driven rain, I can stop worrying. No headshrinker can do that for me, erase my suspicions like that. He tells me she's been fooling around, then I know, at least. I have the details. I can put it to her and she can't hand me some lame excuse."

"You're nuts, is what it is," Ted insisted. "You've been married six months and you're talking about hiring a detective to follow your wife around?"

The green was perched up on the next hill. A flock of starlings swooped into the hollow below them.

"Okay, maybe I'm jumping to conclusions. But let me put it this way, Ted. I've knocked around as far as women go. All my life I've played loose. Now, Felice, I absolutely love her to death. Crazy? I am crazy about her. And if I ever find out she's cheating on me, I honestly don't know what I'd do. I'm afraid to think. What are you using here, a six?"

"No detective is going to straighten your head around, that's what I'm saying. I think I'll go with a four-iron. My arms haven't got the snap they used to."

Gina was waiting for Sal when he arrived home.

"Where have you been?" she demanded.

"Where have I been? I've been to the moon. Where have you been?"

"I told you I'm taking this dancerobics. Twice a week. Laura recommended a class to me. You said you were going to be here when Mario got home from school."

"So I got held up. So what? He can play with the kids next door."

"He was here when I got back. Alone. Sitting in here watching TV all by himself. Is that smart, Sal?"

"I figured—"

"Will you wake up! What's the matter with you? It's just what they want. We become lax, it leaves them an opening."

"They? What they?"

"Oh, for Christ sake! Don't pretend. They could grab him at any time. I'm worried sick over it. They could appear out of nowhere when you least expect it. They won't hesitate—"

"Hold it. Mario, get the hell up to your room right now! I catch you listening behind a door again, boy, I'm going to whip your ass good."

Gina was wringing her hands.

Sal said, "He listens to that shit, he's going to get spooked. You watch your mouth."

"Sal, this whole thing is twisting me around. Every night almost, I wake up terrified. I hear a noise, I'm out of my skin. I'm walking in the mall, see somebody who doesn't look right, I turn and—sometimes I actually run. I'm scared, can't you understand that? And it's getting worse."

"This is funny, you harping on this. You were the one who wanted this life."

"I know I did. I thought it would be an opportunity. It is, I mean. It is an opportunity. It's just, I get thinking about the danger, it crushes me. I think about them harming Mario. I think about you—every morning when you go out I wonder if you'll come back, if I'll ever see you again."

"Cool down, will you?"

"We can't relax, that's the important thing. We have to keep up our guard at all times. It's just common sense. And Sal, most important, I need you. Don't desert me. Ever."

Sal sighed. "Gina, it's me. Remember? I can handle this shit, anything comes down. Just play it cool."

She pressed the bottom of her palm against her forehead and took some deep breaths. "I'm trying. Okay? I'm putting it out of my mind. All gone. Hmm? Look here. Look what I got." She showed him the additions to her collection. "See the little ballerina? And the prince of Siam? Look at the detail, those fingernails. And this collie, look at that expression. Lassie. It almost looks real, doesn't it?"

"I don't think I've ever seen a real collie four inches high before."

"Funny. But wait, I got one for you. The 'Naked Maja.' I thought you'd appreciate this."

The pink female figure was stretched out on folds of purple.

Sal laughed in his throat. "Nice bod," he said. "But not as nice as yours."

"You're so sweet. I need this stuff, Sal. I need my things. I'm going bananas here."

"Going? Did you say going?"

"Honestly. Don't laugh. Can't you feel it? It's so strange. Life is so strange. I feel like I don't know who I am sometimes."

"All you have to do is face it, Gina. Deal with it. Sometimes I think it's too easy. I find myself slipping into that suburban security. The biggest worry any of these people have, somebody's going to steal their garden hose. Violence, it's something they see on the tube."

"I wish to God it was easy. I just can't seem to fit in."

"Hey, have a drink. Relax for once."

They fixed cocktails and sat out by the pool. A robin was sending arrows of sound into the eggshell sky.

"My main worry," Sal said, "is that I'm slipping, losing my reflexes. Tell you the truth, I'm kind of getting to like this life. It's so soft. These people, you can con them without trying. I'm out there making the moves the way I used to and they're dropping like flies. Business is just plain old hustling, as far as I'm concerned, only with paperwork. Ted, he can't get over it. Keeps saying, how do you do it? All the years he's been in the racket, I come in, overnight I'm a superstar. Of course I let on everything I know I learned from him. He's starting to believe it, thinks he's pretty hot shit himself."

"You want to be careful, though, Sal. These people aren't what you think, maybe."

"Sure they are. They're fish. That ding Maynard put up a bundle to get us started, we're cruising. He's good for more, I know he is. And the jerkwater bankers in this town, it's literally like taking candy from a baby."

"Don't talk that way. I mean it."

"I know what I'm doing. Hell, Ted's getting into it himself. He kicked about the posh offices, okay. But next thing, I hear him bragging to his old real estate buddies about the place, giving tours, wagging his tail. We hired that kid Don you met at the barbecue, just so Ted would have somebody to order around."

"If everything's so hunky-dory," Gina said, "I wonder why Laura told me Ted was worried sick."

"He's a born worrier. Sure we're running up debt. That's the way you go. Sure it's a pain having to deal with these bureaucrats and paper-pushers. But I just landed an option on some retail space at eighteen-a-square-foot. We can turn around and rent that for twenty-four, twenty-five, we find the right tenants. Ted's too timid, likes to cling to the shore."

"She said he was afraid the old-age deal would blow up."

"Golden Age, babe. Remember that. We call them that because they're a pot of gold for us. Or we hope they will be."

"What do you mean, hope?"

"Well, there are a few minor technicalities. I keep telling Ted to look on the positive side. He's worried because the whole ball of wax stands or falls on that deal. Make or break."

"She said he was risking his life savings."

"So? I put a few bucks in it, too. Que sera sera."

"I'm telling you, you have to watch out for these people, Sal."

"What? I know what I'm doing."

"I hope you do. I hope you're not underestimating them."

"Day I can't keep a step ahead of these straights, I give up. Besides, I like Ted. He's a real schoolboy."

"Laura's sweet, too. I just wish I could feel more relaxed, more at home here."

"You will," he said. "It's a matter of adjusting. It's psychology. I never thought I'd fit in, but look at me."

They sipped their drinks, soaking up the quiet evening. She watched his eyes move, his face darken. Despite all his talk, she knew the memories were beginning to get to him.

Jenny and her friend Debi crouched, peered through the rhododendrons.

"Oh God, Jenny!" Debi whispered.

"Is he cute?"

"He's hairy. He looks like that actor, what's his name, Burt Reynolds?"

"He's better-looking than Burt Reynolds," Jenny said. "He could be a star in the movies. He could win the Academy Award just by looking at you with his beautiful brown eyes."

"That's her?"

"His wife. Gina. Look at the makeup she wears. Gross."

"Gross. And tipped hair. Double gross."

"She has to cover up, her skin is like leather."

"Like my mom," Debi said. "Have you been, you know, seeing him much?"

"I was. Because, I told you Sal and my father started this business together. And at first they had their office at our house. But then they got a place downtown. So Sal doesn't come around much anymore. I have to peek."

"That's his punching bag?"

"Yeah. He works out out here, skipping rope and doing push-ups and all."

"So how about it, Jen? What's keeping you?"

"I have a plan," Jenny confided. "Twice a week she goes to her aerobics class. She's trying to sweat off her saddlebag hips."

"Good luck."

They giggled.

"Good luck for me," Jenny said. "He, a lot of times, comes home just after she leaves. He doesn't spend his life in the office like my stupid father. So, if I can get my mom to take the twins somewhere and their kid, too, I'll have him all to myself for a couple of hours."

"How will you get him to . . . you know?"

"I'll go over and I'll say, like, I thought I heard a noise and I'm scared. Or, could he help me get the top off this jar of pickles, I want to make a pickle pie."

"Or pickle soup."

"Or something in my eye."

"Or you could have a cramp. You need him to massage it. A cramp in your hip."

"In my lip."

They both covered their mouths to mute their laughter.

"Anyway, that's my plan," Jenny whispered. "I'm just waiting for the ideal moment. But I can't wait much longer. The way he looks at me. I just dissolve, Deb."

109

"I don't blame you, I—"

A sound like a crack of lightning split the air between them. Both girls screamed.

Looking for the source of the sound, which appeared to come from all directions at once, Jenny saw Sal sprawled on the patio. Gina was covering her face with her hands.

"You're dead!" a voice shouted.

Leaves rustled near them. Debi continued to scream hysterically.

Sal had crawled out of sight on his belly.

More shouts burst from the bushes.

"You're dead! You're fragged! You have to surrender."

"We scared you! Ha ha!"

"Scaredy-cats! Scaredy-cats! Look at 'em crying!"

"They're prisoners of war. We have to torture them according to the Geneva conventions."

Seeing Sal approach very quickly, Jenny stood.

"You little bastards!" she screamed. "I'm telling Dad on you. Get away from here."

"This is no-man's-land," Robbie said. He emerged from the bushes in camouflage gear. "It's a free-fire zone. You're spies. You're spying on Mr. Vincent."

"What the hell's going on here?" Sal demanded, his face distorted by anger.

"These little brats," Jenny explained. Debi was staring through her tears at Sal.

"Who set off that firecracker?"

Josh and their friend Brian now stood with Robbie.

"I think a spark from it hit my leg," Jenny said. She pointed. Sal looked.

"Well?" Sal said, frowning at the boys.

"It was Mario, sir," Robbie said. "We were just playing."

"Where is he?"

"Over there."

"Mario!"

Mario came out of the bushes, his head hanging.

Sal took hold of Mario's arm and slapped him along

his head with the flat of his hand. Mario closed his eyes and puckered his mouth.

"You gonna cry?" Sal asked him.

Mario shook his head.

"You better not." Sal swatted him hard across the seat of his pants. Again. Again. All the while he kept watching Mario's face.

The other children, unaccustomed to being spanked, were petrified by the intensity of the punishment. Even Jenny gritted her teeth and put her fingertips to her lips.

"Get in the house!" Sal ordered his son. "Now!"

Sal glared at the rest of them. He turned, walked back to the patio.

Chastened, the children tiptoed back to their own yard.

"Oh, oh, oh!" Josh whined after the long silence.

"What's the matter?" his brother asked.

"I think a spark hit my leg. Oh!"

"You little brats!" Jenny screamed. She lashed out at the boys. Laughing, they dashed for the security of their tree house.

11

Laura worked part-time at an art gallery. She'd been putting in extra hours lately. Driving home she felt the strangeness building again. She was distracted. What was it exactly?

Fatigue? Changes? The summer had been hectic, one thing after another. The kids. Ted completely preoccupied with the new business. She'd been under a lot of pressure in her own job, arranging for three shows this fall, including a big retrospective. The new neighbors.

Quite a change from the Bennetts. The Vincents appear on the scene and inside of six months Ted's quit his job and started a successful real estate firm with Sal. And Gina—well, Laura had to admit she was an interesting person.

At first, the two women had kept their distance, felt each other out. But then Laura began to catch glimpses of the fragile, gentle person beneath Gina's sometimes vulgar exterior. Laura had come to appreciate Gina's inner toughness and her refreshing frankness, her lack of false delicacy.

Gina often called her over to see some new item she'd bought to decorate their house. Laura found most of Gina's additions hideous—the green velvet drapes, the painting with the lurid sunset, the massive brass lamp whose facets were a compilation of Rodin's greatest hits, the bric-a-brac, the Franklin Mint porcelains.

She recognized that Gina had a certain sophistication—Laura almost envied her. Yet behind it she was strangely naïve. She was—what would you call it? Lowbrow. Yes, sophisticated lowbrow. You could see it in the jewelry she wore—heavy, ornate gewgaws—and in her musical taste, which ran to Elvis and Barry Manilow, and in all the soaps she watched, not to laugh at, as Laura and her friends sometimes did, but with genuine interest in the silly stories.

Laura preferred blond oak, beige carpets, clean lines, pastels, wicker, sunny windows. She'd studied the baroque simplicity of Japanese flower arranging. She couldn't understand why Gina kept her drapes closed so much.

Laura glanced at the Vincents' house before she pulled into her own driveway.

Her neighbor was obviously neurotic. She smoked constantly. She often drank a couple of bloody marys for lunch. Her mood could swing from euphoria to melancholy, from excited chatter to dark silence, in a matter of minutes.

Laura had diagnosed her as mildly paranoiac. She was always suspicious of people, of the world. Do you know this person? Who's that over there? Some basic insecurity, some flaw probably in her self-esteem. She was obsessive about keeping track of Mario. At first she hadn't let him out of her sight. She admitted that many nights she was so racked by indefinable fears that she couldn't sleep. She sat up, she said, reading cookbooks. Not because she liked to cook, but simply for their bland, unthreatening perspective.

Laura undressed and stood for a long time under the

shower, the water as hot as she could stand. Had Gina's nervousness infected her, too? She could never seem to relax anymore. She always sensed a vague agitation in the back of her mind.

Reaching for a towel, she watched herself in the full-length mirror. She automatically inventoried all the negatives—the little bit of flab in the hips, her stomach not as taut as she'd like. But she looked good for her age. For any age, God damn it. She took some time to admire herself, to try on a couple of seductive poses.

Gina's moods hadn't kept her and Sal from an active social life. They'd quickly expanded their circle beyond the suburban group that contained most of Laura and Ted's friends. A woman Laura knew through the gallery actually asked her if she could get her an invitation to a soiree the Vincents had held at the end of August. She'd made some coy reference to Sal.

Laura dressed and went downstairs.

Jenny had arrived home while Laura was in the shower. She came bounding down the stairs and was heading out the door.

"Jenny."

"What, Mom?"

"Where are you going?"

"Over to Sal and Gina's. They—I wanted to ask them something about baby-sitting."

"I'd rather you didn't."

"What are you talking about?"

"You've been over there, I think, practically every night this week. It's getting to be too much. And dressed like that."

"I have to ask them what time. What do you mean, dressed like what?"

"Look at you, shorts that are two sizes too small for you. In October?"

"It's not that cold out."

"Don't think I don't know what you're doing."

"What am I doing?"

114

"Jen, he's a married man. A girlish infatuation is fine, but there are limits. I'm sure that Sal is getting pretty fed up with your campaign, your spying."

"Who's spying?"

"I've seen you. Look, girls get crushes at your age, I had them myself."

"It's not a crush!"

Laura involuntarily responded to Jenny's anger. "What do you call it?"

"Sometimes you have a special communication with somebody," Jenny insisted. "You don't have to say anything to each other, and it doesn't matter what kind of measly little barriers may separate you."

"The man has a wife, Jen."

"It doesn't matter, I said. If you have something bigger with a person, nothing matters except that—nothing in the world. You may find it hard to believe at your age, but I actually have a very mature attitude toward men. I am not infatuated."

"It's your emotions dictating to you. Your going gaga over Sal—"

"I am not going gaga!"

"Your interest in Sal—"

"He's an interesting person. He's civilized. If he happens also to be very sexy, that's not my fault."

"Of course he's interesting. But with you, it's your hormones that are interested. I can remember when I was your age—"

"Remember? You were never my age! You were you. I'm me. I'm not replaying your life. You don't know what I feel. You don't know anything about my hormones. Things are different today. That's what you can't understand. You're so damn smug!" She stalked out, slamming the door behind her.

Laura regretted immediately having mentioned the thing with Sal. She'd razzed Jenny about it a couple of times before and realized it was a tender nerve. A case of hopeless love always hurts.

She shouldn't tease Jenny. It was good for a girl to have an infatuation at that age, healthy psychologically. As long as it didn't go too far.

Ted arrived home twenty minutes later.

"Anybody home? Why have you got all the lights off?" he asked. He still had his suit on, though he'd pulled his tie to the side. Circles underlined his eyes. It had grown quite dark.

They kissed. They'd sworn they would never fall into exchanging the habitual peck of the long-married. They always put their tongues into it. Ted always caressed her behind. But that in itself had become habitual. She could sense his mind was elsewhere.

"I smell Old Grand-Dad."

"Don't start."

"Ted, I'm not starting, all right?"

"Okay. I stopped off with Sal for a couple. He insisted."

"Rough day?"

"You could say that. Before, we had problems, right? Okay, every project is going to have problems. But now we are absolutely and totally screwed. We're dead in the water." Ted kicked an imaginary dog.

"Why, what's the matter?"

"There's an old cemetery out there on our site. Nobody even knew about it—at least we didn't—a weed patch full of bones. But it's almost impossible to get a variance to move a cemetery. You know, sacred ground and all."

"Can't you build around it?"

"Not according to the zoning board. Anyway, that would look beautiful. That'd be a real selling point for the old duffers. Look folks, your very own boneyard. When you croak, we just wheel you out the door and dump you. Plus it would screw the whole plan architecturally."

"What can you do?"

"Nothing. We can't do anything. The project's kaput. Just when we need more capital to meet operating costs."

"I'm sorry," she said.

"Well, sorry doesn't pay the bills. Sorry doesn't save your ass when you go into bankruptcy. Sorry doesn't mean diddlyshit when you're on that slippery slope we know so well, the one Ted Reed always seems to find himself on just when he thinks he's managed a little breathing room."

"Don't you think you're being a little overly dramatic?"

"Don't tell me what I'm being. I explained to you when we took out the home equity loan that if Reed-Vincent goes seriously belly-up, we could lose the house. Do you understand that? Laura, this thing is extremely serious. This is do or die, literally. And the way it looks right now—shit."

"I'm sure you and Sal will find a way."

"Sal? Don't talk to me about Sal. The guy's crazy. One minute he's brilliant, the next minute he's totally off the wall. He doesn't show up for meetings, he doesn't do what I tell him, he's not detail-oriented at all. What's he care? He's Mister Happy-Go-Lucky. Meanwhile, we are desperate for capital, we need to somehow, miraculously, break through this bureaucratic red tape, we need—I mean, I need a drink. You want one?"

"Just a Perrier. Or, no, I will have a rum and tonic."

"You look nice."

"Thanks."

He mixed the two highballs. "Here's to the guy with the big ideas. Here's to the guy who was going to tackle the world and ended getting knocked on his can."

"Don't talk about yourself that way, Ted. You're going to make it, I know you are. I'm sure you and Sal can—" She was unknotting his tie.

"I told you, I can't depend on Sal. You know, I'm not kidding about this. This situation could get very very sticky if we don't find some answers soon. The bottom can drop out of your life, Laura. It really can. It happens to people. You can lose your way so easily in this business."

"With your experience?" Holding both ends of the tie, she pulled him forward, almost within kissing range.

He shook his head. "My experience is in residential.

117

Even when this thing was going well I felt in over my head."

She hated to see him upset like this. She began to unbutton his shirt.

"What the hell's Sal doing in this crisis, you might ask?" he continued. "I'll tell you. He's spending all his time making arrangements for the party next week. Can you believe this guy? The thing is a goddamn lark to him. He's spending big money on a party when we may not even be around next week. What's he care?"

"It sounds like it's going to be fun, though." She was against him. Her hair was glowing, her skin, her smile.

"I hope I'm here to enjoy it. I had a feeling this afternoon—I know it was just indigestion from gorging at lunch while I tried to sweet-talk a jerk from the building inspector's office. But at the time I thought it might be the big one. You know, the tightness in the chest they talk about?"

"Oh my God, Ted. Have you had a checkup lately? They say stress—"

"It was just indigestion, I told you. And it's not stress. Stress is when you worry about something that *doesn't* happen. This is more than stress, Laura. This is real."

"Okay. I'm real, too."

"Laura, the boys are going to be in here in a minute."

"We'll just have to move the party upstairs, won't we?"

She tilted her head back. Ted's hands closed around her throat, then slid up to hold her head while he kissed her. He kissed her very very hard.

"Whoa!" she said with a giggle.

He followed her up the stairs. In the bedroom, two buttons from her blouse clicked onto the floor.

12

R eal suburban," the girl said.

"I took off a place out here once." The man steered his Camaro into a spot across the street from Ted's house. Cars already filled Sal's driveway and spilled along both sides of the block.

"Around here?" She was a *Playboy* bunny. Tight satin squeezed her breasts, a collar and bow tie circled her throat, and rabbit ears flopped over her blond hair.

"About three blocks from here. Me and Billy. Remember, during the time when everybody was so gone on gold, melting down their gold? This guy was supposed to be dealing it under the table. And I always said, if the joint is clean, look for the stuff stashed high up. So this guy's joint was neat as a pin. And up on the top shelf of his closet we got—"

"Oh, those gold chains."

"Right. And twenty-three hundred cash."

"You bought those 'ludes."

"That's it. And remember, we found that caviar in his refrigerator."

"Which tasted like rotten fish." She wrinkled her nose remembering.

"I told him, I said, I ripped a joint out your way a few years ago. He said he's only been here since spring. He said, I hope you try to take off my place sometime. He's got it wired, floodlights, infrared sensors or something. I really hope you try it, he says."

They got out of the car and chugged the doors closed. The sky was sprayed with stars. Crickets were hard at work. The man wore a black leather jacket, tight blue jeans, and heavy boots. As they crossed toward the house, he slipped on a pair of sunglasses.

"Who is this guy, Tony?"

"Sal? He's just a guy, a straight Joe, pushes real estate. I run into him now and again down at the Pair of Deuces. He's cool. Come to this party we're having, he tells me. Gonna be a blast. He's straight, but he's not. He talks the lingo. He's very interested in what's what in town."

"Sounds like a cop."

"No way. Cop, I'd know it. Think I can't smell a cop after all this time? I could smell a cop at a skunk convention. I think, what it is, he was in the CIA, something. He let drop a few times about, you know, covert operations."

"I just hope you're right."

"Sal's no cop. He doesn't try to pry into your business. He knows people. I asked around. They said, Sal knows some heavy people in this town, some actors. Whether he's in the game or not, I don't know. But if he is, he's major league."

"Is he cute?"

"Sure, Doris. He's cute as a pistol. The guy's very bright. And he promised this was going to be one dynamite party."

Ted was looking at himself in the mirror. He stretched his hands out to the sides, beat on his chest, and yelled, "Aaah—ah-ah-ah, ah-ah-ah!"

He had to laugh. Tarzan? Somehow he didn't quite have Johnny Weissmuller's wild greasy hair, sincere expression, or flashing muscles. He tried puffing his chest. No good. Damn.

He thought back to when he'd played a decent game of basketball in high school. His legs had never been spindly in those days. His stomach had been flat. Now the body that peeked through the leopard-skin costume Laura had rented him was the body of a middle-aged man. How the hell had that happened?

Well, as soon as the pressure was off at work he'd be down at the Y pumping iron. Get back in shape in no time. If the pressure was ever off.

He had to admit, the costume party was a good way to kick off the business. It would definitely loosen people up. Just the thing to make them remember Reed-Vincent Properties. Sal had knocked himself out on the preparations.

Forget about the fact that Ted had refinanced his house, that he'd encouraged Maynard to jump in with both feet, and that the business was on the ropes. Sal claimed he had an ace in the hole, and in spite of himself Ted was getting into the habit of trusting Sal to come through. How, he couldn't figure. But Sal would find a way, Ted knew it.

Sal's balls, Ted's brains. It was hairy, but— Ted hammered on his chest and laughed.

"Vincent," Robbie scoffed, "you look like a very."

"What?" Mario said. They were in Josh's bedroom.

"A very. A very's a fairy, a queer."

"I'm Mr. Spock. From 'Star Trek.' " Mario wore rubber pointed ears.

"You can't come with us because you're out of uniform. You look like a dimp. A dimp is a wimp." Robbie had on fatigues and combat boots. He'd spent an hour applying camouflage paint to his face and hands. Josh wore a mask that was crisscrossed with lacerations, the left eye dangling.

"I'm going with Mario," he said, "so if you don't want to, great."

"Okay, he can be a spy."

"I can give the Vulcan death grip."

"You're an alien who's a spy for our forces. We're going to be behind enemy lines. This is a vital mission. Code name—Sunset."

"You really want to go down there tonight?" Josh asked.

"What's the matter, you a yellowbelly?"

"No, it's just, there'll be a lot of those kids out."

"I know why you're chicken. You've been hanging out with enemy forces. Haven't you, Romeo? Oh, Romeo. Where are you, Romeo?"

"What do you mean?" Mario asked.

"I mean Josh the Bosh is a lover boy. Aren't you, lover boy? I mean Amber. Ha ha, I know all about Amber."

"Shut up, you jerk."

"I think Amber's one of the prettiest girls in our class," Mario pointed out.

"Pretty?" Robbie guffawed. "She's a scuzz. She stinks. All the girls from Sunset stink."

"You're full of it," Josh said. "She's not my girlfriend."

"What is she?"

"Nothing."

"You walk with her in the hall. You got caught passing a note to her in science. And at night I hear you moaning, Amber, Amber, I love you, Amber."

"You're cracked."

Robbie checked the combination stopwatch that hung from his neck. "It's almost H-hour. Take these and put them in your pockets." He handed Josh and Mario each a piece of candy corn.

"What's this?" Mario asked.

"Cyanide. If you get captured, you have to eat that and you'll be dead. Then the enemy can't torture any information out of you."

Josh held his cyanide capsule between his teeth and grinned.

"That's a demerit, mister," Robbie said. "Now, first we're going to raid places to get our C rations. But only candy bars or M&Ms. No popcorn balls or apples or junk."

"Remember that one year?" Josh said. "Your bag broke on the way home 'cause it started to rain and your candy went all over the road, a whole bag of it. And you cried."

"Did not. I never cried, ever."

"You bawled your head off."

"You're out of order, private. Now, let's prepare to move out." Robbie fixed his gas mask, which resembled a Porky Pig face, over his nose. He waved his hand. "Forward, ho."

Laura was still in the bathroom. Ted went downstairs.

"Jenny," he said, "I told the boys to be back here by ten thirty. You can let them stay up for a while, but not later than midnight."

Mario was staying over with the twins, Jenny baby-sitting.

She said, "You already told me twice, Dad. Dad?"

"What?"

"You really look bizarre."

"Thanks. It's a costume party. What do you want, you want me to wear a shirt and tie?"

"I can't believe you're going out like that. You know? I'm really mortified."

"We're trying to have some fun here."

"How do you think Mom feels to be seen with you? Don't her feelings count?"

"Jenny—"

"Okay, do what you want, I don't care. What's it to me if my father makes a fool of himself?"

They were interrupted by a commando, an accident victim, and a Vulcan marching down the stairs.

"I think you look great, Dad," Josh commented. "You look like the guy on wrestling who always gets beat up."

"You shoulda been the Lone Ranger, Dad," Robbie

advised. "Then you could wear a mask and a gun. That'd be cool."

"And your mother would have had to be Tonto. I don't think she fits the role."

"The leopard is an endangered species," Jenny pointed out. "Don't you care about the planet?"

"Is rayon an endangered species, too, Miss Silent Spring?" he said, tugging at the spotted fabric.

Laura bounded down the stairs. She was Jane. Lean and robust. She wore sandals, a rugged rawhide miniskirt, splotches of burnt cork on her legs.

"We'd better get going, Ted. We're supposed to be hosting this, too, and I see people arriving. I don't want Gina to have to handle everything."

"Aren't you going to be cold?" Ted said. The night was luxuriously mild for October.

"Oh, Ted. Bye, Jens. Thanks for holding down the fort."

Ted felt a nervous excitement during the short walk next door. The preparations—the tents, the caterers, the Japanese lanterns, the live band—were all on a grander scale than the parties they usually attended. This was going to be a real blast, an event to remember, not some drab suburban wine-and-cheese affair. And, Sal had assured Ted, it would be great for business.

"Excuse me," Ted said when Gina answered the door. "Afraid we're a bit lost, old sport. Kindly direct us to the nearest jungle?"

"Let me guess," Gina said. "The Two-thousand-year-old Man?"

"I'll give you a little clue. Jeepers creepers, where'd you get those cheetahs?"

"Oh, I know. You're Fred Flintstone's accountant."

"Getting warm," Laura said.

"Another clue." Ted snorted, scratching both armpits. "Gwonk, gwonk."

"Ted," Gina laughed, "that's good, that's very good. You've come as a lawyer."

They all laughed.

"Her Tarzan, me Jane," he said. "No, you Tarzan, me—"

Gina wore a crisp tuxedo and black tights. She clicked out a staccato welcome with her tap shoes.

"You look great." Laura smiled into her face.

Gina said Laura looked fantastic, too.

Ted said Gina looked so great he might knock her over the head and carry her to his tree house before the night was over.

She said she didn't want any monkey business from him.

Laura asked what she could do. Gina told her nothing except to enjoy herself, the caterers had done a terrific job.

"See you around, as they say on the bomb squad," Ted said.

As they started to move away, Gina took hold of Laura's arm and pulled her aside.

"Are you sure Mario will be all right?" she asked. "I'm worried half sick over it. I never should have let him—"

"He'll be fine," Laura assured her. "The boys have strict instructions. They won't leave the neighborhood. I told them, Crestwood Street's the limit. There are plenty of other kids out. They're as safe as can be."

"I hope you're right."

"I am. Don't worry."

As she walked away Laura could still feel the pressure of Gina's fingers on her arm.

Early arrivals were scattered through the house. They spilled out onto the patio, where two tents had been erected. One covered a buffet of hors d'oeuvres and salads, chafing dishes and crudités. Glistening glasses and a regiment of liquor bottles crowded a spacious table. The other tent was for the band and a small dance floor. Smiling young men in white coats dispensed the refreshments.

Ted waved or winked at the people he knew. He beat *mea culpas* on his chest. He smiled broadly. He introduced

Laura to several groups of people he'd met through Sal.

"Did I tell you it was going to be an affair?" Ted said to his wife. "Sal knows how to put on a shindig."

"Nice crowd."

"He's perfected the art of networking, I've got to hand him that. Christ, his guest list was longer than mine, and they've only been here, what, not even six months."

The scope of the affair overwhelmed any twinge of envy Ted might have felt of Sal's vast popularity. After all, Ted was special. He was Sal's partner, his neighbor—his best friend, for that matter. He was the one who'd taken Sal under his wing, who'd recognized the man's vast deal-making capacity, who'd trusted him. The party was to kick off their business, their dream, their great adventure.

The five-piece jazz combo was oozing a samba. A few couples were gliding around the boards. Ted and Laura ordered drinks, nibbled some morsels, and mingled.

Half an hour later Ted said, "There's Maynard and Felice." It took them a few minutes to push through the growing crowd to reach their friends.

Maynard wore a tie-dyed shirt, patched blue jeans, and water-buffalo-hide sandals. The lapel buttons on his leather vest proclaimed "Peace" and "Flower Power." He stared at them through his pink-tinted glasses and flashed a V with his fingers.

"I love it," Ted said.

"Heavy," Maynard answered. "This is a real cool love-in, ape-man."

"And who's this ravishing enchantress? You look radiant, my dear. More than radiant. You look . . . buoyant."

"Oh, Teddy, you're so-o-o-o gallahnt."

Felice wore a flashing tiara, a white mask, and a dramatic red satin gown. The neckline was one that made men rise a bit on their toes when they spoke to her. Ted kissed her cheek and pulled her close, his arm around her waist.

"You believe in free love, don't you?" he asked Maynard.

"Hey, dude, take her. My old lady is your old lady.

We don't have any of those bourgeois hang-ups. You gotta do your own thing, man."

"Ready for some real loving, Mata Hari?"

She draped herself over him. "Anytime, big boy."

Maynard said. "Laura, you're looking sensationally primitive tonight."

She smiled at him.

Ted asked Felice who she was supposed to be, the Good Witch of the East, or what?

"Lucinda—she was a princess in Atlantis. I actually, through hypnotism, have explored my previous existences," she said to Laura, ignoring the men. "I found out I was in the court of one of the royal families of Atlantis."

"You look lovely," Laura said.

"She did the weather there in old Atlantis, too," Maynard said. "Partly sunny with a fifty percent chance of tidal wave tomorrow. Going out, better wear your scuba gear."

"Oh, funny. Actually, you'd be amazed," she told Laura.

Both men chuckled.

Ted asked if they'd seen Sal. They said they hadn't.

"I hear your man's a real sensation," Maynard said. "Real wheeler-dealer, high roller."

"Everyone's talking about him," Felice said.

"He does have a knack for the business," Ted said, "when he applies himself. Absolutely confident. You'd be surprised how important that is. And he sure gets around. Look at this."

Maynard stepped close to Ted and lowered his voice. "How's it going, really? Did you get those problems you were talking about ironed out? You seemed a little concerned there, Teddy."

"Well," Ted admitted, "there are always a few hitches with these deals. If there weren't, *then* you'd start worrying. But the basic idea, the demographics—" He skimmed his hands together and sent one pointing into space.

Felice interrupted. "There's Melody Klein from the *Record.* I have to talk to her. See you folks later. You look nice, Laura."

Laura told the men she was going to find Gina.

"We'll get together and touch bases on all this soon," Ted assured Maynard. "You want to look at the whole thing, the big picture, rather than concentrate on the negatives. Another thing about Sal, he's a great judge of people. That girl—woman he hired as receptionist? Turns out she's an absolute whiz. Set up a whole computerized accounting system for us, just between answering the phones."

"I saw what a whiz she was when I was up there that time," Maynard said. "I'd like to whiz *her*."

The night was full of dark smells—piled leaves and hemlock and rotting apples. Figures were moving in and out of the cones of light under the streetlamps. A breeze made a ghostly sigh in the pines along the edge of the lawn. The three boys stepped carefully into pools of black.

A scream pierced the air. Robbie leapt back, plowing into Josh and knocking Mario to the ground.

"I knew it was you," Robbie said. "Brian's second-in-command," he explained to his companions. They greeted the three other boys, who were friends of Brian. "What's your report, Lieutenant?"

"All clear, General. Present and accounted for."

"Prepare to issue ammunition. Listen up, you guys. Your life may depend on this. These are your claymores. Don't drop them or you'll lose a leg. They can stop a tank if you wait till the last moment and get a direct hit. You each get three."

He and Brian handed the water balloons to the others.

"These are fifty-caliber machine guns," Brian said, passing out bars of Ivory soap.

"When you spot an enemy vehicle, you use this to disable it," Robbie said. "Do you know how to disable an enemy vehicle, Vincent?"

"Soap their windows?"

"You write *shit* on the windshield. Or you can write *tish* on the back window. That's *shit* backward. So when they look in the rearview mirror they see it and they're

128

grossed out. Private Vincent is in charge of the tactical nuclear weapons."

Mario had insisted on retaining control of his stash of M-80s.

"If he has to use those," Robbie explained, "it's World War Three."

They rang doorbells and waited patiently while the householders, civilian dupes unaware that they were supplying armed commandos, dropped Snickers and Three Musketeers into their bags.

They encountered numerous enemy patrols. But most were with their mothers, so Robbie decided not to engage them in combat. Josh was able to write *shi* on a gray Oldsmobile, but the porch light came on before he could totally disable the vehicle.

They passed Crestwood Street, which divided the suburban development on the hill from the poorer tracts down by the highway. Robbie informed them that they were now really in enemy territory. They would be approaching the Sunset sector any minute. They were on red alert. There was no turning back.

The neighborhood did grow more hostile. The houses were shabbier. There were more vacant lots.

They plunged on, down streets they'd never traveled at night. At a big house an old lady made them take off their masks before giving them homemade popcorn balls. They counterattacked by scrawling obscenities on her cellar windows.

Their mission was to attack the ammunition dump at Sunset Mobile Home Park. The feud between the children from the Maplecrest suburb and those from Sunset was legendary. For them to come down the hill and even approach the sprawling trailer park was a feat of bravery. To pull off the mission that Robbie had in mind was reckless, but it would be something they could brag about forever.

They couldn't turn back now, Robbie insisted. They had to locate and destroy the detonator for the world's largest hydrogen bomb, the KB-777.

Laura felt herself deliciously exposed. Wandering through the crowd, she answered looks with nods and smiles. A man she thought was dressed in a waiter's costume turned out to be a waiter. He offered her champagne from a tray. The bubbles tickled her nose.

The party had gathered speed and lifted off the runway with a surge of unified noise. It seemed to be held aloft by a spirit of expectancy, as if everyone were waiting for something to happen but no one knew what. Many of Ted's real estate cronies seemed to lounge around with aggressive nonchalance, like car dealers on a slow day.

About half the guests had come in full costume. The others made their concessions with Lone Ranger masks or funny hats. There was a continual stream of laughter and the kind of animated charades that a costume party brings out in people.

Laura spoke briefly with Elliott Fishman and his wife. He was an anemic Popeye in a sailor hat and pipe. She had the bony physique that needed only workshoes to turn her into Olive Oyl. Fishman asked Laura if she'd seen Evelyn Winner, with her six-shooters. His wife said she thought Evelyn looked cute as Annie Oakley.

Laura had noticed a number of glamorous, effervescent women in their early twenties. One of them, whose eyes were highlighted with glitter, approached her. She asked Laura if she'd met him yet.

"Who do you mean?"

"This guy Sal. My girlfriend knows him, her friend does. I've heard he's like a soldier of fortune. Rambo, kind of."

"Of course I've met him."

"What's he like? I've heard all kinds of stories. He's supposed to be incredibly sexy."

"Yes, incredibly. But I don't think he's your type."

"No? Why?"

"Because he has taste."

"Oh, yeah? Well, who are you, anyway?"

"I'm his wife."

"You are? Look, I didn't mean anything, I just heard these stories is all. Really."

Laura walked away. Why had she said that? I know his wife, she'd meant to say. The champagne.

Crowds made Laura nervous. They were too chaotic.

She filled a plate and sat down with a couple who had a daughter in Jenny's grade at school. Everyone agreed that this would be a party to remember.

She couldn't stay still. When she finished eating, she drank another glass of champagne and wandered along the landscaped paths of the yard. It had been almost hot during the day, but the air had a pleasant crispness now.

"They getting to you?"

She couldn't see where the voice was coming from for a second. Then, through the bushes, she saw a narrow opening that led to a tiny gazebo. She stepped into the darkness.

"I can only take so much, myself," Sal said. He was sitting smoking a cigar, dressed in a double-breasted suit.

Laura sat beside him. She told him it was a great party, she was having a great time, great bunch of people, great music.

"I was thinking of you when I hired that group."

"You were? That's—I love it. We don't get out to listen to much live music. Ted has sort of a tin ear."

"They're not the MJQ, but they're decent."

"I think they're great."

"You're in a great mood."

"Am I acting silly? I've had more than my quota of champagne."

"I like your costume."

"Thanks."

He smiled at her. It started as his usual half-smile, but the other side of his mouth relaxed into it, too. It made Laura think of the times during the summer that she'd caught glimpses of Sal when he thought no one was look-ing. She'd seen a roughness to his face, a brutality that

131

reminded her of a construction foreman or a trucker. But this smile embraced her, wrapped her in a warmth of assurance and conspiracy.

She had trouble swallowing for a second. She could smell the sharp tang of cigar smoke in the air. The silence became too complicated for her.

"I—I have to apologize to you," she said, to say something.

"For what?"

"I know Jenny's been making a pest of herself. She's going through a phase."

"She's a nice kid, what do you mean?"

"Well, fabricating excuses to come over all the time. And imposing on you to let her swim in your pool, traipsing around in her bikini. And all the giggling and eye rolling and what-have-you."

"Is that a crime?"

"I just hope you don't mind. She has a terrible crush on you, I guess you figured that out."

"Hey, what do I know? She seems like a swell kid."

"We like her. But I'm afraid she's hopelessly in love with you."

"I'm flattered."

"Just keep in mind that a young girl's crush is absolutely ruthless. I pointed out to her, Sal's married. That's purely a formality in her romantic way of looking at things. Love conquers all, full speed ahead and damn the torpedoes. Jenny thinks of you as a kind of celebrity, thinks you should be in the movies. These things—every girl goes through it, I guess. I suppose there's some psychology behind it."

"I think I'll survive. Some guys make a show of how they know nothing about women. That's not my style. I do know something about women—plenty."

"I believe you do." Laura laughed. She touched his arm. "I overheard her describing you to her girlfriend on the phone. I mean, you sounded like a Greek god or something. This scar? I guess she saw it when you were swimming. She described this scar on your chest and said it made you look so erotic she couldn't stand it. Erotic—you know how girls go on."

"I got shot."

Laura stopped laughing.

"Want to see?" Sal said.

She licked her lips, shrugged almost imperceptibly, moved her eyes away from his. He slipped the knot from his tie, unbuttoned, and pulled his shirt aside. She looked at the line etched through his tan. She reached tentatively, hesitated, touched the flesh. She pulled her fingers back as if she'd received a shock.

"It's nothing," he said.

"I'm sure that she'll—"

"What?"

"Get over it. I guess you want to get back to your guests." She stood.

"Just the angle. Otherwise, I'd have been dead. It deflected off the rib."

"You're lucky."

"I'm very lucky, Laura. I've ridden my luck so long, I just take it for granted." He stood. "Life is a gift, that's how I see it. You don't ask to be born, how can you gripe at how it turns out, how long it lasts?"

Her lips were parted and she could feel them playing with a smile. He changed his eyes in a way that gave her a shiver.

"I guess I'm getting cold," she said. "This is a wonderful party, the way you've organized it. We're not used to such affairs around here."

"You've gotta let go once in a while."

They both headed back toward the house.

"Save me a dance?" Sal asked.

She smiled over her shoulder. "Sure."

13

As he followed Sal out to the pool house, Ted became acutely aware of the difference in their heights. Though he was over six-two, Ted never thought of himself as tall. Sal, at five-ten, seemed to fit into the world much better. Ted felt awkward, especially wearing this ridiculous ape-man costume. He should have chosen something sensible, more like the pinstripe double-breasted suit Sal wore. Sal looked like a character from the Roaring Twenties, complete with snap-brim fedora and gold watch chain.

But Ted felt important. He experienced a rush of anticipation at the surprise Sal had promised. Sal and his surprises. Ted's swagger was a mixture of pride and more drinks than he normally allowed himself.

A man was waiting for them. He didn't rise when they entered. Ted knew him immediately. Leon Lujak. Lard Lujak, people called him. What the hell was Lard Lujak doing here? he wondered. The one and only. He was somebody Ted had never expected to meet in person. This should be interesting—the infamous Lard Lujak.

Sal made the introductions. For some reason he kept calling Lujak "Nelson."

Lujak's hand was cool and damp and soft in Ted's. It did not grip back.

Lujak pointed to his St. Patrick's Day tie and said he was dressed as Robin Hood. He pulled a thick wad of bills from his pocket and waved them in the air and said in a humorless voice, "I steal from the rich."

"You having a good time, Nelson?" Sal asked.

"Blast. I'd like to get my hands on some of these babes. Where'd you round up the talent, Sal?"

"Better be careful, some of them are married," Sal said, fixing drinks at the bar in the corner.

"So'm I." Lujak roared. He already had a glass. He took a big swallow of liquor and hissed through clenched teeth. "This guy puts on a real shindig, don't he?" he said to Ted. "See that number in red? Some fucking talent out there. Huh? Am I right? Is that talent or isn't it?"

"Talent," Ted said. "Fantastic talent. Talentedest talent I've ever seen."

Lujak guffawed. Ted, thinking of Laura, frowned. What the hell was he saying? What did you say to *the* Lard Lujak when you met him?

Lujak leaned over to him and lowered his voice. "I like the way you lads play ball."

"You do?"

"Your pal took my best boy with his own iron. Lifted eight bills off him. But then Sal comes straight to me. I think this is yours, he says. Hands me the dough. I like that."

"I'm not quite sure I—"

"You've got a tough podner there. Savvy."

Ted nodded gravely in reply to Lujak's squint.

They were always talking about Lujak in the papers. And the rumors he'd heard. What was it people said?

Sal passed around drinks, heavy rocks glasses with doubles of premium scotch.

They talked about some of the people who were there. They talked about baseball and about the fool the Democrats were thinking of running for mayor this year. They talked about German cars and Italian food and Japanese women.

Lujak was a professional character, that much Ted knew. He'd once brought a baseball team to the city, a double-A franchise. He acquired a real bison for mascot. But the Apaches could never recruit any quality pitching. The buffalo got loose, was crippled by a UPS van, and had to be destroyed. The club folded during its second season.

He wasn't sure what business Lujak was in. Photo developing, was it? A large kennel that had gotten in to the news over some SPCA thing. Other rumors connected him with gambling and prostitution. Some said he was behind the rise of crack use in the local schools. Ted felt a spasm of parental indignation. Why did Sal want him to meet this clown? Hadn't the man been arrested once? Acquitted, but still.

Sal kidded Lujak as if they were old friends. Ted felt himself a step behind in the conversation. It was the booze, he decided. Just needed one more drink to cut through the cobwebs and allow his mind to take a deep breath. Even as he was thinking this, Sal refilled the glasses.

He drank. Good. Needed that.

"Here's to talent," Ted said.

Lujak laughed and said, "Here's to senility. Huh? What we're here for, huh?"

"Senility," Ted repeated, closing one eye and taking a swallow of liquor.

"So, you, Ted, you're our quarterback," Lujak said.

"Yeah. Joe Namath. I'm your Joe Namath." Ted waved "we're number one" with his finger and flashed a Joe Namath grin.

"Ted's the man who's making this happen," Sal said.

"I'm making it happen." He smiled broadly. "What am I making happen?"

"Leon's interested in the Golden Age project."

"This nursing home you're doing. I want to make a little een-vest-mint."

"Not a nursing home."

"Nursing home, old-folks home."

"No. No, sir. This is a different concept."

"Concept, Nelson," Sal said. "Listen to this concept."

"The concept." Ted closed his eyes briefly to search for the concept. The room began to somersault. He held his breath to pull himself together. "Dignity. That's the concept. A person, later in life, hasn't got—the children are gone, don't have time for them—the wife, the husband, maybe, passed on—the person hasn't got anything left. 'Sgot nothin'. Except dignity. The dignity of the individual human being." He fought the tide of tears behind his eyes.

"And dough," Lujak said.

"You're dealing with genuine human beings here," Ted explained. "A person doesn't lose being a human being because he gets old. Or she gets old. This, it's something you have to understand."

"Leon thinks he can help push the deal through," Sal said.

"Well, I'm certainly, certainly . . . ," Ted said.

"Podners," Lujak said. "I'm the, what you call it, quiet podner?"

"Silent," Sal said.

"I'm the silent podner."

Lujak looked so hilarious with his finger to his pursed lips, Ted had to laugh. But he was suddenly serious.

"Have to tell you, there are problems here. Deal is not an easy deal to deal. 'Snot a done deal."

Sal said, "Leon might be able to help out with some of the problems, Ted. He thinks he has a pretty good chance of swinging it."

"Swing it," Ted said. "Swing low, sweet char-i-o-ot. Comin' fo', carry me home."

The room exploded into laughter. Ted laughed until tears ran down his cheeks.

Some indeterminate time later, Lujak was explaining

137

why he couldn't stay. He had a date to go night fishing. Some people, some important connections. Nice night, sit out in the middle of nothing and cast for walleyes. Bring a case of champagne, a couple of broads for ballast, you could make a night of it.

Not that this wasn't a pisser of a party.

Ted agreed. It was a fantastic party. Absolutely fantastic. His friend Sal was the greatest friend a friend could ever have. He knew how to make things happen. The man was a dynamo, he was a sensation, he was a phenom. This party, incredible. And the talent.

"Nelson," Ted said, resting his hand on Lujak's knee. "There is some kind of talent here tonight. Talent to the right of me, talent to the left of me, into the valley of talent rode the—" His own laughter choked off the rest of Ted's recitation.

Ted found another glass of scotch in his hand. Looking across at the fat man, he had to narrow his eyes to focus.

"Listen, Sal," Lujak was saying. He made his lower lip into a question mark. "Let me ask you something. Could I ask you something?"

"Sure."

"Who are you? Will you tell me that? Who the fuck are you?"

Ted looked at Sal. He felt the room go icy. Tension had entered Sal's posture. He was staring back at the fat man, thinking.

Finally, he said, "Dillinger."

"Dillinger?" Lujak echoed loudly.

"The bank robber. John Dillinger."

"Shit. The guy, they shot him down coming out of the movies?"

"Yeah. A Romanian broad turned him in so they wouldn't deport her. Biograph Theater, they shot him like a dog."

"Isn't he the one," Lujak said, "they have his prick pickled in the Smithsonian?"

"Sure."

"That's—you know what that is?" Lujak said. "Huh? Ted, my pal, you know what that is?"

Ted stared at the hard fat face. He said, "I don't know."

"History. That's history."

When walking alone, Robbie habitually imagined himself at the head of a company of commandos. Marching as he was tonight in front of six boys, he was the commander of armies, the leader of a ravaging horde.

The children in the trailer park had always enjoyed privileges denied most of the boys on the hill—to wander around in torn and scruffy clothes, to stay out until intriguing hours at night, to engage in forbidden pranks. The Sunset boys claimed the railroad yard across the highway as part of their kingdom and enjoyed all the mysteries of that exotic territory.

Most of the suburban youths had at one time or another been harassed or chased or pelted with cinders or jeered at by the aliens down the hill. The prospect of retaliation glimmered brightly in their eyes.

Now the troops had reached their objective. They hid in shadows directly across from one of the trailers. Josh was the only one who'd actually been inside the park. The times he'd gone secretly to visit Amber he'd become intrigued with life in the narrow trailers. He wished that his family would move to a mobile home.

Trees hung their claws over the roadway. The wind, picking up, blew night into their faces. Robbie coughed a few times. He had trouble clearing his throat.

They looked across at the mobile home with the small porch built on. A line of wash hung ghostlike in the dark side yard. An elaborately carved jack-o'-lantern was balanced on the railing beside the front door.

"They've got intercontinental ballistic missiles there," Robbie whispered. "Pershing 2s and B-1 bombers. That's the KB-777 detonator on the porch. Now, who's going to volunteer?"

"For what?" Josh said.

"I have to have a volunteer. This man could win the Congressional Medal of Honor."

"Why don't you go?"

"A commander never endangers his mission for the sake of false heroics."

"I'll volunteer," Mario said. "I'm not afraid."

Raised eyebrows were accompanied by taunts of "Sure," and "Oh, Jeez," and "Yeah, the scaredy-cat."

"You're too inexperienced," Robbie said.

"You'd chicken," Brian added.

"I would not."

Robbie stared intently at the smaller boy and smiled. "Okay, kid. We'll give you a chance, see what you're made of. You're going to deploy at oh six hundred hours and proceed to Checkpoint Charlie."

"What do I do, though?" Mario asked.

"You proceed to your objective and terminate it with extreme prejudice, soldier."

"Grab their pumpkin," Josh explained.

"And smash it," Brian said.

"I know, I'll blow it up."

They agreed that would be even better. It was what he'd meant all along, Robbie said. Blow the sucker.

Mario moved up toward the house. He felt a chasm opening behind him. He looked around once, plunged on.

Except for Josh, the guys were always needling him. They made fun of his name. They didn't believe his father carried a gun. Sometimes he'd forget and say things he wasn't supposed to, so he'd have to take them back and then they'd jeer. They called him liar, chicken. But he knew he was braver, tougher than any of them. His father told him so.

A gust of wind rattled a flap of sheet metal leaning against an abandoned refrigerator. Mario crouched for a second. The place smelled funny, like wet dog. He continued forward.

Through the window of the trailer he could see the flashing blue of a television.

He was at the porch. The jack-o'-lantern loomed bigger than it had looked from the street. Perched on a narrow railing, it was ready to leap on him. The expression on its face was barely human, an insane leer.

Mario took one step up onto the wooden structure. He waited. He peered backward into pure darkness. Then he stumbled, thudding up the last two steps. He almost fell in front of the door.

He crouched for a minute, waiting. Nothing.

He stood and took hold of the big orange head. He gripped the cool ridges of the skin. The smell of pumpkin was overpowering.

He turned the jack-o'-lantern toward him. It glanced at him out of one eye, questioning. It was much heavier than he'd expected. It almost slipped from the rail.

He knew the others were watching. He felt like shouting with the sense of power.

He pulled a handful of M-80s from his pocket and inserted them in the gaps between the pumpkin's teeth. He turned the face back toward the road so the others could see. Reaching around with a plastic lighter, he lit the jutting fuses. He ran.

He just made the bottom of the steps when the blast came—a quick rip of detonations that not only obliterated the pumpkin's face but knocked it off onto the ground, where it collapsed into an orange lump.

Mario was about to turn to acknowledge the cheers of the others when the door of the trailer opened and half a dozen enraged children poured out.

Mario sprinted across the yard.

Robbie stood, his arm raised, caught in an eddy of indecision. Finally, he screamed: "Charge!"

Mario tripped. A boy was bending over him as Robbie ran up. Robbie threw an uppercut that caught the boy square in the belly and lifted him off the ground. Robbie was astounded to see the kid fly through the air and land on his side, winded and gasping. He tasted an unfamiliar metallic excitement.

Four or five brawls raged around him. Robbie grabbed a child indiscriminately from one of the fights and effort-

lessly pushed a fist into his face. In the dull light he could
see the blood begin to stream from the boy's nose.

Mario lit another M-80.

One of the Sunset kids ran back toward the trailer.
Then another. Robbie's troops concentrated their fury on
those who remained, kicking and punching wildly.

They were just erupting into screams of victory when
the door of the trailer opened again and a man emerged.
He held a shotgun in his hands. He shouted six guttural
syllables and pumped the gun.

The Maplecrest boys sprinted toward the darkness
across the road. Robbie turned to make a last gesture at
the man. He laughed as he ran. He'd left behind his trick-
or-treat bag. He didn't care.

Laura was trying to identify the emotion that gripped her.
It felt like fear, but what was she afraid of?

Was she anxious about Jenny? Afraid of losing control
of her daughter? Was she afraid of what Jenny might do?
With an older man? What trouble she might get into? Get
pregnant? Drugs? Marry a brutal older man? A man who
would get drunk and beat her?

Was she afraid for Ted? He always put on his glad
face—nearly always. But she knew he was deeply concerned that the business might not succeed. He'd put so
much into it. So much of himself. Not to mention the
money. She knew how devastated he'd be if his dream
didn't fly.

Yes, Jenny and Ted. She was the mother, the wife.
Those were her fears, her comfortable concerns, natural
concerns. Like Gina's worrying about Mario.

Maybe some of Gina's anxiety had rubbed off onto
her.

She was talking with a couple that she and Ted knew
slightly. They were community-minded. They were discussing the bike lanes being proposed for the community.
The community needed bike lanes. The highway was impossible. All the development that was going on, it would
be a small thing to add bike lanes. With bike lanes, people

could ride downtown. Laura agreed. She rode a bike. The kids wanted to go on their bikes. Bike lanes would be good for the community.

Bike lanes were a comfortable topic. The man had gray hair and a big gray mustache and a voice like a Pekinese. His mustache surveyed Laura's costume and asked her fluffy little questions.

She wanted to keep talking about the community, about nice things, things that weren't scary. But she was swept up by restlessness, by the momentum of the party.

She excused herself, moved off alone. She drank another glass of champagne.

What was this feeling? Had she been on automatic pilot for so many years? Life had suddenly come to life for her. Vague possibilities swarmed around her. Dangerous possibilities. She felt giddy, girlish.

She was standing next to three young women. One of them was saying, "He was in the CIA. The Russians captured him and they had to trade some top spies to get him back. It never came out. He was in the CIA."

Laura looked around for Ted. Where had he disappeared to? She was afraid he might be drinking too much. Ted couldn't drink.

Immediately she thought, to hell with Ted.

Felice broke away from a group of men and came over to talk to Laura.

"Cripes awmighty, these men," she said. "They see me on television and they think that gives them the green light or something. Your voice, Felice, they say. And they always assume I'm getting it on with Jerry, the sports guy, who's a fruit and a half." She yawned gracefully. "It makes me tired."

"I can imagine."

"You know, we should get together, Laura. We never get together, chitchat."

"I'd like that."

"I'm sure you could give me some pointers. You handle yourself so well. Maynard is always singing your praises, what a lucky guy Ted is. I say, a Sagittarius and an Aquarius is why. The classic combination." She gave a brief explanation of astrological compatibility.

Laura barely listened. She was thinking how young Felice seemed, how she glowed with confident spontaneity. She made Laura feel like a mature woman, someone with all the fizz of youth gone. At the same time, Laura felt like a schoolgirl, felt a sharp mixture of expectation and despair.

A man in a motorcycle jacket had been watching Felice. Laura saw him gesture with his eyebrows. It was comical. Felice noticed. When you're young, Laura thought, it's not comical. The man smiled and walked toward them.

"You a model, Cleopatra?"

Felice laughed. "I don't think we've met," she said.

"Tony."

"You're a friend of Sal?" Laura asked him. The man smelled of cigarette smoke.

"Me, I've known Sal for years."

"Most people seem to have just met him since he moved here," Laura observed. "Where did you know him?"

"Around. We're asshole buddies from way back. What is this, cross-examination time? Think I crashed?"

"Just curious," Laura said.

"I know Sal. He invited me. I come as a biker. Huh? Pretty good, huh? The Wild One." He was talking to Felice. She said, "You look—authentic."

"I am authentic, sweetheart," he said. "I don't have a phony bone in my body. You know, I've been watching you. You're quite a number."

Felice rolled her eyes at Laura. "Fresh, aren't you?"

Laura envied Felice's easy coquettishness.

"You like them stale?"

"No, not really."

"What if I asked you to dance with me?"

"I don't know. Why don't you try it and find out?"

Throwing Laura a tight smile, Felice stepped over to the dance floor with the man.

The band was playing an upbeat Beatles tune that Laura couldn't remember the name of. She watched Felice improvise fluidly. Felice seemed oblivious of her partner. Now and then she favored him with a look, a suggestion of a smile.

Laura's feet hurt. What time was it? She knew Ted had gone over the edge. When he got to drinking, he never wanted to go home. She wished she was in bed.

She spotted Maynard on the other side of the dance floor. She thought of asking him to help persuade Ted to call it a night. He knew Ted couldn't drink, shouldn't drink.

But from the look of him, Maynard had put away quite a few himself. He'd removed his tinted glasses. His face was compressing and expanding like a bellows. He was staring intently.

The band segued into a ballad. The drummer was setting a lush rhythm, the bass thumping roundly, the horns along for the ride.

Tony now had Felice in his arms. They were moving in unison. He said something in her ear. She laughed. He pulled her closer. Her cheek touched his black leather shoulder.

He was kissing her neck. Felice leaned her head back, but she was smiling. His hand rested low on her waist.

His mouth went to her neck again. Then suddenly his head snapped back.

Laura gasped. Felice stumbled forward. She almost fell before he released his grip.

A fierce mask glared over Tony's shoulder. Maynard.

The younger man was sitting on the floor now. Maynard let go of his neck and thudded a fist against the side of his head.

"Maynard!" Felice cried. "Oh my God, stop it!"

The band blasted into a raucous version of "Perdido." People pointed at Maynard, his rigid face, his loud shirt. They laughed.

His opponent was not laughing. He twisted. Maynard, in a gesture of fair play or uncertainty, allowed him to stand.

Tony rushed him. Maynard let loose an adrenaline

punch. It surprised Tony, smacking him smartly across the jaw. Maynard threw another. Tony moved his head back to avoid it. He jabbed at Maynard's face. A gush of blood erupted from Maynard's nose.

Maynard roared back, trying to grasp the man with his hands. A short right caught him in the belly and made him retch. Tears came to his eyes.

Felice's fingers were laced over a silent scream.

A few people continued to dance. Others were watching the confrontation. Some cheered.

Laura saw the young man's arm move. She saw danger materialize in his hand. The movement was so quick, she didn't know where the knife had come from. The dim light gleamed on the blade.

Maynard was turning to face his opponent again. Rage and hurt were fighting a battle on his features. The young man crouched like a rattlesnake.

Some of the other dancers were just now turning curious faces toward the action.

The young man drew his arm back, ready to thrust.

Consumed in self-righteous wrath, Maynard lunged forward.

Then Sal was between them. He was holding Tony by the shirt. He was pointing a small black gun in Tony's face, very close. He was saying something. He nodded. Tony took up the nod. They nodded in unison. The knife disappeared. Sal pushed Tony off the dance floor. A girl in a bunny costume joined Tony, her eyes full of questions.

Somebody laughed. Somebody else pointed and laughed. Sal tucked the gun back into his Dillinger coat. He smiled around at his guests. He took Maynard by the elbow and led him away. Felice followed.

14

Mike Ryan removed the smoldering stub of Chesterfield from his mouth and drew a circle with it in his ashtray, pushing the other butts aside. He stared across his desk at the woman in the lavender hat. He thought, yeah, there was a spirit he'd like to have her contact for him, she was so good at contacting spirits.

The woman wore a feather anaconda and a clanging excess of jewelry. She must have had a nice figure once, but the years had left her top-heavy, with an overdeveloped bust and skinny legs. She was flashing her bones at him, her knees and knuckles, her elbows and prominent cheeks. He was barely listening to her, thinking of this spirit he'd like her to conjure.

The spirit's name was Mike of Old. He was an elusive ghost, a chameleon who changed his shape to suit whatever nostalgic, beery, boastful, or bathetic mood Mike Ryan happened to be in. He was a sharp young cadet at the police academy, a crackerjack marksman, a black belt in judo. He was the second youngest officer on the force to make sergeant. He was the proud father of Mike Junior, Rose Ann, little Maureen. He was proud to be a cop, proud to be the son of a cop.

Mike of Old was as honest as the day is long. Mike of Old was brave. Mike of Old was loving. Mike of Old enjoyed respect throughout the city. Mike of Old's build brought to mind a Greek god. And Mike of Old had one of the sweetest baritone voices west of Killarney.

Mike of Old was smart as a whip. You couldn't put anything past him. These merchants wanted to violate the blue laws, who was going to kick? But there was no reason why they shouldn't chip in a little of the profits they made on the Lord's day to their favorite charity, their neighborhood protector and pal.

And when they abolished the blue laws, well, Mike of Old knew all about that plant store in which a single dying rubber tree made up the entire inventory and don't ask what went on behind the steel door at the end of the counter. Mike of Old knew how to keep his bread buttered. No, he'd tell them, you can't have a good time on nothing.

Mike of Old's bravery was legendary. Truly legendary. He'd walked up many a dimly lit alleyway with his pistol drawn. He'd sapped down a wino wielding a potato peeler. He'd faced an angry mob of college kooks protesting the nuclear reactor they were building out on the river. He'd given *them* a good taste of his nightstick where they sat.

People knew not to mess with Mike of Old. An Hispanic woman had thrown him the bird just because he was a white cop doing his job. Mike of Old couldn't let that go by. He'd twisted her arm and held her hand in the door of his cruiser while he slammed it shut. There had been a little stink about that one and they'd had to reprimand him. But Mike of Old caught the glint in the captain's eye and knew what he was signaling—that it was understood Mike of Old had done right.

Mike of Old believed in the sanctity of the family. His wife didn't. He continued to try to teach her, even after the separation. She'd gone whining to a judge, showing off her bruises, until a court order convinced him finally that his love was unrequited.

Mike of Old was proud of his heritage, proud of the Old Sod. Nobody matched him in sentimental inebriation on each and every St. Paddy's day. And 'twas one such green day he'd taken it in his head to strip-search a girl, a sophomore at St. Agnes's, a lying little hooker whose father should have been grateful—grateful that an honest cop was trying to straighten the girl out. The incident made the papers and the authorities were forced, regretfully, to bring Mike of Old up on departmental charges. And God damn the politicians who'd made hay out of that one. For the good of the force, mind you, he had turned in his badge.

Ah, but you should have heard Mike of Old lay into "Danny Boy"—though there were those who said his voice was as flat as Kansas.

He wanted the woman's help to contact this spirit in order to warn him. If Mike of Old had a fault, it was his innocence. This world, laddie, is filled with people who want to tear you down, destroy you. Watch out for them. Backstabbers and talebearers, the covetous and the impotent, the little people whose only ambition is to drag others to their level. Watch out for them, I say. Don't tolerate them. Smash them in the face as soon as you meet them. They're out to get you. They're out to destroy you.

Mike Ryan lit another cigarette. What, he sighed, was the use? Mike of Old was beyond redemption, beyond warning. This broad couldn't reach him. They'd already torn him to bits. They'd already taken all the good he had to give and kicked his teeth in as a reward. He was a goner, was Mike of Old.

"It's the silver hair, Madame LaGrecque," Ryan said. "The ladies go for that Cesar Romero look, I don't know why."

"It isn't," she hissed. "He's been threatening my ladies, spreading stories, spouting spurious slander about me. The man is destroying my reputation. I want him stopped. What do you know about my ladies?"

149

"You wanted the list, I made you the list, I'm telling you what I think."

"I will destroy him. I want that he should writhe in agony, burn in the fires of hell, I want."

"Would you like me to talk to some of his clients?"

"*My* clients! *My* ladies!"

"Your ladies who are now doing business with him—talk to them, try to establish grounds for defamation?"

"Yes! Most certainly. He is a slimy son of a serpent, this Naji. Master Naji—humph!"

Mike leaned well back in his chair to avoid the spray that accompanied her consonants.

The case was as simple as a horse's turd. Madame LaGrecque and her partner had been operating a channel scam. She was the pipeline to the beyond, he was a swami for all seasons. She could contact spirits. He doubled as herbalist, reflexologist, kinesiologist, you name it. He softened them up with foot massages and high colonics while she delivered the knockout punch from her trance. Good team.

But she came to realize that Master Naji was massaging more than feet. She caught him in the act with a reincarnation of an Egyptian high priestess and went through the roof. After the split, most of the clients chose Naji's ministrations over LaGrecque's hoodoo. LaGrecque's lawyer was encouraging her to pursue her grievance in court.

"None of them will speak to me. He tells them I'm an agent of Beelzebub. I heard it from Mrs. Horngren. She said that that man had informed all my ladies that he'd seen me on Johnny Carson, that Lucifer was sitting behind the desk."

"Guest host probably."

"What?"

She was Mike's meat. All he had to do was to sit outside Naji's house for a week, taking down the plate numbers on the cars of his visitors. A friend in Motor Vehicles supplied names and addresses to go with them. Mike charged a grand for the service.

"I can interview these former clients of yours if you

want, Mrs. LaGrecque, determine if, you know, he's made specific accusations."

"How much would it cost?"

"Well, it would cost. And I don't know how cooperative they'd be. I can't force them. I still think it's the silver hair that did it."

"I don't care what you think. It's his manipulations. I think he's giving my ladies drugs. I want you to get to the bottom of this."

"Whatever you say. I'll see what I can do."

Mike knew her lawyer well. He was an alkie whiplash specialist from way back who survived by looting widows' annuities. Otherwise Mike would have suspected somebody had set him up, sent this dame over from central casting to make a fool of him with the hocus-pocus stuff.

Early in his life, Mike had developed the distinct feeling that there were two kinds of people on the earth, the Mike Ryans—of which he was the only living example—and a race of aliens that included everyone else in the world. The aliens' sole occupation was to create an illusion of reality for Mike Ryan. When Mike wasn't looking, they lounged around, just waiting. Or they conspired together, planned their next charade. When his eyes fell upon them, they sprang to life and acted out the latest scene in the absurd drama of deception. They were manikins, puppets whose strings trailed out into the universe.

Mike had long been frustrated by his inability to prove or disprove this notion. He tried to catch them off guard. He peeped into windows, spied with binoculars, swung around to reenter a room he'd just left and catch the occupants relaxing into their true postures. But they never forgot their lines, they never stumbled or slipped.

The Joke lacked a seam. Mike could never see the point. If there was a punch line, he failed to catch it, though he knew the world guffawed behind his back. Over the years he became resigned to being the perpetual Butt. His attempts to catch a glimpse behind the scenes of the cosmic masquerade led him, years later, into a career as a private eye.

Mike stood up, lifting his prominent potbelly, his "Milwaukee goiter," as he affectionately called it, over his desk as his next client entered.

Mike worked out of his home, a two-bedroom bungalow in a postwar development. He didn't need an office. He was in the field most of the time. He simply hired the answering service that he felt had the sexiest-sounding telephone girls.

He watched the man's eyes roam the room. A dozen framed and autographed glossies decorated the wall behind his desk: Mike shaking hands with the mayor; Mike throwing a mock jab at the chin of the Democratic county leader; Mike with a fatherly arm around the shoulder of the teenage winner of the local Miss Rose of Tralee contest. On the opposite wall hung a mounted marlin. Mike caught the client looking at the dusty seven-foot-long specimen and went into his standard icebreaker: "As the Irishman said, the man that caught that fish was a liar."

The client smiled and made a noise in his throat.

Mike sized him up quickly. One of these guys full of paper courage. Mike could see it in the uncertainty that showed in his mouth. He noticed the guy slip his thumbs into his waistband. Sitting down he let one hand creep briefly between his legs as he crossed them. The case, Mike knew, would be a matrimonial one. Yes, the guy definitely had wife problems. Of course, Mike had to admit that three-quarter of his cases were matrimonial.

"Yes," the client said, replying to nothing. "Now, Mr. Ryan—"

"Make it Mike. What do your pals call you?"

The client's name was Maynard, Maynard Barker. What a dumb name, Maynard.

"I have to tell you right off, Mr. . . . or, Mike," Maynard said, "that I never dreamed—I mean, I'd seen detectives on television and all, but I never imagined that, you know—"

"It never occurred to you that you'd have anything to do with a private dick. Right? You thought they were just in Mickey Spillane or something. But here you are. Do I carry a gun? Sometimes. Why? Because it makes the clients think they're getting their money's worth. I'm licensed by the state and bonded to a quarter mil. Now, what can I do you for?"

"I want a person—watched."

"Yes?"

"She's, uhm . . . she's my wife." He chuckled. "This sounds so odd when I say it out loud. It seemed like a good idea when I was thinking about it. But now that I'm actually doing it, I mean, it's ridiculous, it doesn't seem right."

"A guy in your situation is going to go through some funny feelings, Maynard. Only natural. I've been inside about three hundred divorces, including my own. Always—always it comes down to a question of feelings. Incompatible, what's it mean? One man's incompatible is another man's bliss. Feelings, attitudes, emotions—these things, Maynard, are the great imponderables, the variables that make a horse race. Am I registering? You can expect to feel a lot of funny feelings here—and I don't mean ha ha. It's what you *do* that counts."

"I want to *know*. That's what's important to me, knowing. What I do is another matter. First I have to know."

"Finding out *is* doing something. It's the smart first step."

"I'll admit to you, I'm upset. That's why I'm turning to a professional. I'm a . . . I'm in a profession myself, I know do-it-yourself is never the way to go."

"What are you? What profession?"

Maynard told him. Mike smiled without baring his teeth. He said, "And your wife? She work?"

"Yes, she's a meteorologist, on television, channel eight."

"Oh, the weather girl."

"That's right. She was a patient of mine and it just went from there. She needed a lot of work done, crowns and all."

Funny, the guy had to try and justify marrying her, Mike thought. He'd seen her on the tube. Lot of woman for a little man, for a dentist.

"Kids?"

"No, not yet. We're—we were just married in April."

"I have three of my own. I see them every other weekend. Sometimes I can't go, I'm on a case. They don't even notice. To them I'm a stranger. Their mother's made me a stranger. Hey, I don't care. They've got my genes, that's enough. Rest of it's sentimentality. You can have it."

"Yes, well . . ."

"Why am I telling you this? I'm telling you because I want you to open up to me—and why should you open up if I don't? I want you to know that I'm a human being, too. I can sympathize, I'm not sitting here on this side of the desk making anything light out of your problems. I've had more problems than most people in my life and I've dealt with them. We're brothers, Maynard. That's how I look at it."

"Listen, I want to keep this as simple as possible. All I'm after is to find out if my wife's—what she's doing with her time."

"What do you think she's doing?"

"I don't know. If I knew, I wouldn't need you."

"What do you think?"

"It may be nothing."

"Suspect?"

"I just want a report. I doubt if you'll find anything. I doubt very much if there is anything to find. But for my peace of mind, you understand—"

"You think she's out fucking some other guy."

"I didn't say that."

"Do you?"

"I suspect she may possibly be involved in an affair, but I'm also pretty sure I'm wrong."

"Be frank with you, Maynard. Most of them that come to me aren't wrong. Those feelings are uncannily accurate. I'm not saying they are in your case, but in most cases. Don't worry, I'll find out all about him."

154

"Assuming there is someone."

"I never assume. Never. What I tell you is what I see. I see her go into a motel room with him, come out three hours later and her lipstick's on crooked, I'm not going to tell you that this man had carnal knowledge of your wife. That's only an assumption. I'll tell you what I saw, inclination and opportunity. That's all you need in order to file the separation, if you were to file."

"You may find that she's not seeing anyone at all. I may be completely wrong about this."

"As you say."

"This may be just my own paranoid fantasy."

"Want some advice?" Mike said. "I'm not in the advice business, but from the little I've seen of you, I like you and I'd like to give you some advice from somebody who's a professional in these matters. My advice is, don't take it personal—if it turns out she's fucking somebody, that is. Don't take it personal. Don't dress it in some kind of mythical getup, you're goddamn King Arthur or something. A man is not lost because his woman's unfaithful to him. It's been going on since the beginning of time. You can bet your ass women were sneaking out of the cave and getting it on in the bushes with the Java man next door. So fucking what? You're a man—I can see that looking at you— you're a man and you're a man in spite of anything she does."

"Look, you're blowing this up. You say you're a professional. You say you don't make assumptions. Fine. Don't start any lectures with me, what it means and all. I know what it means."

"I'm not—hey, I'm no preacher. I'm giving you my perspective as a professional, that's all. You imagine it. I've seen it. I've seen them do it in cars, goddamn Corvettes. In motel rooms you rent by the hour, the ones with the water beds and the blue movies. In boats, you could see the thing rolling. In the trees, on the ski slopes, in a swimming pool, on the garage floor, up against the wall of a ramp in the Coliseum at a Tom Jones concert. I've seen it all. I know. 'Cause what it comes down to, Maynard, is

155

this"—he tapped his temple—"not this"—he pointed to his groin. "See what I mean?"

"No."

"Maybe, you find out your lady isn't really doing it, you're just a nervous nelly, you'll learn something out of the whole thing. You'll be happy to pay my bill because you'll be able to say, I'm a little wiser now. I know myself a little better. I've got it straighter, the whole loyalty thing now. I'm not going to let her play with my head no more. That might be something you can take with you."

"You talk a lot for a private detective."

"It's a lonely job, pal."

15

The official groundbreaking was a week away. Sal had ordered some chrome-plated shovels and arranged for a few city officials and a local beauty queen to attend.

But machinery was already at work and Ted wanted to observe the first progress, wanted to watch his dream begin to materialize. Two backhoes pecked like mechanical vultures at the abandoned graveyard. Men in slickers the same yellow as their machines were collecting the uncovered bones and putting them in plastic garbage bags for the transfer to the new site.

The November sky spat and sobbed. Dirty clouds were being torn to shreds on the pines higher up the hill.

Sal's car pulled in behind Ted's. Ted watched him complete a call on his car telephone before he got out. Sal turned his collar against the wind and came over to stand beside his partner.

"You know what you always hear, when they do this?" Sal asked.

"What?"

"When they move a cemetery they open a coffin that's been in the ground for a long time and they find deep scratch marks on the inside of the cover. Huh? The inside."

"Nothing left of those coffins."

"Why do people want these new vaults," Sal said, "lead or copper or whatever, permanently sealed? What are they afraid of? What the hell are they afraid will happen?"

"Just the idea of it, I guess."

"I heard about a jerk who was so afraid of being buried alive he had a phone put in his, just in case. I mean, that's taking fear with you."

"Why does anybody have a fancy casket at all? Because if you don't people talk."

"The undertakers have it sewed up."

"Tell me about it," Ted said. "I had to for my old man. Don't you ever waste money on one of those mahogany buffets, he always said. Plain pine is what I want. But they hit you when you're vulnerable and put on the subtle pressure—you're cheap if you don't go top shelf, your last chance to show you cared. I shelled out some pretty good coin for his box."

"Let's take a closer look."

They trudged down the hill toward the work site. Ted had thought to bring galoshes, Sal seemed oblivious of the mud on his dress shoes.

"He used to bring me up here hunting," Ted said.

"Who?"

"My father, when I was a boy." He pointed down to the highway. "This was all open then, all along there, just orchards, fields, and woods. Now this is really the only available land left that's at all suitable for building. We were lucky to grab it."

In the gloomy late afternoon the sodium lights were already glowing over the mall parking lot, already illuminating the cars clustered around the dealerships. In the gathering fog the neon and the lighted billboards seemed unnaturally bright. The scene pulsed with the flashing brake lights of the cars that crowded the roadway, shoppers rushing to beat the Christmas rush.

"What did you hunt?" Sal asked.

"Pheasant, grouse, rabbit sometimes. I was never much of a hunter. I didn't have the kill instinct, I guess. Anyway, I could never hit anything. My old man would get furious when I'd miss an easy shot. This is serious, he'd tell me. Nothing more serious. And I'd agree with him, but it didn't improve my aim. You ever hunt?"

"No, I wasn't an outdoorsman."

"Yeah, my father loved the wild, loved to sit and fish, wander out in the woods. Always trying to get me interested, but I just didn't appreciate sleeping under the stars or dangling a hook. This, he'd be sick to see what they've done along here. He hated development, housing tracts, shopping plazas, even paved roads. To him it was a desecration. What we're doing, it would just make him sick even though it's to benefit people like him."

They stood on the edge of the graveyard. A rail of wrought-iron fence was lost in the weeds. All the gravestones had long since been flattened.

Ted leaned over to try to read the name and dates on one of the old stones, but it was too eroded to make out the letters. He continued, "You know, I've always had a lot of animosity toward my father. It was like he made me pay the price for not being the son he wanted. I resented him for it. And yet what really got me thinking about this Golden Age project was the way he had to spend his last years in a human warehouse. If there'd been something like this available, it would have meant so much more than a fancy casket. I guess I have the feeling I failed him and this is my way of making it up or something."

"My papa was a sonofabitch," Sal said. "Sweated his life away working for some asshole who ran a machine shop, drank most of his pay, and beat my mother for recreation. He dropped dead when I was twelve, and good riddance. You watch a drunk beat your mother with his fists when you're six, you don't ever have too much feeling for him."

"I can't really imagine. I guess it happens often enough."

"It happens, all right."

The architect they'd arranged to meet there arrived. Ted walked back up the hill to confer with him. Sal stayed where he was.

It was a night like this you torched the packers, he thought. A filthy New Jersey winter, the same fog, same sick light.

Paulie calls you in, screaming Corsi's not going along, the rulings of the Association. Corsi's taking over stops that belong to Paulie's carting companies. Corsi's men roughed up one of Paulie's drivers when he was picking up a dumpster. Corsi has to be taught. He thinks he has backing out of Philly, he's invulnerable in Jersey. He has to be taught a lesson.

You go out on a day like this, a day close to night. Eight packer trucks in a row. You put a jar of gas in the cab of each one, a newspaper down the pipe. Light them.

You stand watching. God damn. These dirty white trucks flaming and flaming, belching big balls of fire. And he's got some shit stored in barrels off behind. That catches. It's sending up green and blue and orange flames. One of the barrels blows like a rocket thirty feet in the air. Solid-black smoke lit from within. They have to pull you away, you're watching and watching, still a kid at heart. You're fascinated that you can actually do this, do whatever you set out to do, get away with it.

Ted came back down the hill. He explained a point the architect had made, but Sal wasn't listening.

"You know," Ted was saying, "I wondered at first about bringing Lujak into this. I thought maybe you didn't realize exactly what his reputation was around here."

"I knew. First thing I found out, checked the man's limitations. He's no mystery to me."

"You know the kind of dirty dealings they talk about that he's been involved in?"

"Reputation's his strong suit. He probably had nothing to do with half of what you hear about."

"But I see what he can do," Ted said, "the strings he can pull. I was afraid this boneyard was going to stymie us."

"You use a guy like that. Let him think he's a big cheese, great. He throws his weight around at city hall, you toss him a few crumbs, you keep your momentum."

"Yeah, speaking of that—"

"Momentum is the thing. Tomorrow, a guy like Lujak, we won't want to deal with him, he'll be irrelevant. Where we are right now, he can grease the wheels for us, fine. You don't want to become bogged down or they're all over you. Am I right?"

One of the backhoes was struggling. A stump desperately gripped the earth, gave way with a crack, flew up, a Medusa's head of roots.

"Who's all over you?" Ted asked.

"Them, the little people. Little people run the world, didn't you know that? Look around. Everywhere it's the guys with the small brains, the puny hearts, the tiny balls who control things. Bureaucrats, clerks, lawyers, politicians. I mean, who makes it up the ladder—in business, politics, anything? The brownnose, the toady, the yesman."

"Sure, but you do have some—there are some leaders."

"Yes, and they're almost always independent. They're guys like us who have to be free, who have to make it on our own in the face of all the bullshit the little people throw in our way. That's what's wrong with this country."

"People don't want to take risks," Ted said.

"You've hit it, my friend. These little people want to be sure of tomorrow, and the day after. Absolutely sure. They don't like thin ice, making your way as you go, taking a chance now and then. They're so worried about tomorrow, they're completely out of what's happening today. And today is the only time anything ever happens. And you have to make it happen. Am I right?" He held his hand up, Ted held his up, they slapped them lightly together.

"What I was going to tell you," Ted said. "I talked to this caterer today, called me up. And he says, you've got this Golden Age thing going up, you're gonna need food service, I can give you a very good deal, all this, and Leon told me to call you, I'm a good friend of Leon. I said what do you do, he tells me, a regular catering setup. I explained to him, this—there's going to be some complicated dietetics involved in this operation, this is not just laying out plates of ham at a Polish wedding. Anyway, I said, we'll bid it out, you're free to— Wait a minute, he says, I don't think you heard me. I'm a friend of Leon's. I said, I don't care if you're a friend of the pope, you bid according to the specs, that's it. So he starts giving me a little lip. I told him to go to hell. Can you believe that? Just because he knows Lujak."

"Yeah, well."

"Was I right? I told him to go to hell."

"Sure, you were right. Just, an actor like Lujak's going to be unpredictable. Not that I can't handle him, but you don't want to throw it in his face."

"What's he expect, all the jobs on the site are going to go to his buddies? I'm not letting him push me around. We allowed him to buy in, he's helping us by pulling a few strings—that doesn't mean he takes over. Does it?"

"Not at all."

"He isn't—dangerous or anything, is he?"

"I said I can handle him," Sal said.

"I mean, we're not getting in over our heads here, are we?"

"Like I said, you can't always be sure how the man's going to react."

"I just hope he understands that we operate according to our rules, not his."

"I hope so, too. Hey, I'm going to get one of those."

"What?"

"Look." Sal stepped over to a pile of clay the shovel had dumped near them. He picked up and brushed the muck off of a skull. "I always wanted one of these. I wonder if—you know, once this might have been the head of a gorgeous broad. Huh? Nineteen years old and long blond hair and look at her. Where's the come-on wink now, babe? Huh? Makes you think, doesn't it?"

The night was settling in quickly now. They started back toward their cars.

"You're going to keep it?" Ted asked.

"Sure. Conversation piece. Make a good ashtray."

Laura had a couple of days off because they were remodeling the gallery. The kids were at school. She found herself wasting time. She wasn't storming through her daily "to do" list as usual. That morning she was sitting in the quiet kitchen over a second cup, idly reading an article in a women's magazine.

She started thinking about what she and Ted would tell each other later in life. Did people tell things when they got old? Affairs and all? She remembered hearing of an old man who committed suicide because, after his wife died, he found love letters that had been written to her forty-five years earlier by his best friend. Would it still hurt? Why?

Ted, remember when Sal and Gina first moved in? You won't believe this, but I had this mad infatuation. Why? I don't know why. I guess I was just at that restless stage—you know, almost forty and all. Did I what? I came so close, so very very close, but I always loved you so much.

Or: Did I have an affair? Yes. You suspected? I figured you did. It was a very brief fling. It made me appreciate you all the more.

No, that wasn't how it would go. People don't tell. There are secrets that must go to the grave. "To the grave"—what a line.

Better not to tell. Though, face it, nothing to tell. Yet. She'd allowed some men to go too far in the corners of cocktail parties. She'd flirted. Teased. But she'd had no real adventures.

Why did she think about sex so much? Had she always? No. In fact, how many months ago was it she'd been wondering if her interest had not departed in the night? "Life after sex"—she remembered herself coining the phrase. Things had gone black and white between her and Ted. She'd been startled to realize how little she missed it.

Then, around the time of the costume party, her world had flashed Technicolor. Suddenly everywhere she looked she found stimulation. She'd started noticing ads for men's underwear. Started noticing herself in the mirror, trying on alluring looks, tugging down her necklines, testing a pair of shorts she'd judged too tight years ago.

Maybe it was Jenny. Her daughter's tempestuous romances carried Laura back to her own girlhood. They reminded her of the rush of passion, the giddy rapids that you suddenly encounter after the placid flow of life that precedes adolescence.

The funny thing was, Ted had also become a more ardent lover. He, too, seemed—

The doorbell rang.

Startled, Laura listened. No, it had only sounded in her mind, as if her yearning had set off a gong.

The doorbell would ring, she thought, and it would be Sal.

I was going to slide it under the door.

Sal. What?

The carrier put it in our box.

A bill. They would say what people always say about bills.

Want to come in? I was just going to put on a second cup.

He hesitates. She fights to control her eyes.

Why not?

She closes the door behind him. Gina's off shopping. He overslept. He's a son of a bitch to get out of bed in the morning. He has an excuse, Latin blood. Wops are from a lazy climate. Hey, this is good coffee.

164

Anyway, here she is sitting around in her bathrobe and slippers, going on ten o'clock. That blue silk looks very nice on her, by the way.

And she'd probably guessed that he'd taken that bill out of their box, just as an excuse.

She first feels the chill at the door. The outdoors cold grabs at her belly, rakes nails down her bare throat.

Sitting in the warm kitchen, she still feels raw. She grips her mug. Her fingers do not absorb the heat. The coffee scalds her throat without warming her.

Why does he act so goddamn casual?

Jesus, she's cold. She pulls the robe close around her neck. She talks, not knowing what she's saying.

She looks across at him, at his eyes.

Sal is saying how he has to get to work. He doesn't rise immediately. She tries to keep her face from assuming the mask that she feels coming over her features. But she can't control the shivering anymore. She's never been so cold in her life.

If she didn't feel so cold, she wouldn't. If the chill wasn't shaking her heart like a pompon. If black ice wasn't streaming inside her veins.

If she had the warmth to, she would draw back her hand before it touched his. If she didn't have to clench her teeth to stop them chattering, she would say something that would let her stop right there. If her hand did not glow warm as soon as it brushed his skin, she would laugh it off. If the chill did not flash to body heat as he took her fingers in his, she could still manage a sisterly smile.

Her awkwardness is as big as a kitchen table. She stands stiffly. She steps toward him. A chair scrapes. He does not rise.

She immediately sees his genius. Ted would reciprocate, would mirror her passion, match each gesture, affirm each forward step. Sal does not.

His eyes are blanks. His mouth immobile. His hand consents to be held.

He is to be the clean slate of love, on which she can

finally write her full sexual message. With Ted she's always run into his well-intentioned ego—reassuring, accommodating, stifling.

She presses Sal's face to her. The silk slides away. Her chin lifts toward the ceiling.

He is not eager, he does not resist. He lets her be the one who gives.

She has a giddy, muscle-wrenching sense of danger. Eyes are already upon her.

At any moment they could appear. Ted. Jenny. The twins.

But as the chill leaves her, soaked away in the bath water of her lust, the line of danger and the line of passion fuse. The hidden urge to exhibit herself makes her revel in the danger. The potential for catastrophe fuels her warmth.

She draws him up and wraps herself in his arms. He kisses the lips she gives him, the neck. The teakettle, forgotten, whistles its urgency.

His lips push the nightgown from her shoulder.

Danger follows them up the stairs.

He remains passive, silent. He allows her all the room she needs. Acts and words absolutely strange to her flow from her. He is her instrument, cool or ardent as she demands.

The violation of their bed, hers and Ted's, is a terrible thing. She knows that. Knows it as if she'd read it in a newspaper, a small item on page three. It cannot compare with the headlines of her own arousal.

The acrid smell of scorched metal brought Laura back to herself. The kettle had boiled dry.

16

The school smelled the way all schools smell. Sal and Gina walked down a corridor lined with metal lockers. Yellow buses stood in ranks outside.

Sal was thinking of Paulie's school bus thing. Paulie'd had an arrangement with the union, he could pay below-scale wages to the drivers. Eight separate companies, they all operated out of the same yard. They rigged bids to get the contracts.

Paulie saw Sal was a comer, so he put him to manage it. Sal built it into a profitable arrangement. Plus they could add guys to the payroll from Paulie's outfit, guys who needed a job, something to show the probation officer, the parole board. Easy work. They'd sit around Sal's office and bullshit.

Fort Lee Jerry going on and on about these little girls, little thirteen-year-olds with their miniskirts and tight pants and the things he heard them talking about, how he was going to arrange to get up a party, him and three or four of them.

Eventually the newspapers picked up on it, mobsters driving your kids to school. The reporters were sharks on a feeding frenzy when they started running stories on that. So the politicians yelled and charges were brought. But Paulie slipped out of it, cashed in some of his markers with people at the district attorney's.

"You're a what? A psychologist?" Sal said. "Hey, what is this, we're supposed to talk to Mario's teacher, and they're sending us to a psychologist? The kid's supposed to be crazy or something?"

"Sal, let her talk, will you?" Gina said.

"Mr. Vincent, I can assure you, this is a routine matter. Many, many children evidence this kind of disturbance."

"Disturbance? What the hell are you talking about?"

"First, you must be aware that Mario is a very bright boy. I've reviewed some of the standard tests we give, for evaluation purposes, and he's scored consistently in the top percentile."

"Don't tell me he's gifted," Gina said. "I couldn't live with gifted."

"What are you talking about?" Sal said to his wife. "Of course he's gifted. Isn't he, Miss Loo—Loo—what?"

"Lucazinski." She had dark Polish eyes, a wide mouth, and a sharp chin.

"Isn't he gifted, Miss Lucazinski? I mean, the boy is a whiz. I ask him, you done your homework? Sure, he says, I done it on the bus. On the bus, and he's all finished. Of course he's gifted."

"Or he does it watching 'Three's Company,' " Gina said. "And he still gets a beautiful report card. I hope he's cheating. I wouldn't want him to be gifted."

"Why?" Sal demanded. "You want him to be a dummy?"

"I was gifted myself. I know what it's like. It's agony."

"You gifted? Don't make me laugh."

"I was very gifted as a child. It makes you a kind of a freak. I always knew the answers and kids hated me for it. I could read before I went to kindergarten. Gifted is very stressful."

"Gift of gab, maybe."

"At least I went to school—more than I can say for some people. Gifted children are usually oversensitive, aren't they, Miss Lupinski?"

"I don't think the problem here has to do with Mario being gifted."

"I want him to be normal," Gina explained. "You don't know how I've wished so often I could have had a normal childhood. Too much sensitivity can actually hold you back in school. I was never given the understanding I needed."

"Hey, we're not here to talk about your problems."

"I feel that the difficulties that Mario's been running into are all related to a central underlying cognitive configuration," the psychologist said. "To begin with, children of Mario's age generally have begun to establish a stable conceptualization of right and wrong. They may do wrong—in fact, it's normal for them to test the limits of their personal moral system—but they see it as wrong, understand it's wrong. With Mario, the distinction doesn't seem to be there."

"How do you mean?" Sal said.

"I see it in many little ways. He expresses a disdain for authority. His sole criterion for deciding moral questions seems to be whether he can get away with something."

"Well, he needs to learn," Gina said. "That's kind of why we send him to school. To learn all that stuff."

"What you're talking about," Sal said, "is attitude. He has a bad attitude? He needs a little talking to."

"I'm afraid it goes beyond attitude. Closely tied in is Mario's inordinate fantasy life."

"That's bad?"

"It is if it keeps him from correctly constructing reality. I've had many talks with him. The story keeps changing, but he repeatedly has told me his father's a gunfighter, like in the Wild West. He says your home is full of guns. He insists you're hiding out, that people are after you, they want to kill you. Some men are trying to kill him, he thinks.

He says they appear from nowhere, he sees them when he's out playing and has to run away. His last name isn't really Vincent. He has a secret name that he can't tell anybody."

"Didn't you ever have fantasies, Miss Lucazinski?" Sal asked.

"I beg your pardon?"

"I said, haven't you ever had fantasies? Don't you ever see some guy walking down the street, somebody you don't know at all, and think about coming on to him, doing all kinds of things that have got no psychological relevance? Never think of marrying some rich Saudi squash player, give up your job? You know, see Dean Martin on television, imagine him making love to you?"

"Dean Martin's a drunk," Gina said.

"So, she can dream, can't she? Or fantasize you're a successful singer yourself, sell a million records. You really do have a gorgeous voice."

"She's obviously not a singer, Sal. Jesus. See what I have to put up with?" she asked the counselor.

"I think we should focus on Mario here. Uhm . . . I think there's a confusion of identity involved that prompts Mario to attract attention to himself with these stories."

"Come on," Sal groaned. "The kid's just bullshitting."

"I believe that Mario has had some trauma, some dislocation in his life that remains unresolved. He's a very frightened little boy. All children have fears, but something's undermined Mario's basic trust. He sees the world as a threatening place."

"So?" Gina said. "It *is* a threatening place. It's a dangerous place. I mean, just the traffic out there. People are getting in accidents, kids are being run down all the time. Diseases they've got going around now. Who knows what somebody else's kids have? Or kidnappings. I don't want my child to end up on some milk carton somewhere, Miss Luzinski. Scared? Good he's scared."

The counselor narrowed her eyes.

"What we've tried to teach him, to be tough," Sal said. "Not scared, tough."

"Mrs. Vincent, he's a nine-year-old boy. He's a sensitive child. He doesn't need continual lessons in the brutality of modern life. He needs support, guidance."

"I live in dread," Gina said flatly.

"The kid picks up on it," Sal explained. "That's what the woman is saying, Gina. You're paranoid and Mario picks up on it and you're turning him into a timid little sissy."

"We have to keep alert," Gina insisted. "We can't get lax. We have to watch out, all the time. There's no other way. I hate this life. I hate it." She bit on the knuckle of her right fist.

"What do you do for a living, Mr. Vincent?" the psychologist said after a long pause.

"Me? I'm in real estate developing. I have my own company."

"I see. These wild stories about you being a gunfighter—I thought maybe you were an actor even."

"You know how kids are. I was a paid killer, actually."

Miss Lucazinski's pencil stopped writing.

"For the government, that is," Sal said, smiling. "I was connected with army intelligence. I can't really talk about it."

"Oh. Well, perhaps that explains some of the boy's ideas."

"I'm sure it does," Sal said, standing. "And don't you worry, dear. My wife's been under some strain lately. We'll make sure Mario reins it in. The kid won't cause you any more problems."

He gripped Gina by the shoulders and helped her to her feet.

They left the psychologist alone in her office. She spent the next half-hour writing notes in Mario's file.

"Jason," the woman on TV said, "if you really love Mitsy, the last thing I want to do is to stand in your way. But, it's just—"

"What is it, Heather? I feel there's something you want to tell me."

Gina sat on the sofa, holding her ankle and staring intently at the picture.

"No, no, I can't. Not yet. You're not—you're not ready."

"I've trusted you, Heather. You told me I had to, and I've trusted you. There's something I should know, isn't there? Or is it—is this amnesia—?"

"No, Jason. It's just that sometimes I wish I wasn't your therapist, that's all."

"But why?"

"Why? Why? Why do you think?"

Gina turned off the sound during the commercial. The blare set her on edge. Yet she was reluctant to switch off the set. She'd been following the show for years. And she didn't like the silence that would pulse through the house. That got on her nerves, too.

She was feeling especially rattled. She was trapped inside a soap opera herself. If she were still in New Dorp she would have called someone. Anyone, just pick up the phone and dial any of half-a-dozen close friends. Talk to somebody who understands the life, understands Sal, knows what kind of crap you can run into.

The people here, you couldn't do that. Oh yeah, they bubbled over with friendship at first. But their open, cordial faces were fronts for shrunken souls that they kept locked up tight.

They didn't know her. They weren't her kind of people. Especially the women. They judged her. Of course they did, she knew they did.

She picked up and petted a porcelain cocker spaniel. She was having headaches. She imagined she was developing arthritis. Backaches. The doctor gave her pills to sleep. Maybe she had a tumor. She requested a CAT scan. He said she didn't need one. The stress, he said. That's all. That wasn't all. She knew that now.

Her mother and sisters were fading into the mist of the past. Their letters, forwarded through the drop box, were becoming increasingly infrequent and impersonal. And with them she felt herself fading.

172

She was drifting away from her own life. She was out on an unknown, terrifying sea. Sharks were circling below her.

What was left? Sal? Sal Vincent? Was Sal Vincent any different than Sal Veronica? Sometimes she let herself hope so. Sometimes she nearly persuaded herself it was true, that she had achieved the new life she'd dreamed of.

Dreamed? What dream? This was no dream.

Gina had a secret. When Sal found out—he'd have to find out very soon—he'd use it against her. Use it as an excuse. The way he had the first time. Him and his theories.

He'd desert her. She would be left on this stark sea of unfamiliarity all by herself. She couldn't take that. She couldn't allow that.

She turned the sound back on and watched the well-groomed actors suffer their make-believe dilemmas.

17

Sal lay in bed turning over memories of redheads, waiting for her to show. A mirrored sphere was revolving, casting snowflakes of light on the walls. The room was half dark, with cracks of brightness seeping around the edges of the shades. Sal was listening to Miles, "Straight, No Chaser," on the tape deck built into the wall.

Listening and thinking about redheads.

Like the ones with the crinkly orange hair who were cute and freckled and blue-eyed, always full of energy, spitfires when they got mad. They were skinny and had pug noses and high-pitched voices and small feet and slender shoulders.

Like that one you picked up hitchhiking in Florida, you and Tommy Pitano. That was when you were making the first moves into the coke business. Paulie'd heard about the profits people were turning just driving cars up the East Coast. He got word to Traficante in Florida. Traficante gave him the okay. He connected with some Brazilians who were supposed to be saner than the Colombian cowboys.

It's your first trip. You drive down in Tommy's Riviera with the trunk full of stolen Oxy Pete bonds, earning in both directions.

Drive all night and hit Daytona just as the sun is skimming the Atlantic. Tommy wants to stop and look at where they raced stock cars on the beach, though they haven't run the sand course since the fifties. The air is like a sigh. You stare at the lapping waves, buy paper cups of coffee, and head back to the highway.

Nobody is around at that hour, except for these two girls. They're standing just beyond a gas station. One wags her thumb at you. The sun is setting fire to her hair. Tommy says no, but you pull over.

Eighteen, nineteen. What was her name?

They're planning to get off in Cocoa, but you make contact with the redhead in the rearview mirror. You talk her into riding farther south. Her girlfriend giggles and gets out.

Tommy has people in Pompano Beach. The place sits on stilts out over a marshy inlet. You make love to the girl while rain hammers on the tin-roofed wing of the house.

You can still bring to mind her freckled shoulders, her long girlish legs with their sharp knees. It isn't smoky lust you see in her eyes, but an eagerness, an excitement with life that takes your breath away. Eyes clear as water.

Still on a burn, you drive alone into Miami that afternoon to unload the securities and make the buy.

You return in the sweaty evening. She doesn't want to let you into the bedroom at first. The side of her face is swollen. She's still licking a trickle of blood from her nostril. Your friend wouldn't listen to no, she says.

Tommy is sitting shirtless over a plate of shrimp and a quart of beer. You're ready to take his head off, but you think better of it in time. You have business to take care of. No time for sentimentality.

But you remember six months later when you catch Tommy holding out on a score. You're glad of it.

Son of a bitch. You invite him over, relive Florida all through dinner with him. Remember that little redhead you knocked around, Tommy? You laugh about it with him. You laugh, you put a couple of .22 slugs in his head.

The memory, like the memory of all your work, comes back to you with a stunning clarity. You felt satisfaction then, popping Tommy. But now the slugs behind the ear don't balance the girl's bruised face, don't make up for it. They're part of the same tapestry, as if *you* had beaten that beautiful girl, marked her, raped her.

So there was that type of redhead. He struggled to keep his mind off the other thing. Think about redheads.

Okay, then you had the ones, they had green eyes and white skin that couldn't take the sun. Gold highlights in their hair. They were delicate and fierce, not cute, with wild curls and sharp nails. They were touchy and full of imagination. They never knew what they wanted from one minute to the next.

Tommy Pitano had screwed up the way so many guys screwed up when they got into dope. The money was too easy, the temptation too great. Guys would skim or guys would start snorting. They'd like it and then they'd get ideas. Ideas meant trouble.

Another type. The auburn beauty, all satin skin, dark tan, and brown eyes. They were moody, deep. They had firm flesh and high proud cheekbones and rich lips. Like Vanessa. Oh, yes, there was that type. That type was the most dangerous of all. They got under your skin and made you take chances, made you try and buck the house odds. That type.

You got around to blowing coke yourself. Vanessa encouraged you. You played all kinds of bedroom games with it, for hours. But then you made the big mistake. Paulie actually laughed. Broads, Sal, bad enough. Broads and dope both, forget about it.

To hell with Paulie.

She wasn't bad, this one. She almost made him forget.

176

She knew how to play the game. She was a natural. She was no actress, but her imagination worked overtime.

Usually, they were strangers, the two of them. Strangers meeting at a movie. They'd pretend the television was the screen and they were only strange hands, strange mouths in the dark. Furtive and alien.

Or he was an escaped convict and she was the schoolteacher he took hostage. And though she was innocent of the brutalities of prison, though they came from radically different backgrounds, the violence of their meeting threw them into the grips of passion. Their play rescued him from the thoughts that kept tightening wires in his brain, gave him a brief respite from the memories that loomed out of his control.

Christ, here he was, lying in a squeaking bed, in a cheap motel, in a strange city, in the middle of nowhere, and these thoughts that had never bothered him all along were coming back to haunt him.

And he thought he needed a broad to make him forget. He'd told himself that one enough times. Or he needed her in order to show up these straights, show them he could boff their wives. Or he needed her because it was only when they were wrapped up together in the coil of passion that he could be himself, come back to himself.

Yeah, need. He'd actually convinced himself he had to have her when, looking at it stripped, he didn't need her. He didn't need her at all. It was nothing more than . . . what? Loneliness? It was nothing more than goddamn softness.

Because softness was one thing they couldn't accuse you of back then. Not that night Paulie called you in, looked at you with his one eye, said it was time to break your cherry. Started raving about Corsi. Corsi hadn't learned his lesson. Corsi was going to have to go away.

You want this, Sal?

You know I do, Mr. Amato. You know I've been waiting for the chance.

No piece of cake, your first one.

I can handle, no problem.

He'll be ready.

He's a dead man right now.

I have all the confidence in the world in you, Sal.

A chance to make your bones. A chance to become a man. The fly balls sailing into the sky.

And how many other times after?

Lot of guys couldn't. Tough guys, they couldn't—you learned that later. They didn't mind bending a knee the way it wasn't supposed to go. Punching a guy's kidneys to pieces. But when it came to killing, they couldn't.

Like Ricky Lopresti. Lotta mouth, good with his hands. You take him to meet those two punks said they lost the skim from those cruise boats off of Lauderdale. They thought you were going to help them rob a big-money crap game to pay Paulie back. Climb in behind them. You take the driver. Ricky sits there, his lip running spit. The other guy is going for a pistol under the seat. You drill a .22 into his spine and he jerks into a dance. Ricky just looks and looks.

You would always start to feel cold. Didn't matter, even in the thick wet heat of the steam room you felt chilled. It's the chill of everything stopping. You shut down. You shut down and you're more capable than ever. No friction. You're a coiled spring and when you move, there's no friction. Because of the cold. The cold rush in your veins. No resistance. No doubt.

But you're getting so far away from that. You're getting soft. You need to exercise your reflexes. If you don't, they're going to catch you flat-footed someday. You need to breathe a little real oxygen. Take a risk.

Hell, Ted crowing about risk. What the Jesus does he know about risk?

The trip will take care of that. The trip will wake you up. Talk about risk.

Sal tensed, sat up on the bed. Footsteps. She entered.

". . . at eleven and a half," Ted was saying into the phone. "I said, what are you talking, eleven and a half? That's shylock rates. He says, unsecured this and high-risk that.

I said, don't talk to me, unsecured. This, we've already started work at the site. Well, he's going on and on about the definition of a commercial property and what they can accept and all. I said, I thought I was doing you a favor bringing my business to you guys. Hell, you think you're the only bank in town? What?

"Yeah, yeah. Well, you know, everybody's a goddamn vice-president at a bank. They're a teller or they're a vice-president.

"Okay, you know what we need. Tell them if they want in, now's the time. We'll be putting these places on the market as soon as we get the go-ahead from the attorney general. After that, it's a new ball game. I mean it. Okay, just tell him. Right. Listen, I've got another call coming in. Talk to you later, Steve. Right. Bye now."

Ted hung up. He massaged his eyelids with his fingers and blinked a few times.

So much to do. But he was enjoying it. He couldn't think of a happier time in his life. Sure they needed money. They were going through cash so fast they could hardly keep solvent from day to day. Sure tomorrow was uncertain. But it seemed that the future had approached him. Before, he'd always thought of it as a long way off—next year, the year after, when he retired—that was the future, the unknown. Now the unknown was next week, tomorrow. He was dancing with the future on his arm and he loved it. He was making things happen. He had no time to worry about it. Okay, he was definitely over his head. But he found, much to his pleasure, that he could swim. He could swim just fine, thanks. So being over his head was not so bad.

Well, he only had six more calls to make, a stack of papers from the attorney to read, and some new projections he wanted to run through the computer.

He needed more coffee. He shouldn't, he'd been trying to cut down his cups a day after the article that Laura read him about the effects of caffeine. No, he really shouldn't.

Before he could pick up the phone, it rang. Margot

told him that a Miss Nalgas was here to see him. Did she have an appointment? No, Margot said. Ted told her to have Don take care of the woman, whatever she wanted. Margot said that the lady had a real estate matter to discuss and that she insisted on conferring with Mr. Reed personally. Ted looked at his watch and said he'd give her a minute, and could Margot bring him a cup of coffee?

Miss Nalgas was a serious-looking woman who wore a worsted blue suit and large tinted glasses and carried a briefcase. Ted shook her gloved hand and asked her to have a seat. He offered her a cup of coffee, but she refused.

"I might start by advising you, Miss Nalgas, that as a rule we don't handle residential real estate. If you're looking for a home, I could put you in touch with an excellent representative who—"

"Oh, no. That's not it at all. I . . ." She removed her glasses. "You see, I've recently inherited a sum of money, quite a lot of money, actually. And I was advised that real estate was an excellent investment, that it was practically a sure thing."

Her voice was rather husky. She crossed one leg over the other. Ted glanced at her calf.

"Nothing's a sure thing, I can tell you that. In fact, real estate is one of the more volatile areas for investment. While it's true the profits, the potential profits are large—"

"Yes, that's what I'd like, some large profits. I've always been struck by that expression 'let your money work for you.' Mr. Reed, I want my money to work for me. But I'm really so ignorant when it comes to these financial matters, such a child, I need some advice, someone I can trust."

"Maybe a financial adviser would be what you're looking for. I know a man who—"

"I don't trust them. I've heard so much about scams and swindles."

"Yes, there are a lot of wolves out there, no doubt about it. How much did you plan to—I mean, how much of an inheritance were you thinking—? Excuse me."

"Sorry to interrupt," Don said, entering. "Sal and I

180

were going to go over the Portman file, he said I could find it in your cabinet. And here's your coffee."

"Thanks, Don. Miss Nalgas, Don Dixon, our associate. The one on the left, Don. Second drawer from the bottom."

Don squatted at the filing cabinet.

"You were asking how much my inheritance was, Mr. Reed," Miss Nalgas said. "I'm not entirely sure, but I think in the range of, approximately somewhere around four and a half million."

Ted held the noncommittal smile on his face. "And how much of this were you thinking of putting into real estate ventures?"

"Oh, all of it. I don't believe in going halfway with anything, Mr. Reed. Or—do you mind if I call you Ted?"

"Not at all. Now, it just so happens that we—"

"Isn't it awfully warm in here?" she asked.

"Well, I don't—"

"Do you mind?" She slipped off her jacket. Beneath it she wore a recklessly low-cut blouse that revealed her generous development.

"I was saying, we—excuse me." Ted cleared his throat. "We're putting together a project right now that may be along the lines of what you're looking at—for."

Sal came in. "Sorry, Ted. Don, did you find it?"

Ted said, "It should be in the second drawer—"

"I found it," Don said.

"The reason I'm interested in letting my money work for me, Mr. Reed, I'm a singer. People in the entertainment industry, as you know, don't make a lot of money, unless they're Barbra Streisand—it would almost be worth looking like that if you had her voice, don't you think?"

While she spoke she was removing her gloves with a series of delicate tugging and twisting motions that held Ted's attention.

"I really feel you have to hear my promo tape," she said. She already had a cassette recorder out of her case. She placed it on the corner of Ted's desk and turned it on.

181

The woman is a nut case, Ted was thinking. But what a nut.

The music sounded very much like Tina Turner. Miss Nalgas stood up and mouthed the words to "Proud Mary." As she did so, she whipped away her skirt. Black seamed stockings covered her dancer's legs. Red bangles flashed from an abbreviated G-string. As she pulled her blouse over her head she removed the combs holding her hair in a bun. Her indigo pasties had tassels, and it took no effort for her to make them spin.

By this time, Ted had caught on and was enjoying the show. When the music faded out, he joined Sal and Don in applauding.

Margot came in carrying a cake covered with flaming candles. They all joined in singing Ted "Happy Birthday."

"Ted," Miss Nalgas said, "you've just been treated to a Stripogram from Stripogram, Incorporated. And I have a little present here from your partner and good buddy."

"A ticket to Las Vegas?" Ted said, looking inside the envelope she handed him.

"One way!" Don cracked.

Sal pulled out an identical one. "You and me, baby. We're going to go out there and have a dynamite time, guaranteed."

"No, I can't—with the work I have to—"

"Forget about it. One long weekend. You need the break."

"Well, I guess, hell, why not? I'd forgotten it was my birthday, I really had."

They served the cake.

"You should have seen his face when she said four point five mil," Don said. "I think his tongue hung out more then than later."

Sal paid the stripper and turned to Ted, grinning behind his cigar.

"I needed that," Ted said, smiling sheepishly.

"Gotta live, babe."

"You serious about this Las Vegas thing?"

"Why not?"

"It just seems, you know, hokey, sort of Bob Hope-ish. What's there but gambling?"

"You'll see. You go somewhere and lie on some beach, it just makes you lethargic. Oh, do I have to go back to work already? Take a break in Vegas, it's like a blood tonic. You get a taste for action and it pumps you up for bigger and better things."

"I don't know. I'm not much of a gambler."

"Ted, I don't agree with you. Look at this thing. We're out there on the high wire, babe, with no net. You're a risk taker. You're a ballsy sort of guy, you just don't know it. You go to Vegas, you play a little. You throw away some money. It's healthy. People who never take a chance, they develop a kind of anemia. You have to realize money's just a tool. Wealth? Wealth's what's between your legs, my friend. Money is just the flow of things. They proved that in economics. Hoard, stop it up, you're interfering with the flow. Gambling's therapy. Trust me."

"I do. That's the funny thing about it. I do trust you."

"You're going to love Vegas. You'll see."

It wasn't unusual for Gina to join Laura for coffee in the late afternoon. Laura would be home from work before Ted or Sal arrived. The kids were out playing. It was a relaxed time before the supper rush.

Laura had come to enjoy their talks. Gina could be so fresh, so unaffected. She would entertain Laura with funny stories about her family, her Uncle Frank, who ran an Italian restaurant, or her cousin the compulsive gambler.

But today she was in one of her moods. They'd become more frequent lately, more somber.

"It's certainly been a mild winter so far," Laura said to break the silence.

Gina crushed out her cigarette. There was a tiny rattle as she replaced the cup onto its saucer. She leaned closer to Laura across the table.

"You're really my best friend here, you know that, don't you?"

Laura smiled. "I'm glad."

"Laura, tell me something and be completely honest. I mean, I know you're honest, but tell me truthfully—you haven't heard anything. Have you? You know so many people. Nobody's said, mentioned about Sal, have they? Hinted?"

"Mentioned what?" she said too quickly. "What do you mean?"

"About Sal and some other woman."

"Why, no, of course not. I haven't—nobody's said anything like that to me."

"Seriously." She lit another cigarette. "I know—I'm sure something's going on, that he has someone."

"Oh, I can't believe . . ."

"I can tell. I feel it, as if it were an earthquake a long way away. This is just the way it started when I was carrying Mario. I mean, you know how vulnerable you feel, how shaky. I was pregnant when we got married. I was so—just so thrilled to be this man's wife. Then I found out and I was crushed. He used the baby as an excuse. He had his own theories about the whole thing."

"Gina, let me assure you—"

"No. I know. I can sense it. If he's not actually doing it, he's getting ready to. And so help me, I'm afraid to tell him. I just see it happening all over again."

"Tell him what?"

"I'm pregnant."

"You're—why, that's wonderful. That's exciting."

Gina shook her head. "I'm afraid to tell him about it. I'd love to have another kid, but if I found out for sure he was cheating, I don't know what I'd do. I really don't. I can hurt him very badly, Laura. I have a way."

"I thought you—you said you had an open relationship, that it didn't bother you, that you were both adults about it."

"Those are words. You like to keep up a front, just in case. But when it happens, when you find out, it's a terrible, terrible feeling. And it never gets any easier. You think you're tough, but each time is as bad as the time before. Worse. You find out that the person you love most in the world, who's everything to you, who you've given your life to, that to him you're somebody on a list, and not even at the top."

"I know how you must—"

"No. You don't know. Not if you haven't been through it. You raise his kid—okay. But the best moments, the really sparkling moments, are all going to somebody else. Everything you thought he was doing out of love he was doing to blind you. You find that out—Oh, Jesus." She pressed her hand over her mouth.

Laura's fingers floated, half reaching across the table.

"I don't know what to do," Gina sobbed. "I don't know who I am. And I'm pregnant. And I'm scared."

Laura herself was overcome by a profound sense of relief and disappointment. She recognized it as the type of comfort and regret that a traveler senses on returning home after a long trip. Back home, no longer in fantasy land.

The feeling was accompanied by a flash of fever, of near panic. She realized that she'd narrowly averted a danger of which she hadn't even been aware.

18

Ted, who rarely drank while the sun was up, decided to have a bloody mary before breakfast, hair of the dog. He was, after all, on vacation. And what a vacation.

He was sitting by the window in the hotel restaurant. Outside by the pool a tall blonde in a spandex suit was settling onto a deck chair. The morning sun was relentless.

Muzak was seeping from speakers in the ceiling, a movie tune, "Chariots of Fire" or "Rocky," it had to be one of them. It was two hours earlier—no, later back home. The thought, for some reason, made him feel younger. If he were home, he'd be at work by now. The kids would be in school, life would be completely normal, without magic.

But here, in this magic land, two hours ahead of—or was it behind?—your own life, you felt the armor of adulthood slipping off.

The waitress came. He indulged his appetite. Fruit

cocktail and eggs and sausage and home fries and Danish and coffee.

Ted considered himself a faithful husband. Even in his fantasies of infidelity, which were legion, he always set the scene in such a way that the imagined Laura would be protected from ever knowing. Sometimes, his precautions were so elaborate that they consumed the entire fantasy. In theory he felt that the occasional fling was okay if you were scrupulously discreet. A stew needed spice.

He knew he had a double standard in this regard. Not that Laura would want to cheat on him.

Oh, he was liberated. He didn't refer to women as girls. He pitched in with the dishes. He cooked occasionally. He was genuinely concerned about the lack of equal pay. But you couldn't deny real sex differences. Promiscuity was more naturally a male trait, that was obvious.

Still, butterflies had fluttered through his stomach when he saw Sal enter the lounge the day before with two girls. Sal knew how to fit in here: his clothes, his manner with the bellhops and casino dealers, the sunglasses that he wore all the time. Ted was hardly surprised that he'd managed to pick up a couple of extremely attractive young ladies.

Sal introduced the one as Lorna. It was clear he'd chosen her as his own companion. Lorna—Lorna Doone, Ted thought. A real cookie. And she looked like she'd just come in from the dunes. Her wide face flamed with tan, freckles sprayed her shoulders, her hair carried some of the orange of the desert evening. She was, Sal explained, a friend of a friend.

The were both very glad to meet Ted.

"We're partners. We have a real estate business in Chicago," Sal said.

"Chicago," Ted repeated. He picked up the little deception, though he wasn't sure of the reason for it. Combing his mind for specifics about the Windy City, he added, "The Loop."

They sat down. They'd been talking golf—everybody in Vegas seemed to talk golf when they weren't talking gambling. Ted talked with animation, ridiculing his own game. His initial breathlessness passed. Why shouldn't he spend his time in Vegas with a pretty young girl on his arm? What happened happened.

The one with the short-cropped hair and pointed chin, the one he already thought of as his, said it was Scotland, not England, where they'd invented golf. She was a thinker, Ted observed. Good.

Then he had an awful realization. He hadn't caught her name. That wasn't like him.

". . . never been here before?"

"No, I never had," Ted answered. "Have you—ladies, are you from around here?"

"I'm from San Mateo," Lorna said. "She's a native."

"Oh, really? From Vegas, Las Vegas? You actually live here?"

"Actually."

"I mean, I don't think of anybody really being from Vegas."

"My hometown." She had frank inquiring eyes that made him think of a co-ed.

"It's sort of like being from Disneyland or Hollywood."

"You mean like Mickey Mouse?"

"Yeah. But your ears are too small." What was he saying? Sal and Lorna were talking. "I mean, they're nice ears. You have very lovely ears."

"Thanks." Her smile was a crooked one that emphasized her youth.

"You know, I remember everybody's name. In my business you have to. But—I guess I was nervous, I didn't get yours."

"That's all right. It's Savannah," she said.

"What is?"

She gave him a slow smile. "My name."

"Oh. Oh, that's a lovely name. Savannah. Very beautiful." Georgia peach, he thought. Her breasts are Georgia peaches. Savannah, Georgia.

They exchanged smiles. Ted said, "It must be different growing up here."

188

"It's not different, really. We don't learn craps in kindergarten or anything. The Strip isn't the city."

Shy at first, she warmed once the ice was broken. She told him about herself. She was going to school, majoring in English at a community college nearby. Her favorites were Frost and Mark Twain. Ted agreed it was a pity people didn't read more. She loved to ski. She loved horses—she'd practically grown up in the saddle.

"You look like the athletic type," he said.

"I always wished I'd been a boy. I would have gone in for rodeo."

"I'm glad."

"What?"

"You weren't a boy." He felt a quick flush wash over his face.

"Thanks."

She could be my daughter, Ted thought. No, she couldn't. Wait. He did some mental arithmetic and figured that it was conceivable. Conceivable, that was funny. He'd have to tell Sal that later. *Conceivably*, she could have been my daughter.

He told her about himself. He was careful of what he said. There was golf, and he did a little woodworking. He jogged, not that he was a fanatic about it, but you had to keep in shape. He rode a Harley Davidson motorcycle. He'd rebuilt the engine on it. It was true he'd once owned a bike. No need to mention that he'd sold it ten years earlier. She said she wished she was handy with mechanical stuff, but she just wasn't. He said he'd like to take her for a ride on his bike. Out here in the desert you could really wind it out. In his mind he saw himself doing it, her arms wrapped around his waist.

Occasionally, Ted glanced across at Sal. He felt like an awkward schoolboy on a blind date. Sal was completely at ease. He and Lorna were having a high time. Sal would tell a joke and she would sputter and slap him. Then she'd tell one and he'd chuckle his appreciation. Once when he felt neither of the girls was looking, Ted caught Sal's eye and made a sign that meant hotcha-hotcha.

189

Ted's breakfast came as he relived the previous night. He began to eat slowly, with unusual relish.

They'd been in the middle of their second highball when a man approached the table. He wore a yellow seersucker suit, black-and-yellow Hawaiian shirt, and yellow shoes. His horn-rimmed glasses had yellow lenses. He was bald and had a pliable face.

"Sal? Sal, can I believe my eyes?"

Turning to look at him, Sal's face went hard.

"Sal, good to see you. Jesus, I heard— Hiya, sweetie." He nodded at Savannah. Ted resented the familiarity.

Sal was standing. He shook hands with the man. He kept a grip on him, pulling him forward until their heads were very close. He continued to squeeze the hand as he spoke into the man's ear. The newcomer's eyes jumped from Lorna to Ted to Savannah, making several laps of the table. He nodded. He licked his lips. He said something in Sal's ear. Sal nodded. The man retreated, muttering, "Take care."

With a forced breeziness, Sal said he was famished, they should get out of there and eat. Ted gulped the rest of his drink. Maneuvering around the table, he touched Savannah's elbow lightly.

The restaurant was an elegant one, or at least it put on a show of elegance, with tuxedoed captains and soap-opera-star waiters who told their names and rattled off long lists of specials.

"Who was that guy?" Lorna said. "I know him. As soon as I saw him, I said, I know that guy."

"Him?" Sal said. "He's a guy I know."

"Danny Kahn," Savannah said. She answered Sal's look. "Wasn't it?"

"Yeah, that's who it was."

"You know Danny Kahn?" Lorna asked. "He's funny as hell. He's a funny funny man."

"He's not so funny," Sal said. "In person he's not so funny."

"He's right," Savannah said.

"You know him, too?" Ted asked her. "I saw him in

a movie once. That one where he plays the funeral director? He cracked me up."

"I met him. My uncle knows him."

"That's true, though," Ted observed. "A lot of funny people aren't funny in person. James Thurber, they say, was a sourpuss."

"And Frost," Savannah said. "Robert Frost."

They finished eating and went to another place where there was a show. Sal spoke to the hostess and passed her some money and she put them in a nice spot, about halfway back, on the side but with a good view of the stage.

They had more drinks. Sal lit his cigar and put an arm around Lorna's shoulders and talked to her in low tones.

Ted couldn't think of anything to say for a minute. He looked at Savannah. Their eyes met in a way that was more than casual and she smiled to acknowledge it and he smiled. They kept up the eye play for a few seconds. Then she turned to look because the show was beginning.

The entertainment kicked off. It was the Las Vegas extravaganza of Ted's dreams—a phalanx of girls with long legs, ostrich feather headdresses, swelling breasts, and rhinestone costumes paraded onto the stage. They did a lot of dancing and kicking while the orchestra blared. Then a girl draped in bangles came out and took over. She dropped some of her clothing, then some more. It was an ordinary strip act, and a pretty blatant one, Ted thought. The surprise came when the girl took off the last thing she had left to take off, her wig. She was completely bald under it.

Some hoots arose from the audience. Ted wondered why Sal had picked this place. Surely the girls would have preferred something with more class. At the same time, he felt excited to be watching such escapades with a pretty young girl beside him.

Ted glanced at Savannah to see how she was taking it. She was chewing on her swizzle stick and watching the stage, apparently caught up in the action. Maybe he had a lot to learn about sophisticated night life, Ted thought.

This was actually a good production. It was erotic. So what?

The show finished in a mock orgy. They went outside into the tepid night. Lorna said she wanted to go driving in the desert in her car to see the moon. Savannah protested. She didn't feel like it. Events seemed to proceed like a scripted play. Sal slapped Ted on the back and climbed into the car beside his date. Suddenly Ted was alone with the girl.

She said she'd like to sit by a pool somewhere and have a drink. Somewhere outside. She hated sterile, air-conditioned bars. Ted agreed. He said their hotel had a nice pool, they could sit there.

It was almost three in the morning by his watch, but the intensity of the Strip had not diminished. They sat at a small metal table and looked at the pool. Ted ordered drinks and gave the girl who brought them an extravagant tip. At first nobody was swimming, then a guy with a beer belly and no tan came. He put on goggles and stroked up and down wearily.

In the elevator Ted took special notice of what Savannah was wearing. It was a simple dress, of the most delicate blue shade, like the blue on painted china. It was lovely, absolutely becoming. It draped her lithe body delicately.

His nervousness returned as soon as they left the elevator and began to walk the silent hotel corridor. They'd hardly touched all evening. They hadn't kissed. By the pool he'd played with her hand casually, significantly. She'd played with his hand. She'd slipped his wedding band off— he realized he should have removed it long before—and pretended to swallow it. He'd been frightened and he'd laughed at his own fear and she laughed and it was all right. It was all right about the wedding band. He didn't have to explain or lie about not loving his wife or anything. Laura would never find out.

Sipping his coffee, he relived the magical interlude. He remembered her gesturing with her thin wrists, wrists attached to slim brown forearms, forearms attached to slender biceps, to molded shoulders, collarbones like a bird's, a fragile, vulnerable throat. Little things she'd said, meaningless, banal at the time, became intimations of secrets that they would share in the night.

The remembering accelerated beyond his control. Pretty pretty feet, lightning tongue, pliant spine, her mewing, the fever in her eyes, and back to the smile, looking down on that smile that held all innocence and all depravity. His Georgia peach. Her Georgia peaches. Savannah.

And hadn't he risen to the occasion?

Savannah was good. But she was a baby still. She needed the guidance of a man. She needed someone to lead her through the erotic jungle. Remembering, Ted smiled to himself. Yeah, me Tarzan.

The brimming delight he felt was mixed with delicious sadness. Sadness was an image of Laura. Lovely Laura. Beautiful, wonderful Laura. Of course she could never understand, but he loved her even more now than ever.

How could he have his Savannah and his Laura both? He flirted with the idea of the harem, of a ménage whose impracticality matched its potential delights. He saw himself changing his life—moving to Vegas, becoming a professional gambler, living in swimming pool bliss with his dream girl. But would that be fair to the kids?

No, it would have to be occasional junkets, long awaited, carefully planned. Weekends of ecstasy. Delirious reunions and tearful partings. A luminous secret to brighten his middle age.

Suddenly Sal was sitting beside him. Ted had been looking forward to sharing his joy with his friend. But the look on Sal's face made him hesitate. Something was wrong.

"How's it going?" Sal's voice was impersonal. Ted couldn't see his eyes through the dark glasses.

"Dynamite, buddy. You look like Lorna Doone gave you quite a workout last night."

"We've got to get out of here."

"Huh?"

"I've got the bags down. We're checked out. I was able to get us on a two-thirty flight."

"Flight? To where?"

"Home."

"Wait a minute. Have I lost a day here? I know I haven't been looking at my wristwatch, but didn't we just arrive yesterday? Don't we have two days to go? I thought we were playing eighteen this afternoon."

"Change in plans."

"How come? I don't get it."

"I can't explain it." Sal wiped his hand over his mouth. "I shouldn't have come here. Some guys are looking for me. It's not safe. It's dangerous."

Ted laughed. Then he stopped laughing. "You're serious."

"I'm dead serious, Ted. I don't joke about something like this. We're vulnerable just sitting here."

"Something to do with your army stuff?"

"It's real, that's all I can tell you."

Sal's grim sincerity disturbed Ted. Ted's breakfast made itself known in his gut. Without wanting to, he looked around the restaurant. Sal shook his head minutely. Ted looked out at the pool. The sunshine made the mystery seem absurd.

"Well, listen," Ted said. "I understand everybody has a past, skeletons and all. You go if you have to. No reason I should spoil a terrific weekend."

"They know we're together."

"Who?"

"They're serious. This is not fun and games. I never should have come here. I took a gamble. We have to leave now. Right now."

"Whatever beef they have with you—whoever it is— it's none of my affair," he said, annoyed. "Don't start pushing. If you want to tell me what it's about, good. Otherwise, you do what's right for you."

"Uhn-uh. You're a link to me, to my wife and kid. You're the only person in this town who knows where I live."

"I'm not talking, okay? I won't tell a soul. Don't worry."

What was it? He'd never seen Sal act this way before. Act scared.

"No. You can't have anything to do with them. Stay behind and you will. Your family will come into it, too."

"What's this about families? Are you talking about blackmail? Because of those two girls? Is that it?"

"I'm talking about people getting hurt. I know it seems farfetched to you, but it happens. I've seen it happen."

"Let me guess. The KBG—or is it the KGB, I can never get that right."

"Why are you making a joke? I told you, this is no fucking joke."

Ted felt a flash of real anger. He said, "Because I don't like mysteries. We're out here for three days. I'm having a good time. Better than a good time. You come running up to me with this cloak-and-dagger stuff. Okay, if I'm in danger, tell me about it."

"The more I tell you, the worse it is for both of us. If you stay here, they will find out where you live—all they have to do is to look at your wallet. They will make you tell them where I live. We leave now, I've been careful not to put down any correct forwarding address anywhere here. We leave, we're gone. No more danger."

The sun had reached the point where it was shining on Ted's plate, lighting a crust of toast, a stain of butter. Ted felt Sal's eyes on him through the dark lenses. He picked up his knife and tapped it idly against the dish.

"Listen," Ted said. "This may sound as wacko to you as your story does to me. I had a great time with that girl last night. With Savannah. Okay? That's understood. Great time. But it went a little farther than that. A lot farther. I know there's nothing practical about it, but I'm kind of crazy about her. Don't laugh, it can happen. And I don't think it's all one-sided. She's sleeping up in my room right now. I'd at least have to take time to arrange things, explain things, tell her—"

"She's gone."

"What?"

195

"When I got the bags I told her to get out."

"You—"

"Ted, she's a prostitute."

Ted stared at the other man's face. He knew instantly that he wasn't making it up. If Sal had smiled, if he'd assumed any expression except blank seriousness, Ted would have punched him.

"You son of a bitch."

"I did it for you, babe."

"How much?"

"Forget it."

"I said how much."

Sal told him.

"Shit."

They stared at each other for a long moment. Then Ted smiled. Sal smiled. Ted chuckled. He covered his eyes and laughed. He laughed until his palm was wet with tears of laughter.

He stopped laughing and said, "Whoopie!" Then he laughed some more.

They made the two-thirty plane home. Ted was happy to see Laura. He told her Vegas wasn't that great. They'd done all there was to do the first day and he'd missed her. She laughed at him and loved him for it.

19

The dirty day made Maynard feel dirty. Zinc-gray clouds were draped from one horizon to the other. Drizzle dampened the pavement.

He felt guilty. He knew now for certain his fears were empty. Felice would never ever cheat on him. Ridiculous.

It was insane. He was insane. He must have been insane to hire a detective. His jealousy had gotten the best of him, had warped his thinking. What if Felice found out? How could he make it up to her? This could kill the trust she had in him, the implicit trust.

He'd gone off his head. It had happened how many times in the past? He should learn to recognize the signs.

But wait now. He'd had real suspicions. They were unfounded, okay, but wasn't a private investigator an intelligent, adult way to assuage his fears? He was simply paying for peace of mind. Didn't people go to shrinks for that? Take Valium? You cope. That's it. You cope.

This would be his punishment for being suspicious, having to go through with this.

Maynard mounted the steps to Ryan's porch and rang the bell.

Ryan greeted him brusquely at the door and told him to wait in the living room for a second, he was on a long-distance call. Maynard sat on a greasy love seat and flipped through a copy of *People* from the previous spring.

Five minutes later Ryan stuck his head out of the office door and told him to come in. Maynard entered the office. A tobacco aroma hung heavy in the air.

"Nice day," Ryan said.

Maynard glanced at the gloom that hung outside the window.

Ryan smiled and pointed to the afternoon paper. "See this? Midair collision outside Atlanta. Took the wing right off a DC-10."

Maynard shrugged. "So?"

"These things happen," Ryan said. "That's what I'm getting at, Maynard. They happen."

He leaned back in his swivel chair and pulled a file from a cabinet on his right. He dropped it onto his desk, tapped it with his finger, and smiled. Reassuringly, Maynard thought.

"You've got a problem," Ryan said.

"What do you mean?" Maynard asked impatiently.

"She's playing on you, boy."

"Felice?"

"I have three incidents here over the past six weeks. Inclination and opportunity."

Maynard now realized that in spite of bucking himself up with false optimism this was exactly what he'd expected to hear. A sugary feeling developed in the pit of his stomach. He struggled to control his face.

"You're sure?" he demanded.

"Like I told you before, I don't assume. She's spending time alone with a guy in a motel room. What they're doing in there, I don't try to guess. But, uh . . ."

"Okay."

"Listen, this happens to guys, their—"

"Don't give me any lectures! I don't care what happens to guys." Maynard was shouting. "Understand? I don't care. This is happening to me!"

"Okay. Just hold on. You got the call to come in from the bullpen in a game you had nothing to do with up to this point. The bases are loaded in the bottom of the ninth. But you can't fall apart. You have to make every pitch count. Because the game is on the line. So just let me finish here."

Maynard sneered. He crossed his arms tightly over his chest. Short breaths were dilating his nostrils.

"What I was saying, this happens, it blows over. It's common as white bread. Fine. But you've got problems and you've got problems."

"Talk straight, will you! For God's sake!" He wiped a hand over his clenched jaw.

"You know the guy."

Maynard felt as if he were on an elevator that had suddenly dropped half a floor. Oh, shit. Oh, no. No. First the primal insult—his wife ravaged by another man. Now the far more intimate humiliation. Somebody he knew. He ticked off possible culprits in his brain.

"Sal Vincent. Two eighty-two Ridgewood Drive."

"What about him?"

"He's the guy."

"You mean you saw her with Sal?" Maynard fixed his mind on a gleam of hope. He even chuckled. "Is that all? We're friends, sort of friends. Sal's in business with a buddy of mine. Sure, if she ran into him, they might have had lunch, whatever. You got the wrong impression."

Ryan shook his head. "Bases loaded. Nobody out. Three-and-oh count."

Not Sal. Anybody but Sal. The detective had to be wrong, Maynard told himself. The vacuum in his gut said different. "Anything can be twisted, make it look bad."

"Hey, I'm on your side. I'm not twisting. They might have been in there planning a birthday party for you, wanted it to be a surprise." He opened the folder. "Tuesday the twelfth. She leaves the house at eleven thirty-six. Drives over toward the north side. Stops at a Rexall on Plymouth. Uses the phone there. Then she drives to a motel on Norton. She's inside two hours and twelve minutes. They leave together."

"What do you mean, together?" Maynard demanded. His mind was racing ahead. What a fool. How sickeningly obvious it had been.

"She came out, he held the door for her. They walked to the curb side by side. He's driving a blue Buick, license LMX four oh three. I followed him to the three hundred block of Clinton, which is where his office is."

"What day did you say?"

"Tuesday the twelfth."

"Son of a bitch." Maynard couldn't remember anything about the day. He would have gone to work as usual, having left Felice sleeping. He would have filled teeth as usual, pored over X rays, completed a couple of root canals, just like any other day. Meanwhile, his dear wife . . .

Suddenly he saw himself reflected in a darkened mirror. The whole thing was unreal. Every incident was an eerie reflection of itself. Felice kissing him when he arrived home became a spit in his face. Sal's infectious laugh turned to a mocking jeer. Maynard's own cockiness over his new bride, a pathetic obtuseness.

"That was about three weeks ago. Then a week later, a Wednesday this time, I picked her up, she took a circuitous route to the same place. This time I made him going in. They were inside for an hour and five minutes. They left separately, ten minutes apart."

Only two weeks ago, Maynard thought. He struggled. He could grasp the idea of the Felice of two weeks ago, that past Felice, maybe doing something like this. What roared down on his consciousness like a Mack truck was the thought that now, that the real, this-minute, flesh-and-blood Felice, could be, right now, right this second, behind drawn shades in a cheap motel.

He fought against a sense of unreality. This was not

some soap opera. This was his own goddamn life they were discussing. Felice. Beautiful, horrible Felice.

"Anything else?" he croaked.

Ryan gave him more details. "It's all in the report. As I say, I did some preliminary on him, got you a copy of his driver's license. But you know all the basics—address, place of business, all—already. Like I say, you've got a problem."

"Oh, I've got a problem. Oh."

"Of course, the big question now, what are you going to do?"

"Yeah, sure. Sure." Maynard's hands were gripping his elbows. He knew he was trying to keep himself from shaking and he knew why. Anger had hold of his mind, but his body was afraid. Of what? The way the bottom had suddenly fallen out of his life? How Felice might throw this in his face?

"See, you're entering into unexplored territory, my friend. Wild frontier. I've been there, I told you."

"Hey, don't tell me you know what I'm feeling. You don't know! You don't have any idea! So don't God damn start telling me. This is *my* problem."

"Okay, okay. You just got kicked in the jewels. Hard. With a steel-toed shoe. It hurts like hell. That hurt gets into your thinking."

"I need some time just to— Listen, you don't think there might be a chance you got it wrong, do you? That she wasn't—no that's stupid." For a fiery instant Maynard thought he was going to lose control. He pressed his tongue against the roof of his mouth. He squeezed his eyes shut, scratching his forehead to hide the moisture in them.

"I've been around this stuff," Ryan said. "It's my bread and butter. I'd be lying if I said I could give you an easy answer. But I can lay out the options for you, talk it over, maybe help you implement, once you decide."

"What options are you talking about? I don't have any options." Maynard felt himself physically shrinking.

"Sure you do. Divorce, for one. Go that route, you

want the best terms. You'd be surprised how often a guy finds out his wife's cheating on him, ends up *he's* the one gets fucked over in the proceedings."

"I'm not sure I want a divorce. That's something for down the road." No, he couldn't face a divorce. That would mean he'd have to expose himself. He'd have to go to his friends, to each one of them, and tell them. He imagined the world ringing with laughter.

"Some guys," Ryan went on, "they'd go home, beat the living Jesus out of her. You don't seem like the type to me, though I'm sure you're capable of it, you had to."

Maynard looked down at the way his hands were balled into fists. Beat her? He rolled the idea on his tongue. He'd beat her until— No, that wasn't in him.

"Not her," he said.

"But him? That what you're thinking? Better weigh that one. Guys in your boat get self-destructive. Probably some kind of psychology behind it, I don't know. But you want to avoid something stupid."

"I want to get even. Understand? I have to! I don't know what I want."

"Okay, get even. But what's the best way? What means are at your disposal? Financial? Reputation? You start flinging mud, how do you keep it from getting on you?"

Sal's smile, his silly mustache, the way he'd flash a quick wink—the images loomed now in Maynard's mind. "I'd like to—to destroy him."

"Sure you would. Her, you can administer the Chinese water torture in the home there. Him, he's a son of a bitch scum bastard and you're going to put it to him. How?"

"Simple," Maynard declared. "I'll just go—I'm not afraid of him. I'll go and have it out."

"With what? Fists? Lawn mowers? Bicycle pumps? Think about this. Want my advice, the first thing you do, do nothing."

"Let them continue? Are you nuts? Let my wife continue to—to associate with that bastard?"

"Something you've got to deal with right now, Maynard. They want to keep doing it, this is a free country.

Nothing I can do, you can do gonna stop them. Consenting adults, good night."

"No, no, no, no. Not my wife." To think that they could do it while he knew it was happening—no. No, sir.

"What happens, a guy in your position, he's pissed, he runs right home—I've seen this—lays it on the wife, right? She comes back with her excuses, her explanations, her accusations. Claims *he's* been screwing around—which is probably true, who's a saint? He's on the defensive all of a sudden. He doesn't know whether to believe what I've documented—*documented* for him—or not. He blows his wad, he's got nothing to show for it."

"I knew it was going on, something like this. I knew it, I really did."

"You want what?"

"To get him out of the picture, get even with him."

"No, more. You want to fuck him over. Not get even. The hell with even. He should have left you alone, left alone what was yours. He didn't. Now you're gonna make him wish he did. You're gonna make him sorry his pecker ever stood up and looked around when he saw your wife."

"How?"

"That's what we have to find out. We have to search out his weak point. We find the chink in his armor, and we drive home the blade. Everybody's got an Achilles tendon, believe me."

"He's a God damn Judas."

"Tell you something, Maynard? Talking about thirty pieces of silver? Who hasn't got his price? Maybe it's a woman, it often is. Maybe it's a chance to be boss man. Maybe it's a fat pension. Maybe it's a needle full of dope. You show me a human being on this earth who won't give the Judas kiss once you find what it is, I'll shit. All you can do, he fucked you, you fuck him back, only harder."

"I want him to suffer."

"Look for his weak link."

"How?"

"I'll tell you, there's something very funny about this guy Sal Vincent. I get a feeling. I get a very distinct feeling."

20

As he walked across the carpeting of the posh restaurant, Ted self-consciously tugged at his cuff links. They were a gift from Sal, big gold-and-onyx affairs with a flash of diamond chips. Ted would never have picked out anything so prominent, so gaudy. Yet now he appreciated the way they complemented the understatement of his new smoke-gray suit. He felt he understood the importance of little flourishes like this when you were headed into the kind of high-power negotiations that would take place at the luncheon he was about to attend.

The noise of the diners drifted up toward the high ceiling, where it became lost among the chandeliers and friezes. The waiter indicated a corner table near the window. Ted held out his hand and cranked up his smile as he approached.

One of the three men rose and greeted him. He introduced the others. Ted stared into each face in turn.

They all wore crisp white shirts, quietly expensive suits.

Ted joined them in a drink. They talked the small talk that skirts the edge of real business. They mentioned mutual acquaintances, one of whom Ted had known for years, another he'd met recently through Sal. They touched on politics, on some of the new building that was going on in the city, on the mess they were making putting in a freeway on the east side of town. They made comments on the national economy, on a graft scandal that had been in the news lately.

They ordered another drink before the waiter brought the menus. Ted felt that his personality had the same sparkle as his cuff links. He'd long ago acquired the knack of quickly making himself at ease with strangers. He used a deft combination of humor and earnestness, congenial banter and innocuous opinions, anecdotes and gossip. If well aimed it worked on these moneymen the same way it did on your average home buyer.

While they considered their choices for lunch, Ted took in the carved woodwork, the real plate silver, the bone china dinnerware, the crystal glasses. It seemed like only yesterday that lunch meant a corned beef on rye at his desk at Winner Realty or a club sandwich at the Ramada Inn.

The men themselves were of the same material—their hair silver, their faces mahogany, their fingernails fine china. Each had a resonant baritone voice and small banker's eyes that grasped at nothing but took in everything.

During the meal, the conversation moved on to some particulars of the real estate business. Then over coffee and cognac Ted presented the details of his proposal. He couched their need for financing in terms that made it seem like an opportunity. He was surprised himself at how favorable he made the deal sound. He trembled inwardly at the amount of debt they would have to add to what they already owed in order to keep the Golden Age project flying.

More brandies. He had to watch himself. Drinking had the potential to induce a crucial misstep.

He tried to read their body language, the meaning of the tiny cough, the tilted head, the tugged earlobe. Their comments were amiable but noncommittal.

But when he finished he thought he detected from their questions that he'd scored big. One even asked him about future projects, his ideas for expanding the Golden Age concept, taking it statewide. Ted said they'd already done some blue-sky work in that direction.

They ended the luncheon on a congenial note. Ted told them he'd look forward to their response. They assured him that he'd be hearing from them very soon.

Driving back to the office, he was anxious to let Sal know. In spite of the fact that Lujak's machinations at city hall had enabled them to move the Golden Age project along, they still weren't out of the woods. Interest payments were soaking up Reed-Vincent's entire cash flow and more. They'd bargained away a good portion of the future profits from the development just to raise the necessary capital. They were working without a net, Sal explained, and that's the way it should be.

Though Sal had never satisfied Ted's curiosity about what had gone down in Vegas, in the end the experience had brought them closer. They'd both exposed something of themselves out there: Ted his foolishness, Sal his fear. Sal's momentary loss of composure uncovered a side of him that Ted had long wondered about, a fallible, frightened, human side. Sal made up for the shortened trip by giving him the cuff links, which became an emblem of their deeper friendship.

Back in the office, Ted threw Margot a boyish grin and a thumbs-up gesture. She indicated with her head the man waiting on the couch by the door.

His blazer wasn't cut quite big enough for his shoulders. His flesh, as if it resisted confinement in his clothing, burst from his collar and sleeves in the form of an enormous red face and big meaty hands.

"Reed? We had an appointment, remember?"

Ted glanced at Margot.

"Mr. Ernst," she said. "Two thirty."

Ted checked his watch.

"I'm sorry I kept you waiting. I was detained."

"Oh, you're sorry. You look real sorry."

"What was this about? I can't remember."

"It's something *you* want to talk about."

"I don't understand. What is?"

"You want me to just lay it out for you right here?"

"Come into my office. Margot, if Bannister calls, tell him we got the go-ahead on the lease extensions, he just has to sign the amendment. And Craig should be here"— he glanced at his watch again—"any minute. Tell him I'll be right with him. You can give him the Essex file to look over while he waits. Shouldn't be long."

She smiled her understanding.

Ted led the man into his office.

"So, Mr. Ernst . . ." He sorted through some messages that Margot had left on his desk.

"You're building that old folks home on Route 83, aren't you?"

"That's right. We call it a seniors' community, but—"

"Big project. Lotta bucks."

Ted examined the man more closely. Squinting his eyes slightly against the glare, Ernst resembled a football lineman.

"What exactly is your business? I don't think you mentioned it."

"Me? I'm a consultant."

"Oh, that's right. I don't know as we need any consultants at the moment. If you want to leave a card, we can—"

"You're new in the business, aren't you?"

"I've been in real estate for thirteen years."

"Not at this level, though, am I right? You've recently moved up, you're trying to play the game with the big boys."

"What are you getting at?"

"I told you. I'm offering you a service that *you* want, that you *need*. Labor relations consultant. I can help out a firm like yours because I understand the dough riding on

207

this deal. I understand the meaning of time, how even one day's delay can pinch."

"But I don't see that we have any labor problems. Why would we need a consultant?"

"You don't have any problems—now. But you've got Local 1142 out there. You've got District Council 50. And you're going to have to be dealing with Local 14, putting in your electric. Problems could develop any time. So problems develop, problems could be straightened out, you say. Maybe problems could. But problems could also take time to straighten out. That's what I'm telling you. Meanwhile, you're bleeding."

"I don't see any reason to anticipate trouble."

"People don't see any reason to take out health insurance, they're not sick. Not today. Tomorrow you come down with a massive something and you're flat on your back wishing to God you had insurance."

"I see your point, but I think we're capable of conducting any necessary negotiations ourselves."

The man shook his head. "I don't think so. I don't think you understand what's involved here. I have contacts. You don't. I've built up markers with guys over the years. This labor relations racket, it's all give and take, very complex. You try to jump in after they're acting against you, you haven't got the time to make the right connections."

Ted measured a pencil with his fingers, tapped it on his desk. They really come out of the woodwork when they smell money, he thought.

Ernst continued, "See, there's all kinds of ins and outs to dealing with these people. There's work rules. Well, there's work rules and there's work rules. Understand? Some of them the shop stewards can ignore. Or they can not ignore. There's adjustments to the standard rates. There's supplementary payments, gratuities that always have to be paid. Off the books. Like I said, it gets very complex."

"Maybe we'll just wait and see what kinds of demands they make before we decide what to do here."

"Maybe you'd like to, but these union leaders are

funny. They like to talk to somebody they know. You need a rabbi to help you out. Me. I back you up. They start to give you a hard time, I can assure you you're going to want to be able to say, I'm with Ernst, talk to Ernst, Ernst is my man."

"Well, that time comes—"

"Time comes, it'll be too late."

"I said, when the time comes I'll deal with it. I won't need any back-alley go-between to tell me I have to start making supplementary payments under the counter in order to do business."

Ernst's eyes followed an imaginary fly around the room for a moment. Then he said, "I don't think you fully appreciate what I've been telling you. This is not a take-or-leave sort of a thing. This is a take sort of a thing. There's no time comes, there's no if. Time is now. You want trouble or you want to avoid trouble? I'm no go-between. I'm the man. Get it?"

Ted slowly sat upright. His fists were clenched at the edge of his desk. He felt himself rise up off his chair even though he remained seated. His face lit up with hydraulic pressure.

"Now you listen to me, you son of a bitch," he said very precisely. "You're not coming in here and telling me how to run my business. You think I'm going to roll over and beg, you're crazy. I'll take this whole goddamn project nonunion and you and your labor-hall buddies can go for a ride. Goddamn unions have ruined this country with their gimme, gimme, gimme and I say the hell with them." He almost stopped short when he heard this opinion, his father's, coming from his mouth.

"Why, you—"

"No, you've done your talking. You listen to me. You've already said enough right here for me to take to the D.A. and get an extortion case going. You want to make any more threats or say any more about gratuities or supplementary payments, go right ahead, because it's coming right back in your face, buddy!" He was pointing his finger at the man and shouting.

Ernst managed his first smile as he stood. He cradled his massive right hand in his left and massaged it.

"One thing I learned a long time ago in this business," he said. "Start pushing, know *who* you're pushing, because they might push back. I suggest you talk to your silent partner about this matter, Mr. Reed. He knows me very well. He'll tell you all about me."

"The door's right behind you."

"Ask him about Ernst. Okay?"

"Get out."

"See you, sucker."

Mike Ryan sat in his gray Corolla staring at the Stardust Motel. The old Stardust, Christ almighty. How many times had he sat outside here while some mark he was tailing took advantage of the accoutrements inside? How many times had he testified about those accoutrements in court?

Blue movies are indeed available, your honor. Movies depicting actual, graphic, and promiscuous sexual activity. There are indeed mirrors attached to the ceiling. Yes, the Stardust offers water beds. And video cameras are available for rental. And, your honor, a sign prominently displayed on the structure's exterior advertises quote day-rates unquote.

So the guy was getting a lunch-hour quickie. Big deal. Him and how many thousand other guys in the city? Or if they weren't, wished they were. And Barker's wife was hot merchandise, yes sir doggie. How many guys out there whacking off to the weather every night?

Not that it was any picnic tailing him. As soon as he picked him up, Mike made out this Vincent guy was tail-conscious. Mike could tell by the way he drove—the immediate double-back, the lane changes.

He hadn't actually made Mike. Nobody could make Mike on a tail, even in broad daylight. If the guy's tail-conscious, you pull in front of him. He turns off, let him go. Wait. He'll do his little maneuver, decide he's clean, come back around again. You start off in front and stay there. Takes a close eye on the rearview, but for a guy with Mike's experience, it's playtime.

But why tail-conscious? Of course, the broad could explain it. If you're bopping somebody's wife, you tend to keep your eyes open. But there was a lot more to it. He was just that much too wary, too alert. The eyes in the back of Sal's head were just one piece of a puzzle that Mike was determined to solve.

Mike's intuition was working overtime on this one. Where there was smoke there was fire, and this Sal was all smoke. He was a wrong son of a bitch. Mike was beginning to see the pattern and it was adding up to something big.

People knew the man. They connected him with Lard Lujak. They connected him with this other guy. He hadn't been in town for very long, but so many people knew him, people on the inside. Knew him, but didn't know him.

And his background. Just the background alone, Mike would have known he was a ringer.

It was supposed to be spring, but winter still had its nails dug in. A rain dirty with sleet lashed intermittently. A good day. Mike liked gray days. Sunshine made him edgy. The way the light would sometimes catch a gum wrapper or a discarded beer can and flash at his face gave him a funny feeling, an ill feeling. Gray days you could blend in.

Gray days you didn't have colors to worry about. Mike was always afraid some smart-ass lawyer would trip him up, ask him wasn't it true he was color blind. He wasn't, obviously, but he'd taken a test when he was on the force and they told him he was. Some kind of a trick. Color blind? He could see colors. Colors annoyed him. Like, some of the city's fire trucks were painted a kind of lime green, almost yellow. It was a poisonous color and it pained Mike to see them. Or the vivid orange-red some women smeared on their mouths. Supposed to be chic, it was sick.

So he liked gray days when colors were muted. Best of all were nights. At night, life was all black-and-white, like an old movie. That's when he felt most comfortable, most himself.

This guy was pulling the long scam, no question about it. It irked Mike that he couldn't see the angle. This business, the Golden Age Estates racket, was it a pyramid scheme? Set up a corporation then bust it out? Were they going to gouge the old folks?

Mike settled down to wait. He was used to waiting. His nondescript car was much more worn on the inside than on the outside. The backseat was piled with old maps, Coke cans, hamburger wrappers. He had some newspapers, he could hold them up and pretend to read. Of course, you couldn't actually read on surveillance. Glance away from a doorway for a second and you could end up waiting for six hours for your man to come out of a place he'd already left.

All you needed for this job, he often told himself, was a leather bladder and an infinite capacity for boredom. As the years went by, if his bladder wasn't what it had been—he'd taken to carrying a mason jar under the front seat—he'd become more of an alligator than ever when it came to boredom. He could sit inconspicuously in his car for three, four hours. At times he felt that he could really make himself invisible. He would ride up in an elevator with somebody he was tailing, somebody he'd been on for three weeks, and they wouldn't see a thing.

During the waiting, Mike would make up stories about himself. He was never really bored. He was too busy being everything. Ever since he was a kid, he'd known that he was going to be everything someday. A cop, he'd done that. Fireman, doctor—those were yet to come. Nothing would pass him by in this life. Someday he'd maybe be a real estate developer giving a hot redhead a workout on a spring afternoon, a real estate developer with a shady past.

The long scam. It was something he'd be good at himself, Mike figured. The scam that went on for years while you worked your way inside, became pals with some millionaire. He'd be good at that kind of playacting. Hell, he should try it. The old confidence game. He'd be so slick, they'd never know they'd been fleeced. He could drag it out endlessly, year after year.

What exactly was it about this Vincent? Why did Mike feel, tailing this guy, that he was back on the force? That he was on to something major? No other tail, no other case he'd been on had lit up his instincts in the same way.

Mike fastened his attention on the door to room 17N. They were coming out.

21

"R_{eady, Mr. Vincent?"}

"Burn it by me if you can."

"Okay."

Robbie was pitching from the stretch. There were runners on base. The crowds in the stadium were ominously quiet.

He brought his hands together and swiveled his head back and forth, his face a deadpan of concentration. He kicked his leg high and hurled the ball. It sailed up and in. Sal leaned back and tried to chop at it. He squirted a dribbler wide of the first base line.

"Strike!" Robbie called.

A chorus of "come on" sounded from the field, where Josh and Mario, Brian, and Ted were all waiting with their mitts on.

"Okay, it's two out and the bases loaded and we're leading by one run in the bottom of the ninth and it's a full count and their best hitter is at the plate," Robbie explained.

"Just pitch it across, will you!"

"Give him something he can hit, Robbie."

Robbie rubbed the ball and went through his ritual again. He lobbed one over the plate. Sal golfed it. It sailed high into the evening sky. Josh backpedaled. He had time, but he couldn't decide where the ball would land. He stretched his hand back over his head. The ball just nicked his glove and fell to the grass.

"Two hands for beginners, Reed!" Brian scoffed.

"That error cost us the game, Josh," Robbie said. "I hope you realize that. That was a costly error. That error will come back to haunt us."

Sal knocked out a bouncer and Mario leaped to put a glove on it but couldn't handle it. Ted told him it was a nice try.

"You're letting the ball play you," Sal yelled to him. "See?"

"I should have charged it, right Dad?" Mario answered.

"Right."

"You should have put it on your credit card, Vincent," Brian cracked.

Sal took a couple of practice swings, putting his weight behind the bat. It felt good. How many times had he played ball since the Corsi thing? Three or four times in the park? A few games of catch on their lawn in Staten Island? A father should get out with his boy more often. Mario— maybe the broad at school was right, he needed more attention. Besides, the kid could have talent.

Christ, the best life you could have, pro athlete. Money, women, everything you want. And all you do is play a game. People get down on their knees to you just because of the way you swing the bat. Just because you're one of a million who has the eye, the reflexes.

Baseball always makes you think of Corsi. Your first, the one you made your bones on. Like guys think of the first lay they had. You remember.

215

Sal got some good wood on a ball and lofted it over everyone's head.

"Home run!" Mario called. "Beautiful, Dad!" Sal acknowledged the cheer with his chin.

It's midsummer when the Corsi thing happens. Sal remembered it being perpetually midsummer in those days. Years of sun and sweat and dirt and the pungent city smells.

After you talk to Paulie, you're feeling seven feet tall. The streets are more alive than ever. Your first. You're going to make your bones on this one. Your chance to get on the inside permanent. You're twenty-four, you're on top of the world.

You go over to see Eddie Lazarro. He's a sleepy guy. Any time, day or night, his mother's likely to have to pull him out of bed. And he wears this perpetual grin as if he's imagining getting laid all the time. Lazy-eyed, but not dull-brained. The man never gets flustered. You have to have a yes or no before you explain the who, where, and why to him. Eddie yawns and says sure.

So you tell him the plan and he laughs. Baseball. Of course.

That night you're in the field while Eddie knocks you flies with a softball. Eddie once played on one of the best fast-pitch teams in South Brooklyn and can really whack the ball. You never had time for sports, but you have the easy grace of a natural athlete. You're playing in a field that backs up to Corsi's garage.

The more balls you catch, the more you worry that it will be too dark when Corsi comes out. Two guys playing ball, that's the way you move close to him, get to him when his guard's down. You even parked around the corner and rode over on bicycles in case Corsi or his man is looking out the window when you arrive—bikes would look that much better. But not if it were too dark.

Just as the sky's exhaling the last of its daylight, the steel door opens and a broad man in a polo shirt and seersucker jacket comes out. You know him as Rasp Torrio,

216

Corsi's bodyguard and driver. You know he carries a .45 gun under his arm.

"Hit one here, Mr. Vincent! Another high one."

Sal responded to Josh's request with a towering pop-up in foul territory.

Corsi comes out a second after Torrio. He has a flagrant beer belly, a well-fed nose, and basset-hound pouches under his eyes. They both start walking toward a gray Lincoln Continental.

Hum, babe! you call. It's your signal.

Eddie unleashes a long drive. The ball sails over your head as you sprint back. It bounces three times—you still remember those three bounces—and bangs into the side of the town car just as Torrio and Corsi reach it.

Hey! Torrio says.

Corsi leans to get an angle on the light and see if the ball made a dent in his fender.

Sorry, mister, you say.

There's something about a ball, something attractive. You're depending on that. People topple over rows of seats to grab a foul at a ball game. Torrio steps over to where it's come to rest on the crushed stone. He bends to pick it up. Maybe he's going to toss it back. Maybe he intends to fling it away in anger.

He never gets a chance to do either. You pull your revolver from a holster at the small of your back and smack a bullet into the stocky man's spine. He pitches forward, his face in the stones. It only takes a second. The shot is already evaporating in the still air.

You know you're in now. You feel you've burst through a transparent barrier. You're in a world with different rules, different signals, a different charge to life.

"Nice one, Ted baby!" Sal shouted. Ted has caught a line drive over his shoulder and on the run.

Corsi's hand is still on the spot where the ball hit, as if he would soothe the car's hurt. Stupid fuck, you think. You walk toward the car.

Corsi straightens, looks over at his companion, who's

in the position of a person listening for a distant train approaching on a rail line. Corsi holds his hands out as if testing to see if it's raining.

You step closer. The gun jumps three times in your hand. Three roses open on Corsi's chest. Corsi sighs. His face prunes up in a way that reminds you of the pictures of Oswald getting shot. Corsi folds his arms as if he were holding a baby. You think of yourself as a boxer. You have your man on the ropes. Corsi's leaning against the car. As you measure for the knockout punch, he slides to the ground.

Here the ref should jump in, waving his arms. But, you think, you can't be saved by the bell in this game. You stand directly over your man. You bend down and nestle the barrel of the pistol in his ear.

The pitch came right across the plate. Sal swung hard. The ball flew straight back at Robbie on the mound. The boy had no time even to begin to react. The ball hit him in the face with a dull thud.

Robbie dropped down onto his side, his hands clutching his face, blood streaming through his fingers.

Sal ran to him. He felt an unfamiliar helplessness, a touch of panic. He didn't know what to do. He stared at the blood. He started to bend down, hesitated.

"Okay, boy," he said, groping for a word. "Don't— It's just a bloody nose. I didn't mean—"

The air was terribly still. So much blood.

The other boys ran up. They watched with open mouths.

Ted was slower to come in from left field. He knelt and took his son in his arms and soothed the heaving sobs. He gently pried the fingers away and examined Robbie's eyes and mouth.

"I know it hurts, son."

He wiped the boy's bleeding nose with his handkerchief.

"It's all right, Robbie. It's one of those things. You're okay. Aren't you, boy?"

"Why's he crying then, Dad?" Josh asked.

"Because it hurts, that's why. He has a right to cry. Come on, we'll get him home, put some ice on it."

"He's going to be all right, isn't he?" Sal asked.

"He'll have a shiner for a few days, but he'll be fine."

"I really didn't mean to—"

Ted just looked at him.

Sal felt an urge to explain, to avoid blame for the accident. Ridiculous, but he couldn't escape the feeling.

For all these years, Sal had been sure about that night. It wasn't a question of right or wrong. Who had the balls? Who had the brains to survive? Who was willing to gaze on the brutality of life without blinking? You did a piece of work. You were somebody who could pull a trigger.

Now, for the first time, it didn't seem quite so clear to him. Somehow it had become tangled up with the boy's pain and it didn't seem at all clear to him. For some reason, it set him to thinking. And that kind of thinking, Sal knew, could be very dangerous.

22

The little office, its window-less walls and institutional decor, had not changed, but Sal had changed. He'd been up here a dozen times or more, straightening out details of documentation, picking up mail that had been forwarded from the drop box.

His contempt for Deputy Schimanski had gradually given way to a feeling that verged on friendship. Their talks sometimes lasted several hours. Schimanski was the only person other than Gina who knew his real identity.

This knowledge became a bond. Sal joked about going to Father Schimanski for confession. In fact, the sensation strangely resembled the one he remembered from his first-communion days. Schimanski became the neutral ear listening to his complaints and his hopes, to the memories that had infiltrated his consciousness. Interested, but unjudging. Absolution guaranteed.

Schimanski shared certain qualities with Ted. It had

taken Sal a long time to recognize them, to distinguish a principle from a pose, to realize that honesty need not be stupidity.

They talked about their families. Schimanski had a son. The boy had been born with a defect, both legs malformed. To walk unsupported would be a goal that he could hope to conquer, maybe, by the age of twelve. Hearing about the boy made Sal think in a new way about Mario.

The wariness that remained between them was the comfortable clothing with which they were both familiar, but it covered a genuine rapport. Sal always told the latest Polish joke he'd heard, and Schimanski was always able to top it with one of his own.

"Haven't seen you in a while, Sal."

"I've been busting my hump."

"How's the business going?"

"We have a million loose ends hanging. One of them gets caught, it's going to pull us neck-first into the grinder. I mean, I'm used to hustling, but this business shit is wearing me down."

"Something's come up," the deputy said.

"I figured, the way you called."

"I doubt you saw it, the local papers never picked it up, but Paul Amato was released from jail."

"When?"

"End of last week."

Sal stroked his pursed lips.

"So here's to Paulie," he said. "Jesus only rose from the dead. Paulie burns two twenty-five-to-life terms in—what is it?—eleven months. What did he do, bribe the president?"

"He petitioned for a new trial. His lawyers pushed it through on a technicality. Seems Amato had two Chryslers, a LeBaron, and a New Yorker. They got the order for the New Yorker, to wire it, but they put the wire in the LeBaron by mistake. That was enough to have the case thrown out on appeal. The judge had to give him bail until they could set up a new trial."

"Paulie's back on the street," Sal said. "Isn't that a kick in the ass?"

"I should warn you, you'll probably have to go back to testify again."

"Like hell."

"It's in the agreement."

"What agreement?"

"Check the fine print."

"Hey, Schimansk, you're catching me on the fine print? I testified. I told my story in court. If you guys can't hold on to the man, don't look at me."

"Nobody likes it."

"If I was running your operation, I wouldn't have any of these screw-ups. I would have put Paulie beyond any technicality you can think up. It's because you guys have no incentive. Way I came up, you played your hand wrong, you lost the pot, that was it, you didn't have any chance to say oops."

"But if we played by your rules, you'd have gone down yourself. No deals, no protection, just a short good-bye."

"You'd have to catch me first."

"The trial won't be for another six months, probably. When you go back, you'll be given the same kind of around-the-clock protection you received last time."

"You think Paulie's going to wait? He knows he only has one way out. I don't show up at this trial, he's free. Think a person can't be found? As long as Paulie was in Atlanta, okay. Guys aren't going to knock themselves out. Maybe it's not so bad for them, Paulie stays in Atlanta. But as soon as he's out, he's going to be working twenty-five hours a day to find my ass. And he will. Somehow, he will. I'll tell you something else, a couple times this last week I got the feeling somebody was shadowing me."

Sal had a glimpse of Amato's face as it appeared during the trial. Everybody said about Paulie, you can't tell which eye is real. It was true. If you didn't know, they both looked equally glassy, equally lifeless. You could never be sure whether he was staring at you or not. And the way his mouth rippled with contempt, with malice. Now the face loomed with new menace. Now the eyes gleamed in his memory.

He remembered the face from another time, when Paulie ordered Sal to kill Frank DeGarmo.

Paulie had no closer friend than Big Frank DeGarmo. They'd come up together in the Genovese thing. They'd been through the Profaci wars and a hundred other struggles. They'd stood up for each other's kids at confirmation. They spent their Christmas dinners together.

When Paulie had become boss, he made Frank his underboss. Frank controlled the garment district, all the shylocking and gambling and hijacking. He had big operations in Jersey, in Atlantic City, and in half a dozen small cities up the Hudson Valley.

Big Frank still paid Paulie tribute, tokens of respect for Paulie's position. But Frank was building. He was expanding his range and breaking more and more from Paulie's control. Dom Petrello, one of Frank's button men, had taken off an electronics warehouse that Paulie's people had been casing for a week. Without permission, without approval. Frank was on the verge of becoming too big for Paulie, of forging an organization that Paulie would have to think twice about challenging.

But this was not like the Corsi thing, stamping out somebody who was giving him a hard time. DeGarmo was a made man himself. He was a man who knew the same secrets as Paulie. He was a man well versed in death, a man of substance.

He was also cautious by nature. He lived in a big estate in Westchester protected by walls and dogs and razor wire. He traveled in a caravan. He only appeared at places he was positive were secure. He was always surrounded by a squadron of bodyguards who knew their business.

Paulie's face was sadder than usual when he called Sal in that day. Sad, but determined. This man, his friend, had to be eliminated. He's been like a brother, but that is all the more reason.

Sal was surprised. Big Frank was a man whose reputation he'd known since boyhood. That Paulie could coolly order him murdered, without a word of warning, without a chance to redeem himself, showed Sal a new depth to Paulie's ruthlessness.

At first, Paulie had interpreted Sal's surprise as a reservation.

No, Sal said. *I can handle Big Frank.*

Who do you want on the job? Take anybody.

I'll do it alone.

Alone. At the time, he felt as if he could have fought the Russian army alone. He was at the peak. Point to a man and that man was dead.

Paulie picked up on the way Sal was looking at him. His instinct, he said, was to give Frank a chance. Kill Petrello and the other two involved in the robbery, call Frank in and show him their heads. That would be enough to teach most guys.

But in the inferno, Paulie said, you can't let up. You can't hold back. You have to be hard at your core to pass through the valley of fire. And if you let sentiment in, you'll slip and perish.

Sal caught up to Big Frank DeGarmo in a steam room.

"You say they'll come looking, that they'll find you," Schimanski said. "But from what I heard, they won't have to look too hard."

"How do you mean?"

"Vegas."

"You've been reading my mail."

"Word gets around in this town, Sal."

"What's wrong with Vegas?"

"I told you, the protection's only good as long as you stay out of the danger areas. You were Amato's proxy in Vegas at one time. You know people there, you're definitely known by them."

"I just went out there to clear my head."

"Clear your head."

"I needed to limber up my reflexes. This city, I'm growing goddamn cobwebs in my brain dealing with these people. I needed a taste of action. Call it a fix. I needed it."

"What happened?"

"Nothing."

"Let me tell you," Schimanski said. "You ran into some pit boss or some dealer or some hard guy. And they said, Sal Veronica, of all people. Or, better yet, a woman, some show girl you used to have the hots for. She couldn't forget your face. She ran up and kissed you and you pleaded mistaken identity and she created a scene right there in the lobby of your hotel. Or did you deliberately get in touch with somebody, somebody you thought you could trust?"

Could trust. Sal knew he didn't have to worry about Jimmy Dee. Jimmy had hated Paulie ever since Paulie accused him of cheating in a poker game in Vegas back in the fifties. But even Jimmy was worried when Sal contacted him. There was heat out, he said. There were too many guys with too much to gain by turning Sal up. Okay, he could arrange for the girls, no problem, but he had to warn Sal to keep his eyes open.

What really developed was worse than Schimanski's scenarios.

Nothing had happened. Nothing except that he'd run smack into Vinnie Dellacroce, Paulie's number two lieutenant. Sal was buying a cigar in the tobacco shop off the hotel lobby. The big man came in and stood beside him. Sal felt him looking. When he turned, Vinnie made him. Neither man said anything. Their faces were masks of oblivion, but their eyes exchanged voltage. Sal nodded as the clerk gave him his change. He walked out wearing leaden boots, imagining Vinnie pulling a gun and taking care of him right there. He crossed straight to the desk and told them he and Ted would be checking out immediately.

Exercise his reflexes. He'd told himself that. But you don't exercise anything with a weekend in Vegas. What the trip had really proven was how quickly you lost it when you were away from the life. Sure, he had some instincts left. He'd done the right thing. He'd made the moves needed to get him out of trouble. But he hadn't enjoyed it. He'd experienced, for the first time, some of the confusion of an ordinary citizen faced with imminent violence. He'd come close to panic.

Sal wasn't about to admit it to the man across the desk, but Vegas had served as a warning to him to avoid those danger areas. It had made him think. And thinking, he couldn't really explain to himself why he had made the trip. He was beginning to feel that he didn't need that stuff.

As if echoing his thoughts, Schimanski said, "You're actually making some progress, I think, Sal. You had to go back. Officially, I can't approve. But I think it was a good thing you did. You felt you were losing yourself and you went to Vegas to look. But you weren't there. Sal Veronica wasn't there. You could play the part, sure. Sal the Veil, back in action. But you couldn't be the part."

"Hey, babe, I just went out for a good time. I needed a break, I got one."

"Okay, you don't want to go into it. I just hope that you did catch a scare. Might have been your first. Very therapeutic."

"I have too much on my mind to worry about what's therapeutic."

"Business?"

"That's one thing. You know, when I went into that, I thought of it as something to occupy my time for a while, then I'd bust it out, move on to something else. But I have to admit, there's something gratifying to have people look up to you for yourself, for your ability, your—what would you call it—who you are, simply—and not just for your reputation, what they're afraid you might do to them."

"You change. People actually change. Hard to believe, but it's true."

"Plus, what the hell am I doing answering to somebody like Paulie Amato? I don't need that, some boss telling me what's what. Independent, that's my thing. I've been considering lately—I guess it was something Ted said—it made me wonder about Mario. What the hell do I want my son to think of when he thinks of his old man? A killer? Or a—somebody he can respect?"

226

"You're starting to care. Think you've been walking on thin ice before? Caring can make you damn vulnerable."

"I know what you mean," Sal said.

"I'm not sure you do, but you're learning."

"I'll have plenty of opportunity to learn. Gina's six months pregnant. And I'm actually—you know."

"Hey, buddy, welcome to the human race."

23

Felice came in from the bathroom drying her hair. Sal stared at the abbreviated imprint of her bathing suit. She sat cross-legged on the bed beside him.

"... was reading this book by Krishnamurti, and he says we all have to look at our fears, not try to suppress them, because that never works. It's like, your fears are you. If you push them away—he calls that creating conflict. So I'm going, what are my fears? What is it that I'm most—Hey, you aren't even listening to me."

"I'm listening." He was examining her toes. Her pretty feet ended in a friendly row of slender, pink-polished toes. She could pick up a full glass of wine with them. Once they'd pretended she was an amputee, no arms, and could only use her toes.

You don't need her. You know it's the end, time for hello, good-bye. Do it now. Don't linger. You never lingered before. You always knew when it was time to cut it off.

"You weren't listening. You never do. I'm trying to be open, trying to tell you what I *feel,* and you don't pay any attention. How are we going to build a relationship if you ignore me like that?"

"Have I been ignoring you?"

"I mean when I talk to you. These things are important, they're important to me. The gentle things are important, Sal. Everybody has things they're afraid of. Maybe even you."

"So what's the big deal? What are you getting like that for?"

"Because you don't care. You don't care about me. You're—a lot of the time, I don't think you're even there, Sal. Two people have to have some feeling if they're going to make it work. I don't get that with you."

"Certain feelings, Felice, I just don't have. I've programmed them out. That's me, who I am. Anyway, what are they good for? Sentimental isn't real."

"It *is.* Is it phony to be tender? To care about another person? The way you take me for granted, it hurts. You know it does."

"Yeah, well— Listen, you're a beautiful lady, Felice. I mean that. You're very sensitive, very open to what's happening. I've always noticed that about you. You pick up on things. I think in this case, you're really hitting on what's wrong here. I think it's obvious we're going to have to make some changes."

"Wha-at?" Her eyes widened and narrowed a couple of times as if she were trying to shake off a spell of myopia. "What do you mean, changes?"

"This has to be the end. We'll drop it cold. It's the best way, the only way."

"Sal, what the hell are you saying? The end? Just like that?"

"Clean. That's what I'm saying."

"Clean? You can't cut off feelings that way."

"You can if you have to. This is the last time. We just accept it and that's the way it will be."

"Sal, please, don't—oh. Oh, I get it. This will be our last desperate encounter. You're going on a secret mission and I'm never going to see you again. We—"

"Felice, listen."

"We have to pack a lifetime of love into this one brief moment. Is that it? It's a moment we'll both treasure for as long as we live—if we live. It'll be the fiercest, most passionate, most intense—" She made her eyes as round and excited and guileless as her breasts. But she spoke quickly, knowing he wasn't playing.

"I mean it," Sal said. "This is no joke."

"Sal, don't play around this way, okay, hon? You're scaring me."

"Look, the best thing you can find out in life, save yourself endless grief, is to know when you've reached the end of something and cut it off clean. It's a hard thing to learn, but you'll see what I mean later."

"I want to be what you want me to be, Sal. You know that. How can you treat me this way?"

"Hey, wake up. The game now is good-bye. We deal the cards and we play out the hand. We don't try to change the rules. Make it clean and nobody gets hurt."

Felice crossed her arms over her chest and tilted her head at him. "You said you loved me. Were you lying? Is that it?"

"Felice—"

"You said it!"

She fought back tears.

Sal was dressing. He pulled up his left pant leg and strapped on the pistol. The pistol had fascinated Felice at first. They'd played games with it.

"I'll kill myself," she said, hiding her mouth behind her fist.

"Go ahead."

"No! You know I won't. That would be dumb. Am I dumb, Sal? Am I dumb to you? Is that the way you see me? You always act so goddamn superior!"

Sal shook his head. "You're not dumb. It's just, you haven't learned when to let go. That's a very important lesson in life."

"Look at the philosopher."

"You have a lot of good times ahead of you. You're a girl who knows how to have a good time. You'd be surprised how rare that is. You're a sweet sweet lady and you have a beautiful mind. I'm not going to forget you. We'll be together up here. Always." He tapped his forehead.

"That's a great line. You think that up yourself?"

"Someday you'll look back and you'll be glad we broke it off at the peak. You'll thank your stars we were so lucky. We both will, knowing that for once—for once, God damn it—we had it good from start to finish, no letdown."

"We will, huh?"

"Sure." Sal was measuring his tie around his neck.

"So we'll really always be one flesh in spirit. Is that it?"

"Yeah, in memory."

"A golden memory."

"You got it."

"Like a myth almost. More real that real. Only, Sal?"

"What?"

"Can't we? Huh? Once more? Please?" She got out of bed and moved toward him. "Once more for all time?"

"I've got an appointment."

"Sal, Sal, Sal."

Clean, Sal thought. You break it clean. Not one last time. Before, you never would have allowed yourself one last time. Sal Veronica wouldn't have.

But her body pressing against him convinced him—just once more.

He didn't notice, as they plowed onto the bed, the look of cold malevolence that twisted her features.

The day was fragrant but unsettled. Rain had fallen.

Walking toward his car, Sal felt a familiar shudder as his attention ratcheted up two notches. It was a shifting of gears. He became like those numbers players he'd known in New York, for whom the world was alive with arbitrary significance. They saw an omen in every detail. The trees were unfolding sticky leaves, the air was round with the smell of mown grass, a robin was celebrating spring, but for Sal everything had an edge, a flavor of pain, of danger.

He turned the opposite way from where his car was parked. He strolled briskly up the sidewalk.

He had the gun in his hand before he half realized what he was going to do. The man was sitting in his car, reading a paper and paying no attention to Sal. Sal tapped on the glass with the barrel. When the man looked up, Sal sighted down his arm and with the trigger drew the automatic to full cock.

There was a brief frozen tableau. Sal nodded for the man to roll down the window. He did so very slowly.

"Ace boon coon?" Sal said pleasantly.

"What?"

"Tail job?"

"Look, if you're going to rob me—" Everything about the man, his small eyes, the way he wiggled his chin back and forth when he talked, said he had a major attitude.

"You fuck!" Sal snapped the short barrel down on the man's nose. "Get out, come on."

The man was out of the car. Sal grabbed him by the collar. He pushed him along the sidewalk. They walked a very fast walk down an alleyway. Behind the motel was a cinder-block garage. The ground was littered with broken glass as if it had rained from the sky. A dumpster overflowing with garbage sat close to the back of the building. Sal pushed the man into the space between the wall and the metal container. He frisked him quickly but felt no gun.

"Listen, don't—I'm just—you can't—"

"Get down on your knees. Now."

"In this muck?"

Sal made a sound and lifted the pistol. The man covered up. He murmured his assent. He knelt, sneering at the mud.

"You're going to get in a lot of trouble for this," the man said. "Believe me, you're—"

"Open up."

"What?"

"Open your mouth."

The man reluctantly opened his mouth. His eyes crossed. The barrel of Sal's pistol clicked against his teeth.

He could do it. He knew the routine, his body knew, his nerves. He could pull the trigger, twice quickly. Then simply walk slowly away, saunter. He'd registered in the motel as J. Dillinger.

But he knew, too, that he could not pull the trigger.

The man wore a light windbreaker and plaid slacks. Sal saw he'd wet himself. He removed the gun and yanked him down by his collar, forcing him onto his face.

Sal lifted the wallet from the man's back pocket. He sorted through the documents.

"Michael. Local boy. So whataya say, Mikey? Huh?" He threw the wallet down. "Paulie send you? Huh? Answer me."

"I don't know what you're talking about."

"You'd better start thinking fast what I'm talking about, or you're dead fish, Mike."

"I said I don't know—"

A hard kick up under the ribs cut him short.

"I've seen you before, Mike, so don't give me that. This is just a little gun. It makes a little noise. And it leaves you a little dead."

"No."

"Talk to me."

"I'm a private dick. My license is in my jacket pocket."

Sal pressed the gun to the man's neck. He retrieved a leather folder and looked at the paper inside the flap.

"So you've got a license. So what? License give you a right to follow me? Huh?"

"It's a free country."

"Since when?"

"Constitution, Declaration of Independence, Magna

233

Carta. Where the hell you get off knocking me around?"

"Who pulls your strings? New York? Or are you in it for yourself?"

"I do this for a living, buddy."

"I'm asking you a question, Mr. Ryan."

"Wise up, whataya think?"

"You tell me."

"A guy hired me, thinks you're porking his old lady."

"Who?"

"Who hired me? Who do you think? The broad's husband. He knows she's beating his time."

"You stink like a cop, you know that? You put in your twenty, figured you could beef up your pension as a gumshoe man?"

"That's right. And I've got plenty of friends on the force still."

"They're not going to do you any good if I see you again. Because if I do, I'm going to kill you. Understand?"

Ryan groaned at the pressure of the gun behind his ear.

Sal said, "What do you know about me?"

"Nothing. You like a piece on the side. You and every other guy I ever met."

"Nothing else?"

"You're in some kind of real estate business."

"Well, listen, Mike, you're getting a reprieve here. You could be spending this time dead. I'd suggest you enjoy the nice spring weather and tell your client you couldn't get a line on his problem. Because you're no match for me. Understand?"

"Yeah."

"Yeah what?"

"Yeah, I'm no match for you."

"I run into any grief because of you, you are going to be very sorry. You forget you ever saw me, understand?"

"Hey, I can take a hint. I don't know what your beef is, but I'm off this case as of now. I didn't see nothing."

"Good. Now I want you to cover your eyes. That's right. Keep your face in that dirt. I'll be standing here for a while, then I'll go away. If you look while I'm still here, it'll be bad for you. Wait a long time."

Sal backed up silently, replaced the pistol, and ducked around the side of the building. The taste in his mouth, as he started his car, pleased him. At the same time, he knew he'd slipped.

24

Maybe it was the weather. The sky was a deep cobalt, yellow-green buds were erupting on the trees. Ted felt good. His life was collapsing around him and, God damn, he was having a wild time.

He finished handing out yellow hard hats to the eight moneymen whom he was going to guide around the site. He'd tried subtly to discourage them from coming out here, but they'd taken it for granted that they should see the physical plant before proceeding further with the deal. Okay, so make the best of it.

Work had been shut down on the project for two weeks now. The ostensible dispute was over a violation of work rules by one of the subcontractors. But Ted knew that that was a ruse. It was a power play, pure and simple. The demands the unions were making to resume work were absurd. What they really wanted, who really had to be paid off, was impossible to find out. Reed-Vincent was facing a stone wall. He and Sal had made zero progress surmounting the obstacle. Meanwhile, the company was hemorrhaging cash at a rate that Ted didn't want to think about.

"Don't mind our friends from the third world down there," he told the bankers as they started out, indicating the band of shouting picketers by the hurricane fence. "Strictly routine. Somebody picked up a hammer who wasn't authorized, that type of thing. It's due to be settled."

"Nobody's working at the moment?" a gray-haired man asked. They stepped around a puddle left over from the downpour the night before.

"Well, you know how it goes, honoring picket lines and all. But we've got our men negotiating, it should be cleared up momentarily."

All of them stared down the hill at the strikers, who responded with a burst of garbled chanting.

"Now, if you'll just step over here," Ted said. "This will be the Keep Fit Center, this excavation. That's going to be a definite draw, all the interest in health and exercise today."

The site was a turmoil of heaped earth and gashed landscape. Some of the foundations for the Golden Age buildings had been completed, the reinforcing bars jutting in rusty rows. Weeds were already beginning to sprout in the mounds of clay.

Ted was amazed at the assurance that he heard in his voice. Reed-Vincent was absolutely on the ropes. Their accountant had made that graphic enough for them. Not only was the work stoppage killing them, but the quick revenue stream they'd anticipated from the advance sale of Golden Age properties had failed to materialize.

They hadn't kept a careful enough rein on costs, Ted told himself. Their expenses had pushed the prices of the units past the point where they were widely attractive to the elderly customers he'd targeted. He still wasn't ready to accept the possibility that his idea was simply a bad one.

"Down in this general area," he continued, "will be the Garden of Tranquillity. We envision this as a multi-faceted amenity that will allow residents to sit together in

237

small groups and pass the time—the whole community thing. And we'll set aside certain plots where they can have their own gardens, raise their dahlias, mums, what have you. Your senior today is much more hobby-oriented than he or she was in the past. And gardening, of course, is a favorite."

Two of the men asked questions as the group stared down into the muddy hollow. Ted answered with such zeal that, from a distance, his gestures resembled those of a boxer taking the attack to a weary opponent.

Down by the gate the crowd of picketers had increased in both numbers and volume. Ted knew that the unions were bringing in extra picketers from the ranks of idle hod carriers in order to make sure the operation was thoroughly disrupted. A man with a foghorn voice yelled a singsong slogan whose final phrase was ". . . you asshole!"

"You can see how the layout of the buildings, a rather unique achievement of our architect, will be conducive to fostering our principle marketing concept—community. Our spacious community meeting hall will be located here, convenient even to those in wheelchairs, a true town-square sort of idea."

A scrubbed young man with powder blue eyes raised a question about a particular aspect of their cost projections. He annoyed Ted. Ted was trying to sell them on the concept. He was doing a damn good job of it. He didn't need anybody coming at him with these negatives. He brushed the issue aside with a few smiling words.

Ted hadn't been sleeping well lately. The business had his nerves in a jangle. Too much coffee, too many thoughts pulsing through his brain. Yet as the situation moved relentlessly toward a crisis, he felt an odd kind of manic vigor. It was a shaky feeling, but exhilarating. The blare of this primary predicament drowned out the whispers of his usual concerns. He wondered why he'd ever given them so much weight.

"What I want you to focus on, gentlemen, as you look over this site, is the guiding principle, the value that informs the whole Golden Age Estates project. I'm talking about dignity."

Accompanied by cadenced shouting, the union men were pounding their picket signs against the fence and against several pieces of construction machinery parked nearby.

"Dignity. The absolute worth of the human being. The idea that old age can be an oasis in life, not a desert. That a residence can be a true home, not a warehouse. The bottom line is community, not isolation. Inclusion, not abandonment. The bottom line is a flower on the breakfast table every morning, a smile from our staff, companionship, warmth, dignity."

He was hitting it just right. He went on a little longer softening them up, then drove home the kicker.

"And gentlemen," he said after a pause. "Just look at the demographics. America is getting old."

Adversity brings out the best in us, Ted thought. He socked them with numbers and statistics, with profit projections and return-on-investment rates that he knew in his bones were winning them over in spite of the desolate, essentially abandoned work site. That was selling. Anybody could sell a sure thing. It took a pro, somebody with a deep line, to push a venture as shaky as this. Ted cocked his eyebrow in just the barest hint of his deal-closing hex.

He'd made sure the moneymen came in through the rear entrance, where there were few picketers. He now walked them back to their limousines, fielding questions and winding up his pitch. He shook hands all around and sent them off with a thumbs-up salute. He walked back to the contractor's trailer in the middle of the site and picked up his briefcase and some paperwork. His own car was parked just down from the main gate.

The crowd of strikers, grown larger still, revved up its clamor as they saw him coming down the slope. Someone had apparently identified him, pointed him out not only as the boss who was unjustly depriving the men of their livelihood, but also as an archetypical symbol of the entire ruling class.

Shouts of "Reed!" tore through the air like thrown rocks.

For a second, Ted hesitated. One of the men climbed up onto the gate, clung to the chain link with his fingers, and flung an orangutan scream through the wire. The others pressed forward.

These were the type of men that Ted had always felt intimidated by. In the back of his mind he was convinced that their lives, their vulgarities, were justified by the grit of their labor. They had an authenticity that made him uncomfortable. He felt much more at ease with the middle class, with people who, however ornery, were properly tamed. Those were people he could handle.

Yet he found himself opening the gate, walking straight into the pack of workers. He held his head up to the torrent of abuse.

Enraged by his placidity, one of the men put a hand on Ted's chest and pushed him half a step backward. The mass of arms and fists and hard bellies congealed around him.

Ted didn't run. He didn't lower his head and hurry away. He was surprised by his own audacity. He was directing a string of curses at the man who'd touched him, words that felt unfamiliar in his mouth. He was jabbing his finger at the man. He was looking in the eye one, then another of the strikers. Several of them surprised him by looking away from his gaze. His courage swelled.

A chorus of jibes and complaints broke out. Ted quieted them with the sheer force of his words.

"Don't tell me about fucking work rules!" he barked. "The goddamn unions are what got us into this mess. You people never cared one iota about quality or productivity or competitiveness. All you ever gave a damn about was the almighty paycheck. And you ended up pricing this country right out of the world markets. You screwed yourselves, don't you see that?"

The workers leaned over each other's shoulders to express their passionate disagreement. But they'd listened,

Ted thought. And not one of them could come up with a coherent reply.

Ted now moved forward, turning his back on the jeers and slanders they hurled after him. He stepped carefully to avoid showing that his knees were wobbly. He covertly reached for his handkerchief to wipe the perspiration from his brow. But he was buoyed by his small victory.

He remembered Sal saying, what can they really do to you? When it comes right down to it, what the hell can they do to you? What, in the final analysis, is there to be afraid of?

Yes sir. Things were getting out of control. But Ted was capable of getting a little out of control himself. He had balls, damn it.

The spring air seemed especially cool and sweet to him. He swung the door of his car open and was already climbing in when he realized that something was wrong. He stepped out and looked. All four tires were dead flat, slashed. Behind him, the band of strikers erupted into a howl of laughter and abuse.

"Can babies be afraid," Gina asked. "In the womb, I mean?"

"What?" Laura said. The preparations—the sandwiches, the cake, the lacy decorations—were all completed. She and Gina were waiting in Laura's living room for the guests. "I don't know. I guess there's a certain amount of controversy about what they feel, whether if you play them music they're more relaxed. Who can know, really?"

"Wouldn't that be a terrible thing, to be afraid that early? They're so helpless, they have absolutely no way to cope with it. Do you think the mother could—something in her blood could make the baby afraid?"

"No, no, I'm sure. It's very cozy in there."

"God, what would it be like? But you're right. It's after they're out that it begins. Isn't life a nightmare, Laura? You always have to be ready, that's the first thing. But when in God's name do you have time to *get* ready?"

241

"Are you sure you want to go ahead with this? You seem—"

"I'm positive. I'll be okay. After all the trouble you've gone to."

"So many of the girls were asking. They haven't seen much of you lately and they wanted to do something for you. I thought, why not a shower?"

"No, it's fantastic. It's so nice of you, of everyone. Even though I know what they think of me."

"Gina, they admire you. You're very, very popular with everyone. If you'd just— Listen, they want to be close to you. We were thinking of a surprise, everybody get together and—"

"No! Never! Laura, never surprise me. I'm—I'm clinging by my nails as it is here. I couldn't take any surprises."

"Okay, I figured. Try to relax and enjoy, all right?"

Gina shook her head. "I can't relax. I have to keep concentrating, keep focusing my attention or I'm afraid I'll dissolve. I really am. During those first weeks, when I had the sickness so bad, I thought I was going to puke myself right down the toilet. Every morning I'd be kneeling on the bathroom floor—and you know how you retch and you still feel queasy as hell? And I'd start thinking of the labor, of what I went through with Mario, eighteen hours. Christ, how I dread that. But what am I saying? You know. Twins yet."

"I do know. And I know when it's over it's over. You'll do just fine. What is it, eight weeks left?"

"Two months more. I just can't handle it. Look at me, I'm already a blimp."

"You look good."

"I have to keep a grip on myself. That's the main thing. I can't start thinking the wrong thoughts. Just make sure—" She stopped, turned her head, listening. "Where is Mario? Laura, my God—"

"Jenny's taking care of him, Gina. They're just playing next door."

"Oh, that's right. I have to not think about the dangers. Not think about Sal. See, I know too much."

"You're going to be fine."

"Laura, has Sal ever—did he ever approach you?"

"Of course not. Stop worrying. Sal loves you. Anybody can see that. I think I hear them arriving. Are you okay?"

"Yes." She touched the corner of her eye with her pinkie. "I'm ready."

The women arrived, a wave of subtle perfumes and exuberant good wishes. They babbled and cooed and whispered to Gina. They teased and soothed, consoled and reassured. Each had a hilarious horror story about her own pregnancy, always with a blessed ending.

Laura was glad to see that Gina brightened. Her neighbor had become increasingly isolated, increasingly suspicious in recent weeks. She'd begun to drive Mario to and from school. The bus, she said, was too dangerous. She kept the television blaring from morning till night. The curtains in their house were always drawn now. Lines of insomnia showed through Gina's heavy makeup.

Talk and laughter washed through the house. Her friends poured attention on Gina as if she were a sick child.

Felice was among the last to arrive. Laura had debated with herself whether to invite her or not. There had always been a little poison between Felice and Gina. But Felice was a regular member of their circle. Laura worried that it would look worse not to invite her.

Felice entered in a bubbly mood, sparkling, slightly overdressed. She slipped onto the couch beside Gina and embraced her.

"You darling, how are you? My, you're blowing up like a balloon there. Is he kicking yet—or she? Did you do the thing where you find out before? I don't think I'd want to. It would be like opening your presents before Christmas. Can I listen?"

She placed her ear against Gina's belly. "Yes, I hear it. I felt a little foot there. I really did."

"I think that was my lunch," Gina said. She tried to chuckle.

Sitting opposite them, Laura noted that some of the anxiety on Gina's face had been replaced by maternal serenity.

Felice laughed. "You're so lucky, Gina. And the little darling will be born in Cancer. Compassionate, like its daddy. I have a friend who can do the baby's chart as soon as it's born. I think this is going to be the luckiest baby in the world. Can you imagine, a brand-new life. Maynard's anxious for us to have one, but I tell him there's plenty of time. I want to concentrate on my career."

"Of course you do," Gina said.

"You know, you are so privileged," Felice said. "You really are. I'll bet half the women in this room would give anything to be having his child."

Gina's smile faded in half a dozen little steps.

"What did you say?"

Felice leaned closer to her. "He's a very, very special man. I'm sensitive to these things. I know he has a terrific aura about him. A power."

"I don't know what you mean, special," Gina said flatly.

"There are no scientific explanations for these things," Felice went on. "But some people are just magnetic. It's a kind of intuitive force they give off. I mean, how can you not notice?"

"A force?" Gina said. "What do you know about him?"

"It's a kind of spiritual thing. It's hard to explain. People are on different planes. Sal's just—" Felice's face lit up.

"Hard to explain? Why don't you start explaining?"

Laura broke in, "Gina, it's a way of talking."

"It's like an emotional resonance he has. The way he cares about people. Listens to them. He's so tender. It's obvious to everyone." Felice's grin was stony, mirthless. "Know what I mean, Gina?"

"Oh, it's obvious? Is that what it is?"

"Why don't we open the gifts now?" Laura suggested. "You feeling okay, Gina?"

Felice clicked her tongue. "You don't look well."

"It's obvious. Of course. Where is Mario?"

"He's okay, Gina," Laura said, taking her hand.

Gina jerked away. "Where is he? Spiritual? Spiritual bullshit!"

Felice looked at Laura and shrugged. Laura threw her a sharp frown.

"Where's my son?" She looked around quickly. "Who are these people?"

"They're your friends," Laura said. "Mario's all right, he's perfectly safe."

"He's not all right. Sal's special? You think he's special? We'll see who's special."

"Maybe you should lie down for a few minutes."

"Mario! Laura, where is he?"

"He's fine. Come on."

Gina's face went gray. Laura put an arm around her shoulders, spoke to her in a low tone, led her upstairs.

An embarrassed murmur rippled through the room.

"Poor thing," Felice said, shaking her head.

25

These people should be put in jail, in cages, Ted my friend," Lujak was saying. "This hoodlum element, this scum is taking over our country, am I right, Sal? Peasants, peons, they're in the driver's seat today."

Lujak's office was in the back of a seedy Victorian mansion in the oldest section of the city. A video rental shop and title office shared the building. The room had a moldy feel, with shelves of dusty books, sea-green velvet drapes, and antiquated radiators hissing against the dank day. The tropical atmosphere was reinforced by a blue parrot that sat chained to a perch and occasionally burst into the conversation with a squawk that sounded like a Chinaman saying, "Cadillac, Cadillac, Cadillac."

"This guy Ernst," Ted said. "The labor relations man, he said he knew you. Let on he was a close friend of yours. Implied you owed him a favor."

"Implied. I hate that word." Lujak, dressed in an indigo satin smoking jacket, sat behind an enormous desk. Only when he spoke did he look up from a methodical game of solitaire.

"These people are always implying," he continued. "That's all they do, imply. Twerps, assholes, five-time losers, they're coming out of the woodwork. Know why? Dope. Dope, dope, and more dope. It attracts them like flies to shit. Dope means big money in small hands. Means automatic weapons. Ten years ago a machine gun was a novelty item. Today every punk who wants one has an Uzi, a whatever."

"This has got dick to do with dope, Nelson," Sal put in.

"I'm telling you why everything's a mess, there's no order anymore, the world is overrun with creeps. They murder, they rape, they slash a man's tires. It's just the same as that poor kid, that girl, pregnant girl? Hear about that? She was hanging out with these Hell's Angels, or some bikers, not Hell's Angels—anyway they were, what else, into dope. So she was going with one of them and somebody got busted and she was pregnant at the time. Oh, I heard your wife's knitting booties, Sal. Congratulations.

"So she's pregnant and they, somebody says she was the reason this guy went down—or, I think a few of them got popped. She, they thought, turned them in. These people are animals to begin with. You get some dope into them, look out. So." He hesitated in order to transfer a black queen.

"They wanted revenge. What did these crazy fuckers do? They opened her up. Strapped her down and slit her belly with a razor. She's still awake, right? Pulled the baby out and showed it to her, then whacked it with a two-by-four. I mean, come on. And she lived. Testified against them."

"What's the point?" Sal said.

"The point is scum's taking over the earth, Sal. That's the point. Ted here, they intimidate him, I'm not surprised."

"Is this guy your friend or not?" Ted demanded. He'd

resisted making any concessions to the unions or to the men who pulled their strings. It was extortion pure and simple, he pointed out. Though Sal favored dealing with the realities of the situation, he assured Ted he was ready to back him up. Now they'd reached the point where they had no choice. Some kind of deal had to be struck or the firm would go under.

"Ernst? I know him," Lujak said.

"Well?"

"That doesn't make him my friend. And who says he had anything to do with your problems out there? Though, you tell the man to get lost, a guy like Ernst, talk about shooting off to the D.A., it strikes me a little, how you say, green?"

"What the hell's that supposed to mean?" Ted asked.

Rain was beating on the windows. Lujak took his lower lip in his fingers and wagged it thoughtfully back and forth.

"Guy with Ernst's connections, good man to have in your corner. I mean, you guys are the businessmen here, but I think I would have handled it a little differently."

The close air in the room, the smell of the radiators, the fat man's phlegmy voice, made Sal think of Frank DeGarmo in the steam room.

Big Frank DeGarmo hates to exercise. He thinks he can sweat off the pounds lounging in a Turkish bath. He hangs out there, talking with the garment-district cheeses who come every day to cleanse their pores.

Outside two of his boys are giving the once-over to everybody who enters. They nod as you pass, a towel wrapped tight around your waist.

DeGarmo greets you.

Sal, how's shots? You boys know Sal.

He introduces you to a few noses, a few potbellies, naked flabby chests.

Frank's a big man. Not just fat, like Lujak, but big bones, big shoulders, a big sweating forehead. His feet are long slabs with misshapen hammer toes, protruding nails.

A half-dozen men are sitting around, lying around on

the benches. They're all naked or draped with towels. The steam is thick. Water's running down the tile walls.

You have a silenced .22 tied to a thin cord and hanging against your balls. You undo the knot and pull your towel off, the gun wrapped inside.

You've been working out, Sal. You look in good shape, kind of shape I was in, your age. How's Paulie? Haven't seen much of him lately.

You sit right beside Frank and make with the small talk.

He starts in about a prostitute he hired. He was able to play chess with her and they did it to Mozart. That's rare, he says, a hooker with brains. And she read philosophy. She read Nietzsche, she read Kant. They have a lot of fun with that one. And somebody is telling an elaborate joke about a streetwalker and a priest.

You're laughing and whooping with them. Working your hand inside the towel. You can feel it coming. The heat drops away and you're icy. No more steam but pure oxygen you're breathing. It takes forever for Frank to reach a hand up and wipe his brow. His face slowly revolves toward you, slowly folds into a smile. You smile back.

You're on his right. You smile and reach over and slap his back. Your hand is in the towel.

"They're ready to jump in with both feet," Ted was saying. "Positive commitment. All they want to see is solid progress, a project without problems. As long as this crap goes on, they're going to sit on the sidelines. And we have to have that capital they represent. They are simply our last chance to get this thing off ground zero. I hope you understand what I'm saying. The situation is critical."

"But you see, I agree with you. I am not exactly an ignoramus when it comes to business." Lujak looked around the room and made a limp-wristed gesture that seemed to vaguely indicate the scope of his business acumen. "Without the big money behind us, what can we accomplish? But I don't understand what I can do. This, isn't this all out of my hands? In the hands of God, so to speak?"

"I guess that's what we're asking, what do you know about it and what can you do?" Ted said. "Sal seemed to think that—Well, never mind what he thought."

"You guys, you guys. You are not sensitive enough. That's your problem. You gotta be sensitive in this business. There are feelings involved here. People must be persuaded."

"We're willing to make concessions," Ted said. "Not because I'm afraid of this goon squad. But we're on a tightrope here. I can see now that this labor consultant— he's not just a go-between, he actually has these unions in his pocket. Okay, so be it. We're on a tightrope and we have to keep moving or we go down. I'm accepting that now."

This isn't the way, Sal thought. You don't deal with a Lujak this way. This is not the way Sal Veronica would handle. But where is Sal Veronica? Where is Sal of the steam room?

"Cadillac!" the bird croaked. "Cadillac!"

Lujak scratched his lip up and down, up and down. Finally, he said, "Hokay. We are podners, yes? Of course I will do whatever I can. I will talk to Ernst. No, not just talk, lean. I will lean on him. Am I right, Sal? Do you understand? I will persuade him."

"That's all we want," Ted said.

"This is a matter of communication only. Communication not with words but with symbols. Bank notes."

The guy, the Seventh Avenue ding in the steam room, reaches the punch line.

I could if I knew which was the right end, father.

They all guffaw. You guffaw. The tiles echo the laughter. You slap Frank again and pull him toward you. You're going to tell him a secret.

They're still laughing. Frank's laughing. You cough loudly.

As you cough you pull the trigger. You have the towel by his ear.

You cough again.

Frank slumps. You make as if you're trying to hold

him up. You direct his head into the corner of the bench opposite. A gash to explain the blood. You let him drop to the floor.

A .22 slug is good because it doesn't make a pencil hole right straight through. It's small enough to ricochet inside the skull.

Still, Frank isn't dead. He lies in the wet, his face registering all the short circuits.

The others jump up, concerned. What's the matter? Has he fainted?

Keep back, you say. *It might be his heart. Heart attack. DeGarmo's had a heart attack.*

A naked man runs out. One of Big Frank's boys comes in, incongruous in his jacket.

Frank's eyes are groping. He knows. He's trying to shape a word with his tongue. His lips are moving in a mime of speech. He's trying to control the spasms of breath to make a sound. His finger, all his fingers, are trying to point.

You walk out naked, leave the gun and the towel under the bench. You dress and are on the street just as the ambulance arrives.

". . . true podners, don't you see?" Lujak said.

Here it comes, Sal thought, suddenly weary.

"No, I don't quite understand," Ted replied.

"Of this project, the old folks, sixty-six percent signed over to me."

"Sixty-six percent? Are you—?" Ted's hands floated wildly.

"Of course I am."

"For what?"

"For using my influence. Of the parent company, fifty-one percent. True podners, you see?"

"Is this a joke?"

"My terms, exactly and precisely—yes-yes, no-no." Lujak clapped his hands together twice.

"You're crazy." Ted looked around the room as if this statement were literally true, as if he were searching for a suitable restraint in case Lujak began to froth.

251

"No, Ted my friend, you are the crazy one. Sal here is more wise, you should have let him guide you. He approached me, wisely. He requested me to make my small contributions behind the scenes to the success of your business. I did so. But your lack of sensitivity upset the delicate arrangements I had made. Now, for me to become interested once more in your affair, I would need greater incentive. I would also want enough control to assure that your innocence does not interfere with the viability of our investment."

"Don't ever say 'our'!" Ted snapped. "This is my idea, my work, my sweat, my worries, my efforts, my dreams. Mine and Sal's. You want me to give up control of something I've been planning for ten years? You want me to let you grab all the fruits of my sleepless nights? You want me to concede that jerking a few chains, handing out a few bribes is equivalent to the effort I've put in on this, the risk I've taken?"

"But there you have it," Lujak said, his calm voice mocking Ted's fury. "You've taken a big risk. You can easily be ruined. This situation makes you—how would I say it—vulnerable."

Ted shook his head. "You planned this. You came in and established a foothold and learned exactly how you could screw things up for us. You knew we had loans that had to be rolled over. You knew we needed to attract more capital. You and Ernst worked it together to put us to the wall so you could move in and take over."

"Ted," Lujak chuckled. "Your imagination. Ask Sal. He understands the way things are. He knows dreams are dreams, don't you, Sal?"

Sal took the cigar he was smoking and looked at it, as if calculating the time it would take for the ash to reach his fingers.

He said, "Nelson, you're making a big mistake. It might be the biggest mistake of your life. You're playing games. We come to talk business, you tell us to kiss your ass."

"I'm simply saying—"

"You're small. You're a lightweight, babe. You're looking to get your brother-in-law in the food service. You're
looking for a rake-off on a sweetheart deal, you're looking
for a kickback on the ready-mix contract. That's all you
ever think about, how you can feather your nest off this
project. Always the small-time scam, the petty rip-off.
You're a punk."

"I'm a power in this city."

"You're a toadstool."

"Listen, my friend—"

Sal stood. "I'm not your friend and I never was. I
offered you an opportunity. You wanted in. Unfortu-
nately, in your little pea brain you got the idea you could
horse me around." He laughed a mirthless laugh. "Let me
tell you something, Nelson. You may think you know me,
but you don't. You may think you're holding the high hand
here. But I've got cards that will top anything you lay on
the table. Wild cards. If it comes down to it, I'll trump
your ace, man. And you'll be one sorry fuck."

Lujak tried unsuccessfully to pry a laugh from his
throat. His mouth twisted into a snarl. "You couple of lousy
bastards. You think you can operate in this city without
Lujak? You are nothing! You're salesmen! Two weaselly
little salesmen who talk talk talk. I push the buttons around
here. Me." He pounded his fist on his desk, scattering some
of the cards. "I know who I am. You will find out. You
will find out the price of defying Lujak. You will find out
that this game can become nasty. Very nasty. And very
dangerous."

Sal sipped smoke from the cigar, tapped some ash onto
Lujak's carpet. "Nelson, you've insulted my friend. You've
insulted me. And I think you're going to find that I'm the
one person in the world that you'll wish you never insulted."

Sal smiled at Ted. They walked out.

26

Dr. Pangnaw? Was that his name? Dr. Achegall? Was that it?

The few minutes he spent waiting for Dr. Barker, Mike Ryan relived his earliest encounters with the dental profession. He remembered one old bird, probably an alkie, but Mike was too young to realize it at the time. His breath always smelled of violets and his veined hands trembled as he approached with the needle or the drill.

Every time Mike went, the guy would find a bunch of cavities. Now Mike knew it was just a scam, the old man was simply ruining good teeth and sending Mike's father the bills.

They were all the same, these dentists. Okay, this guy had pastoral paradise photos on the walls and piped music and a nurse with a tight white wiggle, but that was just a cover.

Mike never went to a dentist now, hadn't been for years. And guess what? No problems. None at all. That

254

proved conclusively that these guys were a bunch of quacks.

"Sorry to keep you waiting, Mike," Maynard said, appearing at the door of the waiting room. He wore a white tunic and was pulling off a pair of creamy latex gloves. "I didn't expect you."

"I pick up a lot, dropping in on people when they don't expect it, when they're not prepared," Ryan said.

"Well, I have a pretty heavy schedule this afternoon, but I can take a few minutes if it's important. I assume it is."

"I have your answer for you."

"Good, good. You were able to run Vincent down, find out—"

"Vincent? Sal Vincent? Ha. There is no Sal Vincent. Sal Vincent doesn't exist."

"Come into my office. Maria, we'll be a few minutes here. Have Mrs. Rangewood make an appointment, she needs a patch on that filling, number eight distal."

They sat down in Maynard's office. Ryan cast uncomfortable glances at the demonstration set of teeth on Maynard's desk. Something about naked teeth gave him a sour feeling.

"The wise man and the fool," he began, "are separated by one thing. Surface. The fool stays on the surface. The wise man always digs. Because there's always something behind what we see. Things are never what they seem. Fall for the surface and you'll get screwed every time. I don't care if it's broads or business or bullshit, you've gotta dig." Ryan touched a crusted scab across the bridge of his nose.

"So Sal changed his name?"

"Sure he did. But you know why he changed it? Know what his name was before he changed it? Know who he really is?"

"Why don't you tell me?"

Mike could see that, like a lot of guys in his situation, this Barker was putting on a hard shell, a no-nonsense attitude meant to shield his hurt feelings.

"Let me walk you through it. You gave me the man's

255

résumé and all. I started checking. Everywhere I touched it, it crumbled to dust. The school he had listed as his alma mater burned down years ago. No records. Very convenient for Sal. Too convenient. See, I'm sort of a suspicious guy, Maynard. I take nothing at face value. I had a guy I work with up in Buffalo go out and find somebody with a yearbook from when Sal was supposed to have graduated from that school. No picture. No mention. Nobody ever heard of the family. His army records—I have a connection at V.A. headquarters. They couldn't find his serial number. Was he ever even in the army? That company he claims to have done consulting for? It doesn't exist. The guy is one hundred percent bogus. Nothing fits, nothing backs him up. He's a complete ringer."

"I don't understand. What's this supposed to mean?"

"Let me finish. I looked at his social security number. Then I looked up his wife's number. They have them on the tax records at the county clerk's office. Know what I found? His is 457-62-8892. Hers is 457-62-8893."

"Social security numbers?"

"Consecutive numbers. Phony. Phony, but issued by the government. So? The government's helping this guy go underground. They give him a story, a background that looks plausible on the surface. But Mike Ryan sees through it."

Maynard waited, arms crossed, for Ryan to continue.

"So I now have a pretty good idea what's going on here. Then he tries to kill me and spills the whole thing."

"Kill you? Sal?"

"Waved a gun at me. Usually I don't let a guy get away with a move like that. My standard operating procedure, that man very quickly becomes a corpse. Pulls a gun, I make him eat it. But this guy, this Sal, I decide to string him along. Sure enough, he talks too much. He lets slip a name, Paulie. Paulie, I'm going. Paulie, Paulie."

"I'm not following you."

"They have this program, this witness protection thing. It's operated by the feds. Takes these mob guys that will talk and gives them new identities."

"You mean you think Sal is an informer?"

"Pretty elementary, really. You have a hard guy who carries a rod. He's been given a new identity with government cooperation. So I start looking at trials during the six months before he landed in our lovely city, especially back east, New York or Phillie. I got that from the way he talks. I'm looking for the name Paulie. After a great deal of searching I found Paulie. Paul Amato. Convicted of conspiracy, extortion, bribery, a bunch of other things— all on the testimony of our key witness, one Mr. Salvatore Veronica, otherwise known as Sal the Veil, otherwise known as our friend Sal Vincent. The trial finished up a week before you said he moved in next door to your pal. Here's a picture I got from the Associated Press library. Look familiar?"

"This is hard to believe. Add the mustache, it's him, it's Vincent."

"What I found out, I'm glad I'm here to tell you about it. I checked with New York, talked to some people I know on the force there. The man is an animal. I mean, we're talking major criminal here. He was Paulie's enforcer. He killed people, that's what he did. He was a punk, a thief, and a strong-arm man. This Paul Amato—maybe you've heard of him, he's a wheel in the New York mob. He's been in *Time*. Sal became Paulie's personal hitter. The man is a genuine sociopath, psychopath, whatever you want to call him."

"What about the time he spent in the army, Afghanistan and all that?"

"Bunk. Handy cover for not having a legit background. Our friend is a killer, Maynard. A professional killer. He helped this Amato reach the top. Then Sal the Veil took a fall. See, when he's not gunning people down he's peddling dope. To kids ultimately. Took a heavy fall, he's facing a stiff term behind bars. So he talks. So they send a couple of guys to stop him talking. But Sal lucks out. Kills them and escapes. Testifies. Government rewards this creep with a pension, a new identity, VIP treatment at the taxpayers' expense. It's criminal."

"I thought there was something not right about the guy. I had a feeling," Maynard said.

"You thought, you were right. You smelled it, just the way I did."

"But who would have imagined this? The mafia? God almighty!"

"This is the information age, Maynard. What you have here is one hot piece of information."

"Jesus, I guess you could say that."

"Do you understand what I mean, hot?"

"Sure, like a state secret, federal thing."

Mike shook his head. "What you have here is dynamite. This man has killed people, nobody knows how many. He's a professional killer. He's a made member of La Cosa Nostra. Do you have any idea what that means?"

"Of course. I mean, law enforcement isn't my line. But, of course, you see it on television." He smiled wanly.

"Television? This's got nothing to do with television. This is real, my friend. You know who he is. Let's say he finds out you know. The next thing your wife knows, she's holding a check for fifty grand and it's your life insurance. This man is dangerous. Do you understand me? He's unpredictable. Listen, a friend of mine, when I was on the force, they put him on rackets. He was tailing some organized-crime types right in this city. Know what happened to him? Five bullets in the back of the head. Left a wife and three kids. That's the reality of it, my friend. So this information is hotter than hot. Question is, what are you going to do with it?"

"Sure, that's the question," Maynard agreed.

The jerk still doesn't get it, Mike thought. He said, "Hot information is also valuable information. To some people it would be very valuable."

"Who?"

Mike didn't answer, only stared. He was starting to feel an ache develop in one of his molars.

"Oh," Maynard said.

"I can assure you it will all happen very, very fast."

"Are you suggesting—?"

"He's a degenerate criminal. The government should never let these guys out of a cage. They're putting them in among law-abiding citizens. You have no way of finding out who they are. The next thing you know, they're in bed with your wife."

"What would they do?"

"Do? They'd take him for a long walk off a short pier. I don't know. They'd handle him, that's all you care about. He wouldn't be beating your time anymore, I can assure you of that."

"You mean they'd kill him?"

Mike's tooth was killing him. He had to get out of there. "You gotta understand two things. First, he may look like a respectable citizen to you, that's part of the gimmick. But he's from the underworld. They have different rules there, a different kind of justice. Second, you or I don't want to know what they're going to do to him. That's between him and them."

"I don't know. This is all—"

"Listen, this is a dream situation. You're doing everybody a favor. Yourself, to begin with—the guy's made a fool of you. Your wife—I'm sure she doesn't know she's in bed with a snake. Society—it's only because of a technicality that this guy isn't locked up for the rest of his life. You have an obligation. And it's easy. It'll be over like that. Good-bye, that's all she wrote. Only cost you five grand."

"Five thousand dollars?"

"I'm running a risk here, Maynard. These goons, it's too easy to get caught in the cross fire."

"Let me think it over."

"Think it over? Are you a man? Don't you care what this guy did to you?"

"Sure I care."

"Well, let me assure you, this is not a situation you can sit on. I was a cop, remember. I know whereof I speak. You want to think about it, fine. But you give me your answer by tonight. If you don't, the case is closed as far as I'm concerned—he's your problem entirely. Got that?"

"I understand."

"Whatever you do, don't mention this to anybody. Anybody."

Mike left the office. Think it over? Fucking jerk. You don't play around with a situation like this. The hell with think it over. Mike was going to get word to Nick Prado. Nick was the man to talk to about this.

He walked to his car, his fingers pressed against his throbbing lower jaw.

27

Summer was already shimmering in the air the Thursday before Memorial Day. Ted was finishing his breakfast. He had to take Jenny over to have her braces removed—finally. Laura had already left for an early meeting with a couple of Japanese collectors who'd flown in that morning. Jenny was flitting around the house, almost giddy at the prospect of shedding this symbol of childhood. After dropping her at school, Ted would have to hurry down to the office and get to work dismantling his dream.

He gulped the rest of his coffee and asked Jenny if she was ready. She was. She just had to . . . He didn't catch what it was, but he knew it'd mean at least a five-minute delay. Out of habit he looked over the real estate ads, checked what Winner was pushing these days.

Then they were in the car. As soon as he turned over the engine, Ted knew something was wrong. From under the hood came a high-pitched whimper that reminded him of a puppy on its first night away from its mother. When he put it into gear the car bucked, coughed, and stalled. He tried again. This time the motor wheezed and died immediately.

Jenny was drumming her fingers on the armrest.

As a formality, Ted got out and opened the hood. He stared at the stew of hoses, belts, and pipes, jiggled a wire, then told Jenny they'd have to run next door and see if they could borrow Sal's car.

"Take the Buick," Sal said. "No problem. I'll have Gina drop me at the office and ride back with you later. Only thing is, Margot phoned a minute ago. A guy from the city called her as soon as she got in, some kind of inspector. Said it was very urgent. I'm supposed to be meeting him out at the site right now. I think it's a matter of a little sugar for his tea, but we should take care of it. We don't want any more complications at this point."

"I can see about it on the way," Ted said. "The orthodontist is out that side of town anyway. Save you the trip."

"Okay, if you want to handle it. I'll see you when you get in. Here's the keys."

"And we're meeting with the representatives from the consortium at what time?"

"Eleven thirty," Sal said.

"I'll be there."

"You'll have to give me a kiss without the metal in your mouth, sweetheart," Sal said to Jenny.

"Oh sure," she answered, wrinkling her nose as she smiled.

Let go of your dream, Ted thought as he steered the car onto the highway. That was the lesson he'd learned. How many had been ruined by following an illusion, an empty hope, right down the drain?

Golden Age Estates was Ted's pipe dream. He'd fallen for his own happy talk, sold himself.

What we're offering costs money, was how Sal put it. And the people with the money weren't interested in dignity or community or shuffleboard.

They'd given it a try. Okay. But now the fact that they hadn't been able to move the concept would work to their advantage. Lujak thought they would play his game in order to hold on to a piece of the Golden Age profits. But if there were no profits, they could liquidate.

Ted really did have an eye for value. By instinct he'd picked up some of the last substantial acreage on that side of town. With the problem of the cemetery gone, the new expressway being built, land values had jumped substantially just in the time since they purchased the property. Sal had already managed to locate an interested party, an investor group looking to develop a 1.2-million-square-foot commercial-retail project.

"You look tired, Dad," Jenny said.

"Things have been busy at work."

"You should take more time to relax. You're in the danger zone, you know."

"I am?"

"For heart problems. I read this article. Mid-forties to mid-sixties. That's when most heart attacks happen."

"That's cheery news."

"You have to be realistic, is all. Exercise and reducing stress are very important, it said."

"I can't argue with you. Maybe I'll have a chance to take some time off over the weekend."

"You really should."

So the strike was actually saving them money. They would complete the deal with the developers on the best terms they could manage. They'd take care of their creditors, pay Maynard back his investment. Sal knew ways, he said, to squirrel some of the assets. Reed-Vincent Properties would be left a shell. Then they'd dissolve the company, pay Lujak ten cents on the dollar for the money he'd put in, and start fresh.

Ted knew it wouldn't be quite so easy, but the prospect of getting out from under the burden was a gleam of light in the dark. Once they were free of the Golden Age albatross, he and Sal could move into a new business. He was sure Sal would have some good ideas.

" . . . actually better drivers than if, you know, they wait till later."

"What? I'm sorry, Jen."

"That's all right, I know you have a lot on your mind."

Ted looked across the seat at his daughter. Something about the way she was sitting, the tilt of her head, the fold of her legs, sent a flash up his spine. She was growing up, damn it. She wouldn't be his little girl much longer.

"I was just saying that studies have shown it's better for a person to learn to drive at as early an age as possible because—something about motor reflexes."

"You want to get your permit."

"Yes."

Ted made a left turn onto the highway that ran past the Golden Age site. He checked his watch. "And your concern about my coronary health is simply the butter you thought you'd use to grease the wheels."

"Dad, how can you say that?"

"You've got the right idea, hon. Just keep in mind, you can't kid a kidder or sell a salesman."

"You promised."

"Wrong. I never promised. I learned a long time ago with you, don't promise."

"Dad, Debi has her permit. Gretchen has her license already. So does Kerry. What do you want me to do, be a freak?"

"You got it. I want you to be a freak. And I want you to start earning your keep by displaying yourself on public streets and begging for money. Or maybe you could join a circus. Step right up, folks, and see this amazing, this pathetic, this horrifying sight—a teenage girl with no learner's permit."

"You think it's so funny."

Ted slowed and turned up the road that led to the rear entrance of the site. There were no strikers picketing this early. "Jenny, you have three more weeks of school. The day after school lets out, I'll take you down to get your permit."

264

"Three weeks?"

"Be gone before you know it."

"Do you promise?"

"This time I'm going to make an exception. I promise."

Ted turned in past the sign that announced: Golden Age Estates, Luxury Senior Living. Against the summer vegetation, in the glare of the morning sun, the excavations seemed like cruel gashes, as if some wanton child had taken a giant rasp and carved his meaningless hieroglyphic into the green meadows.

And now, instead of the beautifully landscaped grounds of Golden Age Estates, the site would be forever scarred by exactly the type of mindless sprawl that Ted, in his heart, hated—that would have caused his father to spit.

He stopped outside the contractor's trailer.

"We're going to be late, Dad."

"This will only take a minute."

"What if Dr. Wilkinson cancels the appointment? I'll have to keep my braces on till next week."

"Just cool it, please. It doesn't look like he's here anyway. If he doesn't show in two minutes we'll go on."

At that moment the door of the trailer opened a few inches. Had somebody left it unlocked? Ted wondered. The inspector must have found it open and gone inside to wait. But why didn't he come out?

Ted opened his door and put one foot on the ground. The buzz of a cicada charged the air, then stopped abruptly.

The door of the trailer swung back. A heavyset man in a gray hooded sweatshirt stepped out onto the top wooden step. He was holding something down along his far side.

Ted rose, one leg still in the car.

"Jenny, get down on the floor." He heard a voice say it. It didn't sound like his voice.

"What?"

"Do what I tell you right now." The voice had a quality that made her slouch down in the seat without another word.

Ted followed the eyes of the man by the trailer. Over behind a bulldozer he spotted another man. He was younger, wearing sunglasses, holding a large stainless-steel pistol in his hand. It gleamed in the sunlight.

Ted felt suddenly like an old old man. He was sending signals to his muscles to move, but they were responding with a horrifying sluggishness. By expending an enormous effort he was able to sink back into the car.

On the steps, in the shadow of the trailer, the man was raising a shotgun.

Fumbling, Ted started his engine.

The other man was running toward him from behind the bulldozer.

It took a torturous amount of time for Ted to engage the gearshift. In the periphery of his vision he saw Jenny's wide eyes.

Too late. A crack. The windshield went white. Glass pebbles sprayed them.

Ted's right foot pushed against the gas pedal. The car wouldn't budge. What the hell?

The man with the pistol was almost on them. Ted could see his lips stretched into a grimace. The man was crouching. He was taking hold of the gun with both hands.

Suddenly the scene was obliterated. The back wheels, which had been spinning on loose gravel, took hold. The car lurched backward at full speed. A cloud of dust flew up around them.

Ted craned backward as the car accelerated. The steering wheel seemed to have come disconnected. He couldn't control the car as it lurched from one side of the road to the other. One swerve practically threw him across the car.

A low pile of reinforcing rods leapt into their path. Ted was lifted off his seat as they humped over the obstacle. Then, of its own volition, the car twisted off the road and crashed into the chain link fence near the gate.

266

Ted could see nothing through the dust cloud he'd raised. He switched the gear to drive, but the car wouldn't respond to the howls of its own engine. He backed hard into the fence and tried again. The car surged but didn't come free.

He had to get out. Get Jenny out. Sprint, both of them. Or carry her if she couldn't.

He jerked the gearshift and pounded the accelerator. The car hurtled forward.

He hit the brakes, skidded. He yanked the lever into reverse. They roared out of the site.

Jenny's thin cry reached his ears as he grappled with the wheel, the shift lever. The windshield was a blanket of shattered glass. Ted had to thrust his head out the side window to steer. As he accelerated down to the highway he glanced briefly at his daughter's white-boned face. He started to reach out to reassure her. The car swerved. He gripped the wheel again with both fists.

He made the turn into traffic and proceeded up the road, keeping a close eye on the rearview mirror. Spotting no pursuers, he decided to take a chance. He pulled into a Mobil station. He had no idea how fast he was going until he applied the brakes and skidded ten feet before stopping.

A few pairs of eyes in the busy service station turned toward him. He stared back at them, feeling his heart pound, amazed that people were going about their mundane business. Didn't they know that the world was a dangerous place?

He pulled Jenny to him and hugged her. She was trembling.

Yes, the world was a very dangerous place.

28

A .22 bullet ricochets in the skull. You made your rep with it.

Sal parked up the street from the lounge, the second of Lujak's hangouts that he'd tried. A pink neon cocktail glass shone brightly in front. The night was mild.

Ted had reached him just before noon. Trouble at the site, he said. Big trouble. Sal immediately felt himself begin to harden, to prepare.

A .22 was a light gun, a compact gun. It made a noise almost like a toy, a noise that rarely drew attention. Not much recoil, easy to shoot.

Approaching the bar, he pulled his cap down and put on a pair of tinted glasses.

He'd stopped wearing the gun regularly months ago. He slid his hand into his jacket pocket and gripped the butt briefly before he pushed through the door.

Sal took a place at the end of the bar, ordered a Chivas and rocks. He had a view of the carpeted lounge beyond.

After a minute he spotted Lujak at a table with four other men in the far corner.

You can't let down. He'd really lulled himself there, gone to sleep. You can't let that happen. There are more dangers in this world than just Paulie Amato and his people.

You were lucky. Your luck again. You let your guard down and came out of it with a near miss.

At least this guy Lujak is dumb. Christ, does he really believe you won't make the connection? Does he think you're not going to come back at him? He's a fool. Leaving himself wide open, giving you the advantage.

Business in the bar picked up during the half-hour Sal sat nursing his drink. Most of the tables and all the padded stools at the bar were filled. A smoky, noisy haze hung in the air. Some Sinatra fan had monopolized the jukebox. "My Way" was coming on for the third time. On the television near the ceiling in the corner a beauty pageant was progressing without sound.

Several people approached Lujak's table, spoke to him, moved away. Who does it remind you of? Sal asked himself.

In the mirror Sal occasionally glanced at a weathered, deep-bosomed woman down the bar. But when she twitched the corner of her mouth at him he looked away.

Now. He stared at the quarter-inch of amber in his glass, the gleaming ice, the soggy paper napkin, the folded swizzle. Now. He could simply walk over. Grab Lujak. Yank his head forward. Produce the gun. Deliver two to the temple. Turn and slip away in the confusion, tossing the gun under a car outside.

Now was the time. Nail him. Nobody would see anything. Nobody would remember him. Or rather, they'd all remember him. The cops would have a dozen different descriptions. Just like in the steam room.

The memories of the life now more and more found their focus in the steam room. He sometimes actually felt the clinging damp, the suffocating air. The conversational drone in this bar reminded him of the murmur of talk

269

that had drifted through that fog. He could almost hear the snick-snick of the shot inside the towel. He kept envisioning the massive naked man stretched on the tiles. Kept seeing the red trickle from his ear. Kept watching that confused expression, as if the man's life was being projected, vastly accelerated, onto his features.

Now. But Sal heard a glass break in the storeroom off the bar. A man behind him was laughing and his laughing changed to a violent cough. The bartender stared at Sal, his arms crossed, then came over and asked him if he wanted another. The mouth of one of the contestants on the television seemed to be shaping a warning. A bottle of some kind of liqueur caught the light with a funny, off-color glint.

All of these sensations took the shape of omens. Now was not the time. This was not the place to pull the audacious act, to spit in the face of fate.

Better to wait. Follow Lujak outside. Do it in the dark. Much better.

As if on cue, Lujak rose to leave. Sal turned his face away and leaned his chin on his hand. He watched out of the corner of his eye. The other men were all going with Lujak.

Sal waited for about fifteen seconds, then followed. Outside he turned and walked past the parking lot beside the bar. Lujak was saying good-bye to one of the men. The rest waited to ride with him in his stretch limo. The lot was well lit. Sal crossed to his own car.

He followed Lujak to a seafood restaurant in a shopping plaza out on the highway. Sal parked among the flock of cars outside a triplex movie theater nearby and waited.

Christ, you walk out of that steam room, walk clean away, and they don't even find the gun until after they've rushed DeGarmo to the cardiac unit. Some guy pulls the towel out from under the bench and the .22 falls on the floor.

And they know it's you.

The cops are all over the witnesses with questions. Who? What guy? I didn't see nothing. Big Frank, he just fell over. Didn't hear nothing. I thought he had a heart attack, what did I know? Sure there's guys coming and going, but who sees? Naked men, they all look the same.

But everybody knows. Sal the Veil turned out Big Frank's lights. I don't know how he did it, but he did it. Just sat down next to him and made him go bye-bye. I mean, has the man got balls or what?

It's as if you've just won the lottery. Suddenly, everybody's your friend. Everybody's got a smile for you. You're ten feet tall and still growing. You inherit all of DeGarmo's garment-district business, all the shy operations, and the books. Guys you hardly know walk up and hand you five hundred, a thousand for goodwill.

You're on top of the world. You're invulnerable. The brightest parties, the sharpest women. You own the streets. Every day's an adventure with a happy ending.

Who's that saying watch out? Who's whispering, keep your guard up? Primo. Must be Primo. Murmuring in your ear like a good cornerman so only you can hear. Telling you he sees something, something you're doing with your hands, some way you're leaving yourself open when you move in to hook. You're setting yourself up and you don't even know it. You're ahead on points but you're leaving yourself wide open for the knockout.

But you're punch-drunk. The life has softened you up. A shit kicker from Bay Ridge like you. You get a taste of the good life, the easy money and the easy women—it softens you up. You think you have the world on the ropes. No way you're going to cover up. No way they can hit you.

You take the chance, fate snaps her fingers, and you're suddenly staring at ten years hard time. And before that sinks in, Paulie pulls the plug on you and you're out in the cold.

And Primo's the one who gets it.

The way DeGarmo's thighs trembled—you can't forget it. It started in his legs. It didn't mean a goddamn thing at the time. Now it's as if it splits time in half, that trembling. When they tremble, when the brain rips and they let go, a new time starts. It's the time you live in and they don't. Their time is all over. But your time is different, too. Your time is never the same again.

What the hell? Why in Jesus' name was he thinking this now?

There's a power in that trembling. But the memories outlast the power, replace the power. The dread outlasts the illusion of immortality.

By the time Lujak finally finished eating and emerged from the restaurant, only a few cars were left from the cluster that had surrounded Sal's. Sal followed the limousine out of the parking lot. They headed back toward town.

He'd often been struck by the desolation of the city's business district after dark. Sal was used to the hot, crowded nights of New York. Here, with all the cinemas fled to malls and the night life scattered, the streets were deserted after the stores closed.

He watched the car stop to let out two of the men. Then it turned down a seedy side street and pulled to the curb just beyond a small tavern with a sputtering beer sign in the window. Lujak and his remaining companion, a blubbery young man who could have been his son, went inside.

Sal parked and stepped into the doorway of a shoe store in the building next door. He was out of the light and could catch Lujak coming out, before he reached the limo, which the driver had parked twenty yards up the street.

Patience. It was a virtue that came easy for Sal. Guys would get so nervous they couldn't make themselves wait for the moment. In a game where timing was everything, they'd rush it.

It was good to be back in the groove. He savored the acrid taste of adrenaline, the ice crystals that pricked his veins, the brilliant details that emerged as he cranked up his concentration—the broad transparency of plate glass that he leaned against, the minute tug of the weight in his jacket pocket, the single star that winked through the clamor of streetlights. He loved the coiled feeling, the sensation of being in charge of the world, not buffeted by events.

Christ he'd been lulled. The mild suburban view of things. He'd forgotten how charged up he felt in this world, the real world, how alive.

He saw a hooker working the opposite side of the street. They weren't uncommon in this neighborhood. She'd lounge in the illumination of a streetlight and smoke and wag a knee at a car passing slow, nod, smile, look away abruptly if they kept going.

A figure came out of the bar. He was sure it was the chubby young man who'd accompanied Lujak. Sal watched him step up the sidewalk, stop at the limo. He leaned and spoke to the driver, continued on. Perfect. Sal once more felt for the gun.

"Do you have a light by any chance?"

Sal shuddered. The girl had walked right up to him without him noticing. She stood on the pavement in the light. He was a half-step higher in the angle of shadow. He slipped a book of matches from his pocket and handed them to her. She lit one, cupped it over her cigarette, blew smoke from the side of her mouth. She continued shaking the match long after it was out.

"So?" Her fingers removed the cigarette from her smile.

He took back the matches, smiled abruptly, shook his head, looked away.

"Shy? Lots of guys are. I like you, I like your looks. I want to get to know you, that's all. Have a drink, talk. Hmm?"

The childish lilt of her voice enticed him to look at her, size her up. Her chestnut hair was cut short. Her body vibrated with youth, the youth of lean muscles and firm buttocks and upturned breasts and slender arms and taut thighs. Underneath her makeup her cloudy face had the shape of youth—innocent eyes and soft cheeks and round nose and creamy lips. She'd tried to heighten her allure with mascara and shadow, silver lipstick and powder and rouge. On top of that she'd imposed a false little-girl look,

273

with fake freckles and pixie bangs and an expression of depraved modesty.

Seeing him looking, she touched her leg below the leather miniskirt and propped her other hand on her cocked hip.

"Beat it," Sal growled.

"You're going to love me," she said as though she hadn't heard him. Her face glowed with naïve confidence. " 'Cause I know you're dying for it."

Laughter sounded up the block. Lujak emerged from the bar. A tall black woman was with him, her arm hooked loosely around his. The streetlights caught the emerald sheen of her dress.

Sal spit three obscenities at the young prostitute.

He knew the moment had arrived. Now was when he should begin moving swiftly up the sidewalk. But something made him look once more at the girl's face. At the narrowed eyes, the small mouth. The lips were forming words that weren't reaching him. He stared at her for an instant, then turned and brushed past her.

Her voice, a tiny screech, slapped at him as he walked away.

Lujak and his woman were already halfway to the limo. Gripping the pistol in his pocket, Sal jogged to catch up.

Lujak made a gesture, a circle in the air with his hand, as if he were a politician delivering a campaign speech.

The night was singing. Sal heard his soles smack against the concrete. He heard himself breathing.

Lujak had the car door open. Sal was still ten yards back. The woman slid inside. Lujak followed.

Sal ran. He came even with the rear bumper as the door chugged closed. The windows were black glass.

The limo pulled away.

Sal stood watching the car's taillights. Under his jacket he was soaked with sweat. His hand on the butt of the gun was clammy. He saw very clearly what he should have known from the beginning of the evening—he'd lost his instinct. His edge.

29

Laura wanted Ted to take the day off, but he wouldn't hear of it. If they were able to swing the deal to unload the Golden Age property, the transaction could very well happen today. If the consortium backed out, they'd have to scramble to hold off creditors and find another buyer.

The events of the day before hadn't rattled his nerves as much as he'd thought they would. Maybe the impact of the thing hadn't soaked in yet. In any case, he enjoyed a luxurious sense of composure, almost a numbness. Plus, he'd have the long Memorial Day weekend to recuperate.

The vents were blowing chilled air into the car. The weather, waking up to summer, had turned suddenly muggy. Ted was driving a sporty loaner that the dealer had let him have when he dropped off his car for repair.

You never know how you're going to act when the shit hits the fan, he thought. There's just no way to tell. Ted figured he'd given a good account of himself. He'd made his calm call to 911. He'd waited at the gas station, tense but with no sign of panic, breathing a small sigh when he heard the first siren approaching. Three police and sheriff's cars had swooped down on them in the first few minutes. Others raced past on their way to the Golden Age site.

Jenny stood by throughout, her fingertips over her mouth, swaying slightly as her eyes followed the spectacle—officers questioning her father and examining the damage to Sal's car. She came close to tears when the lieutenant suggested they return to the site—officers on the scene had searched to no avail—and reenact the shooting.

Ted asked her if she would prefer to be taken home. No, she wanted to stay with him.

They drove back in a police car less than forty minutes after they'd first arrived. It seemed that a lifetime had passed since they'd driven up the dirt road. Ted pointed out where the gunmen had been hidden. The police lieutenant praised him several times for his alertness, his driving skill in backing out at high speed.

Ted answered questions for almost an hour. He described the strike, the raucous picketers, the slashed tires on his car. The police picked up on that, seemed to think the case was as good as solved. There was an annoying amount of paperwork to be completed before they could leave.

When they arrived home Jenny hurried in first to tell Laura. She began nonchalantly, complaining that she'd have to wear her braces through the weekend. She grew more voluble as she poured out the story of the shooting.

Alternating waves of concern and disbelief swept Laura's face.

Jenny's narrative became frantic. Her words tumbled faster. She ended out of breath and sobbing.

Laura wrapped her daughter in her arms, held the girl fiercely. Her eyes pleaded with Ted for an explanation.

Ted's instinct was to reassure his wife. It must have had something to do with the strike, the rabble-rousing unions. That was the rational explanation. They were just

276

trying to throw a scare into him. It was a brutal form of threat. These things happened.

"But they *shot* at you!" Laura cried.

"Well, yes."

"And they hit the car? Bullets went right into the car?"

"It was a truly frightening thing, I'm not trying to say it wasn't."

"Daddy knew just what to do," Jenny said, wiping her eyes. "He never hesitated or anything. I didn't even know what was going on. He saved my life. He did. He was great!"

"Now, come on, Jen, don't—" He felt his own eyes burning.

"You did, Daddy! You should get a medal or something. I mean it."

"Ted, for God's sake, you could have been killed!"

"I don't think they really meant—"

"We could too have," Jenny insisted. "They were shooting right at us."

"We were lucky." Ted needed to sit down. He was shaking. Laura took his hand and gripped it very hard.

Sal's first question had been how much Ted had told the police about Lujak. Ted said that he hadn't really thought to say anything. It had not occurred to him to connect Lujak's threat with the shooting.

Sal was certain that Lujak had ordered it. Lujak's strategy was to put a scare into them in order to prod them to accept his terms. The fat man had made a classic mistake, underestimating his adversary.

"I think the sooner we break all our ties with Lujak, the better," Ted said.

"I'm with you, babe. That's where we're heading right now. I never should have brought the bastard in to begin with. I should have done it on my own."

"I'm not blaming you. I went along. I walked in with my eyes open. We learned."

"And Lujak's going to learn, too."

What had he meant by that? It was absurd to think Sal would do something rash, wreak vengeance on Lujak, take the law into his own hands. Or was it? He remembered the gun Sal had pulled at the Halloween party. Christ, it was conceivable that he might just—

The deal was moving quickly when Ted arrived at the office on Friday. Sal had already arranged a late-morning meeting with their accountants and lawyers. With luck they'd have a firm offer by the end of the day. The price that was on the table would be enough to take care of most of their debts and repay Maynard, with even a small profit left over.

"We've got them by the short hairs, babe," Sal said. "They're talking in the six-fifty range, but I'm sure they're going to be willing to go higher. We've got 'em, I can feel it. I dropped a few not so subtle hints that we had several other parties interested in the property. I swear these guys are sweating battery acid. I'm wondering if we should come back at them with a deadline—final offer by one o'clock or it's off. Put some pressure on. What do you think? Huh?"

He paced up and down Ted's office, punching his fist into his palm as he spoke. Ted had never seen him quite so hyper, so obviously jumpy.

"Well, it's going smoothly at this point," Ted answered. "I don't think we should box ourselves in with any kind of a bluff."

"No, no, no," Sal snapped. "No bluffing, no way. Who said anything about bluffing? I don't bluff."

"Hey, cool down. We just wait them out, that's all. And speaking of bluffing . . ."

"What? What are you talking about?"

"Lujak. I was thinking, you know, if we—if you really believe he was behind that stuff yesterday—"

"I'm sure of it."

"Okay, shouldn't we go to the police with it?"

"Hey, we don't need the cops. I'm going to read the riot act to that motherfucker. That was small-time, what he did yesterday."

278

"I don't know what you call small-time, my daughter could have been killed."

"I told you I was sorry, didn't I? What the hell do you want from me? I never should have brought the guy in, okay?"

"Sal—"

"I'll take care of the man. He's a punk, I'll take care of him, forget about it."

Ted started to say something. Sal shot a look at him that made him stop. Sal muttered something and was gone.

"Can I getja?" the waitress asked.

Mike Ryan said, "Johnnie Black shooter, club soda on the side, and a smile."

"Same again," Nick Prado said. When she'd gone, he continued, "So he gets there, then what?"

"His car, I know his car."

"The other guy driving?"

"Yeah, the straight one. But I couldn't see, the glare and all, I just saw the car, I said, that's him. So your man's got his gauge all jacked up and ready to go, he's at the door. But then the car stops and I go, wait a minute. Your boy says, I ain't waiting."

It was midafternoon. They were sitting in the Loon Lounge, a small tavern that Nick owned. Nick's narrow eyes peered at Ryan. They glanced to the door in front. A wash of daylight brightened the dark room every time someone entered. An air conditioner strained against the heat outside.

"He's looking?"

"He's got the door open, looking. I—by this time I can see it's not Sal. It was obvious. So I said, hold on. But he's gone, he's already out there. And your other boy's ready on the other side."

"This guy Reed, he get a good look at them?"

"He's in the sun, we're in shadow. I don't think he saw much."

"He going to pin them in a lineup?"

"I doubt it."

279

"You doubt it? This is crucial, Mike."

"I'm giving you my opinion, I don't think so. I did plenty of lineups on the force. Robbery, something, maybe they can say. But where it's just bang bang, they're trying to get out of the way, they remember shit. But of course, it's your neck."

"Yeah." Prado looked at his watch.

"They be here soon, these hard boys? I'm looking forward to it, get it over with. They'll have the dough?"

"They're bringing it."

"This arrangement, it suits me. It ups my profit margin, getting paid twice for the same shot. Just—it might be harder this time. I hope these boys don't screw up."

"They won't."

"I hope not. Because if your boys blow it when Sal doesn't even show, I hate to think. The man is a real hairball, believe me. Not that I couldn't take him myself. I'd do it, I told you I would. You want to make it a team effort, that's fine. I'm not complaining, I just want it known I could handle the son of a bitch myself. Thanks, darling. Where's my smile?"

The waitress finished setting down the drinks. "You're sitting on it."

Nick laughed. Ryan blew her a kiss.

"You said you had a run-in with him?" Nick said.

"Sure. Pushee-shovee. He's super-paranoid. After the bullshit yesterday, I hate to think. Very few people ever made me on a tail, but this guy, I guess he's got a guilty conscience. He sneaks around and gets the jump on me. Pulls a big fucking .45. We had a pretty tense little showdown. I say, this is a free country. Since when? he says. I'm telling you, these assholes get on the government tit, they think they own the world. I almost took the man's head off and handed it to him."

"From what I hear about him, you're lucky you didn't try anything."

"I was born lucky, Nick. Where are these hotshots anyway? We've got to get this show moving."

"You're nervous, Mike. Denny went to the airport. They'll show."

"What was I saying? I noticed something funny about Sal from the start. I asked this dentist, I said, didn't your buddy know who the hell he's throwing in with here? He never checked the man's background at all."

"The feds give them a new identity, don't they?"

"Yeah, but I'm going through it, his cover's full of holes. When you dig, that is. On the surface it looks fine. But I've got a nose for it when they're trying to put it over on me. You don't put anything over on Mike Ryan."

"He turns out to be a nice meal ticket for you, ten grand more for today's action."

"Nothing. It's nothing. Though I'll tell you something, confidential. I picked up another five from the dentist." Mike snickered. "I had to have that, implicate him, make sure his conscience don't work overtime after. It was a bonus. And I bet if I'd said to your people twenty, they would have. I should have said twenty. More. I'm cracking this witness protection thing wide open. It's not just this one guy. An awful lot of people are going to be thinking twice once this gets out. You realize that? This is going to be national news. This is going to be headlines back in New York. Sal Veronica. This is going to be big."

"Sure, big."

"This is a win-win situation, Nick. You get brownie points. I get the dough. The world gets rid of one more Sal Veronica. I mean, the man is vicious. You, the average guy, you're a businessman. You yourself are in some tough businesses, you have to be a guy to be reckoned with, okay. But this Sal character is an animal. He isn't human. Absolutely no redeeming social value."

"Only don't say it to his face."

"Hey, they shouldn't allow these dudes to walk the streets. You know, they're turning them loose to prey on ordinary citizens. Living next door to a mass murderer, you don't even know it. And the taxpayer is supporting them. They're supposed to be reformed, they aren't reformed. Is it hot in here?" Ryan finished his drink for the third time. He removed his sport jacket. Circles of sweat were soaking through his white shirt.

"You don't reform a guy like that," Prado observed.

"One thing I've been kind of wondering about, though," Mike said.

"What's that?"

"Been troubling my mind a little. I work with these guys, I'm fully cognizant, you know what I mean? I'm an eyewitness. What's to say they don't send me off on the same train as our friend?"

"Mike, don't even think that. You have my word."

"Can I cash in your word in hell? They know you down there?"

"You're questioning my word? Do I understand you, Mike?"

"I'm using my brain, Nick. I've found it stays limber if I take it out and exercise it once in a while. And when I think this whole thing out, I can't see any good reason why they shouldn't make me go bye-bye as soon as I've done what they're paying me to do. They leave with the cash and no witnesses."

"That's not the way I do business. I give my word, it means something."

"I understand that, Nick. I trust you implicitly. You're Plymouth Rock to me, literally. But can you blame me for taking a precaution?"

"Oh, you're taking a precaution. I see."

"That's right, a letter in my safe-deposit box. My lawyer has the key. In the letter I lay out all the details of this little arrangement, all of them."

"Interesting."

"Something to dwell on. You know I can keep my mouth shut. Trust me. Don't try to shut it for me, or you're going to pay a sweet price."

"I don't know if I like that, Mike."

"I don't care if you like it. Just keep it in mind. And it's not just about this one thing. I put information in there about other deals I know about. Some very sticky deals.

Names, dates, times, and where to go for corroborating. Copies for the D.A. and the federal strike force if anything happens to me."

"And how about, you're driving home tonight, you have a heart attack?"

"That happens, Nick. I'll go to my grave knowing that there's at least one soul out there who'll cry at my funeral."

"It's only your suspicious nature, Mike."

"Tool of my trade."

They had more drinks. Ryan, feeling an urge to talk, told a story about a divorce case. In the middle of it, a man came over to Nick and whispered in his ear. Nick nodded.

"They're here," he told Ryan.

Ted sat at his desk feeling hollow and spent. Yesterday's shock and the stress of the day's business had caught up with him. The consortium had made an offer they could live with. There would be a lot of dickering over details, but essentially it was a done deal.

Now Ted imagined someone had turned up the force of gravity. Everything was twice as heavy as normal. His feet were lead. His hands felt swollen, chalky.

Margot tapped on his door and entered.

"I pulled the file on buy-out provisions, Ted," she said, placing the neat papers on his desk. "Also—"

"Margot, you know what this deal means, don't you?"

"I've already sent out my résumé."

"There'll be a big chunk of severance pay for you, don't worry about that. I know Sal promised you an equity interest, but we were never in a position—"

"You've been great, Ted. Sal's been great. It's been fun here. What are you planning for yourself?"

"Oh, I might get out there and start pushing real estate again, residential. I kind of miss that, relating to ordinary people instead of these wheeler-dealer types. Then, eventually, I'm sure Sal and I will get something going again, some business."

"You make a good team."

"We do, don't we?"

Margot went back to work. Ted started to look over the file.

The buzz of the intercom prodded him back to head-achy reality. Margot informed him that Dr. Barker was there to see him.

"Put him on," Ted said.

"No, he's right here, in person."

"Oh, of course. Send him in."

Maynard wore lime-green pants and a polo shirt that molded itself around his plump belly. He was agitated.

"Christ, Teddy, I was on the golf course all day—you know, we had that tournament. And I guess Felice talked to Laura and she got a call in to me. I wish you would have called me last night."

"There wasn't much to tell. You know we've been having those union problems out there. It got out of hand. But I did want to talk to you, we just pulled off a deal—"

"Ted, Ted, that's what I have to tell you. It wasn't the union thing."

"What wasn't?"

"That shooting. Oh God." He walked to the window, pulling hard on the back of his neck. "I really screwed up, buddy."

"I don't know what you mean."

"Remember there last fall, I was talking about Felice, about hiring a detective? You practically laughed at me. Teddy, my suspicions were on the money."

"What? Felice?"

"I haven't told anybody. She doesn't even know I know."

"Jesus, buddy, I'm sorry."

"And it was your goddamn fucking partner that did it!" Maynard's shoulders came up and he clenched and reclenched his fists.

"Sal?"

"Goddamn scum! And that wasn't all my guy found out."

Maynard told the story. Several times his anger swept

284

his narration into incoherence. A one-eyed mobster, a Chinese restaurant, phony social security numbers.

Ted squinted his disbelief. Was Maynard having a nervous breakdown? But in his gut, Ted had a sick, panicky feeling that what his friend was saying was true, that Sal was an imposter.

"What it came down to," Maynard said, sighing to compose himself, "was, what was I going to do? I had to do something. A guy fucks your wife, you have to do something. Don't you? This detective—he's an ex-cop, by the way—said he could have Sal taken care of. I was in a white rage, Teddy. My wife, God damn it. You don't know how that feels. It's like getting kicked in the nuts, only it doesn't go away. To know that that son of a bitch—"

"Maynard—" Ted began. Maynard interrupted.

"I never thought they would try and kill him, I really didn't. You have to believe that. I just figured they'd throw a scare into him, something. I thought he'd have to—you know, the government would have to put him in protective custody, or—I don't know. I wanted to teach him a lesson. He's ruined my marriage. He's ruined my life."

"And you think it was some kind of organized-crime deal yesterday, that they were trying to kill Sal?"

"I was sick when I heard about you and Jenny. I called the detective immediately. He wasn't in. I even stopped at his place on the way here. I swear I'm going to insist he call this off, I won't put up with it. I just didn't think."

"Listen, I know that Sal—that women like him. Okay? Felice is a very attractive lady. I guess it's possible that if—"

"No if, Teddy. I have proof. Dates, times, photographs, everything—down to the minute, the second."

"Okay. I'm not going to offer any excuses for the man. But the rest of it, to accuse him of being a professional criminal, a murderer . . ."

"Don't you see? I had to take action to protect myself. If he had found out that I knew, he might have come after me. I had to protect Felice. She—I'm sure she doesn't know who he is. I had to do something. I had to act."

"Are you positive this detective character wasn't handing you a line? I mean, I know Sal pretty well."

"Do you? Teddy, he carries a gun, we know that. His stories about being in army intelligence always sounded phony to me. You yourself told me there were a lot of things about him that didn't seem to add up. Of course I'm positive—he showed me a picture, even, from the paper. Sal Veronica. Sal the Veil, they called him. It just never occurred to me that you'd be involved."

"Well, let's see what he says."

"No! No, no. Are you kidding?"

"We'll see what he says," Ted said.

"Uhn-uh. First, I—I'm afraid of what I might do. You know me. When I think of him and Felice, what he did, what he's done to me—"

"Look," Ted said, "if what you've told me is even partly true, we're dealing with something here that's quite serious. We have to tell Sal, there's no question about that."

"The guy brought it on himself. He's a criminal, Ted! He should be locked up. The reason I'm telling you this, I want you to keep out of it, keep away from him. Driving around in his car, that was a fool thing."

"Fool thing?" Ted shouted. He banged his palms down on his desk. "My daughter came that close to being killed. Do you understand what I'm saying? My daughter."

"Okay, I'm sorry. I can't ever tell you how sorry I am. But that's it—these guys have their own rules. You have to keep your distance until it's over. These people are animals."

"Sal is not an animal."

"He is, Teddy. They act normal but they can turn vicious so quickly." Maynard was stroking his hand down his throat as if testing to see if he needed a shave.

"Listen, if you found out he was messing around with Felice, you should have come to him then and told him face-to-face to butt out. I would have backed you a hundred percent. If you're right about this, you've endangered him and his family—and me and my family."

"He deserves it. I'm telling you, he's scum."

286

"Deserves to die? What are you saying? What he did was wrong. Okay? But you know Felice. You know as well as I do that she probably deserves half the blame, if not more. I don't like to say that, Maynard, but it's true."

"He—" Maynard's face became small. "You know, I thought Felice was going to be my ticket to a happy life. I put a lot of commitment into that relationship. To you it's just, yeah sure, a guy's wife getting it on with somebody behind his back. That's not what it is to me."

"You took the coward's way out. That's what I'm saying. And even now you won't accuse him to his face. You tell me I should steer clear of him while some thugs sneak up and murder him?"

"He's unpredictable."

"I can't go along with that. You and I go way back, buddy. But Sal's a friend of mine, too."

"You don't know him. You know Vincent, but you don't know Sal Veronica."

"I know him. I'm not saying what he did to you was right. But if he's in danger, I'm going to warn him."

"Which side are you on?"

"I'm going to call him in here now. If you want to leave—"

Maynard stopped at the door. "He could come after me, you know."

"I have to do it," Ted said. "I'm going to."

30

Laurel and Hardy, Mike Ryan thought. Couple of hotshot clowns, just what he'd expected. Should have insisted on doing it alone. He didn't need these jokers. Nick hadn't introduced them, so to Mike they were Laurel and Hardy.

Hardy bulged his clothes. His puffy features crowded a too small face, pinching his eyes. No neck. Hair combed with some kind of glue, a big prong erect at the back of his head. He kept playing with a boil that was erupting near his right ear.

In Laurel's excessively long chin Ryan thought he saw a sign of madness, of degeneracy. It was the chin of a hillbilly, a throwback, a guy whose mother got whacked by a tire iron while she was pregnant. The man's eyes were raw and colorless, like a newborn baby's. They had Stan Laurel's lazy blink. He followed the conversation closely and always seemed to be on the verge of saying something. So far he hadn't spoken a word.

Mike looked at his watch. If they moved soon they could catch him just at dusk. That was the perfect time, that fading time just before darkness took hold, when nobody could be certain of what he saw. He hoped that these two characters were better than they looked.

Punks is what they seemed like to him. Hadn't Mike seen enough of the type when he was on the force? Arrogant. Cocky jokers until you got them alone and started to prod them in the right place with a billy. Then they crapped their pants. Then they said yes sir. Punks.

"I'm a traditionalist," Hardy was saying, "I go for— my favorite is the Smith M27 and the magnum semi-wadcutters. Five-inch barrel. That's a solid gun and it doesn't weigh you down. I like the Python, too, you want to get into a real piece. My buddy used one of those Charter Bulldogs on a job, snubbie in .44. I told him, you're blowing most of your powder out the end, you're not getting anything for all that flash, a barrel that short. I say, give me a Walther PPK any day. Any day at all. That's a classic. But the Bulldog did the work, he says. Yeah, but it don't make sense, I told him. Life's got to make sense or where are we? We do things for a reason, don't we? A fucking sledgehammer works, too. A chain saw, a stick of dynamite."

The guy couldn't shut up. While his partner talked, Laurel shifted his glance between Nick and Ryan, nodding his formidable chin and blinking his blink. Maybe he was a congenital idiot, Mike thought, a cretin.

The thing with the safe-deposit box was a stroke of genius. It didn't put Mike's anxiety entirely to rest, but as insurance it was invaluable. Too many cases he knew about, somebody helps these smart guys out, they reward him with a busted skull. Ryan was too sharp for that shit, way too sharp.

"So what about this guy?" Hardy asked Nick, wagging his head in Ryan's direction. "He okay?"

"Sure," Nick said.

"Sure what?"

"Sure, he's got information to sell. I'm not his mother."

"He's a cop."

Ryan said, "You want to talk about me, talk to me." He almost added, "Sonny."

"I'll talk to you plenty. I don't like cops. Cops make me sick to my stomach. You can't never trust a cop."

"Former cop," Nick explained. "He got run off the force. Had a little girl for breakfast. He's okay."

"That was—" Ryan began.

"You like little girls, dick?" Hardy asked.

"Her old man set me up."

"He commit insects?" Laurel asked, lifting his mouth in a tight, lipless grin.

Ryan said, "Fuck this bullshit. I'm not here to join the K of C."

"No, it wasn't insects," Hardy explained. "That's when you do it with your ant."

Nick laughed. Laurel showed his bad teeth. Hardy bobbed his head around as if searching for the source of his inspiration.

"A cop is a cop," Hardy said.

"Mike always does the right thing. He's helped us out. He was my bodyguard, time I needed a legal gun handy. He's smart. He found out about this, he knew he should come to me. Came to Uncle Nick and offered to do the whole setup. He's a good boy."

"He's a fish," Laurel said.

"What the hell is he on?" Ryan asked Hardy. He waved at the waitress for another scotch.

Hardy answered, "Should see him when he gets hyper. You're not going to get hyper on this job, are you?" he said to Laurel.

Laurel let his head droop to the side and stared at each man in turn, his mouth agape. The waitress set a scotch in front of Ryan.

"Job?" Laurel said.

"Veronica, remember?"

"Christ," Ryan muttered.

"Sal the Veil," Hardy continued. "I met him once. The

broads he had, I'll tell you. Always. Not just the Grand Tetons, stacked all the way up and down—these quiffs were gorgeous. They could—I think some of them were in the movies. And one of them set him up for the good-bye."

"I heard," Nick said. "Shot his way out."

"The man had one weakness," Hardy continued, "but what a weakness. Broad set him up in a chink restaurant. They sent in two of their top shooters—from Miami. They had him sitting there like a goddamn pimple on a whore's ass and he blew them both away."

"He ain't so tough," Ryan stated.

Hardy challenged him. "No? I guess you are?"

Ryan snorted.

"What's your favorite number?" Laurel said to Ryan. "What's your lucky number?"

"Thirteen, what else?"

"Know what mine is? Zero."

"Very interesting."

"Zero. Goose egg."

"Speaking of eggs, you guys ready to settle here?" Ryan said. "Green, that's job one with me."

"Nada," Laurel went on. "Void."

"After," Hardy said.

Ryan drained his drink and stood up. "Nick, I'll be seeing you around."

"Sit down, he's just humping you."

Hardy grinned. He removed a manila envelope from his coat. The stack of bills inside wasn't tall, but they were all hundreds.

Ryan started counting. He knew how to handle these boys. After, that was a good one.

"It's there," Hardy said.

Ryan kept counting. Handling the bank notes gave him a very secure feeling.

"Okay," he said when he finished.

Silence hung over the table for a minute. The others seemed to be waiting for Laurel, who'd developed a sudden concern about his manicure. He looked at his nails out flat, looked at them curled under. He looked at them out flat again and brushed them with his thumb.

Finally he turned his eyes to Ryan and said, "Map it."

Ryan said he'd cased the house. He described it, the layout of the grounds, the kind of neighborhood. But they'd have to hurry, he said, if they were going to get there by dusk. Friday before Memorial Day, traffic would be criminal.

"You know him when you see him?" Hardy asked.

"Of course. He has a mustache, dark hair. Just, you guys have to be ready. You have to move fast before he has a chance to react."

"Listen, Ace, we got this turkey's number," Laurel said. "His number is zero."

"Car here?" Hardy asked.

Nick answered, "It's not here, I don't want it seen here. Denny will take you to it. It's rented on a phony card."

"Is it a red one?" Laurel asked.

"Nobody said anything about red," Nick said.

"Red is the color of my true love's eyes," Laurel sang.

"Don't worry," Hardy said. "Any fucking color."

"In the morning, dah dah dah."

"Just leave it at the airport," Nick said.

"Veronica in the trunk," Hardy said.

"So everybody will know," Ryan added. "It'll be—Dan Rather will have it."

"You like candy?" Laurel asked Ryan.

Ryan raised his eyebrows to no one in particular. "No, I don't like candy."

"I like candy a lot. He can't eat it," he said, indicating Hardy, "he's on a diet. I love it. I could eat candy from now to eternity."

"Good for you."

"Good for me, that's right."

"You need any boys to go with you?" Prado asked.

"No," Laurel said. "We got a boy. This boy's plenty."

Ryan began to develop an eerie feeling that it was Laurel, the obvious loon, who was running this show, who held rank here.

"I'm no boy," he protested. "I wish to hell I was."

The waitress brought Ryan another drink. Laurel and Hardy were sipping Cokes.

Mike tipped the shot back quickly.

"To success." He toasted too late. "This thing is going to make a big noise."

"Sure it is, Mike," Nick said.

"Because the shield is no good anymore. The feds brag how nobody's ever been found, went into the program. But wait till they hear about Sal Veronica. Everybody will be talking about it. Everybody will be going, you get the word about Sal Veronica? Nobody's safe. Headlines. Now, a guy thinks about going bad—"

"Now?" Laurel said. He turned his head to spit on the floor. "Forget about now. This is yesterday. Open your eyes, Leroy, you want to play with us."

"All I'm saying is they'll be looking over their shoulders. Mention grand jury, they'll be looking over their shoulders before they think about talking. This is going to be a hell of a thing. This is going to make waves. All because of Mike Ryan."

"Who the hell's Mike Ryan?" Laurel said.

"Me. I'm Ryan."

Laurel said, "So you're Ryan. So hot shit. You'd better wake up. This whole vehicle's getting ready to shift into high gear. You on the stick, man? Huh? You ready for warp speed zero?"

"Yeah, I'm ready," Ryan said, dubious.

"Let's go," Laurel ordered.

"Nick," Ryan reminded him. "You forgetting something?"

"What?"

"What about the safe-deposit? That's your concern. You don't want to tell these boys about the safe-deposit?"

"That's all right, Mike."

"Shouldn't they know? I mean, they have to know about that."

"No. It wouldn't matter."

"It wouldn't matter? What do you mean?"

"Don't worry, Mike. Be good, okay?"

The sun was an orange ball on the horizon. The ringing in Ted's ears hinted of an angel chorus humming in the cloudless sky. Warm light fluttered on the dancing chrome of the rush-hour traffic.

Sal jammed on the brakes. Ted lurched against the seat belt. Sal blasted the horn, swore.

Back in the office, Ted had barely begun relating Maynard's story before Sal cut him off. He'd immediately picked up the office phone and dialed. No answer. Gina must be out.

He was going home right away. They'd go together, Ted told him. Sal maneuvered as quickly as he could through the holiday weekend traffic.

"Maynard and I go way back," Ted said. "He's a decent guy. He's been a good friend to me. It's just, if you were involved with Felice—"

"Of course I was."

"I don't think it's right—not with the wife of a friend. But I'm not going to judge. I'm sure—"

"There's nothing to judge. There are just some things, Ted, you never learn—I never learn. There are things I'm destined to never ever wise up about."

"It touched a very sensitive spot for Maynard. I guess—"

"Hey, there's no blame here, babe. He did just the right thing, you ask me. I underestimated him, that's all."

"No, he didn't do the right thing!" Ted insisted. "Somebody could have been killed."

Sal accelerated to beat a light that was changing.

Ted said, "I still can't grasp the idea that you're—that you've killed people. It seems like—"

"Ted, I am Sal Veronica! That's the real me. You have to accept that because it changes things. You're finally getting to know who I really am."

"Yeah? Who did I know before? Huh? My friend? My

294

partner? The guy I learned from? Was that all a facade? An empty shell?"

"Yes. No, who am I kidding. Listen, *I* hardly recognize Sal the Veil anymore. It's like, you see somebody on the street who looks really familiar. Who the hell is it? And it's yourself."

"What I don't understand is how you could actually do it. How could you go around killing people like that?"

"No mystery to it. Killing is simple, Ted. Child's play, literally. And what a thrill. Believe me, taking a man's life is a thrill."

"Thrill? Are you serious?"

"It's the ultimate rush. You go up against a man who's carrying a gun. You know that whether it's him or you is just a matter of timing. You whack him. You feel great, you feel fantastic. Hey, I never did anybody who wasn't scum. And that's the truth. They deserved what they got. All of them."

"Wait a minute. You're talking about human beings, I don't care who they are."

"I come out of a world you don't know. The game is survival. How did I kill men? Without thinking. I never thought about it. I swear, all those years, not a second thought. I was on the streets when I was younger than your kids, younger than Mario. You didn't think, you acted. You learned to act right, or you didn't make it. Eventually I got a chance to clip some jerk, some wrong-ass guy who ran a carting business. I jumped at it. He was a piece of shit. I thought nothing of it. I just did it. And then I did a lot more of it. It was work."

Sal felt an odd exhilaration, a heady pride at finally revealing himself. He was taking off the sheep's clothing. He wasn't like Ted, like these suburban dings. But at the same time, maybe from the habit of playing straight, he couldn't shake off a clinging sense of shame.

"It's just impossible for me to conceive of it," Ted said.

Sal made a sharp turn to cut across a lane of traffic. Horns blared. They bumped down an alley and swung onto a side street.

"It's impossible for *me*!" Sal said. "It's become like a dream. But back then I thought I was hot shit. I *was* hot shit. I had a million and a half on the street in shylock loans. A dozen bookies paid me every week off the top. I had women. Ted, I had women you wouldn't believe. And people knew me, respected me, feared me. I had power. I never picked up a tab anywhere I went, the best joints in New York."

Ted reached to grip the dash as Sal pulled into the other lane and accelerated, rushing toward an oncoming car. That car veered to the curb at the last minute. Sal whipped around a corner onto the highway that led toward the Maplecrest suburb. A creeping line of cars stretched as far as they could see.

Mike Ryan could hear Laurel in the backseat of the rented Electra working the clip of his pistol. Despite the air conditioning, Mike was sweating. He felt as if he wanted to yawn but couldn't.

Ryan was driving. Hardy sat beside him. He had a half-grin fixed on his face and was humming what sounded like "itsy-bitsy spider went up the water spout." Laurel was now the one doing the talking.

"I'm ready for a little piece of cake here," he said. He sniffed after each phrase. "I want this gazoony. I want him so bad I can taste him. Time to get up and go to bed. Panic city. I say panic city, you. Yeah, I'm talking to you, dick. You all set? You got a notion for the motion?"

"Sure, whatever you say," Mike said.

"Whatever I say? I say you'd better be with the program here, buddy. You give this guy an opening, he can be very, very dangerous."

"Against three guys? I don't think so."

"Well, you'd just better not think. Because it's show time. In a minute you're going to be walking on stage. You hear me?"

"Yeah, I hear you perfect. You're making me nervous."

"Nervous? I hope you're more than nervous."

296

The traffic held them up. Ryan swore at all the ass-holes on the road, how the hell did they get a license any-way?

"You guys from New York?" he asked.

"What the fuck's that to you?" Laurel snapped.

"Just talking."

"We aren't from New York," Hardy said. "We're from the moon. Get it? Aliens. Don't ask us are we from New York. Where were you born?"

"That's right, you're aliens."

"What?" Hardy shouted.

"Calm down, I'm agreeing with you. I don't care where you're from, it's not my business."

Laurel said, "Start asking questions, you're dead meat, man."

"We almost there?" Hardy asked.

"It's just up here, when we get to that rise."

"You'd better wake the fuck up, Mr. Mike Ryan!" Laurel shouted at him. "You're sitting back in that dive down-ing the Johnnie Walker and you've got business to do. This is no fun-and-games. This, in case you haven't caught on, is the actual shit."

"I'm totally prepared," Ryan said, trying to convince himself.

Hardy was now humming a monotonous version of "Joy to the World." The air was thick with sunlight.

"This is it," Ryan said.

He turned off of the highway. They began to wind up through the placid suburb.

31

Memorial Day had always been Ted's favorite holiday. He remembered as a boy stringing his two-wheeler with crepe paper, watching them shoot off guns to the war dead in the cemetery.

It had always marked the beginning of summer, when the freedom, the sheer possibility stretched endlessly ahead. When summer smelled most like summer and felt most like summer and shone most brightly with summer light.

Death meant nothing back then. When one of his classmates was run down by a milk truck and killed, the teacher had wept telling the class. But Ted hadn't wept, his schoolmates hadn't. It was as if Eddie had gone away somewhere, moved to another town or gone on a long trip. They almost envied him—he didn't have to finish the school year.

What did they care about death? The older you got, the more it meant to you, and it should be the other way around. Shouldn't it?

On those young Memorial Days, when the trumpeter would finish his sour version of Taps to end the service, Ted and the other boys would scurry around the graves looking for the spent shells.

Once his father had taken him to Indianapolis for the 500. Neither of them was a race fan. Why had they gone? Why had they driven all those miles and joined those thousands to watch cars circle the big oval over and over?

Somehow his father had believed that such a pilgrimage would yield the kind of shared memories that could substitute for a closeness they'd never achieved. The Indy was a strange rite of togetherness endured by two men of different aspects trying unsuccessfully to connect.

The race that Memorial Day was loud and confusing. The engines gave off a deadening whine. The loudspeakers competed with the din, broadcasting information, Ted thought, in some blaring foreign language. The race went on and on.

Suddenly, as if the massed expectation had itself broken into the stream of speeding vehicles, it happened. A car spun out right near them on the fourth turn. It hit the wall. Ted, looking somewhere else, had missed it. When he jumped up with the crowd, the car had already been struck by two others and four more cars were careening across the track like shrapnel.

What he saw then would stay with him, a kernel of memory, down the years. Flames engulfed the car. The driver's hands appeared out of the fire and smoke. They waved, as if, burning, the driver was anxious to assure the crowd that he was okay. Those hands were among the most deeply etched images in Ted's gallery of childhood icons. It was the first time, the only time, he'd actually seen a man die.

They turned and started up the rise that led to the shade of Maplecrest just as the sun was setting. Beech trees stood at attention along the streets. Larches and cottonwoods and a few sycamores were burgeoning with vegetation. Leafy silver maples, from which the hill took its name, were slowly buckling the sidewalks with their roots.

From all of these trees, darkness was seeping. Night was filtering down, a balm to ease the agony of the asphalt still bubbling with the day's heat. Liquid shadow flowed relentlessly, running along crevices and into hollows, gathering in the grass and under shrubs.

A profound order and harmony structured every detail of the landscape. Nothing was out of place. Birds sounded their good-night trills on cue. No litter sullied the edge of the road. No weeds grew up here—no raucous wild mustard or Queen Anne's lace. Every lawn was manicured. The aroma of mowing scented the air. Pedigreed hydrangea and viburnum bushes, mountain ash and Oriental dogwoods graced the yards. Stately roses, dusted against fungus and canker, were flashing their proud blossoms in the gloom. Up the side of almost every garage ran a trellis supporting a clematis vine clogged with flowers.

There was no room for hurry. With the tropical weather, time had assumed a tropical pace. In backyards, the juice dripped slowly from thick steaks as they soaked up the heat of the coals. On a hundred frosted tumblers of lime-scented gin and tonic, moisture gathered and ran down in rivulets. At the Little League field the coaches and uniformed players were collecting the equipment after the game: the bats, the leather-padded catcher's masks, the grass-stained balls.

In a pool behind one of the topmost houses a girl of eleven was taking an after-supper dip. Her mother watched her from a webbed chair. The girl halted on the ladder to gaze at a pink-white line that an invisible jet was tracing overhead. On her tan shoulder a bead of chlorinated water held a perfect image of the mild sky.

The blue glass was gradually fading to milk. The upper air was inhaling all the light from the ground in a prolonged sigh. Down under the trees the first fireflies were beginning to flash.

Sal parked in his driveway. He and Ted stared at the dark windows of the house.

Sal reached under the dash to open a compartment. He pulled out a pistol, a black automatic the size of a paperback. Ted watched him draw the clip out of the butt, look at it, palm it back in. Sal pushed the slide, exposing the naked barrel. He clicked it into place. The gun made a precise, clean, mechanical sound. He handed it to Ted.

"That's ready to go. Ever shoot before?"

"Only a rifle. I don't want it."

"Just hold it by your side as we go in. Or you can wait in the car."

"What do you think might—"

"There's no time to talk."

Ted took the gun. It was heavier than he'd expected.

"Just point and squeeze," Sal said.

He pulled another gun from his ankle holster.

They both climbed out into the moist heat. The pistol felt alive in Ted's hand. He swung the car door but it didn't close all the way. He started to open it in order to slam it harder. The palpable quiet stopped him.

The air, as they walked toward the front door, was a riot of smells. The cool green aroma emitted by the maples in Sal's yard was spiced by the pungent cedars and hemlock shrubs nestling near the house. Some flower was glowing with a cinnamon scent. Gina's roses, perfumed like old ladies out for afternoon tea, nodded their heads along the brick path.

Sal motioned Ted to stand to the side of the door. He stepped to the other side and worked the key in the lock. He pushed it open. It swung silently.

"Gina," Sal called.

He waited. Then he slowly slipped around and into the house. He paused before transferring his weight at each step, as if the floor might give way.

Ted followed. He had the feeling that they were entering the house of a stranger. He'd never been here before. He'd never been in any house where light this dim filtered through the windows. It was like being inside a dark house on the night of a full moon. He'd never been in a house in which the furniture, the lamps, the pictures on the wall waited with such expectation, perked up their ears but remained deathly still.

Ted stayed in the living room while Sal checked the bedrooms, the family room, the den. He thought he saw a movement. He almost pointed the gun. But it was only the way the light reflected on one of Gina's porcelain figures. He went over to look.

He examined with new interest the little statues: the butterflies and tigers; the girl in her nightie clutching a bouquet; a prince of Siam; an adolescent ballerina, her face dreaming the movement that her shiny limbs yearned for. How very delicate they were. A bride and groom, their alabaster hands not quite touching. The same figures in lead or bronze would have lost all their charm. They were so breakable—that was their appeal.

A click sounded behind Ted. He spun, pointed the gun into the darkness. His heart roared into his throat.

It was Sal. He'd picked up the telephone receiver. In the quiet, Ted could hear the tiny mechanical melody of the tones.

"Schimanski? It's going down," Sal said, very calmly. "Yeah, the whole show. Right. I'm at home now. I don't know where they are, I'm trying to determine. You got it."

He hung up without saying good-bye.

"Come on," he said to Ted.

They had not yet turned on a light. With reason, Ted thought, but he didn't know what the reason was. They proceeded to the kitchen.

"I guess we're all right," Sal said, his voice barely above a whisper. "I just wish I knew where Gina and Mario were. If she's going somewhere she usually lets me know. I just want to check outside here, then—"

Sal picked up a piece of paper from the kitchen counter. He'd almost missed it in the dark. He read it and handed it to Ted.

"Broke my water," it read. "Tried to reach you. Laura is taking me in. Jenny is with Mario. Here's hoping. Love xxxx Gina."

Sal picked up the kitchen phone and tapped the buttons.

"Jenny? It's Sal. Hi, babe. Listen, is Mario over there?

302

Yeah, I got her note. I don't know, I just got home. Your father's with me. Do you know where he is? In the yard, or—? Would you check? Tell him to come right home, right away, no fooling. Right, thanks. Yeah, I'm excited. Okay, bye, sweetheart."

He turned to Ted. "Let's have a look outside."

"If you want to go to the hospital, to be with her, I can take care of things here," Ted said.

"Yeah, soon as I find the kid."

"The baby wasn't due for another month, was it?"

"That's right. Come on, I want to check the yard."

They stepped onto the flagstones outside the patio doors. Ted was surprised at the pastel glow that hung in the sky. None of the light was reaching the ground. The backyard was a pattern of shadows and obscurity. All was somber except the pool, which stood out like a relic of transparency, a clear turquoise void with a sheen of reflected sky.

The weight in Ted's right hand reminded him that he still held the pistol. It had to be real to be so heavy, yet he didn't believe it could be real. What chance did it have against this overwhelming stillness? How could it ever shatter this silence that seemed to have locked up the entire world?

"Mario?" Sal called softly.

The word floated. June bugs were ascending from the lawn.

Ted waited. His palm, wrapped around the butt of the pistol, was sweating.

"Veronica!"

Sal crouched. Ted stood staring at him for a second as if from a great height, then instinctively followed his lead. They hunkered behind a brick wall that divided two areas of the patio. Low junipers pricked Ted's hand.

"We've got your boy, Veronica!" the voice boomed.

"Mario?"

"Dad? He's hurting me, Dad." The extreme quiet allowed them to make out Mario's voice from across the pool.

"It's okay, boy. You're tough," Sal called. He added

303

under his breath, "Goddamn bastards . . ." His voice trailed to a growl.

"Veronica, you move fast and you can keep your kid from being harmed. I want to see you. I want to talk. You come over here, hands on top of your head, and the boy can go back to his games."

"Let him go first. I mean it. Right now. Do it!"

"Bullshit I will! I want to see you. I want to see you quick. Don't fuck around, man. We're going to talk to you."

"You let the boy go, we can talk." Ted could hear Sal's rasping breath. He sensed a frightening energy coiling in the man beside him.

"You heard what I said!"

There was a brief silence. Then Mario cried out, a long "ah" and five short gasps, a kind of whimpering. Ted strained to see.

"Fucking . . ." Some animal words caught in Sal's throat. Ted heard a low click. He saw Sal looking down, checking the magazine of his pistol. Sal's face was peeled, his eyes shining.

"Wait here." The whisper came from Sal but it was a voice Ted had never heard before. "I'm going to walk across there. If they take me, okay. If they do anything to Mario, open up. Understand?"

"Listen, can't we—?"

"Don't freeze up on me, babe."

Sal tucked his pistol under his belt in back. He stood.

Ted heard himself breathing, panting. He touched the barrel of the gun with his left hand. It was vibrating. In a tree to his right a bird, settling in for the night, whistled a yoo-hoo that sounded almost human.

Sal advanced step-by-step. He held both hands over his head. He lightly touched his hair as if checking to see that it was combed.

All the while he was talking to Mario in a voice that surprised Ted by its deep gentleness. "Don't worry, son. They won't hurt you. I'll take care of them. Everything's going to be fine. You know you're tough. You're tougher than anybody. You're a man. It'll just be another minute."

Now Ted could see the man Sal was approaching. He stood under a dark maple tree. He was a short fat man. He held Mario with his arm raised so that the boy's head was tilted to the side and one of his feet dangled, barely touching the ground.

Nothing was going to happen. Ted was sure of it. The whole thing was a misunderstanding, a masquerade. He should stand up and say, let's cut out this game. Let's put the guns away. This could be dangerous. The kids see us, what are they going to think? There are laws. There are courts of law for settling these disputes. We're living in the goddamn twentieth century.

But immediately he saw another man, a pale man with a long face, walking quite near him. He was approaching Sal from behind. In a second he would be just across the wall from Ted.

He didn't seem to notice Ted. He held a large revolver in his hand. Ted could smell the man's after-shave.

Ted felt his grip tighten on his own gun.

Should he warn Sal? Should he shoot?

Something else caught his attention. A flicker in the grass behind Mario and his abductor. At first he mistook it for a firefly. But it didn't flash out immediately. It was a tiny flame. A tiny wavering flame. From it an arc of sparks shot out toward the man, landed behind him.

Ted tensed. The darkness held its breath.

The quiet that had shrouded them since they'd gotten out of the car suddenly shattered. It exploded into a million irredeemable fragments.

Now the stillness was replaced by movement. The man who held Mario spun toward the crack.

Robbie's voice from inside the bushes screamed, "Run for it, Mario!!"

Mario twisted out of the man's grasp. He dove into the shrubs.

Sal's hand snaked to the small of his back. He whipped out the pistol. He dove into a crouch.

Sal fired a dagger of flame from his hand. The man shot back twice. The sounds were like the smacking together of wide boards. Sharp, dangerous cracks.

The long-faced man who'd been stalking Sal rose up. Ted stood behind him. The man was trying to draw a bead on Sal. Sal scampered over behind a lawn chair.

Ted could have reached out and tapped the man on the shoulder with his pistol. He pointed it. Something kept him from pulling the trigger.

A vision flashed with lightning clarity into Ted's mind. He was twelve. His dog had been run over by a pickup truck. Ted's father gave him a shovel and told him to put the dog out of its misery. He knew that his father was right. But he could not raise the shovel. He could not crack the dog's skull with it. He remembered now the agonizing minutes he'd waited. Until finally his father had taken the shovel from his hands.

Ted leapt. His foot on the wall lifted him into the air with a bound. He was completely detached from the earth for a second. He was Superman. Tarzan. Flying.

He landed hard on the back of the man in front of him. They both tumbled to the ground. The man's gun scraped across the stones.

Ted used his weight advantage to pin the smaller man flat. But his opponent twisted violently. He turned onto his back under Ted and struck out at Ted's face. The blow raked Ted across the eyes, reddened his vision.

Ted slapped the side of the man's head with the pistol. The man swung again, catching Ted's ear. His knee flew up and pounded into Ted's kidney. Ted brought the butt of the gun down on the man's mouth. He felt hot liquid.

The smaller man's fingers closed like steel talons around Ted's throat. Ted gagged. He tried to pull away. The other's grip held. Ted hit at the face. The blow was blocked by the man's shoulder.

Ted struggled to pull the fingers away from his windpipe. Blackness was beginning to eat into his vision.

Summoning all his strength, Ted twisted and struck at the man's arms. The grip loosened. Ted gasped for air.

Without thinking he pointed the pistol and pulled the trigger.

A blast, a jolt. The bullet caught the man in the throat. His hands leapt toward the pulse of blood.

Ted was on his knees. He could feel the smaller man's hips moving between his legs. He held the pistol in both hands and fired it into the man's chest. The gun jerked.

Now Ted heard a gurgling sound, a sucking. With each breath, a wheeze came from between the man's ribs.

Ted stood. His throat was on fire.

The man with the long face was clutching his hands below his chin. He was pressing his elbows together, as if protecting himself from a chill wind. He was trembling.

Ted was not in his body. He was somewhere above the shadows, looking down from the lucid sky. He fired the gun one more time. A dark spot opened just to the left of the man's nose. Ted looked away.

He sat down heavily on the stone wall. His head was reverberating, as though the chorus of angels he'd been hearing since he left his office were shrieking a few inches from his ears. But he could feel the restored quiet on his skin. He could smell the blood, the acrid fumes from the gun, his own fear.

The yard was almost completely black now. Only the pool glowed with its own clarity. The water was so limpid that the space seemed empty.

Coming back to himself, he thought of the boys and stood.

The air by his head went electric. A shot sounded. Glass broke.

Ted stumbled, banged his knee on the wall. He peered over at the tree where the man had held Mario. A body was sprawled on its face in the grass.

Responding to a hiss, Ted spotted Sal. Still crouching, Sal was frantically motioning him down. Ted squatted. Another shot split the night above him.

Sal gestured. It was a sign language that Ted couldn't fathom. Sal held up his pistol and shook his head. Don't shoot? Out of bullets? Ted struggled to comprehend.

Another blast, this one different. Ted looked. He saw a trail of orange sparks. Again the sharp report of one of the firecrackers.

A real shot sounded. Where it was aimed, Ted couldn't tell. The firecrackers seemed to confuse this last gunman.

An impossible quiet gripped the scene for a few seconds.

Ted lifted his head and saw a figure in a white shirt emerge from the shadows beyond the pool. He was walking a kind of duck walk, keeping low.

Again the flame, the sparks. The M-80 exploded just to Mike Ryan's right. Ryan dove for a metal patio table. He overturned it along with its umbrella. He squatted behind it.

Very quickly he started forward again. He was working his way toward Sal. In a second he'd come even with him.

Ted aimed. But Ryan's course brought him between Ted and the spot where Robbie was hiding in the bushes.

Ted fired over Ryan's head.

Mike spun around. He stood. He twisted first one way, then the other.

Now a new sound. A pounding, as of men running. Ted heard footsteps rounding the side of the house. Heard them snapping through the shrubs. Heard shouts.

Ryan was backing up, skirting the edge of the pool.

A voice boomed from a bullhorn: "Freeze! Federal agents!"

No sooner had Ryan's gun cracked and flamed than an explosion louder than all the others sounded from the corner of the house.

Ryan's arms and legs sprang into an X. He pirouetted, as if in exultation. He half flew, half stumbled backward. The water in the pool convulsed with his entry.

At the same moment Ted saw yet another string of sparks in the bushes beyond. No! he thought.

A word, a scream was halfway out of Ted's mouth as the M-80 exploded. The word was drowned by the answering salvo from the three men with the flak jackets and shotguns.

Ripples were still lapping up the sides of the pool and licking over the edges as Ted sprinted past.

Sal ran ahead of him.

When Ted reached the bushes Sal was already on his knees. He rocked Mario's head in a bloody hand, cradled the wound.

"Robbie!" Ted's voice cracked.

Robbie, his face contorted into a silent cry, stepped out of the bushes. Ted hugged him.

The night exploded in all directions. The marshals gathered. A man was barking orders. Other men were running. The air was full of static.

Two marshals, still wearing flak jackets, took Mario away from his father. One knelt, rhythmically stiff-arming the boy's chest. The other gently puffed air into his lungs.

Sal crouched, holding Mario's limp fingers in his own.

"You're tough," he whispered. "You're tough, boy."

Ted started to reach out to comfort him. But his hand was shaking so badly he drew it back.

The revolving red-and-white lights made the scene unreal. As soon as the lights are gone, Ted thought. As soon as the quiet darkness returns. As soon as the summer dawn eases across the sky. This will all have been a nightmare.

32

Ted unlocked the front door of the Vincents' house and stepped inside. He walked around opening shades and turning on lights. A house stripped of furniture didn't show well. At least it should be bright. From a small bottle in his pocket he drizzled a few drops of vanilla extract onto the bulb in a lamp. It would burn off with a cozy, homey scent.

He stared out at the landscaped garden in back, the pool. He noticed that when they'd replaced the pane of glass they hadn't painted the trim. He leaned over to pick a tiny fragment of porcelain from the living room carpet.

Hearing a car, he moved to the front window. His customers had arrived. He gave them a minute to take in the house from the curb, then went out to greet them.

They were a pleasant young couple. He'd recently been made director of human relations at a local computer software company. She was a lawyer. She carried their newborn in a harness on her chest. Ted liked them.

He assured them that the house was just what they'd been looking for. He knew they were going to fall in love with it. Plenty of room for the family to grow. The type of meticulous landscaping that really added value to a place. Established, quiet neighborhood.

"And very safe," he said. "I can testify to that."

They looked the house over carefully. They noted the bidet. They walked around the pool, the sculptured shrubs in back. They were full of praise.

The house was a lovely house, they said. Just, something about it. Maybe it was a little too big for them. It lacked the kind of ambience that she was looking for. The layout didn't exactly suit him. They couldn't really pin it down, but . . .

"The owner's very motivated, I can tell you that," Ted said.

Yes, of course the place was a good value, but . . .

Ted warned them against making up their minds right away. But he knew that they had made up their minds. He accompanied them out the front door.

They continued down the path, past the Winner Realty sign. Ted fought a sensation of weariness and sharp regret as he locked the door. He hurried to catch up with them.

"I think I see a little better now exactly what you are interested in," he said. "As a matter of fact, I do have a place. It just came on the hot sheet this morning . . ."

Sal skipped down the stairs and out onto the street, into the warm evening. They'd rented an apartment in Queens. Their old place in New Dorp had burned to the ground soon after they moved.

Sal found the apartment comfortable enough. Gina said she had plans to fix it up, to make it a real home. But so far she'd done nothing. Sal would go out, he'd return hours later, he'd find her sitting in exactly the same place that he'd left her, as if she'd been immobile since he left.

Sal waved down a cab. He told the driver to take him to Forty-Second Street and Third Avenue.

It was good to be back in New York. He liked this pungent, late-summer weather, weather you could get your teeth into. He liked the noise, the activity, the grinding relentlessness of the city. He felt that he'd come back to himself.

Schimanski hadn't understood. He told Sal to wait. The marshals would give him around-the-clock protection. Wait till he and Gina had had a chance to deal with things. With the shooting. Mario. The baby, which had lived only three hours.

Sal said no. He'd decided. He was ready to sign the "death warrant" release, the one that let the government off the hook regarding his safety.

Schimanski hadn't understood, but then he'd never really understood Sal Veronica. He could talk to Vincent, yeah. But Veronica, they didn't speak the same language.

You're talking about suicide, Schimanski said.

I don't think so.

You've seen what can happen, how far they're willing to go. You have a chance. There's nothing I can say about Mario. I feel sick about that, but—

No blame, babe. Your guys played it right.

But you can save yourself. You've come a long way, Sal. Don't, for your sake, for Gina's sake.

She wants it, she wants to go back.

She's in no condition to decide.

She wants to go home.

At least take some time.

No, it's not what you think.

It wasn't what Schimanski thought. It wasn't suicide. But Sal couldn't explain.

It wasn't suicide because New York was the last place they'd expect him to show up. Paulie would have the word out across the country and Sal would be sitting right under his nose. All he had to do was to stay on the fringes, keep cool, not contact anybody he wasn't dead sure of.

He wasn't Sal Vincent anymore. He wasn't Sal the Veil. He was Jim Lawrence. He wore a full beard and dressed like a construction worker. He was probably as safe here as anywhere.

He got out of the cab and walked across town. He breathed the carnival smells of the city, the whiffs of cotton candy and diesel fumes, roasting pretzels and stale beer, river scents and human scents. He'd returned from exile. He loved the flaming neon, the busy streets, the elegant women striding the pavement, the anonymity. The warm night was coming alive. Sal was beginning to feel cold.

Ted, maybe, had understood. He said he did, maybe he did. He and Laura had brought them over food—casseroles and homemade bread, a cake Jenny had baked. Laura did what she could to comfort Gina. Told her not to hold it in, that she'd feel better if she just let go, let it out. But Gina couldn't let it out.

He turned uptown along Second. He was acutely aware of sounds, of the blare of horns, the rush of traffic down the avenue, a salsa rhythm seeping from around a corner.

Schimanski had agreed to take care of the moving. The movers were already at work when Ted and Laura arrived. Outside, marshals in blue windbreakers cradling submachine guns stood in front of Sal's house.

Sal was on a deserted cross street now, heading toward the United Nations. He slowed his pace, passed a discreet French restaurant that occupied the bottom floor of a brownstone town house. He stepped down into the areaway of the building next door.

Gina had insisted on packing her porcelain figures herself. She handled them with exaggerated care, nestling each in its box of excelsior.

Sal slipped his hand into the pocket of his jacket, touched metal.

She'd held the ballerina for a long time, staring with vacant eyes, stroking its arabesque limbs with her fingertips. She looked around at the others, gazed at the figure again, hurled it against the wall, smashing it.

She began to take down her figures one by one and

methodically break them. Laura started to approach her, but Sal waved her off. Gina unpacked the pieces she'd already put away, her favorites, and hurled them with increasing violence into oblivion.

Only when all the figures, the prince of Siam, the collie, all the butterflies, had been shattered did Gina finally break down.

Sal stopped remembering. He folded his fingers around the butt of the pistol. The door of a black limousine was opening. A man stepped onto the pavement, looked around. Then another man. A man with one eye.